The Stone

Not a crystal. Too dense. A jewel, maybe. But what kind of jewel had such incredible radiance—

Russ was almost blinded by the brilliance, yet he couldn't seem to pull his gaze away. Cold tears slithered across his vision.

Uranium?

He started to step back, but his feet were frozen to the sand.

Fingers of light were spreading toward him. His skin began to tingle . . . the light crept over him, through his pores . . .

He was on fire! Fire, in a shell of thick-ribbed ice.

Light poured into him from the stone—through his eyes, his nose, his mouth, held open in a silent, frozen scream. It invaded every part of him, spreading through nerves like liquid flame!

He tried to run, and couldn't; tried to scream— his mouth was filled with fire . . .

Tor books by Lisa Cantrell

*The Manse**
The Ridge

* *Winner of the 1988 Bram Stoker Award for Outstanding First Novel*

THE RIDGE

LISA W. CANTRELL

TOR
HORROR

A TOM DOHERTY ASSOCIATES BOOK
NEW YORK

THE RIDGE

Copyright © 1989 by Lisa Cantrell

A TOR Book
Published by Tom Doherty Associates, Inc.
49 West 24th Street
New York, N.Y. 10010

Cover art by Bob Eggleton

ISBN: 0-812-50011-3   Can ISBN: 0-812-50012-1

First edition: September 1989

Printed in the United States of America

0 9 8 7 6 5 4 3 2 1

for my son

Acknowledgments and Thanks

To Chief Mike Joyce of the Walnut Cove, NC Police Dept.; Captain Glen Mowrey of the Mecklenburg County Police Dept.; Cecil Yates, FBI, Ret.; Steve Ray, Jr.; Mike Bottoms; and the Walnut Cove Public Library, for technical assistance;

To the RCC Writers' Workshop—the best support group around—and you *know* who you are;

To Allen Wold for advice and encouragement, past and present;

To Butch Burris, for lending me Curly;

To Linda Hayes and my Alabama family for their enthusiasm and love—and particularly Linda Ruth and Herman for chauffeuring me to book signings;

To Theresa, Reesa, Martin, Billie, and Scott for aiding and abetting—thanks, guys, more than you'll ever know;

To *Toys Don't Hate*, the inspiration for *Kafka*;

To my husband, for patience, love, and support—particularly support;

To Melissa Ann Singer, for again applying her talent, skills, and deep sense of caring to help make this book the very best it could be;

And to Jim Allen for most of the above, and all the rest . . .

"... and the stones themselves shall give Thee dominion."
                    —from *The First Book of Divinian,*
                              Ninth Chronicle

Wind roamed about the old stone house. Outside, waves drummed against the beach.

This couldn't be happening. How could this be happening?

She stubbed another cigarette into the overflowing ashtray and ran a trembling hand through already disheveled hair.

Why *God!* couldn't he just leave them alone?

They might have drowned this afternoon—*both* of them—his own child for Christ's sake! And it hadn't been the current pulling her under, it had been a hand. She'd felt it.

She still couldn't believe he was trying to kill them. Even after she'd called him, proved he wasn't there, she couldn't believe he'd come here. Why now? After all these years, why now?

The night felt close, heavy, pressure budding toward a storm. It was giving her a headache.

She lit another cigarette, glancing across the bedroom at her sleeping husband. She'd have to tell him the truth, now; all of it. Surely he'd believe her. Believe the little series of "accidents" hadn't been accidents at all, believe the threatening messages she'd seen written in the sand.

Wouldn't he?

"Oh, *God!* What am I going to do?"

Tossing her cigarette into the ashtray, she jumped up and began pacing, agitation in every move. Hands plucked at the sleeves of her negligee, arms crisscrossed against the penetrating cold.

The wind blew louder, rattling windowpanes, filling the air with an eerie, piercing whine that seemed to cut through her head from ear to ear—

The sudden shattering of glass below!

She froze, gasped a scream. *He was inside the house!*

Several smaller crashes followed the first.

An ominous rumble began vibrating upward—like vicious laughter, or an explosion deep within the earth.

The house seemed to shiver, as if the very stones had moved.

"What's going on?" Her husband's groggy voice was muffled; he fought the bedclothes, trying to get up. A wine glass overturned on the bedside table.

"—earthquake?" she thought she heard him say, and "—kids—get the—"

"What—?"

"Get the kids!"

She stumbled after him, dazed, head pulsing with the rising pressure, rushing toward Sara's room as he dashed across the hall ... Sara was gone, her room was empty!

Oh my God he was *here! He'd taken Sara!*

"Sara? *Sara!* Where are you?"

Frantic, she descended the staircase, dimly hearing her husband following, Jeffy crying.

The air had come alive. It crawled across her like stinging jellyfish—cold, so cold—and the sound!

That horrible humming sound. *What was he doing to them?* It was driving her insane! "Sara!"

"Mommy . . . ?"

"Sara? Where—"

Her daughter stood alone in the center of the great room, gripping her Fuzzy. Her eyes were wide with terror. But no one else was there. *Where was he?*

"Here, take them!" Her husband thrust the babies into her arms. "I'll get Sara. Just get out. *Hurry!*"

The words seemed deadened, as though they were coming at her down a long tunnel. Her movements felt slack, retarded.

She turned toward the door, forcing her limbs to respond, gasping for breath. A sweet burning filled her lungs. *Was the house on fire?* Karen wiggled in her arms; Jeffy had begun to howl.

Windows abruptly began exploding outward, shards of glass flying into the night. She screamed. Swinging back toward her husband, she saw him falling to the floor.

Wind poured around them. And light. Blinding light! A storm raged inside the house, rose through the stones to embrace them, circling the room with a banshee's wail—

Her head was on fire!

"Mommy—"

She tried to focus on her daughter.

"—get behind my glass!"

Oh God it hurts—

PART ONE

Nick

1

Manhattan, 3:00 A.M.

Silent, rain-slicked streets bisected and stretched past a darkened corner where a man stood watching a warehouse half a block up. Of medium build, the man showed no particular concern at being alone at night in one of the seedier parts of the city. He was aware that several specimens of the night-life populating this area had tagged his presence among them. He had not been approached.

Perhaps it was the eyes.

A match scraped the silence; a flicker danced across the man's expressionless face as he lit his cigarette, hands cupped against the cool night wind. The light seemed to bounce back from those inscrutable eyes, reflect off the pupils like mirrored sunglasses.

Weak moonlight leaked through tattered clouds. The rain had stopped earlier, replaced by a breeze which gusted along the empty streets, rippling puddles that would be potholes again by morning.

The man was as oblivious to this as to other extraneous details around him. His mind remained focused on the adjustment at hand, the culmination of three months' careful planning, painstaking manipulation of subjects and odds.

Three of the subjects had already entered the warehouse. A black, four-door sedan now drew up to the curb, followed by a Lincoln town car, headlights off.

Two men got out of the sedan, a third exited the Lincoln. All wore dark suits; the man from the Lincoln had on a hat.

The trio studied one another a moment in the dimly lit silence, then disappeared into the warehouse.

The standing man lifted his wrist and peeled back the sleeve of his dark leather jacket: 3:07. Steady movement pulsed at the edge of the round watchface, a separate circle of numbers being precisely trimmed to zero. It was a diver's watch, custom made, expensive, very accurate.

A slight frown creased the skin between the refractive eyes. The adjustment was about to go down without the final subject in attendance.

Random chance was always a factor in an adjustment. Tonight's ratio had calculated 7.5 percent.

Any one of a number of things could be delaying the final subject: accident or illness, uncanny premonition, car trouble. The possibility of an incomplete adjustment reared its annoying head. The man had become accustomed to success.

The half-burned cigarette being nested by thumb and forefinger into a curved palm arced toward the gutter. A small hiss marked its landing, a wisp of smoke. Tomorrow it would be the only evidence that someone had stood here during the predawn hours. Tomorrow it wouldn't matter, because he would be gone, and the evidence would be too incidental to consider.

The sound of a car approaching from the opposite direction caused the man to shift slightly, drawing even farther into the shadows and the night. Hooded eyes watched the black limousine glide by, no lights, smoked windows giving as little access to what lay behind as the eyes that scanned them. It moved on toward the warehouse, a sleek black shark cruising the silent waters.

When it reached mid-block the limo slowed and drew over to the curb, opposite the Lincoln. The engine remained on, thrumming softly.

Two men climbed out, one from the front passenger's seat, one from the rear. Right hands tucked inside coat fronts, they panned the silent streets, eyes darting up and down, back and forth, never looking at the same space at the same time.

Finally their searching eased. The one behind tapped on the rear window, said something when it lowered an inch, then reached down and opened the door. Frank Terrell got out.

A massive man, Terrell lifted his bulk from the car with a grace that belied it. Wide shoulders straightened as he leaned back to study the upper levels of the warehouse. He said something to the others, pointed toward an unboarded window.

This action was observed with detachment. Fact: The adjustment was already compromised. Fact: There was nothing to be done about it at the moment.

A wrist was raised, a sleeve pushed back. Emotionless eyes watched the circlet of numbers sequence down, lifting to the warehouse as the final integer clicked into place.

An explosion ripped the night.

The surrounding area froze. It was as though time stopped at the edges, like the circlet on the observer's wristwatch, and only the focal point continued to move forward.

Flames blossomed from within the building; several small explosions followed the first. Smoke began to boil from paneless windows, belching past haphazard boarding, through gaping cracks. A popping, crackling sound danced the air, blending with a deeper rumble swelling in the bowels of the building—a grumbling, angry giant.

Frank Terrell had begun to cross the street, flanked by his men. The trio stood immobile now, like they'd been iced in mid-step and refused to believe it.

Terrell recovered first, swinging around with the quick viciousness of a large cat turning on its prey. An arm raked the nearer man, staggering him, but effectively breaking both bodyguards out of the trance that had held them momentarily enthralled. The second man pulled his gun and began waving it around aimlessly, shouting some incoherence as he backed toward the car, attempting to shield his boss from the warehouse. Terrell snarled a reply, jerking open the car door and diving inside.

The car leapt into motion even as the other two climbed in, squealing down the narrow, one-way street, bleeding rubber and tire smoke in its wake. It ricocheted madly as it gained speed and hit a pothole, casting dirty water and shards of reflected light onto asphalt already glistening with a flickering red sheen.

The man watched it careen into the distance, resembling a wildly lumbering bull confused by bloodlust. The lurching smoothed as the car sped away, taillights winking once when it made a right turn three blocks down. Then it was gone.

The observer returned his gaze to the burning warehouse. Flames surged upward, lapping at the shriveling outer skin like a dog licking a wound. Pieces of the structure had begun falling away, showering the sidewalks and street with a steady rain of fire. Small whirlwinds of sparks and ash spiraled on the wind to merge with the heavy plume of smoke being channeled north by air currents.

Suddenly, from inside the inferno, a thin scream began threading its way out. It rose and fell like the waves of heat reaching the street. A part of the man's brain abstractly noted the inhuman sound, the quality of the agony. He was familiar with both.

The scream crescendoed in a crash of splintering glass and wood as a fireball erupted from a third-floor window. It spread itself on the air, blazing arms arching outward, winglike, flailing wildly just before it hit the street. A dazzling array of sparks eddied upward.

The man lit another cigarette as the descent took place. He eyed the charcoaling form a moment, then transferred his stare back to the warehouse. Fire bathed his face with a shifting, unearthly glow, emphasizing hollows and distorting planes, turning features into illusions ... and the rabid, swirling flames lay mirrored on polished corneas, imaged on smooth pupils like matches behind glass where eyes should have been.

Not bothering to cloak his cigarette this time, he placed it between his lips, freeing his hands to turn up the collar of his leather jacket. In the distance, a siren wailed. It could be headed here; more likely it was answering an earlier call.

But he was not one to take chances.

Lifting the cigarette from his mouth, he turned his back on the scene and started walking, tracing the route the limousine had used earlier.

Thinking of the limo brought the slight frown back into play. Random chance had flawed tonight's adjustment and must now be dealt with. Random chance: a killer named Frank Terrell.

No one observed the man's silent departure. The few who had initially stayed to watch the watcher had scuttled back into their holes within seconds of the explosion. No one would see anything. No one would know anything.

It was the way things were.

The man made a right turn at the first intersection he came to, immediately leaving the glowing red backdrop, the acrid smell of combustion behind. He took a final draw from his half-smoked cigarette and flicked it toward the gutter, oblivious to the small shower of sparks that quickly extinguished themselves on the still-damp street.

Nick Vears closed the front door behind him and crossed the unlit living room, depositing his dark leather jacket on a chair arm in passing.

A soft amber glow from his answering machine signaled received messages. He ignored it, going instead to a small table and pouring two fingers of Rémy Martin into a waiting glass. He took his drink back over to the couch, sat, propped his feet on the low coffee table.

The room held a sparsity of lumps and shapes given vague definition by the glow from the answering machine, several other digitals, and city light climbing nine stories to filter through two casement windows. The few pieces of furniture were strictly usable items, good pieces because Nick could afford it and accepted comfort where he could, but chosen mostly for convenience or a specific purpose.

The single elaborate exception was a U-shaped computer work center where several components emitted various hums and glimmers; but even these possessed the machine's impersonal cool sterility, or at most the deceptive look of high-tech hobby.

Nick transferred a portion of cognac from glass to mouth, feeling the smooth warmth slide past his tongue and spread through his body. His hands cra-

dled the glass against his stomach and he leaned
back, staring at the nearly invisible ceiling ... but
he was seeing a long black limousine careening
down a rain-slick street, a wounded shark swimming through an unexpected breach in a carefully
woven net.

For the first time, the thought did not provoke a
frown. Annoyance had passed; abstract reasoning
had supplanted it.

Frank Terrell was a dangerous man under non-
aggressive circumstances: intelligent, cunning,
highly ranked in his particular branch of the family. Hunted, and aware of it, he could be lethal. And
he'd be doing his own stalking now.

Of course, it would take time to discover Nick—
possibly more time than Frank would expect, as the
path to Nick Vears was circuitous. But Nick didn't
hold any illusions about Frank Terrell's ability to
find him, eventually. Such arrogance could be
costly. And the sophisticated machine at Terrell's
disposal might peg him even sooner than anticipated.

The answer was simple: find Terrell first.

The act was less easily defined. Frank would have
dug in by now, no doubt already oiling his machine
to discover who had set him up, and why.

Nick spent a few more moments contemplating
the problem, then put it on hold. He had to make a
call.

Setting aside his drink, he rose and went over to
the work center. Still ignoring the message light,
he sat at the terminal, booted the system, and keyed
in a special modem access which did not appear on
screen. Within seconds a small green indicator light
winked on at the base of the monitor unit. Open
line.

Nick typed his entry code, using four of the five

seconds allotted, then waited. A second cursor appeared.

He typed: /Adjustment pending. 29./ Not exactly the report he had planned to make.

Another moment, the response came: /Ack./

The screen went blank. The green telltale died.

Nick continued to sit, staring at the darkened screen, recalling the project that had come to him three months ago and should have been finalized tonight:

/Family business being overextended. Account balance in jeopardy. Adjust./

It had taken a month to find the key that would offset the problem, another two to set things up.

Now this.

He started to rise, then changed his mind and, reaching over, activated the telephone message replay. It was a special number, unlisted, routed through several dummy exchanges which he altered from time to time. It was the closest thing he had to a normal phone line.

Only half a handful of people knew it, and of them, only a couple would ever leave a message. Any message left on this line would be noncritical.

A few wrong numbers sometimes came in, an occasional random crank call. They usually hung up after hearing the tinny, computerized: "YOU HAVE REACHED AN UNLISTED NUMBER. STATE YOUR BUSINESS."

Harry Kim's voice entered the room: "Hi, Nick. Got some papers you'll need to sign yourself on that tax thing. Before Friday, that's *this* Friday, April 15th—Oh, shit, if you can't make it, I'll get an extension. If you can, come for lunch. Papa's got a great new pasta verde, made with seaweed. You'll love it. Spock out."

A moment of silence between messages. Nick decided he'd keep the Friday appointment with the Korean bus boy who handled all of his financial affairs from the kitchen of his father's Italian restaurant—

"Why are you trying to kill us?"

The woman's panicked voice jumped out at Nick with such force that he caught himself leaning back reflexively.

"For God's sake, Nick! Your own child! What have we done? Can't you just leave us alone? Can't you please just leave us alone?"

Nick remained motionless for a long moment after the answering machine clicked off, its amber telltale switching to green. Then he reached over and reactivated it, listening again to Carole's hysterical message.

Carole: his ex-wife. He'd recognized her voice, though it had been almost six years since they'd had any personal contact.

Carole: who had left him after stumbling across the results of an adjustment, taking their baby daughter with her. The results had been two dead bodies.

She'd accused him of being a hit man. He'd never told her otherwise.

Standing, he punched a button on the boxlike phone unit, switching to audio as the number automatically dialed. It started ringing, was interrupted: "The number you have dialed is not in service. Please call your operator if you feel you have reached this recording in error."

Nick pressed disconnect, then tried again. Same results.

He did as the recording instructed and received confirmation that the phone was indeed out of order, would be reported to the proper department, "Thank you very much, sir."

He stood a moment, then returned to the couch, taking his former position and another swallow of cognac. Despite Carole's propensity for melodrama, she'd sounded more high-strung than usual, and Nick knew only something extraordinary would prompt her to call him.

Four years ago she'd remarried—a moderately successful artist named David Grant; a good enough man, Nick knew—he'd checked. They had two children of their own now, and had recently moved to a small fishing area on the mid-Atlantic seacoast where they were renovating an old stone house.

The last time Carole had even attempted initiating contact with him was shortly after the remarriage. She'd wanted Nick to allow her husband to adopt Sara.

Although Nick never expected to know his daughter, his only child, and accepted the logic of Carole's request, for some reason he'd refused. The blind trust he'd set up in perpetuity continued to pay a generous quarterly allowance. Nick knew from Harry that Carole had never touched it, but simply allowed it to accumulate in Sara's name.

Fine. Nick really didn't care one way or the other. He'd done what needed to be done. They were well out of his life, for several reasons, most of all their own protection, and in his line of work Nick could ill afford the emotional straitjacket of a wife and child.

He'd wondered sometimes why he'd married Carole—finally crediting it to a last moment of sentimental weakness.

"Why are you trying to kill us?"

Nick's eyes narrowed.

He lifted his glass, drained it, set it on the coffee table.

"Your own child!"

The strangeness of those words caused him to hesitate a moment before going over to the telephone and setting the unit to auto-dial Carole's number every hour on the hour, signaling him when a connection was established.

Until then, Nick headed to the bedroom. He needed some sleep.

+ + +

Waves. Cold, black. Lashing at the edges of her consciousness.

Blinding redness. Swirling all around, mixed with sparkles of crystal white.

She stood, clutching her Fuzzy, eyes twin pools of raging nightmare vision, small bare feet beneath her jammies gripping the stone floor with prehensile strength.

All around her: badness—roaring, shrieking badness, crashing against the glass. She could hear it, but not feel it; she could see it, but not touch it. And
it
could
not
touch
her.

Again and again it charged the glass, wanting to get in, seeking a hole, a crack—big and fierce and cold, so very cold.

She drew her Fuzzy closer, moving away from the glass, not moving at all.

She had seen enough.

+ + +

2

The telephone woke Nick. Not the connection he'd programmed to rouse him, but an incoming call.

He listened as the machine clicked on and the portable extension beside his bed came alive:

"This is Deputy Piner of the Collett County, North Carolina Sheriff's Department, calling Mr. Nicholas Vears. The matter concerns a family emergency and is extremely urgent. Please call Sheriff Seddons at area code nine-one-nine, the number is—"

Nick picked up the phone and flipped a button on the base unit to access an open line while still recording. "Vears."

The young male voice at the other end paused, no doubt startled by the sudden switch from machine to man, but recovered swiftly. "Mr. Vears? Mr. Nicholas Vears?"

Redundancy had once annoyed Nick. Now he accepted it as a penance of life. "Yes."

"You're the ex-husband of Mrs. Carole Allison Grant?"

"Yes."

"Father of Sara Vears—"

"What's this about?" Nick cut through further redundancy.

"There's been an . . . accident, Mr. Vears."

Nick didn't miss the slight hesitation. His eyes narrowed.

"What kind of accident?"

"Your ex-wife, her husband, and their two children have been killed." The voice trailed off, as though expecting a response—shock—grief—whatever.

Nick was silent. The quick-flash vision of a classically beautiful woman holding a baby with vivid blue eyes was from another lifetime.

"Mr. Vears?"

Nick heard the frown in the young man's voice and didn't attempt to cloak his impatience. "My daughter, Deputy Piner?"

"Unharmed, but in shock. She's been taken to a nearby hospital." The deputy paused again, then continued when Nick made no response. "She was a witness to what happened."

"What did happen?"

"We don't know yet. Some sort of explosion."

"Explosion?" Nick heard the frown in his own voice, felt it pull at his forehead. A sudden, vivid replay of erupting flames, of burning debris and a charred, writhing body flashed before his eyes. He felt a small muscle at the side of his jaw tighten.

"An investigation is commencing," the deputy added, and Nick picked up the verbal swagger—at last the caller had gotten a reaction.

"I see." Nick banked the flames.

"No, sir, I don't think you do," the deputy stated cryptically. "When can we expect you? The hospital needs to make arrangements, and there are a few questions we'd like to have answered for our records."

It took only a moment to consider his options.
"Later today."

"Fine, sir. If you'll just give me your address . . ."

Nick gave the address of the Metropolitan Museum of Art and broke the connection.

He went immediately into the living room and fired up the computer. Within sixty seconds the security breach had been reported, his private telephone line rerouted and changed.

Reaching beneath the desk, he accessed a blind storage compartment and removed a small, gray plastic case that was disproportionately heavy. Opening it, he checked the items fitted with minute precision inside, then popped up a second, wafer-thin top whose underbelly was an LCD screen, revealing a smooth, touch-sensitive terminal board.

Satisfied with the ECCO, Nick reclosed the lid, set the unit on the floor to one side, and reached for the phone. Harry answered in three rings.

"Nick, my man. You caught me up to my armpits in dirty dishes. Papa—the old buzzard—had his annual *sakefest* last night, which of course didn't break up until sometime this morning; all the venerables were here. And it'll take me till noon to get the linguini and chop chae stains off the red checkereds. By the way, the pasta verde was a hit."

Nick was acquainted with Harry's rambling style and waited for the lull that would eventually come. The hyperactivity that bombarded Harry's every waking moment fascinated Nick. He could visualize the small Korean whirlwind spinning about the kitchen, dripping soapsuds and soliloquies with equal enthusiasm, and no doubt doing complex stock analyses at the same time, a suspicion proved true as Harry inserted:

"It's time to dump the VelChem."

"Fine," Nick said, with the same interest he'd have in "It's time to throw out the trash," then added, "I'll be out of touch for a while," before Harry could get too involved with the new topic.

"What about the tax—"

"Get an extension."

Harry sighed, but skipped the protest, used to Nick's brevity. "What if I need—"

"I'll call you."

"You're doing it again."

Nick's eyebrows lifted slightly.

"The Radar O'Reilly bit. You don't let me finish my sentences."

"I give you the first three minutes."

"This is true." Harry sounded mollified. "Well, have a good time in—where're you going, anyway?"

"Fishing." Nick terminated the connection.

He glanced at his watch: 9:42 A.M. Reengaging the modem, he accessed a special priority channel and ordered a small private plane for 11:00, transportation to the airfield, a car upon arrival. The requisition was acknowledged.

Nick secured the terminal and went to shower and dress. He'd allowed himself sufficient time.

He knew he was dreaming. It was something he so rarely did; he felt a certain curiosity.

He was in a dark hall—vaulted ceilings, granite floors. His clipped steps echoed across the cavernous room which seemed to go on and on as he walked briskly toward its darkened center, wondering if he'd ever get there. Flames licked the edges of his vision, where strange shapes and writhing forms blended with shadows in an indistinct, undulating union that was vaguely obscene. Jagged scrawls of unknown writing climbed the walls, spreading like a thousand tiny, glistening cracks against the darker sheen of moisture coating the rough stone. Somewhere in the distance, water dripped.

He noted all this in an abstract way; it formed a blurred montage at the periphery of his awareness.

He was drawing closer. His attention was riveted on the slender white pedestal in the center of the vast room. Standing alone, unembellished, it pierced the darkness with clean, flowing lines, gently tapered, its flat, oval surface marble smooth. On it rested a small, brilliantly glowing stone.

The stone was encased in glass—thin, unblemished glass so clear it dazzled with a beauty all its own. His gaze fastened on the brilliance. He couldn't pull away.

And then he was standing at the pedestal, gazing down through the pure glass. Glittering worms crawled around and through the stone; slender, incandescent creatures of liquid, blinding light.

He leaned closer, drawn to the stone's strange beauty yet repelled by the sightless things that slithered at its heart. Something whispered; he couldn't catch the words, yet he heard the voice deep within him, familiar; still, he couldn't quite identify it. Coldness began seeping into him with the light, touching every part of him . . . touching . . .

. . . *closer . . . closer . . . the stone began to pulse and shift, expanding outward to meet his gaze . . . humming softly . . . humming—*

With a start, Nick awoke.

Around him the Cessna hummed its soft, steady drone. Nick glanced at the pilot on his left. The man's profile was a combination of craggy features, concentration, and Ray-Ban sunglasses.

Nick turned back to the panoramic view of blue ocean, blue sky, and green-and-dun seacoast out the forward window, still seeing the stone vaguely superimposed, a shimmering mirage. It seemed etched on his vision, imprinted on his own dark glasses like a photographic negative. Slowly it began to fade.

"Five minutes till landing."

Nick nodded a response, sensing the pilot's glance. He flew when expedience demanded, but only then. It wasn't an acute dislike, just a mild restlessness that probably had more to do with being confined than being in the air. He usually countered with a nap.

He didn't usually dream.

Nick glanced out the side window at the irregular coastline below. Inlets and channels wove through strips of beachland. Long sandbars stretched across the light blue-green of shallow ocean, forming an irregular barrier to the breaking whitecaps that rolled toward shore.

He thought about the balance of things—and that made him think of Frank Terrell. That account would remain outstanding as long as Terrell lived. He'd been the strongest of the rising lieutenants representing several of the bigger families who had advocated a more liberal, aggressive policy. Together, they'd begun swaying enough of the old guard to cause concern among Nick's project managers.

Most of that threat was gone now, of course. The carefully maintained status quo nearly restored. Except for Terrell.

Nick didn't like leaving an adjustment pending, even if the risk was within acceptable limits.

But Terrell could wait. He could afford to take this time out. It might cost him an edge—Terrell would continue hunting him while he was involved here—but not a critical one. He would take care of things when he got back.

"Coming around for landing."

Nick continued staring out the window as the plane banked into a curve. The list was to his side;

it made him feel as though he were weighting down the plane, causing it to sink toward the mosaic of land and water rushing up to meet them.

He remembered something Harry had told him once, about bad deeds being tethered stones thrown out from the body. Too many and eventually the weight would drag you down. Mildly interested, Nick had asked if it were a Korean philosophy. Harry had replied, No—Pink Floyd.

Leaving philosophical thinking in the clouds where it belonged, Nick watched the Cessna straighten into the small, abandoned landing field, felt the momentary kick as it touched down.

They rolled to a stop beside a rusted metal hangar and a patch of scrub brush. He retrieved his nylon tote and the ECCO, and climbed out of the plane, which immediately began taxiing back down the pockmarked runway.

A car was waiting for him inside the deserted hangar, a black-and-gray four-wheel drive that suited the area. He retrieved the key from a small compartment concealed inside the right rear fender. Unshouldering the tote bag, he tossed it on the seat next to the ECCO, got in, and started the engine. There would be other items hidden elsewhere in the vehicle's body and interior.

They could wait.

+ + +

A different place. New.

Soft colors. Soft voices. Warmth.

She lay there, clutching her Fuzzy, eyes closed to the outside world, seeing just the same. Still hiding within her glass cocoon—not so thick, now, but not yet gone.

Her world was under her control as much as she could make it. Small, because she was small and afraid to try for bigger things. Bigger things could hurt, could kill—

Mommy . . .

She backed farther away again, away from the glass and what was on the other side. Mommy was gone, but *it* was still there, cold, shining, wanting to get in.

"No!" She might have whispered it.

"Honey . . . ? Sara, did you say something? Doctor, I think I heard her say something . . ."

Sara felt the warm spot glowing just outside the glass, heard the murmur of voices. They were nice voices. She thought about making a little hole just at that spot, maybe reaching through. But the cold thing was out there too, and it was stronger than the warm, so much stronger. She could feel it in the distance, waiting; see its brightness, glittery and hard. It wanted her to make a hole.

She drew her Fuzzy closer, moving away from the glass, not moving at all.

She couldn't come out yet.

+ + +

PART TWO

The Ridge

3

Special Agent Lew Harris rested his hands on the low stone wall rimming the terrace and breathed tangy salt air deep into his lungs. He could taste it on his lips and tongue, feel the grainy tightness that the sea wind brought to his skin. Overhead a gull screeched, its raucous call echoed by several others farther out. A sky heavy with rain hung low over the horizon, darkening from pearl-gray at the farthermost edges to churning storm clouds converging on the point.

Lew lifted his face to the wind, watched the soaring gulls skim along the currents, occasionally diving, sometimes landing on the sand, always scavenging for food.

The blue-and-white soft spring day had turned hard and gray. A squall might be coming in with the tide. Straightening, Lew buttoned his raincoat against the chill and dampness that was part ocean spray and part spits of rain, and turned up his collar. The surf had roughened since his arrival; heaving breakers now rolled in to crash against the rocks below. Their steady rumble played a backup to the wind.

Shoving his hands into his pockets, he moved away from the rocky parapet that formed an irregular wall around the old stone edifice that seemed a part of the cliff itself. This whole point was an anomaly of sorts, bunched into an otherwise smooth coastal area to form a spiny ridge jutting out into the water. It looked as if some gigantic force had jammed the land together here, causing it to bulge roughly at the seam.

Situated on this rugged promontory was the archaic stone structure that derived its name from its location. Part house, part monastery, part ruin, The Ridge squatted like a huge gray relic of a bygone era, one Lew couldn't quite pin down. He couldn't imagine living here, not even discounting what had happened last night.

Lew's stomach gave an involuntary lurch. He'd arrived hungry because he avoided breakfast and had skipped lunch to make the drive up from the state capital as quickly as possible. Now, two hours later, food was something he didn't much want to think about.

The scene he'd just spent two hours investigating had finally sent him out here to this stone terrace on the side of the house overlooking the sea, seeking to cleanse his eyes and lungs of the carnage that reeked inside the house. The remains of four bodies—two adults, two children—hung spattered from almost every square inch of the great room; walls, ceiling, floor, nothing had escaped the massive eruption of blood and bone and flesh . . .

nothing, that is, but a small circular island in the center of the room, about two feet in diameter, where the child had been standing.

Sara Vears: age seven, long blond hair, blue eyes, quiet.

Lew mentally reviewed the report he'd been given by the first man on the scene: "acting" chief of police for the little unincorporated fishing village of Spiney Point, North Carolina, the closest thing to a town the general area could boast. The chief had been responding to what he'd thought was an anonymous crank call about some disturbance at The Ridge—and had walked onto the pages of a Stephen King novel instead.

Chief Clyde Glenn's position was more honorary than official—such hamlets usually rely on the volunteer system of city management, and rarely have the funds, or the need, for any type of full-time civil servants. But the man had acted quickly and competently in the face of an event so completely out of his scope: contacting the State Bureau of Investigation's main office in Raleigh, getting the proper authorities on the scene, and vocally relieved, Lew recalled with a dab of irony, to shed responsibility for this investigation at the earliest possible moment.

"Never been so glad to hand off a ball in my life," he'd freely admitted by way of greeting when Lew arrived at the scene. Glenn was a former high school quarterback and an avid Carolina football fan.

Despite the chief's tendency to insert vignettes into his conversations, Lew was finding his preliminary reports surprisingly concise and thorough. And a good thing. As a simple matter of standard procedure, this case would be treated as a potential homicide until proven otherwise.

Lew knew better than to underrate the value of the "local law" in this sort of investigation. Particularly a "law" who'd been local for any great length of time, and specifically one like Glenn, who'd been there since birth. It was important, often critical, when the SBI was called in to head up a case, to work closely and smoothly with local authorities. They knew who to go to, what questions to ask. They could tell you things based on knowledge and experience of the area and its people. And they often had answers that explained away even the most tantalizing red herrings.

No one was explaining away Sara Vears, though, and most were avoiding discussing her with an uneasiness that bordered on evasion. But then, how *did* one explain finding a little girl standing unharmed in the middle of a room where four other people had been literally blown apart, finding her completely untouched by the carnage, as though she stood within a small, protected circle that nothing could enter?

According to Glenn, she'd been dressed in pajamas, feet bare, clutching a stuffed animal to her chest. She'd been in deep shock, and was taken to the nearest hospital as soon as a rescue squad made it to the scene. The sheriff's department had placed someone with her, but so far she'd said nothing, acknowledged no one. Still, Lew had hopes that she'd soon come around. He wanted to know what the hell had happened here, and she seemed to be the only witness.

The father was on his way—Lew pulled a small pad out of his pocket and checked his notes: Nicholas Vears, the deceased woman's first husband.

The sheriff's deputy who'd contacted Vears made mention that the man seemed strangely unaffected by the news. Lew filed this thought for possible correlation later. Perhaps the man had simply been stunned; perhaps he was the type who kept his emotions private; and perhaps there was some other, more ulterior, reason for his reticence. Ex-husbands who didn't have custodial rights and perhaps deeply resented a wife's second marriage were sometimes prone to acts of retaliation. And it was, after all, his child who had survived.

A vision of the room inside filled Lew's mind, and he couldn't stop the slight wince. It took a certain kind of monster to be capable of this kind of retaliation. Reaction gave way to reasoning: How was it accomplished? The Big Question.

Vears was due in sometime today. Lew made a mental note to be around when he arrived.

Apparently the only other next of kin was the dead man's sister: Patricia Danielle Grant. They'd had some trouble reaching her. Though she lived in Charleston, South Carolina, she'd been in Key West, researching an article for one of the larger nature magazines; Miss Grant was a freelance writer. Lew thought he might have read some of her work. She'd be here as soon as flight connections would allow.

Lew felt the mask of grimness close down his face as he tucked the pad into his pocket and headed back around the corner of the house toward the waiting mob. He hoped the lab boys would finish soon and they could get the place cleaned up before she arrived. He, for one, didn't want a hysterical relative on site, and he wouldn't wish this nightmare scene on Freddy Krueger.

"Agent Harris, I'm with Channel 2 News—"

"Agent Harris, our camera crew would like—"

"Do you have a statement for the press, Agent Harris?"

Mini-cams pinpointed him. A few camera bulbs flashed.

Lew strode past waving hands and gesticulating microphones, ignoring the crush of reporters jockeying for position on the rocky terrain and trying their best to get at him through police barricades. It never failed to impress him how the news media got wind of these things, often arriving at an acci-

dent or crime scene even before the investigation
team could get there.

They were certainly out in full force for this one,
he noted, running a practiced eye over the milling
crowd. But four people splattered over a room, in
a quiet little fishing commune where violence *never*
occurred, was bound to be something of a nine-day
wonder.

And they were getting restless; no longer content
with the canned-rote speech he'd fed them earlier.
It was becoming harder all the time to stall the
press with standard bullshit lines the department
kept in the can for situations such as this.

Flanking the news cadre, a less vocal crowd had
gathered; locals come to gawk and pander to their
curiosity. They stood grouped along the edges of
the boundary line the sheriff's department had
erected, policed by a couple of deputies who were
stoically fending off questions, and some auxiliary
forces from volunteer fire departments and rescue
squads. Behind them, the rough terrain dropped
away to a smooth, deep stretch of deserted beach-
front.

Lew let his eyes roam left. Inside the barricade,
a relatively flat area held official vehicles of all
sorts: two mobile crime lab vans from the Criminal
Investigations Division in Raleigh; a dusty old station wagon boasting county coroner's insignia; sundry police cars and a couple of fire-and-rescue units;
his own dark, unmarked 1987 Ford that screamed
State Bureau of Investigation from its elaborate an-
tennae to its cheap hubcaps. News team vans and
other vehicles belonging to the uninvited lined the
winding driveway almost all the way down to the
beach road.

Like maggots to carrion, Lew thought—then re-
gretted it as he felt his stomach give another lurch.
But then, they had their jobs to do—some of them.

He briefly toyed with the idea of marching the avid one by one through the great room to see who'd upchuck first, but the lab boys wouldn't thank him for it.

The rumble of distant thunder turned his eyes back out to sea. Shades of purple and slate now blossomed on the horizon. His gaze fell on a small knot of oddly dressed people standing silent and watchful just below the ridge, where beach met rock. One of them seemed to have orange hair—

"Our local group of punk rockers," Chief Glenn had come up behind Lew. "Adds color to the area, don't you think?"

Lew cast a skeptical look at the shorter man, who was wearing a Carolina blue sweatshirt, russet cords, a green-and-yellow baseball cap, and his best Andy Taylor grin, but he merely said: "Where do they live?"

"Rent an old place down the beach 'bout a mile. Pretty remote for kids, but they seem to like it that way. No neighbors to complain about the loud music, I guess."

Or the pot parties, Lew thought, then felt the slight disgust that followed. He didn't like insta-matic labeling—from others, and particularly not from himself.

"Ever cause any trouble?" Lew resumed his walk toward the house, Chief Glenn in tow.

"Not a bit," the acting police chief replied. "One of 'em used to spend summers here as a child, grandmother lived nearby. Stay to themselves most of the time, or off playing. Got a band," he qualified in response to Lew's expression. "Used to be in a band myself. The Seagram's Seven. Played drums."

They entered the stone house through an arched portico and double, solid redwood doors that looked recently installed, except that the glass in two decorative viewports about a third of the way down had been shattered, as though the small windows had exploded outward.

Lew had noticed the broken glass on approaching the house the first time, alerted by the crunch of it beneath his feet. Though most of it had been swept up for testing, a few shards still lay scattered on the flagstone walkway just beyond the doors.

It was a phenomenon repeated by every pane of glass in the great room. Plastic sheathing and plywood boards had been loosely tacked across the broken windows. The shattered glass had initially suggested a natural gas or chemical explosion— coupled with the fact that electrical power to the house had been mysteriously interrupted; the phone line was still out.

Except that there were no gas pipelines in this area, no propane tanks in the house, no evidence of any type of explosives. In fact, the fire department and the mobile crime lab techs had found no residue whatsoever of combustibles or chemical contaminants. No toxic fumes.

The front doors opened into a moderately sized entry hall that rose to the second floor. Facing him, a stone staircase ascended into gloom, a series of shallow steps and interspersed landings that led up, then left, then up again to a level Lew hadn't yet checked.

To the left of the staircase a hallway stretched back toward the unused portion of the house: the original monastic quarters, an old chapel, a further section of crumbling ruins. Mentally comparing the interior of the partially renovated structure to its exterior, Lew realized that the house grew more decayed the farther back it went, as though it had one foot in the grave.

Rooms in use lined both sides of the main corridor: a modern kitchen, well-stocked pantry, and laundry on the left; a coat closet, comfortably furnished den, and bath on the right. The doors were recessed into the stone walls, creating small alcoves along the hall, and suggesting they might have once been monks' quarters. At the end, an archway fitted with a custom-made oak door stained to look old closed off the unrenovated section.

On Lew's immediate left another archway and two steps led down into a formal dining room. The great room was on his right.

Sounds of the lab team still at work filtered through the bifold doors Lew had closed on leaving earlier, along with the smell that would be forever associated with his first homicide. It was a thing one didn't forget.

The sounds came muffled, but Lew could picture the scene inside, like something out of a NASA training film, with techs in their rubber shoes and plastic suits and protective masks. The great room hadn't been furnished yet; possibly the Grants were saving it, doing the more necessary rooms first. Considering what now decorated it, Lew counted small blessings.

Unbuttoning his coat, he pointed toward the upper corridor. "Bedrooms that way?"

"Right." The police chief fell into step, subdued for the moment.

Smudges of graphite powder on the wooden banister marked the print specialist's progress.

"What do you think happened here, Chief Glenn?" Lew asked as they reached the upper landing and stopped at the first door. He didn't usually like pinning down the local law too soon when major guesswork was involved—better to get acquainted before inviting them out on a limb. But this case wasn't fitting any routine pattern, and the man seemed to have something on his mind, despite his obvious desire to dump the ball.

"Curly . . ."

"What?" Lew frowned at the non sequitur.

"The name's Curly. Nobody calls me Chief Glenn—and I'm not sure you want to know what I think."

Lew's frown deepened into puzzlement. "What do you mean by that?"

Evading the probe, Curly took a moment to lift the green-and-yellow baseball cap by its brim and swab his sleeve across an indentation in the smooth skin where it had rested. Setting the cap back in place, he said, "How 'bout I buy you a beer later this evening—you do drink beer?"

Lew felt as if he'd just been tossed a loaded question. Relaxing, he followed it with: "Only in months that have twenty-eight days."

Curly gave him a blank look for the time it took to mentally decode the quip, then dissolved into a lively smile and a chortle of delight. "Damned if I won't have to remember that one. 'Only in months that have twenty-eight days.' That's a good one, Lew, really good." Curly emphasized his appreciation with a slap to Lew's shoulder. "Got a place to stay?"

Lew's momentary relaxation fled. He eyed the beaming chief warily. Had he passed the test too well? Was the man about to offer a spare bedroom? Nice as Curly seemed, Lew cherished his moments of solitude far too much to bunk in with someone if he could help it, particularly when on an investigation. And he was usually on an investigation. A combination of the two could explain why he'd never married.

"Not yet . . ." he said tentatively, preparing to be polite, but firm should the offer come.

"Suzie can accommodate you."

"Your wife?" Lew was still treading cautiously.

"Oh, no. No no. Not my wife. Suzie and I—we—

that is, there was some talk between us once—but
we never, I mean, we *do* but we're not . . ." Curly's
voice trailed off on an embarrassed and rather feeble laugh. His round cherub's face had turned beet
red.

Lew cleared his throat of the laughter that
threatened. "So where is this—"

"Suzie's Bar and Fish Camp," Curly announced
hurriedly, regaining his equilibrium. "It's sort of
an inn, restaurant, and tavern all rolled into one.
Caters to the year-round fishing trade. There's a
couple other places, but Suzie's is best. Most comfortable, too—though don't expect plush, you won't
get it. Good food."

Lew felt it was time to get things back on track.
He gave Curly a quick nod and opened the bedroom
door. "You can tell me how to get there later, and
I'll buy the second round."

The little girl's bedroom—for it was obviously
that—reached out to Lew as he entered. It was as
though a small, serene world existed here, separate
and apart from the ugly reality surrounding it. Cool
green washed the room, the color of shallow water.
Edged with white at curtains and mid-sized canopy
bed, it rolled toward Lew like a gently breaking
wave, all liquid serenity and sea-foam lace. The
sooty remains of the print work was a desecration.

Against the soft gray stone of walls and floor, the
room appeared merely an extension of the view from
the large bay window, an alcove complete with cush-
ioned window seat overlooking the long strand of
deserted beach and the ocean. The lead-paned casements were closed, but Lew could almost feel the
wind blowing through the room, lifting the curtains,
ruffling the canopy, could almost see a little girl with
long blond hair and clear blue eyes standing by the
window gazing out to sea . . . clutching a stuffed
animal.

He stepped into the room, aware that Curly had stopped at the threshold. He was glad. Something about this room made being alone special. It was a child's room, but the ambience felt ageless.

Lew firmly believed that much could be learned about a person from the space he or she inhabited. Particularly a bedroom or office. It went beyond the fact that people always left something of themselves wherever they'd been: hair, threads or fabric lint, a chip of nail polish; no, it was more intrinsic, a permeation. He'd spent many investigative hours testing this theory, and had gotten into the habit of "feeling" out a place, studying even the most minute detail. It worked more often than not—and was much cleaner than scrounging through garbage cans, a job he usually delegated with relish. Details could talk to you sometimes.

A table caught his eye.

He crossed the room to a small pedestal-based table topped by a circle of inch-thick polished marble. It looked like an antique smoking table, the kind found beside a comfortable leather wing chair, just large enough for an ashtray, a brandy snifter, a small reading lamp.

This one held rocks. Pebbles, actually, Lew saw as he gently blew away the faint dusting of volcanic print powder and picked one up, running a thumb lightly across its surface.

Like river rock, these beach stones had been worn smooth by the currents and tossed ashore by the tide. Some were rock, some shell fragments, eroded past identification to anyone but a geologist. There were ten in all, roughly circular in placement except for a single white stone lying in the center and a black one off to one side.

Lew replaced the one he held, careful to put it back exactly where it had been, and lifted the center stone. It wasn't as smooth as the others, but had hairlike erosions in its surface, tiny channels criss-crossing it as though parts had proved more susceptible to the water's effect. He laid it down and chose another, the black one, so polished that its surface was reflective.

A small white wicker rocking chair with soft green-and-white cushions was drawn up to the table. Something told Lew Sara Vears spent quite a lot of time in that chair, at this table, playing with these stones. A child's simple game? He wondered.

Laying the black stone down, he turned to study the rest of the rather pristine room. No clutter existed here, no strewn clothes or carelessly tossed toys. The neatness bordered on sterility—a place for everything, everything in its place. Three dolls sat on a love seat, two on the right, one on the left; a bookcase held two shelves of neatly stacked books, two of games. Teddy Ruxpin gazed down from the crest. A toy chest was presided over by a collection of Sesame Street Muppets. A small glass curio case displayed a miniature crystal zoo.

The only flaw was the thrown-back covers on the canopy bed. Lew strolled over to that section of the room, took note of the soft green sheets patterned with tiny white shells that matched quilt, canopy, and curtains. A fluffy white throwrug lay exactly where small feet would land. A pair of bunny bedroom shoes sat primly to one side.

Her feet were bare.

Something inside Lew hardened at the thought of a child's small bare feet on a cold stone floor.

He turned to Curly. "This is over the dining room, isn't it?"

Curly nodded. "It's the largest of the kids' rooms, but then she was the oldest. Other two are down the hall, this side."

"And the Grants?"

"Their room is above the great room. Sort of a

suite, I guess you'd call it: bedroom, sitting room, big bath. They'd started on a balcony, but it's not finished yet. Never will be, now. At least, not by them." Curly's somber tone piqued another question.

"Were they friends of yours?"

Curly visibly lifted himself from the verge of the abyss he'd been contemplating. "No, not friends. Not yet. Hadn't been time for friendship. Nice people, though. Didn't deserve this."

Lew refrained from the clichéd responses, took one last, brisk look around the strangely compelling room, and walked toward the door. "Let's see the parents' suite."

"Right." Curly led the way toward a large, arched oak door set into the stone wall about a dozen yards down the corridor and to their right. "In here." He thrust the door open and stood back for Lew to enter. This time, he followed the special agent inside.

The sheer expanse of the room was impressive; the view through three sets of double French doors was breathtaking. The ocean had darkened to gray-green. Whipped by the wind, small breakers crested the choppy waves as far out as Lew could see. The surf's muted roar seeped in through the glass, a steady, lulling undertone that conspired with the view to lure the senses.

The sky was a match for the ocean, a darker greenish gray that had smoothed from the boiling clouds of earlier. A swatch of misty streaks to the east signaled rain. It would be here soon.

"Gonna rain soon," Curly spoke Lew's thought, coming to stand beside him at the center set of doors. "But not a nor'easter, won't last long. Expect we'll see the sunset."

Lew nodded absently and turned back to the room. It had been beautifully decorated in rich shades of peach and emerald. Bold colors. A king-size brass bed dominated a large section of one wall, its intricate design blemished by crumpled covers tossed back on either side. An overturned wine glass rested against the base of a lamp on the left-hand bedside table. An open paperback book lay on the table to the right.

Lew walked over and peered at its title: *The Troubled Child*, by a doctor of psychology with a string of letters longer than his name. Carole Grant's side of the bed?

Several large paintings were mounted on the stone walls—landscapes of the area, done in an almost abstract style that was vibrant and alight with the plastic glare of acrylics. No tepid watercolors, these. Lew knew very little about art, but he knew what he liked. He didn't like these. They were stagy. But he thought he could recognize the impact they might have in artistic circles.

In fact, the whole room seemed rather like a stage setting. Lew, who was used to the compact messiness of his Raleigh apartment, the cubicle that was his office, and the string of bed-and-boards that always accompanied out-of-town investigations, simply couldn't imagine calling this place "home." Except, perhaps, for Sara Vears's small world.

He moved across the long room to an offset area that once had probably been an entirely separate chamber. The stone walls that protruded from either side and arched above the opening looked altered to suit. The sitting area within formed a sort of inverted "L," with a short, wide section first, and a longer, thin segment fronting the windowed side. It was here that the deck had been started. Lew could envision the morning sunbathing, the evening cocktails that might have been planned for this private balcony.

A general couch-and-chairs arrangement filled the

initial area, a more personal niche nestled into the far corner. Lew pointed to a door in the closed section to his left. "Bath?"

"Right."

He nodded absently, not looking at Curly, who by his voice was following him through the suite.

Lew walked toward the far end of the sitting area, paying scant attention to the "Better Homes and Gardens" section, drawn to the place he felt certain had been Carole Grant's retreat. There was something decidedly feminine about it, and Lew had an idea that it was here Carole came when her husband was off painting.

The overstuffed lounger looked inviting; a glass-top patio table sat near-to-hand. A too-small bookcase was filled to overflowing, the excess stacked on the floor. Mostly paperbacks, fiction of the best-seller variety. Glitz, glitter, and lurid covers stared up at Lew. He recognized some of his own favorites.

A small portable TV, with battery adapter, rested beside a filled ashtray and a half-full wine glass that matched the one on the bedside table. Here, too, the print specialist had obviously been at work.

A crumpled pack of Salem Lights lay next to another, unopened, pack and a disposable lighter in a silver-and-cloisonné case. Small curls of gray cigarette ash dotted the glass tabletop as though haphazardly flicked toward the ashtray. A couple of cigarettes had been left to burn away, long gray tubes that would crumble on touch.

A natural chain smoker? Or did Carole Grant have a problem? This was not a comfortable messiness; there was an edgy feel to it.

"Do you know of any problems that might have been bothering the Grants, Mrs. Grant in particular?" Lew turned to glance at Curly, who was poised in the archway between rooms.

The chief seemed about to say something, thought a minute, then shook his head. "Nothing I've heard, 'cept maybe the little girl. She was kind of shy, withdrawn even. Coulda been having trouble adjusting to a new place, and of course Grant wasn't her natural father. Sometimes hard for a kid."

The Troubled Child.

Lew nodded and glanced back at the table, reaching for a small blue leather address book half hidden by a cordless phone. It opened easily to where a page had been ripped out. The jagged edges looked fresh.

"Here," Curly said from just behind his left shoulder.

Lew turned, his face a question.

"Picked it up when I checked the room earlier, before you folks arrived." Curly handed him a small piece of lined paper that had obviously been wadded up, then smoothed out. "Thought I'd better keep it on me, what with all the hubbub that'd be goin' on. Stuff can get lost in the shuffle sometimes."

Lew refrained from pointing out that a trained SBI team didn't lose stuff in the shuffle; and if Curly had been referring to his own area forces, enough said on that.

"It's the father's phone number," Curly confirmed what Lew was reading, "Nicholas Vears. That's how we knew where to contact him."

"Where was this?"

"On the floor there." Curly gestured to the corner behind the table. "Looked like it had been torn out, wadded up, and thrown aside."

Lew regarded the paper. The number was one of those special forwarding codes that got routed through independent trunk lines. There was no address. "Do you have an address on Vears?"

"Sheriff got it."

Lew carefully inserted the rumpled paper into the address book, blew print dust from the cover, and pocketed it.

"What else is up here besides the other two kids' rooms?" He pulled out a handkerchief and wiped black powder from his fingers as they walked toward the door.

"One spare bedroom—Grant's sister visited a time or two—couple of unfinished rooms, and David Grant's studio. That's over the far end; probably used as some sort of watchtower once, open to the sea. Grant glassed it in, of course."

A brisk walk and a cursory inspection got Lew through the balance of the upstairs tour in about ten minutes. He'd spend more time here later; right now he needed to check with the lab team.

Kathleen Boyce was just exiting the great room as Lew and Curly descended the stairs. Lew finished getting directions to Suzie's, told Curly he'd see him later, and crossed to where she was pulling the hood from her head. Springy wisps of long red hair had tangled in the mask.

"I'm gonna cut it, so help me God, I'm gonna cut it!" she muttered, yanking at stubborn snarls that wound around the straps.

"Now Kate," Lew stopped beside her and began gently uncoiling hair from elastic bands and groping fingers. "You know you've been saying that forever and don't mean a word of it."

"Yeah?" she stabbed him with a green-eyed glare. "Well, this time I do . . . if only to get the smell out."

The last phrase was muttered as an afterthought, but it held a shudder of revulsion and he could tell she was genuinely affected by what was in that room. *Jesus, weren't they all.*

He finished untangling the headgear and handed it back to her. "Any answers?"

"Christ, Lew. We're still trying to deal with the *questions*." She raked a hand through her tousled hair. "This is the worst yet, the worst I've ever seen—and I was part of the team that did that 'House of Horrors' up in Merrillville couple years ago."

She started walking toward the front door. "So far I can tell you *nada*. And don't count on Bill for much more. Truth is, I'm not even sure we want to know what caused it."

"Yeah." Lew followed her, understanding her need to get outside. "This case certainly has some strange aspects."

"Strange?" Kate gave a little laugh that held no humor. "Fucking *weird* is what I'd call it. There is absolutely no—repeat *no*—explanation for that clean circle in the middle of the room. None what-soever. And it *is* clean; we even sprayed it down."

Lew frowned. There went his theory that some-one had scrubbed the circle. The chemical solution that the CID teams used to "spray down" an appar-ently clean surface would immediately reveal even washed-out bloodstains.

"Whatever ripped those people apart couldn't have missed the kid if she was in there at the time," Kate added.

"But apparently it did," Lew murmured thought-fully, and she shrugged.

They reached the double front doors and Lew gripped the handle, holding it a moment. "How much more time you think you guys will need?"

"Who knows. Another day, maybe. We're through photographing and taking measurements, but there's still the vacuuming to be done. They're scraping remains into body bags now. The ME's gonna have his work cut out for him—no pun in-tended."

"None taken," Lew murmured absently. The pun

ritual was an old game between them, and habit
betrayed him now by popping up a rejoinder about
"off-the-wall shit." He swallowed heavily.

Kate shifted the headgear from one arm to the
other and looked up at Lew with a grimace of dis-
taste. "Shit. I'll be sleeping with this one for the
next six months."

Lew gave her shoulder a sympathetic squeeze as
they went outside. Kate smiled grimly and headed
for one of the vans.

Ignoring the instant clamor that rose from the
media hounds, Lew searched until he spotted Sheriff Seddons standing at the far end of the barricade
talking to someone, probably a reporter. Lew knew
he was going to have to issue some sort of statement, but was determined to put it off as long as
possible. Maybe the threatened rain would end up
postponing it for today, at least. He projected silent
encouragement to the rumble of thunder that
sounded in the distance.

The sheriff had extricated himself by the time
Lew neared him, and he drew Seddons aside, making arrangements for the house to be placed under
twenty-four-hour guard until the lab teams had finished. The area would remain roped off until the
investigation was complete.

And who knew how long that might take.

"How about letting me know when the little girl's
father arrives," Lew said as an afterthought. "I'd
like to speak with him myself."

"Nicholas Vears?" The sheriff glanced back over
his shoulder. "He's already here. Was just talking
to him."

Lew followed the look. "Can you point him out?"

Sheriff Seddons's grizzled head scanned the
crowd, squinted eyes searching. Permanent crin-
kles in the leathery skin made it a face that would

have looked more at home at the prow of a fishing boat. "Don't see him now. Probably left for the hospital already. Was asking directions. Told him we'd be needing to talk to him, get some information for our reports. Said he'd be back as soon as he'd taken care of things out there."

"Did he say where he's staying?"

"Nowhere yet. Asked about local accommodations." The sheriff gave up his search. "Wanted to know all about what happened here, when it happened, how. Didn't tell him much. Gave him your name."

"Yet he left without talking to me," Lew mused. "What's he look like?"

Seddons thought a moment, then shrugged. "Kind of average. Not too tall. About your build. Brownish hair. Had on aviator glasses, dark leather jacket."

Lew quickly scanned the crowd again, thinking: About. Not too. Kind of. Maybe Curly was right. Stuff *could* get lost in the shuffle. Or did Vears have something to hide? "Did you happen to see what make of vehicle he was driving?"

"Well no, I didn't." The sheriff's tone hardened slightly. "There were no orders to detain him. Want me to put a car on it?"

Lew shook his head, recognizing the signs of a man going on the defensive. No need to let his actively suspicious nature antagonize the sheriff over what was probably just a temporary delay. He could always track Vears down if he needed to. He decided he didn't, at least not yet. It was always better to secure a potential suspect's *willing* cooperation as long as possible—particularly when you lacked evidence.

Either Vears had nothing to do with what had happened here, or felt secure enough not to be overly concerned. Whichever the case, he was here now, and wasn't going anywhere for the moment. They'd get their answers soon enough.

But it was interesting, Lew thought as he took leave of the sheriff and headed back toward the house, that so far Nicholas Vears was the one asking questions.

4

Thunder rolled over the heads of the small group trudging down the deserted beach. Three males, two females, all young, feet pushing through the soft, cool sand in an unconsciously syncopated rhythm.

The leader of the group, Set Reynolds, moved with a casual grace that made his lithe body seem almost boneless. Shoulder-length bleached blond strands blew back from an aristocratic face that was a study in thoughtfulness. Wind pasted his white linen priest's shirt to his chest and upper arms, rippled the loose khakis rolled almost to his knees. His feet were bare, like most of the group's. Clear green eyes gazed into the distance as if seeing something visible only to him. It was the look he often had when he played his music—as though the guitar strings were being stroked by his mind, not his fingers.

One golden-tanned arm, with its sprinkle of sun-bleached hairs, loosely draped around the delicate shoulders of a petite, ethereal child-woman whose platinum halo of gossamer-fine hair matched those on Set's arm. Twyla Gerrard looked like a Dresden figurine angel, and possessed a voice to match. Dressed in a long white eyelet skirt and over-blouse, her head came about to the top of Set's shoulders, and she was having to stretch her steps to meet his long strides, a fact he seemed totally unaware of.

Wriggling against his side, she murmured, "Slow down, Set."

He glanced down at her and, grinning, eased his pace, curling his arm to brush the tip of her nose with a long, well-shaped finger. The tiny nose wrinkled a response, and Twyla gazed up into smiling green eyes with a childlike smile all her own.

Behind them the three other members of the band walked along in staggered silence: Hump, their five-foot-five-inch, 122-pound drummer who looked like a skinny, intellectual twelve-year-old in horn-rimmed glasses and a red Peewee Herman hair-cut—he was the only one wearing shoes; Mitch Michaels, keyboardist, lyricist, with his dark good looks, safety-pinned ears, and brooding stage presence; Vesper, Mitch's girlfriend and their flamboyant, orange-haired bass player, dressed like a biker and looking tough.

They called themselves KAFKA, and for almost two years they'd shared their talent and aspirations in a way only those with similar dreams can ever understand. It was a bond that transcended most relationships.

Hump, wearing a frown and trying to keep a lace-less tennis shoe from flopping off, murmured, "This thing at The Ridge, what about it, Set?"

"Shit happens," Mitch remarked from beyond Vesper, not sounding particularly concerned. She gave a little giggle.

"C'mon, Set," Hump ignored them, "I'm really worried—"

"What's to worry, man?" Set tossed a grin over his shoulder. Wind flapped the neck of his collarless shirt; he raked a hand to free the hair caught inside it. "Hey, we got a gig this weekend. You want something to worry about? Worry about that."

"But, dammit, Set. What if they find out—"

"Hell!" Set swung around to face the others, who immediately stopped walking. "Nobody's going to find out, okay? Whatever happened back there's got nothing to do with us. It was a fluke, a random thing. It can't touch us, believe me. Nothing's going to touch us."

"Sure, man, okay," Hump murmured, eyes darting, seeking to light anywhere but on Set, unease giving his narrow face an extra pinch.

"Richard Cranium's gonna be around sooner or later asking questions," Mitch drawled to no one in particular.

Set shrugged, then grinned. "Let the dickheads come. We just live in the neighborhood and don't know a thing."

The small group stood in a loose circle as the wind whipped around them and the thunder rolled over them and the conversation died. No one moved when the rain began: hard, cold drops at first, plopping into the sand and making small craters. Then it was a deluge.

"Jesus, my hair," Vesper wailed, and she and Mitch took off, running toward the rented beach house about a hundred yards farther on.

"C'mon, c'mon," Twyla trilled, dancing out from under Set's arm like a wind sprite, trying to pull him with her.

He waved her on ahead, taking a moment to re-roll the sleeve she'd tugged down, then resuming his steady strides while Twyla and Hump dashed toward the house.

Set watched them all rush into the shelter of the

overhanging deck, saw them laughing, shaking water from their clothes and hair. He wasn't surprised when first Vesper, then Mitch, began stripping off their wet clothing and haphazardly tossing it over an improvised clothesline. Twyla and Hump disappeared inside; the others soon followed. None of them looked at Set as he slowed his stride, then turned and started walking toward the raging sea.

Wind battered Set's body as he neared the violent surf, tearing at his clothes and hair. Golden strands lashed his face and neck as the driving rain beat against him and the buffeting sand stung his legs beneath the rolled-up pants.

Oblivious to all discomfort, he came to a halt at the edge of the breakers where the rain blended with the ocean spray.

"Come on, you bastards!" Set yelled to the crashing waves, lifting his arms to embrace the elemental forces at work on him, in him. He could feel the raw power, the surging energy from the sea, the sky—but most of all from him. He stretched his arms higher, lifting his radiant face to the wind.

He was one with the storm. He *was* the storm.

He *was*.

He was.

Nick eased up on the accelerator pedal and watched the speedometer needle drop back to between fifty and fifty-five. The custom-built, high-performance engine beneath the GMC's hood made speeding easy, particularly on a straight road.

Sand extended to either side of the deserted two-lane, merging with the Atlantic on Nick's left, spliced into stunted vegetation and backwater channels on the right. The quick rainstorm had given way to late-afternoon sun, a huge orange ball mirrored by tinted windows and the darker glass shielding watchful eyes.

Nick kept his speed steady, one hand controlling the sensitive steering wheel with a deceptively light touch. The GMC seemed to strain at the leash, taunting him with the power that could be his at the press of a pedal. He ignored the lure.

Collett County General Hospital had proved to be almost a forty-minute drive from The Ridge, tucked into this sparsely populated coastal region with the kind of reasoning only a grant to a depressed area could explain. Nick's lip twitched at the thought of government grants, wondering if his salary would qualify.

The arrangements with the hospital had taken very little time; he'd met the young doctor in charge of Sara's case—and been impressed enough to reconsider moving her, at least for the moment.

He had not gone in to see his daughter, a decision the young doctor had found incomprehensible. Nick had listened calmly to his remarks, said: "Take care of my daughter," and left.

On the seat beside him the ECCO purred. Nick slowed, spotted a fairly solid-looking verge, and pulled off.

Raising the thin LCD screen, he touched a couple of spaces on the board and watched the information he'd requested earlier rapidly fill the void:

HARRIS, LEWIS ANDREW
SS#427-60-9112
5'11", 170, 44, BLK
SPC/AGT, NC-SBI, 1975-CURRENT

A complete dossier followed.

College . . . a tour in Nam . . . degree in Police Science . . . Nick quickly scanned the data, pressed "Save," and closed the lid. It took only a moment to disconnect the ECCO from the specially designed car phone installed in the glove compartment.

Pulling back onto the road, he drove toward the beach cottage he'd rented about a mile and a half down from The Ridge. There'd be time later to explore Agent Lew Harris, but the information confirmed what Nick had sensed at The Ridge: Harris knew his job.

He felt a frown tighten his forehead. *What had really occurred at that house last night?*

Listening to the crowd, quizzing the sheriff, he'd compiled a rather bizarre tale. Nick didn't like bizarre tales; he liked explanations, solutions.

He was going to have to get inside the place, check around himself. Soon. Not tonight, though—the forensic team might still be working. At the very least the place would be under heavy police guard. No, better to wait another day.

The sun was going down, a red half disk sinking into the water.

Scraps of civilization began cropping up alongside the road. He spotted a gas station/grocery just turning on its neons, pulled in, bought a few staples. Tossing them on the back seat he resumed the drive, stripping off his dark glasses, lighting a cigarette. The match flared briefly against his pupils.

The Ridge ...

Bits of conversation came drifting back, comments from the press, various people on the scene. Nick recalled the familiar prickle of awareness he'd felt when he'd first walked toward the house, like his nerve endings were signaling: Watch out. He'd learned to trust that feeling over the years, use it to advantage.

The Ridge ... *what happened at The Ridge* ... ?

Anger taunted Nick's composure as he thought

about what had been done to Carole and her family, Sara. He repressed it; personal vendettas were for fools. But a faint stirring of something that didn't often enter into his routine scheme of things refused to go away:

Curiosity.

Lew caught Curly's wave and headed for the table at the rear of the small, comfortably lit tavern. A couple of empty beer cans indicated that the beaming chief had been waiting awhile. Lew was later than he'd meant to be, having spent some extra time rechecking The Ridge's upstairs quarters, then contemplating the evidence—or lack thereof—from the window seat in Sara Vears's bedroom, a place conducive to thought.

Shrugging out of his damp raincoat, he draped it over an empty chair and slid into the seat across from Curly, asking the question still uppermost on his mind: "What would make two people get up in the middle of the night, grab the kids, and go stand in an empty room?"

The chief looked momentarily startled, but dutifully mulled it over before offering a tentative: "Fear?"

Lew gave a noncommittal shrug. "Of what? Of whom?" He tugged at his already-loosened knit tie, then rested tweed-covered arms on the table, exposing frayed cuffs without embarrassment. He and the jacket were old friends.

"Intruder, maybe?" Curly suggested, not sounding particularly convinced. "Group of drug-crazed weirdos like that Manson bunch few years back?"

Lew shook his head. "No indication of intruders, and drug heads usually ransack a place looking for money. There wasn't an unusually heavy storm last night, was there? Earth tremors? Tornado?"

Now it was Curly's turn to shake his head. "Nope.

Clear as a bell." He took a long swallow from the full can in front of him, as though gathering his thoughts along with the suds.

A swig of courage? Lew wondered.

"What could have frightened them, then? What rousted them out of bed in the dead of night and sent them rushing downstairs to the great room?" Leaning back, he eyed the chief carefully. "You hinted at something this afternoon. Ready to talk about it?"

Curly's reply was forestalled by the waitress's approach.

"Get you something to drink?" She grinned at Lew, reaching past Curly to retrieve the two dead soldiers.

"Bring him a beer, Janey, and I'm about ready for another. What's your brand, Lew?"

"Whatever's on draft, and can I get something to eat in here?" Lew glanced up at the smiling young waitress.

"Sure," Janey said. "Anything that's on the menu."

Since he didn't have a menu—a fact nobody seemed to notice but him—he simply asked for a seafood platter, figuring it was a sure bet and would include at least something to his liking.

Janey nodded and headed off toward what was presumably the restaurant area.

"Now then." Lew rested his arms on the table again, giving Curly a "you-were-about-to-say" look.

Curly glanced around the near-empty bar, leaned forward, adjusted his hat with a hint of conspiracy and whispered: "Lotta folks around here think it was the Ancients."

Lew wasn't quite sure he'd heard right. "Ancients?"

Curly nodded sagely, looking rather like a small

boy who'd just told his mom, "It was the Cookie Bandit."

"What are the ancients?"

"Who," Curly corrected.

Lew felt the beginnings of a headache. He wondered just how many empties Janey might have carted away before these last two. "Okay. *Who* are the Ancients?"

"People who built The Ridge. Some sort of religious order or cult, nobody really knows for sure. Some folks believe they were a band of magicians, sorcerers like, who held power over the rocks. In fact"—Curly leaned in closer—"legend has it The Ridge just sprang into being overnight, pulled from the cliff by the will of this group of mystics, or whatever the hell they were."

The chief punctuated his recital by a dramatic visual effect ending with both hands hanging in the air, arms arched, fingers pinching hypothetical stones pulled up from the table.

He hovered this way a moment, suspended over the silence. "And they disappeared, Lew, without trace. There's not even any graves."

"Are you talking about what I think you're talking about?" Lew couldn't help the amused grimace that crossed his face.

Curly nodded like an overzealous choirboy, dropping his arms. "I know it sounds crazy, but there's been stories . . ." He faltered.

"Stories—?" Lew raised a quizzical eyebrow as a prompt.

"Well, you know how some people talk." Curly glanced around the bar, presumably to see if "some people" were present. "These stories've been around a long time. Stories about secret tombs, unholy rites, sacrifices, things like that."

"Young virgins, no doubt." Lew tried for a straight face, lost.

Curly flushed, then grinned good-naturedly. "Okay, okay, I'll admit it sounds hokey, and nothing's ever been found. But things *have* happened out there."

"What things?" The amusement left Lew's voice.

"Well for starters, people have tried living at The Ridge before. Strangers come here from time to time, see the place and think it's, I don't know, quaint or something. They move in, begin restoring, changing, adding living quarters"—Curly pierced Lew with a telling look—"but none of them ever stay long, like they're uneasy living there. Wary."

"Of what?" Lew pressed. "What exactly has happened out there? I'm talking documented evidence."

The chief appeared to squirm slightly. "Well, nothing precisely *documented*, from an official standpoint, that is. Still, there's a lot of people hereabouts who think that old house may . . . harbor something."

Lew recalled his own thought that The Ridge was not a place he'd care to call home. But that was a far cry from what Curly was suggesting—if he was reading the chief right. He decided to put it to the test.

"Are you saying that you think The Ridge is haunted?" He felt the fool even asking such a ditzy question.

Before Curly could answer, Janey reappeared, arms laden. An oval plate the size of a small tray balanced between her left wrist and elbow. One hand held a can of beer, a place setting, and a napkin; the other gripped a huge frosty mug of draft.

With the nimble grace of a much-repeated act, she placed the can in front of Curly, the napkin and utensils before Lew, lifted the plate from arm to table, and set the mug beside it. "Anything else?"

Lew looked in astonishment at the pile of delicately braised shrimp, lightly fried oysters, small bowl of scallops panned in butter that, wonder of wonders, had *not* been swollen from soaking, thick, golden-brown fish fillets, freshly made deviled crab—he stopped there, glancing up at the grinning waitress. "Anything else and I'll be here till Christmas."

"Enjoy." Whisking away Curly's current empty, she left.

Lew picked up his fork and looked at the plate. He didn't know where to start.

"Just dig in," Curly suggested with a knowing grin. "Believe me, Suzie's cooking tastes just as good as it looks."

Lew immediately discovered that this was simple truth. For a while he ate in silence, liberally sampling each dish before finally stopping to wash it down with a swallow of cold beer. Thankfully, Curly refrained from further ghost stories, letting him enjoy his meal without conversation destined to bring on a severe case of indigestion.

"Don't you want to help me out?" Lew gestured toward the remaining food. "I'll never eat all this."

"Yes you will." Curly nodded knowledgeably. "Too good to waste, even when you know you'll go to bed feeling like a blowfish. Besides, I ate before you got here."

Taking a deep breath, Lew dug back in, knowing when he crossed the line from "enough" to "too much," ignoring it. At last he pushed back his empty plate. "Unreal." Curly chortled, and they both took a drink of beer.

A companionable silence settled down on the table. Lew was reluctant to break it, but . . .

"Chief Glenn—Curly, are you trying to tell me you believe that a group of ancient cultists, or their *ghosts*, rather, killed the Grant family?"

Curly had the grace to blush. He gave a weak chuckle. "Sounds pretty stupid put like that, doesn't it." It was not a question. He drank deeply from his beer can, draining it.

As if on cue, Janey appeared. "Something else, fellas?" She began clearing away dishes.

Lew shook his head, but Curly said, "Couple more beers is all, please, Janey." He placed his current empty on top of the plate she held.

Lew didn't argue. He'd gotten into this wild tale now; he might as well hear it out, and the alcohol would no doubt help.

"You know"—Curly was watching Janey walk away—"I used to have a drinking problem."

Somehow this revelation didn't surprise Lew.

"But I solved it." Curly turned back around. "Now I just drink as much as I want to. No problem." Slapping his hands on the table, he chortled in delight as Janey came back with their refills.

Lew nodded his thanks, began toying with the glass, composing a tactful exit line.

"It fits, though," Curly said into the momentary silence.

Lew frowned.

"Not that I'm telling you, understand, that *I* believe a group of ancient cultists, or their *ghosts*, rather, killed the Grant family," Curly qualified, quoting Lew's earlier words verbatim. He didn't sound the least bit drunk.

The silence lengthened.

"But it fits."

"You know I can't buy that theory," Lew stated unequivocally.

"I didn't really think you would," Curly replied,

not seeming noticeably upset at being politely called a liar—or a nut.

"What about this anonymous crank caller that made the report?" Lew thought it time to get things back on track. "Male? Female? Any idea who?"

"Hard to tell. The voice was muffled. Not much chance of an ID, I'm afraid."

Curly studied the beer can in front of him a moment, hands loosely circling it. "That's another thing, Lew, crank calls. Get 'em from time to time. 'Course there's always one house in every town, one old place that's been there forever just buildin' up stories and yarns until pretty soon folks don't rightly know what's true and what isn't." He looked back at Lew. "People around here are a superstitious, clannish lot. Keep these stories circulating, prob'bly even beef 'em up a bit, too." Curly made the evaluation as though he were not of the clan. "But every time someone moves into that house there's a new spate of talk about disturbing the—" Curly broke off, a tinge of red moving back into his cheeks.

"Ghosts?" Lew supplied helpfully.

"I was going to say Ancients. You know, Lew, there's a lot of people been expecting something like this to happen sooner or later—anticipating it, so to say. Who knows but what they may have something. Where there's smoke . . ." He shrugged. "Get a few calls now and then; always check 'em out, of course."

"Of course." Could Glenn really *believe* this line of BS?

Lew suddenly realized he'd drunk half the beer he'd had no intention of drinking and his stomach was sending him a vehement protest. He set the mug aside, glanced at his watch.

But before he could utter his tactful exit phrase,

the door to the tavern burst open. Both men looked toward the interruption.

A woman stood in the doorway: tall, slender but not thin, dressed in khaki bush shorts and a "Greenpeace" T-shirt topped by a yellow nylon windbreaker. A travel bag was slung over one shoulder. Crumpled socks and tennis shoes did nothing to camouflage shapely ankles or detract from a pair of long, suntanned legs that automatically drew the male eye. She seemed totally unaware of the effect.

Zeroing in on their table she strode forward, not bothering to close the door behind her. Her long legs chewed up the distance with military precision.

Lew leaned back in his chair, regarding her carefully as she stopped beside the table, barring conjecture from his mind.

"Which one of you is Agent Harris?" she clipped, glancing back and forth between the two men. Her short, dark hair looked as if it has been combed with impatient fingers; circles decorated the hollows beneath flashing brown eyes.

"I'm Agent Harris," Lew said, watching her immediately dismiss Curly to the ranks of the non-existent.

"You're in charge of the Grant murders?" She fairly spit the words.

Lew kept his face purposely blank. "I'm investigating the case, yes."

"They were *murdered*," she stated flatly, glaring down at Lew. "And I know who did it!"

5

The half light of dawn played with the sky, the ocean. Early morning gulls and scuttling sand crabs shared the beach outside the rented cottage; broken shells, seaweed, and a single bloated fish lay abandoned by the tide. The water was calm. No wind.

Nick absorbed these facts with the same detachment he gave most extraneous details: they were there; they didn't concern him.

He'd been awake for over an hour, done the set of exercises that kept his body toned to his particular requirements, gone for a swim, then a walk. He stood, now, on the deck looking out to sea, sipping his first cup of coffee—one cream, no sugar—smoking a cigarette, contemplating the enigma of four dead bodies and one live little girl.

The puzzle had its relative points: Nick was no stranger to ambiguous data or answers that defied archetypes. But questions that challenged logic? He lifted the ironstone mug to his lips. He wasn't quite ready to suspend disbelief to that extent.

To all puzzles belongs a key.

It was this one absolute Nick always sought in making an adjustment. One constant upon which all else depended. Find the key and the rest fell into place.

Terrell and his counterparts had been a key.

The pair of drug traffickers Carole had stumbled across that bright summer day had been a key.

Sometimes an adjustment required no more than simply arranging evidence so that more conventional legal channels could come into play; sometimes it was merely a manipulation of existing facts. Killing was not always part of it, not even usually. Only sometimes.

For the first time in a long time, Nick thought about that afternoon six years ago, thought about the two men who'd been trying to consolidate a principal portion of the East Coast drug trade and triple it in a year. They'd been so well camouflaged, protected by loopholes and payoffs, that the law would never have touched them.

It had been his first major adjustment: one involving a kill. He'd spent five months arriving at the inevitable conclusion, another two setting it up. He almost smiled recalling the first and only time he'd bothered *requesting* major sanctioning from his project managers—and the ease with which it had been granted.

She'd believed he was having an affair. Looking back, Nick realized it was the obvious explanation for abrupt absences, cursory excuses or none at all, a cooling marriage. She'd followed him that day, primed for a confrontation, getting one she hadn't bargained for. He'd allowed it, using the situation as a way out for them all—making a choice that was long overdue, letting her take Sara and run.

A seagull dipped toward the water, pecked at something that apparently eluded capture.

Nick's thoughts stretched further back . . . to the time when he'd been simply a troubleshooter for a large corporation heavily involved in military contracts. He'd made a couple of adjustments—of course they hadn't been "adjustments" then—that had brought his particular talents to the attention of his current project managers.

He watched the seagull follow its prey, skimming along the surface until again it struck, this time with success. The gull soared upward, breakfast in its beak.

Where was the key to The Ridge?

Normally Nick arrived at an adjustment by following a direct sequence of cause and effect. Once a key became evident, an outcome could be charted and controlled.

Events at The Ridge, however, suggested a different protocol, effect being the starting point.

The sun was fully up.

Taking a final draw on his half-smoked cigarette, Nick tossed it over the rail and left the deck through a sliding glass door that opened into a central room. Like most beach houses, this bungalow conformed to a general pattern: small- to mid-sized, mounted on concrete piers, living quarters above, storage and carport beneath.

There were several dwellings along this strip of beach. At the moment, the only other occupied one was an older, two-story house rented by the group of would-be musicians Nick had noticed yesterday among the curious. According to the rental agent, the five kids played the local clubs on a fairly regular basis, stayed out of trouble, and paid their rent on time. Nick would have preferred no neighbors at all, but was probably lucky to have this much of the area to himself.

The bungalow was almost Spartan in its basic furnishings, clean lines. Coolly impersonal, it suited

Nick, who didn't own much—if you don't have anything, nothing matters. He'd placed his duffel in the first bedroom he'd come to. The ECCO went on a shelf in the empty bedroom closet. There were times when Nick traveled with nothing but the Expansion Computor and Compact Ordnance unit, other times with nothing at all; whatever he needed could usually be bought, or requisitioned, when he got where he was going.

Nick made himself another cup of instant and strolled back over to the glass door he'd left open. The tangy smell of salt came in with the cool morning air, the gulls' raucous chatter. He lit another cigarette.

Almost instinctively he began slipping into the catechism that usually preluded an adjustment.

What was the key to The Ridge?

Nick sipped at the coffee, pulled on the cigarette, and thought about it.

Did the key lie with the house itself, or the people who had lived there?

(Why are you trying to kill us?)

(kill us)

(kill us)

What had been going on to provoke that phone call?

Nick searched his mental file of past adjustments, residual enemies who might know of Carole and Sara, use them for retaliation. He wasn't in the habit of leaving potentially dangerous loose ends lying about, but possibilities always existed.

(For God's sake, Nick! Your own child! What have we done?)

Did the key lie in a hospital room forty miles north?

(Your own child!)

Was Sara the key?

She alone had survived.

How?

Why?

Could the stories circulating through the crowd yesterday be true—even partly?

Sara. Nick realized he had no idea what his daughter even looked like.

The sound of a car pulling into the driveway out back disturbed Nick's concentration. He glanced at his watch: 7:10—a bit early for visitors.

Leaving the glass door ajar, he set his mug on the dinette table, stubbed out his cigarette, and crossed to a window on the landward side, standing where he could see and not be seen. A flight of redwood steps led down to a three-car-wide parking area and concrete drive opening to the beach road. Nick hadn't used the carport slots under the house, but instead had backed the four-wheeler into the parking area facing the road.

Another car now sat beside it.

The car was idling softly, positioned so that Nick couldn't see who was behind the wheel, though he had a good idea. The driver had pulled in at an angle, his rear blocking the GMC's front and allowing him egress on the far side of the car—the protected side.

Nick noted these things abstractly, aware of their purpose. Why, he wondered, would Special Agent Lew Harris feel Nick Vears worth such caution?

Maybe he was about to find out.

Nick watched as the engine fell silent, the driver's door opened, and Agent Harris got out.

Dressed in a tan raincoat, a newspaper tucked under one arm—the one opposite his shoulder holster, Nick judged—Lew Harris scanned the house with a seemingly casual eye. He closed his car door gently, not trying for stealth but employing deliberate, considered movements. It was a characteristic suggested by the psychological profile Nick had studied last night.

Walking around his car to Nick's, he peered in through the window on the passenger's side. He didn't try the locked door. Moving to the rear of the vehicle, he took a pencil and small notepad from his pocket, jotted down the license number.

The man's dossier had indicated he was thorough. Nick hoped it wasn't going to be a problem.

Repocketing the notepad, Agent Harris headed for the stairs. Nick spent another moment studying the concise movements of a body in reasonably good shape, then stepped back from the window. He waited until the knock came, waited another few seconds, and opened the door.

The two men stood gauging each other, committing appearances to memory, forming initial impressions.

Nick felt the assessment in the steady brown eyes, not seduced by laugh lines crimping the corners. Skin as smooth as a young man's belied Harris's forty-four years. Overall it could be described as a pleasant face, given to smiles, Nick judged, and thoughtful silences. Women would no doubt find it attractive. One could almost be forgiven for overlooking the shrewdness lurking just beneath the surface. Almost.

He stepped back and Agent Harris entered the room. Nick closed the door behind him. Silence grew as Nick waited. It was Harris's move. When it came, it was not any of the number of openings Nick might have anticipated.

"You made the front page." Harris held out the folded newspaper he'd brought in under his arm.

Nick took the paper, his expression carefully blank. He'd expected as much when he'd seen the morass of reporters on the scene yesterday afternoon. His name would be a matter of local record, easily obtained. It was unfortunate, since it could pinpoint his whereabouts once Terrell had him tagged—and he couldn't count on the improbability factors when making that assumption. The Organization was quite efficient about such matters when pushed, and Terrell would push. It meant he possibly had less time here than anticipated.

It was also academic.

Turning the newspaper around, he glanced at the story, then walked over and laid it on the round dinette table. Harris obviously expected a reaction from him, and the bait was impressively on the mark. But it was a shallow hit.

"I trust they spelled my name right." Nick eyed Harris blandly, until a small upward twitch at the edge of Harris's mouth acknowledged the parry. Surprisingly, he let it drop. Nick speculated on what would come next. Using the lull, he picked up his coffee cup and continued on around the bar into the kitchen.

Harris wandered toward the open glass door and gazed out. "I love the sea. Perhaps I'll retire down here one day."

Nick refilled the kettle, turned on the stove beneath it, waiting.

"Did your ex-wife contact you recently?"

Nick ran through a series of answers, picked one: "She wanted to know why I was trying to kill her."

Harris turned, and Nick gave him points for not showing on his face the surprise his body language delivered. Nick also judged that the surprise didn't stem so much from the content of his admission, but that he'd made it. It confirmed what Nick suspected as the reason for this visit. Had Carole left behind some sort of indictment?

"Coffee?" Not waiting for an answer, Nick pulled

a mug from the cabinet on his left. To forestall the obvious follow-up, he said: "I wasn't."

Harris regarded him carefully, equilibrium restored. "Why would she think so?"

Nick met his eyes across the bar, recognizing beneath the soft brown gaze the relentless bead of the hunter taking aim. "Why are you here?"

Harris left the glass and strolled back to the center of the room, glancing around. "Do you always answer a question with a question?"

Nick said nothing.

"Or use silence as a ploy?" He swung his gaze back to Nick. "Who are you, Mr. Vears? What do you do? Where have you been? And why"—he took another step toward Nick, pinpointing him with a look that was regulation professional—"would your ex-wife think you were trying to kill her?"

"Is this an official interview, Agent Harris?" Nick didn't bother feigning concern.

"It can be." Harris read the answer before Nick gave it.

Nick gave it anyway. "Let's skip the extras." Striding to the dinette table, he tore a corner from the folded newspaper. "Pen?"

Harris pulled out a ballpoint and handed it over.

"Here's the name, address, and phone number of the woman who was with me on the night in question." Nick scribbled the alibi he'd arranged last night across the paper. "We dined out, returned to my apartment about eleven-thirty. She was still there when the deputy called."

He handed the paper and pen back to Harris, who stuck it in his pocket without a glance.

"Was she there when Mrs. Grant called?"

"It was on my answering machine."

"So you don't know exactly when Mrs. Grant called?"

"No."

Harris nodded, a noncommittal gesture. "And, presumably, while she and her husband and children were getting killed, you were . . . involved at your apartment."

Nick said nothing.

"Your ex-wife believed she was being threatened. She was obviously under stress. Based on your past relationship, is there any reason to think Mrs. Grant might have become unbalanced? Or suicidal?"

"Carole was neurotic, not self-destructive."

The agent studied him thoughtfully. "People are rarely what they seem."

Nick let the comment ride.

"I understand you went to the hospital yesterday afternoon." Harris changed directions abruptly. "Why didn't you visit your daughter?"

"I don't believe I have to answer that."

"No, you don't."

The two men eyed each other in silence. Nick guessed Agent Harris was coming to some sort of decision. He broke the stare and went into the kitchen, removing the kettle from the heat before it could begin to whistle.

"I'm hoping you'll consider helping us," Harris said at last, decision apparently made. The sharp edge to his voice had been blunted.

"In what way?" Nick kept his back turned.

"Your daughter is our only source of information, Mr. Vears. The sooner we break through that barrier she's hiding behind, the sooner we'll find out what happened." Harris was gazing intently at the back of Nick's head, Nick could feel it. "And believe me, this isn't just for the sake of the investigation but for Sara as well. I've talked to her doctor, plus I have some experience with this type of shock. The longer Sara retreats from reality, the more dangerous it is that she'll never come out. She's embedded herself in a cocoon of disavowal—and God knows, it's preferable to the reality confronting her. But she needs to be brought out of it, and soon."

"I repeat,"Nick turned around, kettle in hand, "what do you assume I can do?"

"See her, talk to her." Harris strode to the bar separating them and leaned his arms against it. "Try to make her respond. If you're not involved, you should be willing to help us."

Nick regarded his earnestness coolly. "What makes you think I might have any more affect than the next stranger?"

"You're her *father.*"

"Am I?" Nick poured hot water into the empty mug and slid the jar of instant and a spoon toward his guest. Harris didn't misunderstand the question. It took more than biology to make a parent.

The intensity that had momentarily gripped Harris faded. He set about making his coffee while Nick refilled his own cup and returned the kettle to the stove. "Sugar?" Harris glanced from a jar of creamer to Nick.

"I don't use it."

Harris laid the spoon aside, took a swallow of the black coffee, grimaced. "I have a feeling about you, Mr. Vears—"

Nick didn't change expressions.

"—an idea that you'd like to know what happened up at that house as much as I would. Your daughter knows." Harris straightened from the bar, pushing the coffee mug away. "Think about it."

Nick watched his visitor walk toward the door, then hesitate and glance over his shoulder. "That address you gave the sheriff's deputy. Interesting.

No doubt your overnight guests appreciate the atmosphere, but isn't the upkeep a bit steep?"

"I take in tourists."

Harris regarded him another moment; then, giving a faint smile that barely creased the edges of his mouth and didn't touch his eyes, he left, shutting the door gently behind him.

Nick stood there in the silence, looking at the closed door, hearing the footsteps recede down the stairs, the car start up, pull away.

So Harris had bothered to check that address—and wanted him to know it. *Trying to make him bolt and run?*

He finished making his coffee and wandered over to the open glass door, this time stepping through.

Day had arrived, clear and sunny. Waves rolled in toward shore with a nonchalance that cloaked the constant, relentless erosion eating away at the coastline. Somewhat like Agent Harris.

Nick lit a cigarette.

The man was sharp, persistent. He'd garnered quite a bit of information, made some interesting conclusions in a rather short time. He'd tried several different tacks on Nick, all of which Nick had recognized; it hadn't kept them from having some effect.

Nick took a final draw from the barely smoked cigarette and tossed it to the sand. What else might Agent Harris bother to check? Nick wondered briefly, then dismissed it. Should Harris become too much of a problem, he could be taken care of.

Lew drove away with the restlessness that invariably haunted him when he left a situation dangling. He'd accomplished very little of what he'd intended for this meeting with Mr. Nicholas Vears. The man was not easily pegged, and Lew had found himself on the receiving end of a cat-and-mouse

routine he had not liked. A vague sense of being
out of kilter gripped him, an impression that he'd
been fencing with shadows—there was something
about Vears he couldn't quite pull into perspective.

He'd gone to the house primed toward a target,
and felt he'd scored once or twice, even though
Vears had shown no particular concern, not even
for a moment. Harris had watched his eyes—he always watched eyes, often with better results than
a lie detector test—noting expressions, probing for
some betrayal. Vears's gave nothing away, not even
their color, Lew thought, remembering the smooth
blend of shades that was not quite black, not quite
blue, almost gray. They'd been coolly polite and totally devoid of emotion. He'd seen eyes like that
before—staring out of a corpse.

At the moment, Vears was adding up to be a most
attractive candidate for prime suspect, if it turned
out one was needed. He had possible motive, reasonable opportunity—despite the alibi; alibis could
be arranged—and experience told Lew this was a
man acquainted with violence.

More damning, there'd been specific charges
made against him. Lew could still hear the convic-
tion ringing in Danielle Grant's voice as she told
him of recent letters Carole Grant had written her
in strictest confidence, letters expressing an irrational—so Danielle had thought at the time—fear
of her ex-husband and the threat she believed him
to be. Carole had begged her sister-in-law to take
care of Sara should anything happen, making her
promise to do all she could to keep the child away
from her father.

But Lew wasn't quite ready to act on these
charges. It was more than just a gut feeling he
had—Nick Vears constituted too easy an answer to
this thing. There were too many variables, too many

facets still unexplained. So far it had not even been officially ruled a homocide.

And there was still that little matter of *how* the thing had been done. How did one blow up four people in a room while not touching a fifth? Vears might be part of it, yes. But there was more.

Yet someone had seemed to be threatening Mrs. Grant, that much was out in the open now, thanks to Danielle Grant and, oddly enough, Vears himself. Vears had said it wasn't him; Lew had sensed he was telling the truth.

But if not Vears, who?

Lew couldn't explain it at the moment, and he really had no other leads. Unless he could come up with something else soon, he'd have to act on Miss Grant's charges.

It wasn't like he was sitting on his thumbs in the meantime. He'd spent the previous evening at the sheriff's office, running routine data checks on the principals involved. They'd turned up general information on the Grants, nothing that pointed to enemies of this magnitude—except, perhaps, an estranged ex-husband.

They'd coughed up skimpier information on Vears: couple of credit cards, New York driver's license, but nothing he could immediately tag as suspicious. There were no prior arrests, not even a parking ticket; no service record. On the surface it looked pristine enough, average Joe Citizen crapola; but underneath ... was it pure crap? Lew pondered the growing enigma.

And then there was that little matter of the home address Vears had given the deputy: The Metropolitan Museum of Art. That had thrown Lew when it popped up on the teletype.

One such piece of misinformation often suggested others.

Lew had tried the phone number torn from Car-

ole Grant's address book and found it "no longer
in service." He'd sent the number, and another ID
request, back through Raleigh tagged "special priority"—make Records go full-scale and dig a little.
Sometimes a scan got no further than a quick NCIC
check. Of course, that's usually all it took. But as
up-to-the-moment as the National Crime Information Center was, it was not all-knowing.

"Who are you, Mr. Nicholas Vears?" Lew murmured, eyes narrowed against the morning sun.
"And what are you hiding . . . ?"

A pickup truck passed, all-night fishermen on
their way home, Lew guessed from the paraphernalia in back. He returned their wave and watched
them drive by, content to poke along with his
thoughts.

There was something familiar about the way
Vears handled himself, something Lew had sensed
yesterday and recognized today. This man knew
what he was doing. He had about him the aura of
the professional.

But professional what?

Lew wasn't at all sure what he was dealing with
here—case *or* possible perpetrator. He just knew
he meant to find out.

An incriminating amount of evidence had gone
with him to Vears's house this morning, and the
man had done little to counter it. Despite this, Lew
had decided not to haul him in. Probably he should.
He'd been leaning toward it, but now he'd changed
his mind. He wanted Vears's help with Sara, yes.
And there was that alibi to check out. But more
than this, he thought he might want Nicholas Vears
free to act. He'd baited him with that final quip just
to see what might come of it.

He hoped he wasn't making a mistake.

The Ridge came into view, clutching the crest of
the rocky promontory like a huge gray paw. He

turned off the beach road and circled up the winding drive, tires crunching on the broken-shell surface.

People had already gathered, Lew saw as he pulled into the parking area beside one of the crime lab vans, not so many as yesterday but more than enough to suit him. He'd talk to the press corps first—he'd worked up a statement last night—get them off his back. Then he'd check in with the lab team. Hopefully they'd have something positive for him this morning. He suspected the guys had worked all night; they preferred to stay at a job until done. Maybe they'd greet him with the news that they were through, case solved. *I wish*, Lew thought ironically. Their wrap-up usually just signaled the beginning for him.

It would be at least two weeks before all the reports filtered in, from the tests, from the medical examiner. Even the preliminary coroner's report would take days, if not a week or more. Nobody would want to commit on this thing, and Lew was prepared to receive a sheaf of official papers listing what had *not* happened.

"Eliminate the impossible and whatever is left, however improbable, must be true." Wasn't that a Sherlock Holmes theory? Too bad it didn't apply. Four exploded bodies in a room was impossible. A little girl standing untouched in the center of a charnel house was impossible. Yet that's what had happened here, God only knew how.

Lew got out of the car, taking his time. With each step, he experienced a mounting reluctance to go back inside that house, that room the way it was. The aura of it—and the odor—permeated the entire structure. Even the sea air couldn't dissipate the smell, Lew thought, bracing himself to enter the house once more. He hoped they'd removed some of the plywood sheathing and let in the fresh air.

The sooner the lab team moved out, the sooner a cleanup crew could move in.

"Agent Harris, you promised us a statement—"

"Hey, Harris, how 'bout it?"

"Give us a break, Lew—"

He waved at the chorus of voices, the sea of faces, tossing them a: "Gimme a chance to check things inside—fifteen minutes, then I'm all yours," without breaking his stride. Suddenly he was overwhelmed by the certainty that if he stopped now to give them a statement, if his legs didn't continue propelling him on toward the door, he'd never go inside that house again.

The irrational feeling passed as he entered the dark, cool interior and headed toward the great room.

Face your bogies and vanquish them.

Surprisingly, the smell that met him was not as bad as it had been the day before—or was he becoming desensitized to it? Lew crushed this unsettling thought.

To his relief, cleanup was set to begin, just waiting for his okay—mostly volunteer fire department and rescue squad personnel. The French windows lining the far wall had been stripped of their plywood boards, and a tangy breeze brushed past Lew as he stepped through the open bifolds. Despite the macabre legacy that still clung like rust to the gray stone walls and floor, the room was becoming fit again.

He spotted Bill Armstrong squatting on the floor, checking labels as he put bottles back into a carrying case and quietly dictating notes into a handheld tape recorder. Behind him Kate Boyce sprawled on a window ledge, nursing a Styrofoam cup of coffee in one hand, licking fingers on the other, chatting through the window with one of the sheriff's deputies. She waved at Lew, then dug another doughnut out of a green-and-white box at her elbow, obviously back to normal.

"We're just about ready to move out," Bill said, glancing up from the yellow plastic case that looked like a junior chemistry kit. "I'll get to work on these samples by tomorrow noon and should have something for you in a day or two."

"Fine." Lew accepted the routine promise with all the faith it merited. Exchanging a wry grin with Kate, he moved on over to the open casement on the far end, noting that the plywood boards had been propped up outside. Two more guards hovered nearby, one fairly close to the windows, one farther out on the terrace, both looking bored.

Doesn't take long, Lew thought, marveling at the resilience of the human psyche—or was it callousness? No, that wasn't fair. Humanity, like a law-enforcement officer, would never survive if it bogged down in the hideous parts of life. It could rebel, feel horror, but somewhere a saturation point existed, and it swam on. That's what kept it—us—going.

Lew thought he'd put his finger on the crux, what made them all able to deal with obscenities like this, and go on. It was thankfulness to be alive—realization that the horror which has visited someone else has passed *us* by—*we* have a little more time. A heady sensation.

But this was not the time for armchair philosophy.

He left the window and walked back toward the center of the room, zeroing in on the spot he'd avoided earlier.

The small circle was nothing special, merely a lighter shade of gray than the corrupted stones surrounding it. A perfect ring, it mocked them simply by being there. What had protected the child who had stood within it? What had repulsed the carnage?

"There's no reason to believe something's untrue until there's a reason to believe it's untrue," Lew recalled a college professor lecturing a class whose majority couldn't have cared less. He wondered what Professor Barry would make of this.

Reaching a tentative hand toward the clean circle, he hesitated momentarily, almost prepared to encounter some sort of invisible barrier stretching from floor to ceiling, a wall so clear it simply wasn't there . . . until touched. He thought about an energy block of some kind, like in science fiction stories, a force field or something equally futuristic—

A set of fingers wiggling in his face snapped him back to the twentieth century.

"You gonna stand there all day or go ahead and touch that space you're reaching for?"

Kate waved a hand back and forth through the air above the clean spot. "Nothing in there—see?"

Lew realized he'd winced at the gesture, flinched backward as though anticipating a blow. He let out the breath he'd grabbed and stuck his own hand into the empty space. "You're right."

"Don't feel bad," Kate said matter-of-factly. "It caught us all that way. Big Bill"—she jabbed a thumb toward her cohort—"still won't walk through it, even after the rest of us have. Says it gives him the willies."

"Understatement of the decade," Lew murmured, crouching to run his hand through the air about an inch up from the clean circle on the floor, earlier reluctance forgotten. There was no sense of unequalized pressure, no abrupt temperature change. Other than visually, nothing appeared different about the small round spot.

"Want to hear some of the local color?" Kate sounded amused. "Remington Steele over there's been giving me the low-down"—she paused to wave and wink at the deputy who was still hovering just outside the window—"in between suggestions of what we could do with my spare time."

Lew glanced at the tall, rather rakish-looking young man who was trying his best to look macho and suave at the same time. He managed a laugh, but it was a halfhearted attempt, cheerless. "Why not," he answered, anticipating the topic.

"*Well*..." Kate began, dragging the word out for emphasis, "according to local gossip, this place was built by a group of mad monks, fondly called the 'Ancients,' who practiced a specific brand of hocus-pocus that had something to do with mind worship and deriving great power from the rocks—or maybe that should be *great* rocks. Anyway, it seems these mystic weirdos up and disappeared one day, or night, and nooobody knooows what happened to them, though general opinion holds that they dabbled in 'things not meant for mortal man'—and got their dabblers whacked."

Lew cast a baleful eye upward.

"And sometimes, when the moon is full and the tide is high," Kate warmed to her tale, "you can see them rising up from the rocks and hear their chanting on the wind, and you'd better run 'cause they're coming back to claim your soul, and their bodies are mutilated and deformed and their heads are gone—

"Lew, it's supposed to be a joke. You're not laughing."

"Sorry. I already heard the punch line."

"What?"

He stood, glancing back at the clear spot. "Never mind."

Kate followed the look, seeming to absorb some of his mood now. "Still, it's bloody weird, that circle," she muttered, then grimaced as the macabre pun registered. She crossed her arms and ran her hands lightly up and down them as though chilled.

He gave her shoulder a squeeze. "I take it nothing new's turned up?"

Kate shook her head, as much to clear it of unwanted thoughts, Lew guessed, as to indicate the negative. "Not diddly-squat. This one's gonna require the full treatment—criminalistics lab, forensics, even ballistics for possible trace substances we might have missed."

"Anybody willing to call it on probable cause?"

"Sorry. Nobody's calling this one, even tentatively."

Lew lifted his eyebrows at the admission, though he wasn't really surprised. Still, he'd been hoping. The mobile lab techs kept an unofficial scoreboard of the accuracy of their preliminary field opinions. Last Lew heard, their average was 98 percent.

"You?" he urged. "Off the record."

Kate grinned sweetly. "Forget it. Evidence lists are on top of the equipment case over there." She gestured toward a group of boxes stacked by the bifolds, ready to be reloaded in the vans. "Jesse's doing a final dusting for latents. You'll get the full reports when done." The grin faded. "This is a mean one, Lew. Can't say I'd want to be working it by myself."

"Yeah." Lew strolled beside her to the doors. Though the local sheriff's department was there to provide backup, and muscle if need be, and he could always request an assist from Raleigh, for a moment Lew shared her sentiment.

He looked back at the small clean circle. "I don't want that touched. Tell the cleanup crew. Chalkmark me an area at least double what's already there and leave it as is."

Kate nodded. "You got it."

Lew watched her go get the chalk and another jelly doughnut, taking a provocative bite for the young deputy's benefit. Feeling his stomach lurch, he left her to it and was halfway up the stairs before he realized he was heading for Sara's room, for no better reason than its serenity. Changing directions, he went out to the mob instead.

6

Cool night air brushed loose tendrils of hair against Set's cheek as he made his way along the darkened beach. Impatiently he ran a hand through it, then reached into his pocket for a leather thong and gathered the long strands at his nape.

He glanced at the night sky. A pinched moon hung chill and listless, draped in thin, cobwebby clouds.

On his right the surf crashed and bled away, crashed and bled away, each time sounding closer, a giant fist pounding toward him, claiming handfuls of sand with every blow.

Usually he and the ocean *reached*, like the audiences who heard his music. He played to the sea and it listened, carrying his songs to the sky, the wind.

Tonight it seemed alien, beyond his control.

With a muttered curse, Set veered across the sand, heading toward the rocky promontory that was his objective. He quickened his pace until he reached the beginning of the cliff, then proceeded with care, listening for sounds from above.

No light shone from The Ridge, nothing to indicate the R.C.'s were still dicking about inside, though he supposed they'd left a guard posted somewhere to make sure no one crossed their yellow plastic ribbon.

The lab vans had moved out around noon, followed by the fire trucks, the press, and most of the cops; by late afternoon the rubberneckers had even melted away. He'd told the others that tonight wouldn't be a problem. But they'd been too chickenshit to come. *Maybe they still thought this was a fucking game.*

He'd been unable to stay away. They were so close!

Set climbed upward through the rocks, feet instinctively finding toeholds. He slowed even more as he neared the terrace wall, crouching behind it to make his way around to the far side.

Once, he stopped and glanced over the parapet, spotting a single cop car in the parking area. The flare of a cigarette lighter confirmed the cop's whereabouts; the faint sounds of Waylon & Willie drifted toward him. Richard Cranium on patrol. Set smiled and moved on.

Leaving the shelter of the wall, he followed the slightly descending path into the ruins that marked the older, rear section of the monastery. It was an area barely accessible and rarely visited, past renovating. Nothing but an old pile of tumbled rocks.

Set smiled again as he reached the large, roughly circular stone slab with the jagged crack down its middle that marked the opening to the tunnel. For untold years it had lain tightly wedged here, looking like nothing more than a portion of masonry that had given way to erosion and toppled. Probably it would have stayed that way for untold years more had freak storms not buffeted the East Coast.

Set remembered those storms, the gale force winds, the heavy rains and unusually high tides that had battered the coastline, causing severe damage to ocean-front property, eroding whole sections— and opening up the hidden tunnel that had lain beneath the huge stone slab all those years, waiting for him.

"An unusual configuration of the sun, moon, and Earth," the papers had explained. "A rare alignment coinciding with a powerful northeaster, causing exceptionally high tides . . ."

But Set knew better. It had been ordained.

Glancing around once more for any sign of watchers, he shoved the rock aside enough to slip through the small opening, then rolled the concealing stone back into place.

What meager light there'd been immediately vanished. The pounding surf became a muted rumble throbbing in the distance, more vibration than sound.

Set felt in control again. He could feel the Power.

Squeezing sideways, he slithered through the fifty feet or so of ever-narrowing tunnel. Had he not been so confident that first time, he might have abandoned the whole thing.

But the Power had drawn him on, whispering as he struggled with loose rocks and blockage, saying *this way, this way*, reaching out as he dug more and more desperately with hands that had begun to bleed, fingers that threatened to break, tearing the carefully tended nails so that it was weeks before he could again coax delicate riffs from his guitar.

And then he'd broken through.

They were there—as the legends he'd heard from his grandmother promised, as his own dreams had shown—the secret chambers of the Ancients!

And more:

Set had found the Book, the Chronicles of Divinian, leader of the ancient brotherhood, setting forth the rituals that would establish an astral link, a "Mindbridge" to a place of "stones whose power can influence the minds of others."

Divinian had made the crossing, brought back one of the stones . . .

As if from a dream that had lain germinating in Set's subconscious, a new vision had suddenly blossomed full-grown:

What if *he* could re-create this bridge, make the crossing himself, bring back a power stone? Could he enhance the power of his music—reach out to his audiences, influence them?

The stones were there, he knew it, waiting to be used by someone strong enough to control their power.

He was that person! He'd known it all along; even as a kid spending hours listening to the tales his grandmother wove, he'd known. That's why he'd been drawn back here after dropping out of college.

The group had thought he was crazy at first, coming to this jerk-off place, dragging them along; but the music had been his, and the money had been Twyla's, and after a while the gigs had been good. The complaints disappeared. Then he'd found the caves.

Slowly he'd led the others into trying the rituals, pandering to their jokes at first, watching them become caught up in it all. And they'd been getting closer each time—he'd felt it—perfecting the rites, reaching the deep level of concentration necessary to establish the link.

Soon the joining would be complete, the bridge would appear and he would make the crossing, following the very steps Divinian had taken before him. He'd bring back one of the stones . . .

and with its power amplifying his own abilities, he'd have the world at his feet as he played his music and became the greatest performer of all time!

Lost in the vision of what would be, it was a moment before Set realized the darkness was not as total as it should have been. A faint glow marked the end of the tunnel.

He checked his forward motion, stilled his breathing to listen.

Nothing but the muted drumbeat of the surf.

Cautiously he again crept forward. Were Mitch and the others playing games? somehow sneaking in here ahead of him, or—

Shit! Had the cops found the interior entry?

A hidden staircase carved in stone descended from beneath the altar in the old chapel above; but it was so well camouflaged it was nearly impossible to spot. *They'd* only discovered it after finding these tunnels from outside, by following the stone steps upward from the secret chamber. Besides, the chapel was in ruins, probably dangerous even to enter. It had been shut off from the main house long ago.

Coming to the mouth of the narrow tunnel, Set felt for the lanterns they kept stashed just inside the cave. Both were there.

Hardly daring to breathe, he inched forward, then stood still while his eyes adjusted to the faint light. Silence thickened the air, stirred only by the throbbing heartbeat of the surf.

Staying close to the wall, Set passed through the archway that led into the maze of winding corridors and chambers catacombing the cliff. It would be easy to become tangled in their meanderings; they bisected, dead-ended suddenly, and the same chamber could look completely different from another angle.

They'd used fishing line the first few times until they'd learned the way and still kept it tied up just in case.

The secret inner chamber had taken a bit longer

to find, a cave within a cave, an optical illusion from without. Had the Power not whispered where to look . . .

The glow brightened. It was coming from the hidden room. But how could that be? The chamber was totally enclosed, entered through a stone door that became part of the wall. He'd resealed it himself the last time they were here—

Unease pricked the back of Set's neck; a sliver of cool wind momentarily brushed aside the heaviness and touched his cheek.

That night . . .

Everything had been okay at first. They'd performed the ritual—one of the last steps remaining—and if there'd been something building in the air, no one had remarked on it. But as they'd secured the door to the inner chamber, put out the torches and candles, the sensation had seemed to grow, like a shadow from a dream, filling the caves, cold, making Set's skin come alive.

For a moment, excitement had stirred within him—excitement tainted with fear. *Was it happening? Were the rituals really beginning to work?* He'd started to call the others back, then found himself hesitating, remembering the legends hinted that the Ancients might have destroyed themselves. But that was just local bullshit. There'd been no evidence to bear it out, nothing in the cave, no bones—nothing. Still . . .

The first faint rumble had spread with them as they crawled from the caverns. "Earthquake?" someone, maybe Hump, had said, and Vesper had laughed nervously. But they *did* have earthquakes in North Carolina. No one said anything else as they left the trembling stones—the ominous, building force—behind.

The night outside had been dark and still.

It'd been about three A.M. when they'd gotten back

to the beach house; Set and Mitch had gone for a swim. Sometime between then and dawn, the people at The Ridge had died.

For the hundredth time since that night, Set posed the silent question stalking them all: *Had what they were doing caused those deaths? Had they somehow . . . unleashed something?* And for the hundredth time, he dismissed it. So what? Those people had brought it on themselves by staying in the house. He'd tried to scare them away, concentrating on the woman, who'd proved an easy mark.

They'd had their chance to leave and blown it. Too bad. Just too fucking bad. He was too close to stop now, he could taste it, see the visions, hear the voice growing clearer in his mind. Whatever had happened to those people wouldn't happen to him— he had the Power. He would be as Divinian had been. He would claim his destiny. Nothing was as important as that. *Nothing!* And *no one.*

Set abandoned caution. If the others were in here playing stupid games—anger flashed—he'd show the cocksuckers! They had no right to be here without him. None of those fuckers had a right to be here without him!

Quickening his pace, he threaded the maze, anger building as the glow intensified—a sort of cool, whitish light, like fluorescents. It seemed to hang on the air, layer upon layer of thin, rippling sheen moving out to greet him. Again, he felt a breath of wind against his face. It stroked his heated body, cool night fingers wrapping around his anger and softening it to mist. A slight dizziness floated through him; his confident strides slowed . . .

Light became wind, moving brazenly over him in a blending that felt like gentle foreplay. He was part of it now, swimming forward on a tide of glistening sensation, being drawn along by loving fingers in an erotic welcome that soothed and seduced.

Stumbling feet rounded the final barrier—
"God—what?"

Through the waves of sensual fog clouding his mind, Set stared into the secret chamber. Where there'd been a wall, a hole now gaped. Huge stones had been tossed aside like so much gravel. The inner cave lay breached, defiled, ripped open by some unbelievable cataclysm.

Fury tinged with sudden terror surged up in Set like bile. *What could have done this? How did it happen? And if they'd been here . . . ?* He faltered, a hand lifted as if to strike, or ward off a blow—

And then soft fingers were there . . . stroking his mind . . . calming, reassuring . . .

Set's hand dropped.

Slowly he stepped forward, out of the anger and fear, once more embracing the new sensations flooding him. He felt he was on the brink of a great discovery, perhaps the very essence of what he sought. He didn't understand how he knew this, but as the knowledge took hold, he recognized its truth.

The chamber itself looked untouched. No cave-in, no broken rock. He could see the stone dais beyond the Circle, see the Book of Chronicles still lying in place.

The sconces along the walls held only cold, dead torches, thin shadows on stone like dark, brittle spikes in luminous flesh. Not the source of the light.

A soft hum began rising around Set. It seemed to seep from the stones, trace patterns on the wind, whispering

(*Set . . . Set . . .*)

Trancelike, he moved forward through the gaping hole, stepping into the Chamber of the Ancients as though onto a circular stage surrounded by thousands of chanting fans.

His gaze roamed the scrawling designs etched into the dark stone walls—they'd never shone so clearly; his eyes danced with the shadows crouched among the rocks—they'd never seemed so alive. Outside, waves thundered against the ridge—they'd never sounded so near . . .

And then he saw it.

Glowing with a light so pure it drew tears, the small stone, no bigger than his cupped palm, nestled in a shallow crater in the center of the Circle.

Staggering slightly, Set made his way toward it, moving like a zombie to the light.

Rivulets of melted glass flowed outward from the crater, sand crystallized and frozen, fused into strange liquid shapes, seeming to ooze and undulate, glittering serpents filled with light.

Confusion crawled through Set's mind, leaving gaps, emptiness.

With each step, coldness deepened, blurring his thoughts.

He stopped, mesmerized by the painful brilliance, trying to fathom the tiny veins of burning light that darted through the stone, oblivious to the tears streaming down his face and dropping to the sand . . .

and in that moment, Set felt the Power rise within him as never before, felt the light reach out to—*into*—his mind.

Sagging to his knees, he began to rock back and forth, opening himself to the Power, the *Light*, feeling it fill the empty spaces in him the way his music always did. His thoughts took on new shape, new meaning. The gentle hum grew louder, voices singing of the Light.

He reached out a hand toward the stone—

—and froze. *Pain!* He drew back his hand.

(Not yet, not yet) a voice seemed to whisper. And as soft fingers of reassurance stroked his mind, taking away the pain: *(The Circle must be complete.)*

Set reeled with sudden knowledge. He felt himself grow hard with an excitement that transcended mere sexual experience. His eyes clung rapturously to the dazzling stone—

The Mindstone!

It was *his*!

It would *go* with him, *be* with him—on stage, while writing, while performing—

Gazing into the stone's heart, Set felt it radiant within him—and for just a moment seemed to feel other eyes peering through his own.

The moment passed. He drew a deep, slaking breath. He could wait a little longer, now.

Around him the hum crescendoed; wind buffeted the cave, waves pounded against the rocks.

Set spread his arms—smiled—laughed out loud.

He *was* the storm. He was, he *was*!

And in the triumph of the moment Set seemed to see the shadow of an ancient vision rising on the mist, hear an echo singing to the night . . .

"*. . . and the stones themselves shall give Thee dominion.*"

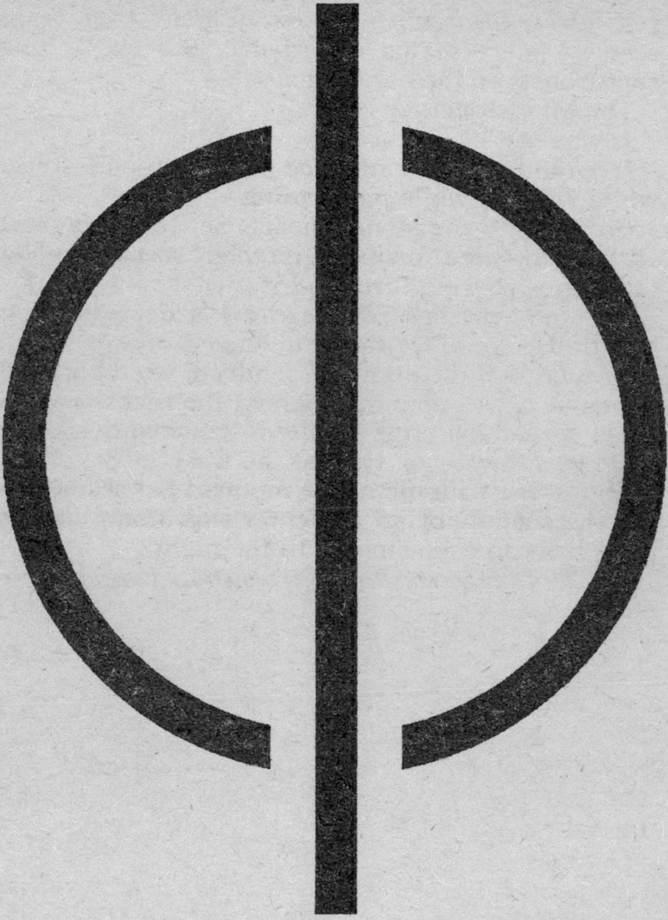

Torches lit the cavern. Candles shivered on the wind. Long fingers of fog crept across the sand to curl about the rocks.

Divinian stood alone before the altar, writing the final words in his book.

Dominion.

He savored the feel of it in his mind.

A smile stretched the pale, withered skin haunting his cadaverous face. So many years since he had led his brothers to the arc of this astral gateway. So many years to achieve the profound meditation, perfect the rites.

And now the moment had come.

Shadows thrown by the sputtering torchlight roamed the hidden chamber, mingling with the glistening symbols etched into the stones, picked out by the flames. He breathed deeply, drinking in the power that filled this place. Anticipation gnawed at the pit of his stomach, a deeply sensual craving spread through his loins. So long he had foreseen this moment, wading through time that had become shadows like those that danced these cavern walls.

Voices chanted in the background, their low hum entwining his thoughts. It was almost time . . .

Divinian closed his eyes against a moment's exhilaration. All was as he'd envisioned. All would soon be his.

Wind wisped around his shoulders, winding through tangled strands the color of midnight fog. It brushed his cheek with a soft caress; the mist coiled about his feet, kissed the hem of his garments.

"The Circle awaits, my brother."

Restraining excitement, Divinian gave a single nod in response to the summoner and set his quill aside. With steady, deliberate movements, he shut the heavy tome, taking a moment to trace a finger over the symbol worked into its faded leather binding: the Circle of One. Soon it would be complete.

So much had been accomplished since the Old Ones roamed the earth, building their tabernacles to the Mind, erecting their obelisks and pillars and icons made of stone. Vainly they had sought the path, gathering the enlightened into the Circle, leaving their monuments of mist behind.

It was said a Child of Light would touch the secrets, walk the holy path—and he was born of Light. But a child no longer.

Turning to the robed figure who stood waiting, head respectfully bowed, Divinian schooled his features into somber lines.

Tonight they would permanently forge the bridge. Tonight he would make his final crossing as a child of this ephemeral existence and return with the Power of eternity.

Tonight he would become God.

Candle flames licked his gaunt features, casting aged skin into transparency, lending wild light to sunken, hungry eyes. Outside, waves pounded against the ridge.

Divinian stepped forward, motioning Brother Tomas to take his place with the other kneeling forms. They had served him well, his brothers; would serve him yet.

The chanting swelled as he moved toward them; their figures swayed to and fro. A gust of wind sped by, laying his robes against him, starkly delineating a body more bone than flesh. Intricate designs woven into the cloth coiled upward with the undulating motion of headless, fawning snakes.

His eyes moved past the bowed heads, seeking the marble pedestal which stood like a glowing pillar of ice in their midst. On it lay the stone, the treasure brought back from his first sacred crossing.

The Mindstone.

Even now its miracle astonished him, awed him with the power at his command.

Crystal light-threads wound around and through it, a brilliant spiderweb of endless motion. Some broke free to stroke the air.

Slowly Divinian stepped into his place at the center of the Circle, gazing deep into the stone. Its cold beauty quickened him, chilling his blood, sharpening his heightened senses like delicate blades of ice.

"Oh Circle . . . Power of the One . . ."

Gently he reached out, touched the others' awareness—

"Unite our minds, our thoughts . . ."

—drawing their strength to his, feeling their energy flow toward him on a sea of shimmering mist.

"Give us Light and Life apart . . ."

The chanting swelled. The wind blew cold. Waves thundered against the rocks.

Divinian felt the power rise within him, spreading through his limbs, his veins. The Mindstone filled his vision, poised upon the pedestal like a glittering white star pulled from a midnight sky. Its brilliance eclipsed the robed Circle, the torches strung along the walls, throbbing an echo to the waves and his own heartbeat as though the three were one.

The acrid stench of burning tar joined the cloying smell of incense, the overwhelming sense of triumph as he picked up the stone. A chill numbed his fingertips. New awareness pierced his mind. His voice grew. He felt the power expand, force pouring through him—bone within bone, skin upon skin!

"Power of the Mind . . ."

A shiver of ecstasy raced through him.

". . . transcend these meager bounds . . ."

Sound came together with Light, swirling about the sand.

"Show us the path, the bridge, that we might cross . . ."

Faster, faster—a spinning cauldron.

The air around the stone began quivering gently, like ripples on a pond. A low hum threw back an echo to the ancient chant, the crashing waves. It vibrated with the promise of a million minds he'd yet to claim.

But soon they would be his. All would be his. Soon.

Divinian raised the glowing Mindstone, tenderly stroking a thumb across its striated surface, closing his eyes to more fully experience the moment of bonding. Again the chanting swelled; he held the moment to him like a lover.

He could feel the power building, hear the rising storm. He drew more energy from his brothers, deepening the link. The Circle must be complete.

Breathing quickened, grew ragged. His eyes flew open. Wind screamed through the tunnels and the caves, extinguishing torches, sweeping candles to the sand.

He raised his voice above the maelstrom, above the rushing air, and the sound grew like a whirlwind in a storm:

"Give us Light and—"

It was happening! Spiraling upward, the bridge was taking shape. Never had it been so clear—so real! He could see the gateway, the silver stairs.

In his hand the stone pulsed wildly, sending violent eruptions of Light arcing through the air. Now was the moment! He would cross the bridge, span the Circle, become One with the knowledge of yesterday and tomorrow, and no one—No one—could stand against him.

And none would stand with him. This was to be his, Divinian realized. His alone.

Relentlessly he began taking total control of the link, sucking power from his brothers, pulling it from their minds. Fools! Did they think themselves worthy to share his destiny? They were tools, chattels, to be used at his command.

Eyes locked on the glittering gateway, he began to climb the bridge, drawing more power, reaching past the last flimsy barriers of his brothers' tiny resistance. They were nothing before him. Nothing!

Fiercely he gripped the stone, opening his mind to the Light, trembling on the brink of an eternity that promised Power only a God can wield.

"Brother Divinian, help us! Please! Take us with you!"

He glanced back toward the cavern, at the nine robed forms, and it was as if he were looking down a long corridor receding into night. For a moment he observed his brothers—his children, their hands stretching, reaching.

"Help us, Brother—please!"

He stared into Brother Tomas's pleading eyes—

"Don't leave us here alone . . ."

—and turned away, gazing up into another realm where all was spread before him—all he had envisioned and more—a shining glimpse that passed beyond heaven and earth, across time and thought itself.

Power strained within him, seeking its own level, stronger than ever before, demanding all he had and more.

Again he deepened his pull on the minds below him, oblivious to their feeble cries, their meaningless pain, gazing from the midnight of ages past to the dawn of ages yet to come.

"Give *Me* Light and Life!"

He must have *all!*

Ruthlessly he plundered their screaming minds, draining them to moaning husks. And still he climbed, raising his cry to the wind, the night, until the power he sought was there, within his grasp.

With a triumphant cry, Divinian held the Mindstone high above his head. The wind screamed around him and the power raged within him and the stone in his hand was filled with Light and Life.

They were One at last! From God—to man—and again to God! Joined in a great union of Oneness that held visions he had barely dreamt of.

Dazzling webs of silk-spun brilliance leapt from the stone to twine about his hand and arm. His mind soared past the bounds that had too long encompassed it. His exultant cry rang out above the storm.

"Soul of My Soul—Mind of My Mind!"

This was the true beginning of eternity.

Triumphantly He claimed the gateway, turning back once more to gaze upon the miserable cave and the pitiful forms who groveled in the sand. He saw their meager resistance, heard their mewling cries, looked into their minds—

There was nothing left. Hollow shells; drained, helpless, empty casks writhing on the ground.

He reached to touch them, anoint His children with True Light—and felt a great surge of power— Had it come from Him?—streaking through the cave and into minds unable to contain such might.

Bodies convulsed, were rent apart. Crimson rain fell within the cave. He marveled as a tremendous eruption spiraled outward on the wind, soaring up on cold black waves and shards of brilliant white, coming toward him—coming—

Pain!

Numbing, wrenching pain!

Waves of pain lashed his head. His mind was a pyre of scalding, blinding pain!

He reached to pull more power to him, protect the Light—but there was nothing there. Nothing left to take!

The bridge began to waver, dim. The Mindstone smoldered within his grasp—searing flesh, distorting bones, turning his hands into brittle, leprous claws. He couldn't hold it!

With an anguished cry, he watched the stone fall from his desiccated fingers and drop into the cave below.

Power ebbed, stripping him of the Oneness he had barely come to know. Groping, frenzied, he gripped the single raveling thread that still bound him to the stone. He must hold on . . .

His body spasmed; his mind began shrinking, slipping back into the mist. He struggled, trying to hold onto the Light—

Around him the gateway shimmered; the bridge trembled beneath his feet. And time, like a fragile memory, quivered on the wind.

Desperately Divinian clung to the slender bond as a chasm opened around him. Unbelieving, he hung between the portals of his mind.

The cave had vanished. And now the bridge was fading, the gateway beginning to dissolve. He felt himself falling . . . falling . . . sliding down, into an endless night. Wind roamed the void like the plaintive cry of lost souls, dying children. Darkness reached up to claim the Light . . .

7

Nick stood at the pedestal table in his daughter's bedroom, eyes narrowed, gazing down at the arrangement of stones glistening in the high-intensity beam of his flashlight. The sudden wave of visual images and sensory perceptions bombarding his mind had begun to ebb, the table come back into focus.

For an instant it had seemed the small white stone in the center of the table was shot through with tiny rivers of moving light. On the heels of that illusion, a blinding sense of déjà vu had clouded Nick's brain with almost numbing effect:

he was back in the dream-place, standing over the glass-encased stone while all around him rivulets of molten ice cavorted with drunken shadows and voices chanted long-forgotten rites

With effort, Nick forced the residual images aside, concentrating on the table, the rocks, Sara's bedroom. Numbness receded, leaving him cold and vaguely nauseous.

Realizing that his hand had tightened on the slender penlight until the supple leather glove felt

welded in place, he immediately relaxed his hold—
and the other hand, which had also formed a fist.

What had just happened?

Nick examined the question carefully, aware
from taut features and tensed muscles that he'd instinctively braced for an attack. He was accustomed to this finely honed awareness, which acted
like an early-warning system in the field—a combination of good instincts, excellent training, and
just plain luck that gave him his edge. This had
been different, almost hallucinatory. It had never
happened to him before.

Nick flexed the fingers of his left hand, then
switched the flashlight to it and did the same with
his right, careful to keep the beam spotted on the
table. Wouldn't do to alert the guard outside.

He glanced around his daughter's room, still feeling a vague sense of alarm

(like an adjustment going wrong?)

What was it that disturbed his concentration?
For a moment it had almost seemed as if he were
somewhere else—some*one* else, seeing himself
through other eyes while his own saw

*a cave ... light, viewed through mist ... cold, so
very cold*

His eyes returned to the peculiar arrangement of
pebbles on the pedestal table. Had this triggered
the strange reaction? The setup faintly resembled
his dream.

The white stone glowed softly in the light,
brighter threads running through it, giving off uneven flickers as he played the flash. He picked it up,
immediately dispelling the illusion.

Hairlike cracks scored the surface, a shallow
crazing etched in milky white. Possible traces of
silicon dioxide reflected the high intensity beam.

Replacing the stone, he played the light over the
tabletop, again noting a familiarity he couldn't

quite identify: white stone in the center; eight others, in varying shades, grouped around it; single black stone off to the side. Sara had sat at this table, working with these stones. What significance did they hold for her?

The black stone's polished surface returned only a smooth reflection, reminding Nick of the windows in Frank Terrell's limo.

A flicker of annoyance intruded. It wouldn't do to become so absorbed in things here that he allowed unfinished business to remain pending too long.

His light clung to the black stone as a sense of danger again stalked him. He frowned, trying to define the source. Was it the sudden thought of Terrell, an instinctive edge of wariness being honed? It was as though something on an elemental level kept sending prickles along the base of his skull.

Turning off the flashlight, Nick pocketed it and stood in silence while his eyes readjusted to the darkened room. Shapes took form, solidified; shadows separated into lighter shades on black. He could make out the window, the door—

Someone's out there

The words came quietly to his brain. Nick wasted no time debating them.

Moving silently to the door, he listened a moment, then opened it, satisfied no one waited just beyond. The dark corridor snaked left, stairwell opening from it. Murky stone steps descended into blackness.

Nick sensed that whoever had entered The Ridge was not up here. Not yet.

Leaving the door behind him ajar, Nick edged along the corridor, a shadow among shadows. The night guard might be making rounds; Special Agent Lew Harris could be stopping by for a late-night check. He meant to avoid either encounter.

A chance existed, however, that the murderer might be returning to the scene of his crime. And Nick wasn't completely discounting a threat named Terrell.

Retracing his earlier path, he moved to the top of the staircase, visualizing the main floor's layout: entry hall at the bottom, great room left, dining room right. Keeping his back to the wall, he silently descended the stairs, sensing no immediate presence, though the prickle of danger still crawled at the base of his neck.

Slipping catlike to the bifold doors, he paused to listen. No sound penetrated the thick darkness, nothing but the unanswered question of a small chalk-marked circle. A faint stirring of cool air eased through the crack and brushed his cheek.

Nick moved across the foyer and into the main hallway that bisected this part of the house and led to the older section. He'd skimmed the unused wing initially, noting several ways one could gain access to the main house. He'd used one himself. The archway door stood open, the way he'd left it when he entered the main house. The danger emanated from there—

The feel of being manipulated suddenly halted him. What if something was luring him on? He melted into the shadows, for an instant experiencing an unfamiliar contradiction of instincts: one whispering *wait*, one urging him forward. Was he being set up? Watched?

A faint sound broke the momentary deadlock: a key being used, a door being opened, closed. Someone had entered the house through the unused wing. Light raked the branching corridor beyond the archway; the intruder was using a full-beam flash.

Nick eased back into a doorway he'd just passed, sliding his body into the recessed opening.

Pulling off a glove, he quietly removed a small foil packet from an inside pocket and carefully peeled back one side, then slipped the glove back on.

Footsteps approached; audible breathing. He watched the light track forward. Whoever this was had a lot to learn about stealth. He didn't think the person was aware of him.

The light moved past.

A shadow crossed his vision.

Nick absorbed information: height, mass, body structure, visible weapons; calculated his move: position, timing, angle of attack—

He stepped out from behind, caught the intruder's left wrist and wrenched it back and up. At the same time, he thrust his right arm around the intruder's neck, jerking the head against his shoulder. Immediately he pressed the gauze pad to the immobilized face, pinching the nose and forcing a gasp of breath.

The intruder had time for one futile moment of resistance before the drug took effect, inhibiting motor reflexes. Choked protests filtering through the gauze pad grew faint, fainter. The flashlight dropped and rolled against the wall. The intruder's body slumped.

Nick controlled the fall, keeping the pad firmly in place until he was sure of complete affect. He checked his captive's pulse, knew he had about ten minutes before the drug started to wear off.

Releasing the body, he recovered the gauze pad and returned it to his pocket. The small Beretta remained holstered in the ankle rig on his right leg. He'd prefer not to use it.

Picking up the intruder's flashlight, he thumbed it off, then swung the body up into a fireman's hold, confirming his initial impression: The intruder was a woman.

Nick carried his burden down the corridor and up the stairs, seeing well enough to avoid a mishap. At the top he turned right, toward a bedroom at the farthermost end, where sound wouldn't carry.

Dumping his unconscious captive on the double bed, he first secured the room, then, working methodically and impersonally, checked the body for weapons and equipment. Clean.

Nick pulled out his penlight and ran it over her: late twenties, athletic, butch haircut. Reasonably attractive for the type. Dressed in jeans and a black, hooded sweatshirt. He'd seen some female contract killers. They ran the gamut from model quality to frump. This one fell somewhere in between.

She wasn't armed, which was a bit unusual given the circumstances. Martial arts expert? He checked the hands. No.

Using a roll of nylon wrapping tape, he quickly strapped her wrists together behind her back, then taped her feet. He was beginning to have serious doubts that he was dealing with a pro here, but amateurs could be equally dangerous, and they were unpredictable.

A soft groan indicated the drug was wearing off. Her head rolled to one side, then she grew still again.

Nick flicked on a convenient reading lamp clipped to the bed's headboard and returned the penlight to his pocket. He slid the small lamp over, aiming the beam to fall on the woman's face. A reflexive tightening of her eyelids indicated returning consciousness. Nick helped it along with a couple of stinging slaps.

The sudden pain brought her awake. Pain had a way of doing that.

It took her a moment to realize her position. When she did, her first reaction was to struggle. Then she saw him: a shadowy form beyond the light. Her eyes grew hollow, and Nick's suspicion that he had an innocent on his hands increased.

"I'm going to ask you some questions," he said quietly. "I want you to tell me the truth. Do you understand?"

She surprised him. "Who the hell are you and what did you give me?"

Nick frowned. He didn't have time for this.

Reaching down, he gripped the sides of her neck with his thumb and middle finger, just beneath the jaw. She tried to scoot her body away from him, to jerk her head sideways. Nick began applying pressure, keeping it minimal but steady, letting the suggestion of pain build toward the reality.

She gasped a faint *"Please—"* going still beneath his hand.

"Do you understand?" he repeated, spacing the words.

She tried to nod, then whispered: "Yes," and again, louder: *"Yes."*

He released her. "That's the only time I'll ask a question twice."

She nodded once, eyes struggling to see him behind the light.

"Your name?"

"Danielle Grant, you bastard."

Nick stood silent as the pieces came together: David Grant's sister; an unlikely threat. But what was Grant's sister doing sneaking into The Ridge?

"What's your business here?" He studied the defiant face glaring up at him, gauging reactions.

"This is my brother's house," she snapped, her husky voice breaking slightly. *"My* house now. You're the one who's—" She thought better of it.

"Why break into your own house?" Nick prompted.

"Because the police won't give me access."

"And?"

Her eyes shifted away from him. "I needed some things."

"What things?"

"For my . . . niece. Clothes—things."

The woman was lying. "Your niece?" Nick's voice hardened.

Again she surprised him, swinging her gaze back around, eyes flashing. "You leave her out of this! She's only a child." Emotion etched her tone—an emotion Nick couldn't read.

"I didn't bring her into it," he said, and her eyes shifted away again.

"You're not a good liar, Danielle." He said her name softly, almost caressingly, and watched her eyes flicker uncertainly back to his. Capitalizing on the psychological edge, he moved a step closer. "How deeply, I wonder, are you involved with what happened here?"

For a moment she didn't grasp the intimation. Then it hit her. Anger wiped the fear from her eyes. "You're suggesting *I* might have had something to do with this nightmare? You son of a bitch! Who the hell are you, a cop? That's it, isn't it? You're a cop. Well, you guys may think you can get away with these Dirty Harry tactics, but I'll have your job for this. Untie me!"

Her breathing came in deep, ragged spurts as though she'd been running hard, her face was clogged with emotion and sweat. Small tendrils of damp hair lay plastered against the sides of her flushed face.

Nick regarded her calmly. "You haven't answered my question, Danielle." He saw the flicker of uncertainty return.

"I'm here to find the evidence you people have obviously overlooked so you'll quit wasting time and go out there and arrest the real murderer!"

"Who is—?"

"Nick Vears!" she blurted, trying to heave her body upward. "*He's* the monster who murdered my brother. And if you won't do something about him, then I will."

Nick met the accusation with silence. So David Grant's sister had him pegged as the murderer; Carole's influence, no doubt. An opinion passed on to the SBI? He recalled the morning's fencing match with Agent Harris, the feeling that Harris was measuring him for a murder rap. Was this why?

She lay there glaring at him, body rigid, eyes glittering, apparently dubbing him the lesser of two evils, now, in her fury at thoughts of Nick Vears. There was a certain irony to the situation.

There was also a certain dilemma: What was he going to do with her?

Every now and then she twisted her body as though challenging him either to release her or come on and do his worst. Ignorance did have its impetuous side, thought Nick, watching her impassively.

He could threaten her until dawn, he decided, and the minute she was free she'd run screaming to Harris. He could hurt her, and she'd probably still run screaming to Harris as soon as he was out of sight; she had that kind of disjoined bravado.

He had no handle to work with. *So what are you going to do, Nick? Kill her?* That would be the safe way out.

"You're not the police," she said suddenly. The fear was back.

She watched him pull out a slender pocketknife and open it, stepping closer to the bed. She shrank back, a look of horror spreading across her face.

And this, thought Nick, was a woman who had broken into a house where four people had been violently killed and held some kind of convoluted notion of confronting their killer? What, he marveled, had she planned to do with him when she found him?

Leaning over, he cut the tape binding her arms and feet, then closed and repocketed the knife.

She sat up slowly, watching him, uncertain of his intentions.

Nick turned his back on her and went to unlock the door, taking his time, searching his mind for some way to deal with this problem before it escalated. He kept coming up blank.

When he turned around, she was sitting on the side of the bed, massaging her abused wrists. The fragments of tape had been wadded and flung to the floor. She eyed him malevolently.

"You're free to go," he prompted, controlling his annoyance.

As though afraid of making too sudden a move, she carefully stood, then took a tentative step forward. "Just like that?" Her tone held accusation, wariness.

"Just like that." Nick let impatience surface. Again, his plans had been interfered with, this time by an amateur. He needed free access to this house; he needed anonymity. He was getting neither. Of course, it would be his word against hers when she finally identified him, which wouldn't take long with Harris. If it came down to it, he could take care of Harris. But this was a glitch he didn't need or have time for.

The situation was fast becoming a three-ring circus, with him as the main attraction. Send in the clowns? They're already here. He speculated on what might be next—the Marines?

Eyes fastened to his face, she began walking toward the door. He stepped back, ignoring her flinch of reaction. She was probably deciding when to break and run for it, Nick assessed, how quickly she could make it to the cop outside, how loudly she could scream. He'd wanted more time in Sara's room. Now he'd have to—

Sara. Knowledge suddenly coalesced in his brain. When she'd spoken of Sara the look in her eyes had been—*protective*. She cared for his daughter. Was that his key to Danielle Grant?

"What makes you so sure Nick Vears is a murderer?" he remarked conversationally as Danielle edged past him.

His question stopped her on the threshold, turning her toward him. He watched her face in the dim light, saw her eyes roam his features as though committing him to memory. He almost smiled.

"Who *are* you?" she demanded furiously.

Nick shrugged, making the only decision time and quick reasoning would allow. "The monster you're looking for."

For a moment she simply stood there, staring at him, unable to deal with what he'd said. Then her features contorted and she lunged.

Nick grabbed her wrists and shook her once— hard. The outburst subsided.

"Listen to me," he said harshly. "I didn't kill these people. But I intend to find out who did. You can help by keeping your mouth shut and staying out of my way. And I want to move into this house."

She gaped at him. "I don't believe this—"

"I'm not interested in what you believe. I'm interested in this house and what happened here. I think you want Sara. I'm willing to make a trade."

"Jesus Christ! You'd bargain your own child?"

Nick drew coldness to him like a shield. "Is it a bargain, then?"

The angry flush drained from her cheeks, leaving a residue of—pain? Nick was surprised he could still identify it. He'd forgotten what most emotions looked like.

"You *are* a monster," she whispered.

He met her accusing look grimly. "Believe me, Danielle, I get worse."

Realizing it was finished for now, he released her arms. "Think about it."

He went over to the bed, retrieved the wadded tape, flipped off the lamp. A sudden return of awareness crawled across the base of his skull.

What was it about this house that bothered him?

"How long do you want the house?" Her voice floated to him from the darkness.

"Until I'm through with it."

"Legal custody, Vears?"

"Yes," Nick lied.

Using the penlight, he walked back over to the door and lightly took hold of Danielle's arm. "Let's go." She let him lead her out into the hall and down the stairs.

"Where are you taking me?" she demanded as they entered the older section of the house. The uncertainty was back.

"To the dungeon to cut out your tongue," Nick muttered, guiding her to the right, away from the door she had obviously used to gain entry, then down a small flight of steps that led into a narrow, musty corridor.

She subsided into silence.

They passed a long row of monks' cells that ended at a small exterior door which had once given access to a private cloister. He let her precede him through the door, then refastened the rusty bolts. The strange awareness had continued to plague him as he threaded through the older section of the house, and it lingered with him now.

What had triggered his instincts?

Tabling the question, he escorted Danielle away from the house and past the night guard. She had the good sense to keep quiet as they threaded their way downhill to the beach road, avoiding the drive-way—or maybe it was his grip on her arm.

"How did you get here?" Nick stopped walking as they reached the road.

"Bicycle." She gestured toward a clump of bushes farther down.

He nodded absently. Somehow it fit. "Have you decided to accept my offer?"

"I'm still thinking about it," she snapped, bravado obviously returning now that the threat of dungeons had receded.

He looked at her a moment, then said softly, "Don't take too long."

Releasing her arm, he turned and began walking toward the beach.

"Vears?"

He glanced back at her, saying nothing.

"You could have killed me."

"I still can."

When she didn't reply, he resumed his interrupted retreat.

"Vears?"

Again he stopped, not turning around this time.

"Why didn't you?"

He thought about it, watching the cold moonlight on the ocean, hearing the waves beat against the shore. From the moment he'd known she wasn't a threat it had ceased to be an option.

He said, "Sara needs someone." A good, manipulative remark. He started walking again.

"Vears?"

Nick turned around impatiently, beginning to wish he *had* cut out her tongue. "What?"

"You didn't kill them?" Her face was a pale, featureless smear in the thin moonlight, but he could sense her expression.

"No," he said firmly, wondering what she'd say

if he added: *because I was busy killing six other people at the time.*

This time he stood pat, waiting to see if there'd be any further discussion. And he'd thought Harry was—

"Vears?"

"Yes?"

"It's a bargain."

+ + +

Sara lay awake in the darkness, eyes staring
through the glass. She'd been this way for a while—
ever since the disturbance had awakened her.

The bright thing had grown stronger for a moment,
swelling like the sun at evening, but cold-white, not
red. She'd expected it to come for her, try to take her
to its cave; she'd started to back away from the glass.

It hadn't, though. There was something in its way,
something . . .

warm.

Sara looked at the warm, tried to see its color,
and couldn't. The color kept changing, reflecting
back the light.

But it was there . . . and it was between her and
the cold, not so big and not so strong but in between.

It didn't seem to be going anywhere.

She hugged her Fuzzy closer, not moving from
the glass, not moving at all . . .

and for the first time in a long time drifted into
dreamless sleep.

+ + +

8

A soft voice woke Sara, the feel of sunlight in the room, a spreading warmth. She didn't open her eyes, but lay there beside the glass, feeling alone and unhappy, wanting her mommy.

(Mommy's gone)

At first, the glass had been her friend, the safe thing between *it* and her. Everything on the other side was horrible—monsters, nightmares, red pain beating to get in. She was never going back out there— *Never!*

(different now)

At first, she'd thought it was a trick, a way to make her come out. And she wanted to come out; it was so lonely in here. She squeezed her Fuzzy, wishing it would squeeze her back. But she hadn't come out. Not even when the warm thing came, not even then. The warm wasn't big enough and she was too afraid.

But the warm thing was still out there, she could sense it; it hadn't gone away, and something about it comforted Sara. The cold was bigger and very strong, but the warm was in between. And it was strong, too, and it made her feel strong.

(friend?)

Sara thought about the stones on her table at home, thought about the black stone that she'd kept to itself because she hadn't known where it belonged, only that it did belong. She thought she knew where to put it now. When she got home, she'd fix things—

(home)

Memories of that night scratched at the glass.

(No! Can't come in!)

Sara didn't want to see them, didn't want to hear them, and no one could make her. *No one* could break her glass.

She wanted to go home. But in order to go home she'd have to come out. She couldn't do that.

The voice beyond the glass murmured into her thoughts, burrowing under her fear like a soft kitten. The voice was soothing, familiar. Sara felt a glow just outside the glass, hovering there the way her aunt Dani would always do with a big, fluffy towel after they'd been swimming. She'd fold her in the towel, bundling it around and around her until only her face was showing, rubbing her briskly dry, giving her lots of hugs and making her giggle.

A giggle eased its way to the surface and Sara let it out. She and her aunt Dani used to laugh a lot—

"Sara? Sara, love? It's me, it's Dani. Please hear me, Sara. C'mon, munchkin, talk to me, open your eyes. It's all right, I'm here now. No one's going to hurt you. Please, love . . ."

(Dani! Dani's here)

Sara edged closer to the glass, wanting nothing more than to make it go away and fling herself into her aunt Dani's arms— But she couldn't. The cold thing was still out there. It would get her. It might get Dani, too. Sara couldn't let that happen. She couldn't!

Tears filled her mind and ran down the glass like rain on a windowpane, blurring her vision of the other side, a further barrier between them.

Please, Sara echoed the word Dani continued to croon softly, *please hold me and make it all go away, please.*

But Dani couldn't hold her through the glass, couldn't touch her, couldn't make it better unless Sara let her. And that meant lowering the glass.

Sara couldn't do that. Not yet. Maybe not ever—

Something touched her. Startled, she refocused on the scene beyond her glass. The bright thing still waited in the distance but it was overshadowed by a swirling cloud. She couldn't see into the cloud, but she wasn't afraid.

(It was the warm thing from last night, between her and the cold. It was growing, changing, coming)

It had touched her through the glass!

Here was something she could wrap herself in, something strong enough to protect her from the cold, something warm and—

Other things swirled within the cloud. Strange things. Dark things. Sara couldn't see them. For a moment she hesitated, giving way to the fear again. She reached for the glow that was Dani, the familiar, the easily understood. The other wasn't like that. But it was strong, and somehow she trusted it.

(Friend.)

Tentatively at first, and then with greater courage, Sara began lowering the glass . . .

Dani felt drained. The past two days had been a nightmare of grief and repetitive body blows. She clung to Sara now, like a lifeline to the past, and the future. Sara was all she had left.

Oh, David, what in God's name happened? The ever-present nausea surged, and she swallowed heavily, blinking back tears that sprang to her eyes and burned like the bile pushing against her throat.

"Sara, love. Can you hear me? It's Dani."

Softly she spoke to the unconscious child, holding the small hand between her own, sometimes rocking back and forth in the uncomfortable straight chair as she kept vigil by Sara's bed.

The doctor had encouraged her to talk to Sara, reassuring her, coaxing her out of her self-imposed shell. He'd said that patients with shock-induced coma often hear what's being said to them, that little by little the mind is building up the necessary strength to deal with the outside world again. And children, he'd said, are particularly resilient.

"Please, munchkin, wake up. It'll be all right, I promise."

But would anything ever be all right again?

Don't go making promises you might not can keep, Dani Grant, she berated herself, heartsick at the thought of further hurt to this child. Too often, she let her tongue rule her head—like last night.

A gush of remembrance burned Dani's cheeks. She should have kept her mouth shut, could have ended up dead. And she'd stupidly blurted something about Sara to that *monster* before she'd known who he was.

But then he'd said he'd give her Sara—legal custody. Could she trust him? Dani went cold, remembering Carole's letters. They'd been adamant in their condemnation of Nicholas Vears; fanatical, even. That's why Dani had been skeptical at first, knowing Carole's tendency to exaggerate things she felt strongly about in order to sway opinion. *I'm sorry, Carole. I'm so sorry.*

But she *had* been wrong about Nick Vears. At least partially. Hadn't she?

Confusion reared its Medusa's head and Dani felt her thoughts weaving in all directions. She'd been so certain Vears was responsible. Yet Agent Harris had spoken of an alibi, and last night Vears had made her doubt her beliefs.

Did that mean a murderer was still on the loose? Or was it all some sort of horrible accident?

Contradictions bombarded her. She banished them and turned her concentration solely on Sara, reaching a hand to brush a tangle of hair from the pale cheek.

They'd always been close. From the time David had married Carole, asking Dani to keep Sara while they went on their honeymoon, a special relationship had seemed to spring up between them. Where Carole saw growing reason for concern, and David bestowed abstract fondness, Dani found only delight. With her, Sara was a child full of laughter, sunshine.

She'd once accused Carole of harboring a changeling, when her sister-in-law remarked that Sara never seemed so carefree except with Dani. Carole had made some cryptic response about wishing that were true, and Dani knew she constantly watched the child for inherent traits of the father. Then, Dani hadn't really understood. Now she did.

How could this beautiful child be *his*? Anger returned at thoughts of what Vears had done to her last night. Maybe he wasn't guilty of murder, but he was far from winning any Father of the Year awards. No matter what it took, she was more determined than before to do the one thing she still could for Carole—keep her daughter away from Nicholas Vears.

Late-morning sunlight streamed into the room through the large plate glass window, depositing a sunbeam on the bed that had slowly crept toward Sara's face. Dani thought she saw golden-fringed eyelids flutter against the brightness, and she leaned over, gently stroking Sara's forehead and cheek.

"Sara? Sara, can you hear me?"

Cautiously she used her hand to shade Sara's eyes from the sunlight, then moved it away, looking for another flutter of reaction. The child lay there, one arm wrapped tightly around her stuffed bear. Smooth lids, with their tracing of light blue veins, remained stoically closed.

Memory of last night again intruded: light glaring in her eyes, a man looming in the background. She'd never been so frightened, so certain she was going to die. She'd learned something last night from Nick Vears: the meaning of true terror. If there was ever a chance to pay him back, Dani vowed, she would.

She tried to conjure up Vears's face and found it nebulous. It remained just out of reach, a vague shadow-form on the darkness. All she could manage to visualize clearly were his eyes . . . like dark, polished stones, when they'd watched her from beyond the light, when they'd glittered into hers as he'd grabbed her in the doorway. Cold. Emotionless. Dani shuddered at the memory.

"Sara, love? Won't you please wake up and talk to me?"

She abandoned her attempt to stimulate a reflexive movement and renewed her soothing chatter. Warm sunlight bathed the small, pale face, but the delicate eyelids were still. There was no response.

Dani watched the sleeping child, feeling love well up within her—love and helplessness and grief. Would Sara be lost to her, too?

A sudden movement startled her. She studied the child's face intently, noting no change, then realized it was Sara's hand quivering against the sheet. As she watched, hardly daring to breathe, small fingers began rubbing the sheet in a slow, rhythmic pattern. The arm lifted, hand reaching out toward Dani with an innocent trust heart rending in its simplicity.

Dani thrust herself forward out of the chair, leaning over the child, gripping the small, cool hand. "Yes, love, I'm here. It's going to be all right now, you'll see. I'm here for you—I'll always be here for you, Sara."

She reached for the call button and pressed it furiously, not taking her eyes off Sara's face.

"She's waking up, I think she's waking up," Dani exclaimed into the activated speaker. She felt a tear roll down one cheek as she waited—*prayed* for Sara to open her eyes and look at her.

As though in answer to that prayer, Sara's eyelids suddenly sprang open, drawing Dani into the deep royal blue that never failed to awe her with its vividness. Like the electric hues of David's magnificent paintings, Sara's eyes riveted attention, startling in their intensity.

Dani's vision blurred as she looked into the wide, clear eyes, seeking contact. But they were looking past, not at her.

The small hand began absently patting her arm as though she, not Sara, were the one to be comforted. Happiness and relief gave way to a prick of fear. Sara's attention was locked on something behind Dani. Slowly she turned her head, following the look.

A man stood in the doorway—Dani hadn't heard the door open. He wore jeans and a loose gray sweatshirt, sleeves shoved to the elbows. A dark windbreaker carelessly draped an arm.

Not a doctor.

How had he gotten past the guard? Did the fool let just anybody waltz right in here?

Medium height, medium build; he was looking at

Sara, his expression remote. His hair was an uncertain shade of brown, cut moderately short and pushed back from his forehead by fingers or the wind. His skin had an olive cast that looked like a tan and probably wasn't. There was an aura of distance about him, and other things less easily defined.

One level of Dani's brain continued to catalog the man, storing up information that had been missing from her recollection of last night.

Oh, yes, sudden knowledge overpowered her. *This was Nick Vears. This was certainly Nick Vears.*

Dani felt her jaw tighten and her gut heave. She'd let Vears intimidate her last night. It wasn't going to happen again.

Placing a protective arm around the pillow behind Sara, Dani glared at him, trying to encircle his child in a web of safety. What was this bastard doing here when he'd promised—

He took a step into the room, moving into a shaft of sunlight. Behind him, the heavy door sighed shut.

Dani's breath stilled. Daylight should have lessened Vears's affect—like Count Dracula. It didn't. She felt a small quiver of the fear that had gripped her so totally last night. Sara's father or not, she was going to yell bloody murder if he tried anything here.

But his eyes were locked on Sara's as though they were the only two people in the room. No one else existed. It was as though the two of them touched, father and daughter.

Where last night his eyes had dominated, today they were opaque, indistinct. Dani couldn't tell their color, only that it seemed vague and misty, maybe gray. Something existed in that look, something Dani couldn't read. She felt almost intrusive.

Shaking her head to clear it of this unacceptable thought, she turned back to Sara, seeking reassur-

ance. But the child's gaze hadn't wavered, and Dani
saw that same strange look of—what?

The small hand on her arm tightened, and Dani
clung to this link binding them. For a moment she'd
felt Sara slipping away again, and didn't know what
to do. *You can't have her, Vears. You can't have her.*

The vivid blue eyes continued to stare past Dani,
and it took all her resolve not to turn back toward
the door. She wanted to. There was something seductive about the man—too seductive. Had he come
for Sara? The thought made her skin crawl.

She sat there, holding Sara's hand, determined
not to allow this odd connection between father and
daughter, not to let Nick Vears assume control.
Sara returned the pressure, but it was her father
who held her eyes.

A sudden influx of people into the room: two
nurses, the young doctor, the guard. Dani moved
out of the way, reluctantly ceding the small arm to
a starched white uniform with a blood pressure
unit. The other nurse went to the opposite side,
checking IV and pulse, while the doctor adjusted
his stethoscope and leaned down, treating Sara to
a disarmingly boyish grin and calling her "Kiddo."

Dani stepped to one side, where Sara could see
she hadn't left her, but Sara's eyes had shifted to
the doctor, now—and she was returning his grin!

"Oh, thank you, thank you, God," Dani whispered, and turned a triumphant glare on Vears—

The doorway was empty.

Affecting a casualness he was far from feeling,
Nick left the hospital through a side door and
strolled across the small patio that bordered the
children's wing. It was almost noon and the patio
was empty.

Retrieving his cigarettes from a jacket pocket, he
shook one out and lit it with a match from the half-

empty book tucked inside the cellophane. A half-hearted breeze ruffled the hair at the back of his neck and scattered the small trail of blue smoke as he walked over to a low brick wall and stood looking out over the landscape.

The view offered a variety of stunted vegetation and patchy sand, not a likely vista for the cover of a regional tourist brochure. The hospital was the only building in sight, as though it had been ostracized from civilization. A few stray gulls roamed the air.

As was often the case in resort areas, the picture-book scenery deteriorated the farther one got from the focal point, but Nick preferred the barren landscape, the uncluttered view and innate silence. As though to mock this thought, the compressor on the hospital's huge air-conditioning unit cut in.

Tossing his windbreaker across the low wall, Nick propped himself against it and took a deep draw on his cigarette, blowing the smoke out slowly, inching his mind back toward the precise thinking that was his norm. He'd been shaken, deeply; it had been a long time since a situation had thrown him off balance like that.

He'd known he'd be taking a chance coming here, understood the risk of becoming too involved with things that had no place in his life. He'd thought to make arrangements for Sara, move her to a private hospital if necessary, find out what happened—and leave. He hadn't bargained for getting caught up in things.

And he hadn't bargained for what had just occurred.

Nick thought about it, starting at the beginning and working through the experience with a mathematician's cold, hard approach:

He'd made the decision to come here today, using it to bargain with Harris—this seemed his week for bargains. He'd try to reach Sara; Harris would grant him access to The Ridge. He'd sensed Harris's internal debate, and marked his surprise when Nick mentioned he had the Grant woman's permission. As a kicker, he'd added that Sara would be staying with her aunt. In spite of his alibi and a lack of substantive evidence, Nick knew Harris still harbored suspicions.

Harris had eventually agreed. The quarantine was due to be lifted anyway now that the investigation teams had finished gathering their evidence. This way the SBI agent would not only be getting the help he wanted with his star witness, he'd be keeping a potential suspect under his watchful eye. Nick expected he'd be seeing rather a lot of Special Agent Lew Harris.

Despite what he'd told Harris, Nick did know something about dealing with violence-related disorders. He'd meant to keep this clinical, impersonal, controller to subject. But what had just happened went past his scope of knowledge or experience.

And what *had* happened?

The first crack had appeared when he'd entered the hospital. He'd known which room was Sara's, gone right to it as though something were directing his steps. He recalled having the same feeling last night at The Ridge. He had no explanation for it.

Nick had opened the door, and immediately recognized Danielle Grant—but he'd have known the child in the bed as his daughter regardless. He could have picked her out of a crowded ward.

The crack widened: Nick hadn't seen Sara since she was a baby; no pictures, no letters bearing descriptions, nothing. Yet he'd known.

And she'd known him.

The thought slid through the crack, increasing the rift in his logic. Sara had recognized him just as surely as he'd known her. The knowledge had been in her eyes.

Nick again saw the startling blue bore into him, touching something at once unknown and familiar, something he wasn't even aware existed, and still wasn't sure of. He couldn't put a name to it, but it went beyond some textbook hypothesis of genetic-level recognition.

"Vears!"

The hail came from behind him, and was distinctively Danielle Grant's.

Nick's eyes narrowed as he dropped his cigarette to the cement, crushed it beneath his shoe, and turned around. He was not in the mood for a confrontation.

She strode toward him from the same exit door he'd used, long legs bare beneath a full cotton skirt and scooped-neck shirt. She wore sandals and a scowl, and Nick found himself confronting a completely irrelevant thought of what she'd be like in bed.

"I want to know what you're doing here, Vears," she demanded as she stopped just short of arm's length.

Nick was not in the habit of explaining himself.

His silence unnerved her, apparently defusing her attack plan. He read her thoughts easily: *Maybe she was jumping to conclusions. Maybe she shouldn't be too hasty in rocking the boat.*

She finally said: "I suppose there'll be papers to sign."

"No doubt," Nick replied, not knowing if she meant to imply hospital release forms or custody documents. He doubted she knew, either. He wondered if she ever fully explored a thought before expounding on it.

"I intend taking Sara with me when they release

her." Defiance edged the husky voice, and more than a hint of challenge.

"Fine." Nick kept his tone even, content in the knowledge that Agent Harris would not be authorizing his key witness's removal from the area just yet.

His complacency seemed to mollify her for the moment. Nick doubted it would last and decided to take advantage of the lull. He straightened from the wall, picked up his jacket, and started to walk away.

It was not to be that easy.

"I want to get this settled, Vears. Today."

Nick stopped walking and turned back toward her. "Go ahead." He maintained his matter-of-fact tone.

She seemed unprepared for this response, and again Nick got the impression of innocence. She knew the ends she wanted, but had no real idea how to get there.

"I want this thing done legally. Legal custody, just like you said." She hesitated, then added belligerently. "I'm not sure I trust you."

"That's your problem," he remarked, sidestepping the legal issue, and saw her bristle. To forestall the inevitable comeback, he said, "Do whatever it is you want to do, and let me know when you've done it." Maybe that would keep her occupied and out of his way for a while. The woman was becoming a nuisance.

Again, he turned to go. The hand suddenly jerking his arm stopped him.

Nick checked the instinctive reflex and relaxed his body.

"We had a bargain, Vears. I'm willing to keep my part, but I'm not sure you are. I want something in writing. Now. Or I'll—"

"Yes?" Nick regarded her coldly, tired of this and through with being tractable.

"—I'll go to Agent Harris and tell him about last night." Belligerence still edged her tone, belligerence tainted by bravado.

"Too late, Danielle," he said softly, moving a step closer and feeling her hand fall from his arm. "The time to make accusations about last night is past. Last night you might have swung it. Today, it's your word against mine. There's no evidence, and no motive to support your claim. You, on the other hand, have already made allegations against me which proved groundless." Nick saw the calculated guess hit home. "And now you're willing to make new ones, irresponsible ones—the grief-stricken, deluded woman who will go to any lengths to gain custody of my daughter. Do you really think you'll be believed?"

He waited as his bluff took hold, watched her attempt to find the flaws that were certainly there. She could cause him some trouble if she called the bluff. She didn't.

"You bastard." Her words came low and hard, her eyes glaring into his. "You lied to me."

Nick's voice was chill. "It's part of my charm."

Whatever she might have said next was forestalled.

"Mr. Vears?" Sara's doctor came across the patio toward them.

"Dr. Craig?" Danielle stepped forward, immediately dismissing Nick in favor of this new concern. "How is Sara? Will she be all right now?"

"I think so." He smiled at Danielle as he reached them, then addressed them both.

"As with many of these cases, Sara has woken up completely alert and responsive. She shows no signs of physical dysfunction, and all our tests are negative. There is some residual trauma—"

Nick heard Danielle's soft gasp, and the doctor quickly added:

"—nothing to be overly concerned about, I assure you. I've talked to her at length, and she answers all my questions right on the money. She's aware that her mother, and the others, are dead. The only thing she can't, or won't, remember at present is the accident itself. And that's fairly normal in these cases.

"I know the SBI is waiting to talk to her, but she really shouldn't be badgered. I'll advise Agent Harris, as he asked me to do, explaining the situation. I'm sure he'll be in contact with you. When Sara's ready, she'll remember. Or it may take some professional help, I'll give you a couple of names," this to Nick. "For the most part, she's just going to need plenty of love and support. She's a little girl who's lost her mother. She needs someone to fill that gap."

He looked pointedly at Danielle, then back at Nick. "I'd like to keep her one more night, just for observation, but I see no reason why we couldn't release her tomorrow."

Nick nodded agreement. "Her aunt will make the necessary arrangements. Sara will be in her charge. I'd appreciate your getting the papers ready for me to sign today."

Beside him, Danielle stiffened and turned to stare at him. He didn't return the look.

"I'll tell them at the desk," Dr. Craig said, a frown touching his boyish features. It was clear he didn't know what to make of Nicholas Vears. "Were you planning to take Sara back to the house where the tragedy occurred?"

"I've rented a beach house for Miss Grant and my daughter about a mile and a half away. They'll be staying there." He sensed Danielle's deepening anger.

Dr. Craig nodded approval. "I think that's the wisest course for now. Like I said, don't force things on her. If and when she's ready to go back, okay. Just being surrounded by a familiar setting may trigger memory. Any problems, I'm available."

With a smile to Danielle, he left them.

"For how long, Vears?"

Nick glanced at her, taking out a cigarette, lighting it. He didn't misunderstand the question.

Nor did he answer it.

9

Today is warmer than yesterday, Dani thought as she took the shortcut across the small side patio that led to the children's wing. Or did it just seem that way because Vears wasn't around? She purposely ignored the spot where they'd stood talking, but couldn't avoid a shiver—like his eyes were still hanging there, focused on the back of her head.

The seesaw emotions of the previous day still had her in knots; she'd felt mauled by them, first with Sara, then *him*. The knot that was Vears clenched tighter. So far he'd intimidated her, scared her silly, infuriated her, physically abused her; then he'd pulled that little emotional wringer yesterday afternoon, letting her think he'd reneged on their bargain, then casually informing the doctor that she was to have Sara, in a house he provided, of course. Bastard!

Dani had intended to keep Sara in town, and as far away from Nick Vears as possible. That was out of the question now, since the doctor had backed up the plan. And *he'd* be right down the beach. But Sara's welfare came first and Dani was willing to do whatever it took to insure this, even if it meant concessions to Vears. As long as he kept away from them, she'd stay in his damned beach house.

Shaking off her sour mood, Dani entered the hospital corridor and turned left toward Sara's room. The midmorning bustle of nurses and aides was brightened by laughter coming from the sunny playroom on her right. She glanced in as she passed and saw several kids in wheelchairs tossing a Frisbee back and forth. She smiled and walked on.

The temporary guard had been reassigned elsewhere. The sheriff didn't think Sara was in any danger, though the department would continue to keep a watchful eye. Dani had breathed a long sigh of relief when Harris had confirmed the sheriff's opinion, assuring her that it was not lack of funds or manpower that had led to the guard's recall. Maybe the whole thing *had* been some sort of horrible accident after all.

A nurse, clutching a blood pressure kit, was exiting Sara's room as Dani reached it.

"Oh, here you are, Ms. Grant. She's all ready to go." The slender, middle-aged woman with kind eyes smiled. "We have the papers at the nurse's station; Mr. Vears signed them yesterday and Dr. Craig this morning. I'm so glad things turned out well"— she hesitated, as though recalling the other circumstances— "at least in this respect."

"Me too. And thank you." Dani walked into the room.

Sara was sitting on the edge of her bed, clutching her Fuzzy, dressed in the new outfit Dani had bought her yesterday. She'd been looking out the window. She turned, and for just a moment gazed at her with such relief that Dani felt like crying.

"Did you think I wasn't coming, munchkin?" She spread her arms and felt the prick of tears as Sara slid off the high bed and literally threw herself into them. She held the small, quiet body until Sara pulled away.

"C'mon. Let's go home." Dani heard that last word and bit her lip, wishing it unsaid. Home was a bad dream, a nightmare memory. She glanced down warily as Sara slipped a hand into hers and they left the room, but the child merely smiled up at her, seemingly oblivious to the dreadful associations the word carried, thank God. Dani suddenly, furiously, hoped Sara would *never* remember that night. Wasn't it enough to know that the people she'd loved were dead?

"Just hand these in at the business office, Ms. Grant." The nurse caught her attention, holding out some papers as they passed. "Good-bye, Sara." She smiled at the child, who said nothing, but offered a faint smile in return.

"Thank you again for all you've done," Dani said. She felt Sara's small hand tighten on her own and, nodding a final good-bye to the nurse, began walking again, suddenly just as anxious as her niece to leave this place.

A pause at the business office and they headed out the front door, Dani fishing through her shoulder bag for the keys to David's car, which she'd been using.

"Ms. Grant?" A voice stopped her. "Patricia Danielle Grant?"

Dani frowned at the man who had stepped out from their left and now blocked their path. Thirty-fivish, stylishly dressed, with the polished good looks of chronic grooming, and the smug expression of the self-approved.

Sara's grip again tightened and she inched closer to Dani's side.

"Yes," Dani said hesitantly.

"The name's Russ Reikert, Patricia—or is it Danielle?—or maybe Patty? I'll bet it's Patty." The man oozed casual familiarity and made Dani think of singles bars and low-slung sports cars.

"It's Ms. Grant. What do you want?"

"Just a moment of your time"—he flashed her a practiced grin, then switched it to Sara—"and the little girl's, here." Pulling a hand from his pants pocket, he reached out as if to ruffle Sara's hair, but she shrank against Dani's leg.

Dani ground her teeth against an urge to kick this smooth-talking jackass in the label of his designer slacks.

"I repeat, Mr. Reikert, what do you want?"

"Perhaps you've heard of me, *Ms.* Grant. 'Russell Reikert At Large.' "

"No."

"I'm crushed. Truly. And you a fellow writer."

A bloody reporter. Dani stepped around him, gripping Sara's hand.

"Now, now, wait a minute. Please, Ms. Grant." He fell in beside the pair as Dani and Sara headed for the parking lot. "This is a big story, surely you recognize that. I'm sorry about what happened to your family, but you can't avoid the press forever." He pasted on his most ingratiating smile. "I'm prepared to offer ten thousand dollars for an exclusive—"

Dani whirled on him. "Get away from me, you vulture, or I'll—"

(a vision of Nick Vears flashed to mind, a sudden urge to say: "Or I'll sic *him* on you.")

"—sue!" She brushed past, fairly pulling Sara along, leaving the jerk standing at the edge of the parking lot, hands on his hips.

Suddenly Dani realized that Sara was almost having to run to keep up, and slowed her pace, glancing down apologetically as she loosened her hold on the small hand she'd been crushing. But the impish face held a satisfied smile, a "We showed him, didn't we" smile.

For the first time in days, Dani felt like laughing.

Sara was quiet during the drive, but it was a comfortable quiet, and Dani didn't push. It was enough to have her there, enough to glance across the front seat every so often and trade grins. Sara always seemed to look across just as Dani did, blue eyes shining in the sun. They could be happy together, in spite of everything, help each other through the pain. If only Vears would—

"Dani, you missed the turn."

Dani glanced at the child, then left, realizing she'd just passed the cutoff to The Ridge. Had Sara thought— "Honey, we're gonna stay in the nicest little beach house just down the road. You'll enjoy it, I promise. We can swim, and take walks, and watch TV as late as we want." It sounded lame, even to her own ears.

"I thought you said we were going home." Did Sara's voice hold a trace of stubbornness?

"We will, darling, but not just yet. Maybe tomorrow." She glanced at Sara, but this time the child didn't return her look.

What did this mean? Dani wondered. Should she turn around and take Sara to The Ridge? Was she ready? Was it too soon?

Inundated with questions that seemed to have no easy answers, Dani kept driving toward the beach house, unable to cope with the idea of going to The Ridge right now. Since that night with Vears, she'd had no desire to return, and sometimes wondered if she'd ever set foot in the place again. She supposed she'd have to, sooner or later, if for no other reason than to pack up David and Carole's things. And the children's. But not yet. Not yet.

Once more she glanced at Sara. The child seemed content, now, with their destination. Dani made the next left turn off the main road, and slowed as she neared the beach house. Maybe it had just been a reflex. She pulled into the empty driveway and stopped.

Together they got out of the car and walked up the steps to the small bungalow. So far, so good. Dani fished out the key Vears had left for her at the inn, along with directions. She'd already made one trip out to make sure she could find the house, see that it was clean, and bring some supplies. She'd found it spotless, like nobody had ever been there.

Opening the door, she stepped inside, then held it for Sara to enter. For a moment, the child hesitated, her head slightly cocked as if listening for something. Then she walked into the house, going immediately over to the sliding glass doors to stare blankly out at the ocean, cradling her small stuffed bear.

Dani sighed, closed and relocked the door, feeling depression sink down on her again. Sara was with her. But the grins had vanished.

"Bitch." Russ Reikert slammed the door of the rented Chevy and gunned the engine to life as if it were his Porsche. Reminded him of the dykes that hung around singles bars just to snub a guy. He glanced in the rearview mirror to make sure the blasted wind hadn't obliterated all the style from his haircut. At fifty bucks a whack, it better not.

What that woman needs is a good banging, Russ decided, remembering those long, tanned legs beneath the denim skirt. He might be willing to oblige, something to while away the midnight hours in this little puke-ass town. "Probably tight as a busload of Scottish nuns," he muttered, and popped the safety brake.

Squealing rubber out of the hospital parking lot, he roared off down the road. Had he been honest with himself, Russ would have had to admit that being snubbed was a response he elicited more often than not, particularly from women. Not being prone to such intimate appraisal, he quickly let sea air blow any possible parallels away, and put the blame firmly where it belonged:

"Bitch."

Of course, a certain amount of snubbing was to be expected in Russ's job; not everyone craved publicity or took kindly to interviews, particularly the sensational variety that drew Russ like a leech to blood. Different strokes to different folks.

But for almost six years, "Russell Reikert At Large" had been the mainstay of *The Exposé*. His feature stories had garnered more response (and upped circulation by a whopping 46 percent) than any other regular column in the history of the tabloid.

Russ specialized in the outré, the unexplained, the horrific. His stories bared the details others couldn't, or wouldn't, publish. He picked up where "tasteful" left off, poked into deeper dirt, where the juciest worms squirmed; and he always got his story—the *full* story. Anything less was like settling for a quick jack in the men's room. Russ hadn't gotten where he was now by jacking off.

He'd known this thing at The Ridge was big the moment one of his staffers stuck the newspaper accounts under his nose. It reeked of the abnormal, the phenomenal, the ghoulish—all the lurid shit his readers craved. He damn sure meant to shovel it to them.

He glanced down at the speedometer, saw it poised near seventy and smiled, confident in his ability to control the car, as well as the situation. Power, in any form. He loved it. His readers had come to expect powerful stories from him. Russ wasn't about to let some smart-mouthed bitch and a kid queer the deal.

Nick pulled the GMC onto the sandy verge that fronted The Ridge, took a moment to look around, then killed the motor and got out. The house was still lined off; the yellow plastic police tape fluttered in the wind, producing a muffled flapping sound.

Though the trappings of quarantine remained, it appeared that Harris had been as good as his word: the on-site guards had been pulled, reduced to an occasional patrol. One had passed Nick as he'd driven in. But, then, he'd expected Harris to keep him under surveillance.

Lifting the yellow tape, Nick stepped inside the barrier.

Silence hugged the old stone house, spacious solitude, the kind Nick usually felt at home with. This time he didn't.

Strolling onto the terrace, he studied the rocky promontory from the new angle, deciding it did resemble a spine somewhat, stretching from the headland into the sea: a vertebrate island picked clean by the gulls, washed smooth by the tides. Angular, high shouldered rocks gave way to more rounded protuberances farther out that dipped beneath the surface, finally disappearing altogether. No doubt they were slippery at all times; afternoon sunlight glistened on small slick patches of moss laid bare by the receding tide.

Nick lit a cigarette, absently wondering what sort of explanation Harris had used to downplay his moving in here, not that it particularly mattered. Maybe none at all. Harris was the OIC, the officer in charge; he could make decisions without making excuses. But the man was detail-oriented.

That little point had caused Nick some tempo-

rary concern. He tossed the cigarette to the rocks
below, dismissing the problem of Lew Harris. It
was being taken care of.

Walking back toward the house, he detoured by
the GMC to grab his duffel and the ECCO, then
pulled out the keys the Grant woman had author-
ized Harris to pass on to him. Harris, of course,
retained a second set. They would remain in his
possession until the investigation was concluded,
which Nick determined would be soon. Though he
intended finding out what had happened here, it
was taking longer—and becoming more involved—
than he'd anticipated.

His morning, and the previous night, had been
spent gathering information. He'd drunk in tav-
erns, eaten in cafés; bought trinkets that ended up
in trash cans, and fish tales that came as cheap as
any other lies. Some of the wilder tales centered
around the bizarre theories he'd picked up at the
scene the afternoon he'd arrived, involving zeal-
ously related gossip about the group of monks who
had once occupied The Ridge. Nick wasn't particularly susceptible to ghost stories.

The need to return to New York weighed heavily.
He wanted to be gone before Terrell located him,
and was wasting valuable time during which Terrell would be setting up his defense perimeter. Nick
might have to leave without the answers he wanted.
The thought annoyed him. He decided he could afford another twenty-four to thirty-six hours.

He unlocked the door, noting that the glass in the
small viewport had been replaced, and stepped inside the shadowed hall. No sounds penetrated here,
not the sea, nor the wind. Stillness lay thick on the
musty air.

Going over to the bifold doors, Nick pushed them
open, allowing sunlight from the great room's un-
curtained windows to penetrate the inner gloom.

His eyes were drawn to the chalk-marked circle.
The room had been cleaned, except for this one
area.

Setting the ECCO and his duffel bag just inside
the door, he crossed to the spot where his daughter
had stood four nights ago, watching her mother die;
stepped into the circle.

What had she seen that night? Nick wondered,
slowly turning around, studying the room from
each angle. Why had she stood here, and how had
she alone managed to survive?

Sunlight streaked through the lead-paned windows, pinpointing dust motes swimming lazily on
the heavy air. Strips of masking tape crisscrossed
the panes, casting tic-tac-toe patterns on the stone
floor where circle, not X, marked the spot.

He thought of his daughter—Sara—saw again
those vivid blue eyes that had held him so trans-
fixed. For a moment he seemed to see them again,
staring from behind glass, looking out to sea. He
closed his eyes and focused more clearly, seeing her
whole face, not just the eyes. She seemed to be
looking at him—

Nick blinked away the strange mental vision, left
the circle and went over to the windows, throwing
them open one by one. The nearly floor-length casements opened directly onto the terrace and offered
easy access to the house, but there was no indication that their double latches had been tampered
with. He supposed that the investigation team
would check the broken glass they'd collected for
the same possibility.

The sound of pounding surf rolled into the room
with the breeze; gulls circled and dove, chattering
shrilly to one another. The sharp tang of salt cut
through the mustiness, freshening the room, and
Nick breathed in deeply.

He wasn't sure what he expected to learn in this

house, but he knew that he needed to be here. Something elusive hovered about The Ridge, circling it like the gulls. It swam just beyond the surface of sight, of sound, of memory, and if he could only brush aside the filmy coating, it would be revealed.

Again, a pair of vivid blue eyes punctured his thoughts. What had Sara seen?

Leaving the great room, Nick wandered through the downstairs, opening windows as he went, studying the house in daylight. The stately dining room fronted a high-tech kitchen, outfitted with all the up-to-date tools of the gourmet cook—Carole's domain. Behind the kitchen a well-stocked pantry and utility/ laundry room shared space. Crossing the hall, Nick opened doors on an elegant black-and-white tiled bath and a cozy den complete with fireplace. All these rooms had been furnished and decorated; only the great room had been left bare.

He scanned the place with a well-trained eye, looking for things that might provoke answers. Only questions met his probing glance.

He was headed down the corridor to the older section when the sound of a car driving up changed his direction. Returning to the entry hall, he paused to reclose the bifolds before crossing to the front door. Dusky sunlight leaked through the small viewports, doing little to alleviate the gloom.

A car door opened, slammed closed; footsteps crunched across the broken shells toward the flagstone walkway and the house. Nick stood to one side, not looking out, as the caller levied a sharp rap on one of the new glass panes.

Nick waited a minute, and the rapping continued. He opened the door.

"Good afternoon. The name's Reikert, Russell Reikert—" The man started to stick out his hand, then stopped when he saw no answering movement from Nick. "I'm with a national newspaper that's interested in doing a feature story on what happened here. I'd like to come in, get a firsthand look at the scene, maybe take a few pictures, ask a few questions . . ." He stepped forward, apparently expecting the man in his path to give way.

Nick failed to do so. He stood, plugging the gap, arms held loosely at his sides, not gripping the door or the wall, but simply standing there—in the way.

Reikert hesitated, reevaluating the situation. "Look, Mister—?"

Nick said nothing.

"I have authorization from the people in charge—"

"I don't think so." Nick reached for the door.

Reickert quickly put a hand on it. "Now look, whoever you are— Who *are* you, anyway?"

Nick almost smiled. "Auxiliary forces." The door swung shut, narrowly missing the reporter's fingers.

A couple of muffled curses filtered through the thick wood to Nick, then the sound of retreat, a car door being jerked open, furiously slammed. The engine in the dark gray Chevy Nick had glimpsed parked beside his own vehicle sprang to life. A heavy foot revved it several times, and with as much violence as could be coaxed from the tires on sand, Reikert departed the scene.

Nick reopened the bifold doors, retrieved the ECCO and his duffel, and headed upstairs. He wanted to finish his inspection tour before dark, and hoped there'd be no more visitors to delay him—except, of course, the one, or ones, who held an answer to this puzzle.

Darkness menaced the small group threading their way through the tumbled ruins, the palpable darkness of a sky seething on the edge of a midnight storm. Thunder grumbled across the lowering clouds. Every so often a ripple of lightning illuminated a corner, trying to fork through a rift it couldn't find.

Around Set, the others—Twyla, Mitch, Vesper, all but Hump, who was still too chickenshit to come—peered intently at the ground, using the slightly lighter sand as a reference point to guide them along.

The anger that had flared in Set at Hump's defection had long since waned. They didn't need him. *He* didn't need him. He had enough Power for them all.

Up ahead, the circular stone loomed, the entrance to the tunnel.

Set hesitated as he reached it, glancing around to make sure they were alone before rolling it aside. Behind him the surf was a booming, invisible presence. Above, the old house etched a deeper shadow on the darkness. He could barely see the fringes of the terrace wall. For an instant he felt the prickly crawl of hidden eyes. But almost as soon as it jarred him, the feeling vanished, and the Power said: *Move on.*

Shouldering the stone aside, Set braced it as the others slithered through the opening, then quickly levered it back in place, working as quietly as possible. Silence seemed to be their particular companion tonight, taking Hump's place as the fifth member of the group, a silent partner they all laid claim to. No murmured jokes, no whispered comments, marred the quiet as they crawled along the tunnel toward the caves.

Their silence was eerie, Set thought, solemn, laced with the tension that sometimes prefaced a gig.

In the darkness, he smiled. This night's work would demand that same intensity from them, the same compulsive drive that took charge on stage and made them more—together—than they could ever be apart.

Since the night Set had found the Mindstone he'd tasted this moment, felt it calling him, seen it play out in his mind a thousand times: They would perform the ritual, complete the Circle, join with the stone—and they would have it all!

He savored the vision in his mind. There was magic in it.

One by one, they reached the end of the tunnel and got to their feet, standing together in the dark outer cave.

"I don't see anything," Vesper said. Her normally abrasive voice sounded sluggish and muddy in the thick, stagnant air.

Set merely smiled again, hearing the sounds of a lantern being located, turned on. Whatever foolish doubts they still held would soon be laid to rest.

Yellow light spilled around them, casting a muted glow on the dull gray rocks and the somber group. Mitch's dark eyes glittered from behind the light, catching Set's glance and holding it with a look both speculative and expectant. Set returned an almost imperceptible nod. They *reached*.

Silently the group moved on, into the catacombs, Mitch leading the way, Set bringing up the rear. For a moment the darkness seemed almost liquid, parting wavelike before the light, closing in again as they passed; a dark, gelatinous tide folding across their wake, sweeping them forward and cutting off any possible retreat.

In front of Set, Twyla turned back, her eyes dark holes of uncertainty and gelling fear. Set grinned, reached out and gave her hair a gentle tug, and she turned around again, following Vesper and Mitch, comforted. He reveled in his growing control, marveled in his newfound strength.

Set felt that strength begin to swell inside him as

they moved closer to the Mindstone, filling him like an icy breath of oxygen, purifying his lungs, illuminating his thoughts. The Power was strong tonight; stronger than ever before. He'd felt its pull from beyond the caverns; even before they'd started down the beach it had called him.

For just a moment, black knowledge stabbed the light, a dark shaft of warning that what happened last time could happen again: people had died—*they* could be at risk.

But there weren't any people in The Ridge. Even the guards were gone. And he could protect his own.

He gathered the Power to him, ruthlessly shoving aside all other considerations. They were too close to stop now. He had the Mindstone, and tonight they would perform the final ritual. Nothing else mattered . . . *Nothing!*

And no one.

Lightning decked the sky over Russ's head, a sky heavy with storm clouds and the threat of rain. A clap of thunder followed close on its heels, then rumbled off across the darkness like a ponderous shock wave.

He glared up at the sky, as if offering an offense to the gods. He couldn't see, with the crashing surf and the growling thunder could barely hear, and now it looked like he was in for a drenching.

"Shit!" He swiped at the cold raindrop that struck him squarely in the left eye and, shivering, pulled up the hood on his sweatshirt—not that it would do any real good in a downpour. Probably ruin the thing. *Three hundred fifty bucks this warm-up suit cost him, and the son of a bitch had to be dry cleaned!*

"Where in the hell did those kids go?" Russ's foot skewered out from under him in the loose rocks

and almost threw him to his knees, but he got a
one-handed grip on a ragged stone and caught himself in time. "Damn!" He felt the sting of scraped
skin on the inside of his palm and lifted it to gin-
gerly brush away grit.

He'd seen the little foursome pass his stakeout
position just outside the terrace wall. They hadn't
seen him, of course. He'd ducked behind some
rocks. But when he'd ventured another look, they'd
vanished into the old monastery ruins.

They were up to something, Russ felt sure. He
had a nose for these things.

Had it been daylight, he could have followed their
trail easily. As it was, he was merely scuffing
around in the sand, running the risk of being caught
or, worse, stumbling into a fall that might break
his neck. This side of The Ridge was proving rough
going, slanted away from the crest of the cliff where
the main house stood, and strung with crumbling
masonry, sudden sand pits, and almost-invisible
gullies.

Another fissure of lightning splintered the night
sky, another blast of thunder. The clouds took this
moment to split open and dump their contents on
the rocky beach, unmindful of dry cleaning bills or
those lacking sense enough to get in out of the rain.

"That's it."

Making his way as carefully as possible in the
blinding downpour, Russ followed the outside terrace wall, circling The Ridge. He could come back
tomorrow, check out the area in daylight, see where
the kids had gone. He didn't think they'd broken in,
though they'd moved too furtively for a legitimate
visit. Maybe they were just snooping, curiosity
seekers, laying low, now, in the rain.

Someone was inside the house, no doubt that
bozo he'd run up against this afternoon; the same
four-wheel drive was parked outside. Apparently

the man wasn't planning to leave anytime soon. All the lights were off.

"Bastard," Russ muttered. "Probably got his girlfriend spending the night."

Sooner or later he'd get in, get his questions answered. Right now he was more interested in a hot shower, some dry clothes—*probably have to give this suit to my sister's kid*—and a double Chivas.

A pair of long, shapely legs stretched a languid hook into his last thought. Russ swiped a wet hand across his dripping face and flicked the sodden hood from his head, feeling his cock stir. He just might have to try *Ms.* Grant again, turn up the old Reikert charm. There was only one decent inn in the little upchuck of a town. She had to be staying there. He idly wondered if they had a hot tub.

Leaving the protection of the terrace wall, he sprinted around the flat, sandy area that was used for parking, glancing again at the old dark house. It seemed to squat there, massive, lumpish, like one of those incredibly ugly Chinese dogs carved in stone, the kind that guarded temples and shrines. A shiver that had nothing to do with the cold slid through him. He felt it twinge his gut and set nerve endings to tingling. The slight tumescence in his crotch went limp.

"Jesus, what the—?" A sudden, eerie sensation washed over him—like he was being targeted by unseen eyes. He whirled around, coming face to face with the buffeting sea wind and the sheets of rain falling in billowing gray curtains from the sky.

He could barely make out the rocky cliff, the beach below it. Waves tumbled violently to the shore, exploding against the sand. A low moan hung on the edges of the storm, a sort of humming, like he'd heard once in the eye of a hurricane.

He started backing up, slowly, eyes darting around him like a defense mechanism. Had those kids come back? Were they lying in wait? intent on a mugging? He'd never been mugged, though he'd lived twenty-eight of his thirty-six years in New York and L.A. Had he come to a small corner of some redneck state to have it happen now?

He glanced at The Ridge again, wondering if his best bet lay there. Someone *was* inside. And it would be a good excuse to get into the place. He took a sidestep in that direction—then hesitated, remembering his afternoon encounter. That man had intimated that he was some sort of police officer on watchdog status; but such lower echelons were usually ultra polite. That prick had been anything but.

People had been killed in there, Russ thought uneasily. Recently. Violently. Inexplicably. Could there still be a risk? He looked at the house through the rain—and had a sudden, fanciful thought that it was looking back at him . . . or that *something* was looking back at him . . . luring him in?

A momentary lessening of the downpour returned some measure of rational thought to his decision-making processes. He straightened, running his hands over his wet face and slicking his hair back from his forehead, for once unmindful of style.

"Beginning to believe your own bullshit, Russell?" he murmured in a rather chagrined tone, and started to turn toward the beach road where he'd left his car.

Movement snagged the corner of his vision, a blur of white down on the beach to the right of the rocks. He focused on it, stepping forward once more as the rain resumed and the wind whipped the sand and the waves impacted on the shore. Putting his hands to his eyes, he tried to shield them from the elements, wishing he had a pair of binoculars.

The misty image fluttered in the wind, pieces of

it strung out behind as it moved down the beach toward the cliff. It was a person, Russ decided, draped in some sort of filmy garment like a tattered white robe. Tendrils of what looked like bleached-white hair flew around what must be the face, though he could see nothing but a blur of white-ness. Hadn't one of those kids had blond hair? But the clothes were different, and where were the others, and how had they gotten back down on the beach?

The figure stopped moving. It seemed to turn to-ward him. Russ froze. It looked straight at him, eyes buried deep within the invisible face—seeing him, watching him, knowing he was here.

Breath caught painfully in his lungs. Sweat min-gled with the rain on his skin.

The wraith began moving again, a floating, dis-joined movement that suggested possibilities Russ didn't want to consider.

Some reflex started his feet moving again, shuf-fling him backward; stammering steps carrying him away from those embedded eyes, that blurry, di-aphanous form. Shivers began rolling over his drenched body, cold, uncontrollable spasms start-ing on the inside and working their way out.

He felt the ground begin its gentle slope away from the house, away from the beach, the eyes. Still he walked in reverse, unable to turn from the apparition that was sinking, now—thank God!— below the dunes.

Visions of things draped in seaweed, crawling from the sea and inching across the sand, cor-rupted his mind. He'd done a story on something like that once: an old flooded quarry that the locals had sworn held the bloated ghosts of some kids who had drowned in it. At night, they said, the ghosts would crawl from the black water, trying to get

home, slithering on their bellies like pale giant
slugs . . .

A burst of lightning ripped the sky, startling a
near-hysterical cry from Russ. And with the sound,
something steadied inside him, made him turn
around and jog for the car like a normal man in a
normal rainstorm dashing for cover.

He'd almost psyched himself out on ghost stories—his own, at that, by God. There were no giant
slugs, no apparitions on the beach. It was just one
of those kids, for chrissake. And tomorrow he'd find
out where they fit into the story he was already
formulating in the back of his mind. If they fit.

Hell, he'd make them fit. Tomorrow.

10

Set's gaze burned into the small lump of brightness lying in the sand at his feet. The Mindstone pulsed eerily. Swirling, visceral colors dove in and out of the brilliance—blood red, umber, bright orange—joining the white-hot dazzle of liquid flame.

Around the circle, kneeling forms swayed with abandoned rhythm. And Set stood at their head—where he belonged, as was his right. *This* was what he'd envisioned through all the weeks and months of waiting. *This* was the beginning.

Light bled into light, colors mutated and swarmed above the sand. He drank them in, marveling at the energy that filled this place. Never before had their bonding been so vibrant, so strong.

Slowly the cave dissolved into pure radiance as Set raised his hands, lifting his voice to the night:

"O Stone ... Power of the One ... Unite our minds, our thoughts ..."

Small lightning tongues leapt from the Mindstone, crackling and sparking the air.

"Give us Light and Life apart ..."

Around Set the chanting increased, matching

voices caught up in the sudden realization that this was no game; this had moved way beyond games.

Whatever initial motivations had led the others to this point lay abandoned on the rock-strewn sand outside this chamber, ripped from them like the force that had ruptured the cave itself. Long, awe-struck moments had passed as they'd stood there, coming to terms with this new reality: *Was the impossible possible? Had the Dream become the Way? Could they truly have it—all of it?* Ambition no longer trembled like a shadow on the wind; it had substance, validity.

Set banished the irrelevant memory—all irrelevant memories—blending the texture of his thoughts to the colors spiraling upward on the wind. He drew the other minds closer, deepening the contact, tightening their link as he lifted his hands higher, and his voice traced patterns in the charged air:

"O Light, come forth . . . Join with us now, that we might be One . . ."

Poised on the brink of vision, he strained for some sign within the stone. It had to be there—*had* to be! Deeper and deeper he probed until it was as if only a veil existed between him and true sight, a tissue-thin membrane that could be broken with one powerful thrust.

Set shivered as the snake began to stir inside him, slithering in and around his thoughts with a licentious abandon that stroked mind and body alike and sent waves of pleasure down his shuddering limbs. A vague undercurrent rippled the air as though something nebulous were trying to form, come together with the stone, with him.

He reached for it . . . blood speeding through his veins, roaring in his ears the way wind had begun to roam the cave, tasting his sweat-slicked skin, molding his thin linen shirt against him. The whisper-sound of unseen voices lay buried in the roar, the musky smell of incense.

Again and again his eyes pounded the brilliance, peeling away layer upon layer of light until deep within the stone Set saw a gaping hole, swelling, growing, rushing toward him like a huge, dark pit at the end of a tunnel, a glittering, dilated eye. He thrust into it—*hard*—and it burst apart, sending little sparkles of glistening blackness to dance the light, shimmery grains of a thousand midnights scattered on the wind—

Power touched him!

Power like nothing he had ever felt.

It was all he could do to keep from dropping to his knees. Power bent him, heaved into him; spasms of wild, ricocheting Power. For a timeless moment, Set knew Power he had only dreamt of—embraced it, reveled in it—made it

His!

—and then he felt it change.

Ecstasy became first uncertainty, then dread as Set felt the Power reach through him, *past* him, a beacon searching the darkness, a beast prowling the night.

No, this couldn't be happening, this wasn't the way it was supposed to—

He struggled to hold on, rein it back in, but it was too strong. Waves of searing energy spiraled around him, flashes of virulent emotion: He felt purpose, a goal, could sense hunger, raw anger, rabid desire . . . and something else:

Danger.

The metallic, coppery taste of fear filled Set's mouth as he felt his control begin to shred . . .

Darkness exploded around Nick. Hard, glittery beads of darkness that burst apart and were immediately gobbled up by blinding light.

Instinctively shielding himself against the glare, Nick rolled off the bed on the side opposite the hallway door, grabbing the Beretta from the bedside table as he went. It was as if a huge spotlight had been turned on him, pinpointing him on the bed, and then turned off again.

Crouched and ready, he panned the now-dark room, certain he was no longer alone. He could sense a presence: cold, dangerous; but moments passed and nothing moved, no sound of breathing, no further attack.

Outside, rain pummeled The Ridge, driving against the cold gray stones as though trying to beat its way in. Lightning stung the darkness, thunder punctuated the constant drone. Inside, nothing moved.

Had it been the storm, then, that waked him?

A tingling sensation spread through the bunched muscles of his legs and arms, the crawl of ants on skin. A familiar prickle caressed the hairs on the back of his neck, touching each one with delicate fingers.

No, not the storm . . .

He remained crouched in position, matching silence for silence, giving nothing away: no sound, no motion, scanning the room that was as dark, now, as it had been blinding moments before.

Through the sporadic bursts of lightning that continued to lick the room, Nick's searching eyes met only emptiness. Still he held his position, playing a game that wasn't new to him, but that seemed subtly altered, threatening on a different, inexplicable level. He didn't like the feeling.

Slowly, using his left hand, he found the flashlight that had rested beside the gun. Silently he gripped it and, holding it above him, thumbed it on, strafing the room. No volley of gunfire replied. No movement.

The door to the hallway was closed, the bolt still thrown.

The feeling of being slightly off-kilter persisted. He was liking it less and less.

Standing, he quick-checked the empty room, then flicked off the flashlight and stepped out into the hall, following his instincts, dressed only in a pair of loose jogging shorts, feet bare.

Gun in one hand, darkened flashlight in the other, he moved silently down the corridor, hugging the wall. A thin layer of sweat filmed his body. A miscellany of possibilities roamed his mind: the murderer? that reporter from this afternoon? Terrell?

Darkness lay heavy in the house, oppressive. It seemed to lap up against his legs. He had the uncanny sensation of slogging through a pool of deep, stagnant water; his body sweat congealed, clinging to him like marsh scum. And yet, light hovered just beyond reach—or, rather, the sensation of light—compelling and repulsing at the same time.

His narrowed eyes bored into the thick darkness as he inched forward, pausing only to check closed bedroom doors. It was as if something was directing his steps, taking him to the top of the stairs, down them, across the main entry hall.

Nick hesitated at the doors to the great room. He'd closed them earlier, and the windows.

The crawling sensation worsened, playing over him like sandpaper fingers, touching every part, inside and out. Stimulated nerve endings sent tiny shock waves threading through his mind and down his spinal cord. Had the murderer returned? Had a failed adjustment come to call?

Slowly he slipped the doors apart.

Beyond the long row of windows the storm blew hard. Lightning flicked the darkness—once, again—illuminating the small, chalk-marked circle in the center of the room like strobe lights. A clap of thunder rolled across the sky, rattling a loose window-pane in passing. But within the room, all was quiet.

Turning toward the long hallway that bisected the downstairs rooms, Nick left the storm behind, remembering the last time he'd made this trek. The feeling of intrusion had visited him on that occasion too, leading him down this same path, luring him on. The lure was strong.

He could still hear the storm raging outside, but in an abstract, extraneous way, as if he were traveling through the belly of the beast, hearing its muted roar from within. The corridor felt like a length of large conduit, a huge pipeline whose thick walls muffled sound and refracted the flashbulb bursts of light filtering in from behind.

Disorientation, faint dizziness, momentarily claimed him; the whisper-hum of voices filled his ears—

Abruptly he came to a standstill, flicked on the flashlight and swung the beam forward toward the closed archway door, then back the way he'd come. He'd thought he heard someone shout "Go back." It had sounded like a child.

He stood there, watching the beam rake empty darkness, listening again for voices on the storm. Only rain and thunder defied the silence.

With the light, his vague disorientation fled and the dizziness faded away. Extinguishing it, he waited to see if his equilibrium would again be affected. It was not. He walked on.

He came to the end of the hall and stood a moment, listening for sounds beyond the archway door. Nothing alerted him; all was silent in the old wing. Standing to one side, he released the catch and slowly pushed the door open with his foot.

Flickers of lightning betrayed only an empty corridor stretching forward, then branching left and right. Nick eased to where the narrow passageway bisected, stopped, listened, flashed the light. The small side door at the end of the left branch, the door the Grant woman had used, led outside to a walled area. There were no obvious signs of more recent entry, and it would be difficult to hide such evidence in this storm. The right branch led to a corridor which angled to the left and was lined with a row of monks' cells. It ended at the door Nick had used for his first entry. This area appeared equally undisturbed. No damp footprints; no unnoticed drops of rainwater or sand.

It took only a moment to check. The locks he'd installed remained firmly in place. The doorless rooms that lined the hall were completely empty, as they had been this afternoon. Were his instincts playing tricks?

Nick retraced his steps, then cautiously entered the left branch that accessed more monks' quarters, and beyond those a narrow passage leading to the chapel. He checked the other door first—it had not been breached—then entered the narrow aisle.

With each step the stones seemed to grow colder against his bare feet, the air heavier, clammy. The sensation of being watched returned, crawling with him down the hall. Nick no longer doubted his instincts. Someone was in here with him.

His hand tightened on the gun . . .

Set struggled to maintain his link with the others as searing energy bombarded his mind, threatened to overload his senses. He managed to block most of it, absorbing some—a blanketlike effect instinctively thrown up as the backlash had smashed over him. But his shield was almost buckling under the brutal, unexpected attack.

He concentrated on the bond, a swirling, churning numbspot in the center of his mind, a positive field holding the negative at bay, keeping them safe inside as this powerful unknown force roamed wildly beyond the barrier.

Set felt the trickling warmth from the others' minds, grabbed it to him desperately, fighting the cold, bright light that swarmed around the edges of his blanket, spreading into the flow like icicles melting in the sun. The light became fingers, a hand of frozen bones touching him *inside*. Fear exploded in his battered mind—

(don't be afraid)

The words formed across the fear: easing it, coating it, converting it to strength.

Tentatively Set touched the frozen fingers, took the icy hand. Little by little, he began to reclaim control. The attack subsided—no, not subsided, exactly, but was tempered perhaps; like a dimmer switch, full current still existed but he could turn it down.

Beyond, the fury raged—looking for some(one?)thing—

(flesh of My flesh)

The thought eased into Set. He didn't understand. And then the words were spreading through him like chilled wine; sweet, cool; coating the inside of his skin until the outer layer felt like a scaly husk to be sloughed off. Other thoughts prodded him from within this new link, first gently, then stronger. There was somewhere he/They had to go . . . something They must do . . .

A strange lethargy began stealing through Set's body. Muted impressions merged with thought; colors drifted by like feathers on a dream . . .

He felt himself beginning to move, sluggishly at first, then with a lyrical grace that flowed, light as mist, onto the keening wind. He smiled down and saw his body, poised within the circle of kneeling forms, hands raised as if to ward off a blow—

(soul of My soul)

Had he really been afraid?

And then They were flying upward, through the stones, through the night, and the cave was gone—yet still there, caught within Their eyes like the scene rushing toward Them:

a shadow prowling the darkness; a star glistening blue in a field of snow—

and Set knew what They must do: They must gather the enlightened, complete the Circle—and the gateway would be opened!

Faster, faster They spread and soared, hungry, seeking, drawing closer to the Power that would soon be Theirs. All must come to know the Oneness. All must worship the True Light!

The part of Them that was Set laughed aloud as clouds raced past, parting at the touch of a thought.

—closer and closer They came to Their goal, skirting the clouds now, blending with the storm, the night, until They were almost there, almost within breath's reach . . .

Glittering blue and dazzling black filled Their vision. The part of Them that was Set felt the Other's rabid desire, and it became his, filling him with blinding lust and fury—

Oh, to be born again—to rule—to live—

(Mind of My Mind!)

(I shall have all . . .)

Nick moved down the narrow hall, past the cubicles that had once housed monks, feeling his way. He didn't want to turn on the flashlight and give away his position, but he held it ready, and the gun.

Spidery sensations continued to haunt the nerve centers in his brain. The intuition that told him he was not alone grew stronger, raising the hackles on his spine as a burst of lightning lit the passage, flickering within the heavy gloom like the glimmer of feral eyes.

Nick glanced over his shoulder and for a moment seemed to be seeing through the house—beyond the pile of stones to a darkness alive with all the crawling, hungry eyes that had been watching him ever since he'd awakened, waiting for him to stumble and fall—

A splash of vivid blue punctured the strange vision, bursting through it like a bubbling, gushing spring. He had a sudden urge to turn around, follow this friendly brook back to the safe eddy of his room. He didn't need to go on

(Go back)

didn't need to see what lay at the end of the corridor.

(bad thing—cold thing—hurt thing—)

Nick shook his head sharply, shoving away the crazy images crowding his mind.

There was no longer any doubt that something here was affecting him physically *and* mentally, causing some sort of stimulation on a subliminal level. A contaminant that had missed detection? Or had he somehow been slipped a hallucinogen? Dark anger swam into his consciousness, further threatening his tenuous control. Unlikely but possible. Nick resolved to have a blood sample tested at the first opportunity. Until then, he suppressed his anger. Destructive emotions were deadly.

The Beretta in his right hand was real enough; the flashlight gripped in his left. He flipped the switch, sweeping the beam up and down the empty passageway. There was nothing there. No one.

A door loomed at the end of the narrow corridor—the door to the old decaying chapel, Nick knew from earlier reconnaissance—a relatively recent addition whose raw wood had only begun to darken. The solid door was heavily padlocked. Nick had picked the lock earlier, but he didn't have the tools with him.

And what could be in there now that hadn't been there before?

Nick recalled the decades-thick coating of dust inside the chapel, the clotted spiderwebs. Embrasures too narrow for human ingress provided the only other access to the room. Double rows of uneven stone benches sat facing a rudely constructed altar backed by a massive stone dais.

He walked toward the door, imagining those rows filled with the cowled, bowed heads of monks at prayer. Ancient heads. He recalled the stories being bandied about town, the strange tales he'd heard concerning The Ridge. Not for a minute was he willing to believe that a group of ancient ghosts had killed Carole and her family. Something extraordinary was at work in this house, that much Nick would concede—though he'd learned in the past that even the most extraordinary acts were invariably perpetrated by perfectly ordinary people—

The air around him seemed to stir suddenly. The prickle of danger intensified.

(Go *Back*)

The warning erupted as a massive shock wave of darkness flooded the passageway, plunging Nick beneath it as though he'd been dragged under the sea. The chapel door and the corridor around him dissolved as he fought for breath, nearly gagging as thick air clogged his mouth and lungs, air syrupy with a fetid sweetness that made him want to retch.

His skin felt corrupted by the touch of unseen hands, stroking his arms and legs, scraping his naked back and chest like a woman on the verge of climax.

Stunned by the reality of the illusion, Nick struggled to retain his sense of balance—physically, mentally—and managed to, just barely. He realized he'd automatically dropped into firing position, gun raised against attack. But where was his enemy?

Nick searched the cloying darkness, unable to make out where the ceiling ended and the walls began, though he knew only an arm's length separated him from stone. He groped for an anchor, found one, and lurched upward, his back against the wall, welcoming the pain as rough stone grazed flesh. The craziness ebbed.

Thunder throbbed in the distance—or was it the waves? He took several deep, slaking breaths. His slightly elevated heartbeat subsided.

Again he felt the air gather around him, as if preparing for another onslaught. It seemed to drain energy from him, suck his strength. He tried to turn on the flashlight and realized it was already on; its beam was being swallowed by the dark.

And then, guttering above and beyond him like a candle flame in the wind, a glint of light trembled faintly into existence.

A vast sense of emptiness opened up around Nick, the feeling of being in a huge chamber with only a pinprick of light. The light began to grow.

A faint hum wavered in the distance, as though of voices rising in cadence; he thought he smelled the acrid smoke of burning tar.

A draft of cold wind coiled about him, bringing a chill to sweat-dampened flesh.

he'd been in a chamber like this before, steeped in darkness except for a distant point of blinding white

The light reached out, touching his body, his face, gently this time, soothing, inviting. He felt drawn by a strange sense of oneness, yet at the same time repelled by something at its core, something he couldn't see.

He swayed forward, certain he had not taken a step, but hearing the echo of footsteps on the cold stone floor. The light swelled, bathing his face, his head, raining against his eyes. It would be so easy to . . .

(NO!)

Nick squeezed his mind against a sudden invasion of blinding light, feeling it stab through his eyelids and into the sockets as if trying to bore through his brain. It was like the sun—like being embraced by the sun!

and then he caught a glimpse of blue sky . . .

Focusing on the blue, dredging a last measure of resistance, he managed to shove back the light—

Awareness rushed into his mind with the needle-sharp prickle of feeling returning to a deadened limb. Nick welcomed the surge of adrenaline that followed, grabbed onto it with the strength of a drowning man. He felt a whirlwind of fury drive against his returning consciousness, a maelstrom raging beyond shimmering glass.

Slowly at first, then quicker, more confidently, he pulled himself out of the sensory pit, sweeping the illusion back to whatever nightmare it had sprung from.

For a moment he thought he could hear keening voices melt into silence, smell the tarry, burning stench of dying torchlight; then that illusion, too, was gone. The corridor was once again a corridor; the beam from his flash gave light.

At some point he'd moved forward and was now standing next to the chapel door. His breathing came ragged, vision slightly blurred, like he'd been running hard for a long time. Sweat beaded his forehead and ran down the sides of his face. He used the back of his arm to wipe it away.

Rain drummed hollowly against The Ridge. Nick concentrated on it, absolving himself, momentarily, of the need to think.

Somewhere in the distance, a phone began to ring.

Fury! Wild, unquenchable fury!
Separation!
Darkness . . . sinking back into the pit.
For a moment They had spanned the Circle, entwined the power of God and man.
For a moment . . .
Fury waned.
Patience again took hold.
Fingers slipped away and sank into the night.
The moment would come again.

Unbelievably, Set felt the Power weaken. Balling his hands into fists, he stretched them higher, attempting to strengthen his bond with the others, pulling their minds toward his . . . but it wasn't enough, and he didn't know what to do to make it enough.

What had they done wrong? Despite the Mindstone, the ritual suddenly felt flat, incomplete, as if it lacked . . . what?

Frustration gnawed him from the inside out. Concentration wavered; his thready link with the others raveled, broke.

The Power slowly sank away.

What had gone wrong?

The stone at his feet pulsed dully, its swirling lightstreams heavy now, ponderous; tarnished arteries gorged on blood. They carried a dingy, rusty glint, not the white-hot dazzle of before.

He dropped his arms. The chanting voices trailed out on a discordant note, off rhythm. Beyond the cavern, the ocean continued its incessant assault, waves impacting on the cliff. Muted thunder rumbled across the background. The promised storm had come.

But not the one Set had envisioned for tonight.

"Damn!" His oath broke the final remnants of the bond apart and scattered them to the dying torch-light. Candles sputtered from their sporadic perches on the rocks. The Mindstone swirled slug-gishly; cloudy, dimming; an opaque puzzle that taunted Set and left a sour taste in his mouth like curdled milk.

"What happened?" Vesper whispered, as if afraid she might disturb what they'd spent the past hour trying to evoke.

For a moment, Set hovered on the brink of mem-ory: *Something about the ritual . . . flying . . . some-thing . . .* "Who the fuck knows."

"Maybe we left out some of the words, or didn't say them right," Twyla offered in a hushed, placat-ing tone that put Set's teeth on edge. "Anyway," her voice trembled slightly, "I think I'm scared of that thing." She glanced toward the stone.

"And maybe that's the problem," Set snapped, glaring her to silence.

"Look, man." Vesper spoke in her normal grating voice this time, taking a belligerent step forward. The dying torchlight cast a strange aureole around her spiked orange hair. "Something heavy's going down here. I mean, we've all felt it. Now I know we've been avoiding this like the clap, but whatever it is *must* have had something to do with those peo-ple getting killed last time. I, for one, don't want to die like that."

"Get real," Mitch muttered, sounding bored.

"I *am* real," Vesper shot back at him with a glare. "Maybe *you* don't give a shit who gets chopped up into meatloaf here—even if it's us— but *I* do. Maybe you even like the idea a little bit, huh? New trip, dying?"

Mitch sneered, "Going chicken like Hump, baby?"

Vesper ignored the taunt. "Or maybe you even think you got immunity. You too cool to die, Mitch? That it, *baby*?"

"Nobody's going to die." Set broke into the charged atmosphere, feeling a sudden surge of possession, control; reveling in it. "Especially not us."

"Yeah? And how can you be so friggin' sure?" Vesper insisted, turning her scared anger on him.

"Because, Vesper luv—" Set met her flashing gaze calmly, holding it until her eyes flickered before his, then shifted away. He turned his expanded gaze on them all. "I got the Power."

For a moment, he experienced a feeling of such total omnipotence over these tiny people it made him giddy. He prolonged the moment, letting it slake the thirst inside him, feed the hunger. Oh yes, he would have it all—more than he had believed possible. Soon.

(Yes . . . Soon . . .)

He eased his hold.

"So, what do you think went wrong, then?" Vesper snapped, as though the suspended moment had never been. "And where did that thing come from, anyway?" She threw a spasmodic gesture toward the Mindstone, giving voice to the question that only now seemed to suggest itself. "Has it been here all the time?"

" 'Out of the nowhere,' " Twyla murmured in a singsong voice, " 'Into the here' . . ."

Vision; a shadow-dream on Set's conscious: a star, falling from a midnight sky; a diamond, slowly sinking in the sand . . . "That doesn't matter. What I want to know is why we didn't make it tonight. The rituals have been working for us, I could feel the bond growing, getting stronger each time. And tonight . . ."

He looked at the Mindstone lying there, its crystallized rivers jutting outward like jagged spokes from a wheel's hub. Its contradictions confused him, infuriated him; its promise hung tantalizingly just out of reach. Tonight he'd felt possessed by it; more attuned, more awakened to its power, and his own, than ever before. Where was that power now?

"There's got to be a reason why it didn't work." Set turned thoughtful. "What went wrong? What did we do different tonight?"

"Hump wasn't here." Mitch's statement fell into their midst like an epitaph.

Set looked at him. "Numbers?"

Mitch shrugged.

Could it be that simple? A slight frown creased the smoothness of his high forehead.

"I don't understand." Twyla's tone had moved toward petulant.

Ignoring her, Set strode over to the stone dais where the Book of Divinian lay in state. Handling it carefully, despite its apparent immunity to the ravages of time, he scanned the pages, having long ago accepted his peculiar ability to understand the ancient script. Though there were repeated references to "Gathering the Enlightened" and "Completing the Circle," there was nothing specific on just how many brothers that took.

Again an impression grazed his mind: soaring, reaching, grasping . . .

Closing the volume, he stood looking down at it, slowly tracing the symbol etched into its cover: a circle with a vertical line through it; the Circle of One . . . zero, one . . . *or*—a one and a zero?

Turning back toward the group, he singled out Mitch, who was picking his fingernails with a small pocket knife. "Ten? Could that be part of what this symbol stands for?"

"Then that means we're only half good enough," Twyla interjected, pleased with her deductive reasoning.

"Shut up a minute, dammit, I'm trying to think!" Set shot back, then sighed in exasperation as the delicate features crumpled. He held out an arm, which she moved into, and gave her hair a quick ruffle. "Look, babe, this is serious. Be quiet a minute, will you?" Twyla lay her cheek against his chest, rubbing it in a nod, and he turned his attention back to Mitch.

"So, if that's the case"—Mitch closed and repocketed the knife—"say five is half as effective as ten, does that mean six is one better than five? And seven one better than six? Like a Marshall amp—eleven is one louder than ten?"

Set shrugged irritably. "Who knows."

"Where're we gonna get five more people, if that's what it takes?" Vesper added caustically. "Drag 'em in off the beach?"

(Patience . . .) The thought brushed Set's mind and stilled the angry words that quivered on his tongue. *(Soon . . .)*

"It'll be all right," Set said tersely. "We'll work it out, I just need time to think."

He tightened his arm around Twyla, not wanting to share this with them anymore, at least not tonight. "C'mon. Let's go home. I'm tired, and I got a hard-on." She giggled, reaching for him, and he tweaked her nose.

They extinguished the candles and torches, then filed in silence out of the cavern, winding their way toward the tunnel entrance. The eerie glow from the Mindstone shivered on the darkness, diminishing as they moved away.

Mitch retrieved the lantern he'd set down earlier about halfway in, flipped it on. Yellow light spilled onto the path their repeated footsteps had packed in the loose sand, a trail pointing the way in or out, depending on perspective.

The trail began to narrow. Set dropped his arm

from around Twyla's shoulders and moved her in front of him, keeping a hand lightly on the back of her neck. Mitch had taken the lead, Vesper following. The tang of salt grew stronger, the pounding waves. Thunder rolled in the distance, a thick vibration on the dense air.

"There were ten that night," Set murmured into their silence.

"What?" Twyla glanced back at him, the only one to hear.

"Five of us, and the five upstairs."

He looked at her without really seeing her; it was as though he were seeing beyond them all, flying through clouds, seeking, touching . . .

(Soon . . . soon . . .)

She shivered, and turned back around.

The small procession continued to move single file through the catacombs. Outside, rain drummed against the rocks.

11

The telephone continued to ring as Nick strode back up the passage toward the main house, making no effort at silence this time, using the flashlight.

Twice, now, he'd experienced some sort of hallucinatory seizure, brought on by cause or causes unknown. His mind ticked off hypotheses as his bare feet slapped the cold, gray stones:

Toxins? Drugs?

Rapid onset and almost immediate return to full awareness argued against these possibilities, though others remained.

Ultrasonics? Neural stimulators? Some form of induced hypnosis?

Unacceptable. These episodes went way beyond any capabilities he was aware of.

Had he simply been caught up in some illusory reality between consciousness and sleep? Jolted awake by the storm, had he gotten out of bed, descended the stairs, and started playing out his nightmare?

No.

What, then?

Rain pounded The Ridge. Questions hammered at Nick's brain.

In the distance the phone continued to ring.

It grew louder as he approached the bisecting corridor, a jarring intrusion on his thought processes. He pushed it off to one side of his mind.

What were *these incidents?*

Were they self-induced? prompted by outside influence?

Did they have something to do with the events of four nights ago?

All this passed through Nick's mind in a matter of seconds, and he turned the flashlight off, halting his quick strides as he reached the bend in the corridor.

Darkness settled down around him, and he stood quietly, testing his perceptions while the muted roar of the storm droned on. Nothing pricked his nerve endings now; no strange vibrations stirred the air; voices didn't call out in the dark. Whatever had been at work was noticeably absent.

He started walking again, easing his hold on the Beretta as he reentered the main hall, not bothering to close the archway door behind him. He didn't like the direction this thing was taking, particularly didn't like the unknown quantity of variables. For the first time in a long while he felt uncomfortable in a situation. It was not a feeling he cherished.

Jagged fingers of lightning raced across the front hall, startling shadows from odd places—but they were just shadows, without substance or ulterior motive. The premonition of threat was gone.

Nick realized he was no closer to answering this puzzle than he'd been when he arrived. In fact, he'd gathered some extra questions since then. Tomorrow he would go see his daughter, prod her memory, find the key to unravel this thing. Then he could be gone.

He should have done it today. He felt a small muscle tighten at the back of his jaw. He'd arbitrarily postponed something he should have taken care of this afternoon.

He again became aware of the telephone, close at hand. It might have stopped ringing, then started again. It might have been ringing all along.

He thought about not answering it, then stepped into the small alcove beneath the stairs, laid down the flashlight, and lifted the receiver to his ear without speaking.

"Vears?" a panicked female voice exclaimed, Danielle Grant's voice. "Vears, is that you? Please, Vears—"

He switched on the small table lamp beside the phone. "What is it?"

"Oh, thank God you're there." Relief spilled from her voice. "Is Sara with you?"

Nick felt something twinge in his gut. "No."

Her relief turned back to panic. "Oh, Jesus, I was so sure—"

"What happened." Discipline kept the words terse, steady. Nick felt himself nearing a boundary line he hadn't crossed in a while.

"She's gone. I got up to check on her, make sure she was sleeping okay, but her bed's empty and—"

"Did you search the house?"

"Yes, of course! Thoroughly."

Nick spared a quick thought to the contradiction in terms "thorough search" was for the amateur and the professional. But surely even *she* could find a seven-year-old child in that small beach cottage.

"She's out on the beach, I know it," Danielle's voice exploded from the receiver. "The sliding glass doors were open. Out in this storm. I think she may be heading for The Ridge—"

Nick hung up.

In seconds he was upstairs, pulling on jeans, sweatshirt, shoes; tucking the small Beretta into its ankle holster and donning a customized Ruger 9mm automatic in a shoulder rig. A searing backlash of anger hit him at this unwarranted interruption, and the Grant woman's incompetence. He'd felt more anger in the past three days than he had in years. This is what happened when you let yourself become involved with people on more than an abstract level. This is how he defined stupidity.

The twinge in his gut he accrued to Terrell. Had he grossly miscalculated that situation? Did Terrell have his daughter?

Throwing on his leather jacket, he pocketed the flash and headed back downstairs. Muted lamplight lit his way to the front door. Nick started to throw the bolt, pull it open . . .

He hesitated.

He could not, at that moment, have explained what brought his hand back to his side and turned him toward the great room. It was sudden knowledge on a consummate level, a marriage of knowledge and reflex that moved him across the entry hall and through the doorway into the huge, empty room.

Darkness banked the inside walls, stacked like props waiting to be brought out at the appropriate Act and Scene. In the center it mitigated somewhat, highlighted by lightning that continued to ripple across the heavy clouds and seep in through the windows, though the brunt of the squall was moving on.

Rain still fell in sheets, forming rivulets on the glass, blurring the scene beyond. At the room's epicenter lay the chalk-marked circle; but it wasn't this that drew Nick's attention.

Someone was standing on the terrace.

Crossing the room to the window directly facing him, he quickly unlatched the double locks and pulled open one side of the casements. A gust of wind rushed in, bringing with it the roar of the ocean and a spattering of rain.

The small form stood by the far terrace wall, looking out to sea, a sea all but invisible through the darkness and sheeting rain. Only the constant explosion of waves as they drove against the rocks below gave evidence of the power churning just beyond. A white nightgown plastered one side of the still body, fluttering from the other like a banner in the wind.

Nick stepped over the window ledge. Rain pelted his face; cold, stinging. He narrowed his eyes against its blast. Several more steps and he was immediately soaked through, except for his shirt beneath the leather jacket, and the guns in their protective sheaths.

Wind rammed him, flattening his clothes against him as he walked forward, leaning into its attack. It howled across the terrace, blending with the resounding waves and the drumming rain.

Sara gave no indication that she was aware of his approach. He kept his motions deliberate as he came up beside her, stepping around in front so she could see him, recognize him. Her arms were wrapped around a sodden stuffed toy, her eyes roamed the rocks; yet he sensed she was aware of him.

The storm swept around them as he looked at her and she watched the sea. Rain battered her face, and she blinked rapidly against it; wind tossed her long blond hair. Gusts tore at her drenched gown, buffeted his wet jeans and leather jacket with a flapping noise that reminded him of the plastic police tape.

He placed a hand on her shoulder. When she

looked up, he stooped, unzipped his jacket, and gathered her against his chest, wrapping the dry lining around her cold, wet body. She made no protest, but seemed to accept him implicitly, as though he'd been expected.

Gripping the edges of his jacket firmly against the wind, he stood, lifting her, carefully shifting her length to his right side, away from the protrusion of the shoulder holster. She nestled against him naturally, wrapping one small arm around his neck in a hold that was firm, but not desperate. He started to walk back toward the house.

"I saw them," she murmured, startling him to stillness, her words nearly inaudible through the howling storm.

"What?"

"The rock people. They came out of the rocks."

Nick looked down at her, and she returned his probing gaze with her own disconcerting stare.

Was she delirious?

Water from her nightgown and the drenched toy she held seeped through the thickness of his sweatshirt as he carried her to the open window and stepped through, not stopping to close the casements behind them. The noise level dropped several decibels. He felt his body warmth blending with her chill. Trickles of rain dripped from his hair and ran down the back of his neck.

As they crossed the great room, a glimmer of lightning picked out the circle in the middle of the floor, and Nick wondered if being in this room again might effectively jog her memory. She suddenly tensed, burying her head against his right shoulder, and he reflexively tightened his hold, surprised by a brush of self-disgust. Had he really become so callous? He felt her tight body relax. He knew she'd shut her eyes.

In moments they were in the warmly lit hall, and

he was setting her down, turning to close the bi-folds. She'd begun to shiver.

"Come on." Nick walked toward the downstairs bathroom, not looking to see if she followed; but when he stopped at the door and turned the light on, she was there, stepping past him into the black-and-white tiled bath. He lifted a large, fluffy white towel from the rack and handed it to her, then flipped on the switch to the infrared heat lamp mounted in the ceiling. "Get out of those wet things. I'll get you something to put on."

For a moment they stood looking at each other, father and daughter, the man examining, the child unreadable. A strange, underlying tension spread through the room, growing thicker as the seconds ticked by. Nick had the uncanny sensation of being measured, as if the pair of them were circling each other, studying strengths and flaws. There was nothing childlike in her evaluation. He was suddenly reminded of the day Lew Harris had come to the beach house: there'd been this same mutual assessment, this gut-level counterbalance.

Water dripped from Sara's hair and gown, and Nick could feel tiny rivers leaving his own body. Small pools had begun to gather on the gleaming black-and-white tile floor.

Her clear blue eyes regarded him carefully, one hand clutching a towel, the other a lumpy wet bear. Nick watched her face for a flicker of expression. It told him nothing. It was like looking into a mirror.

He frowned at the thought, and she shivered violently, breaking the strange spell that had momentarily held them in thrall. She was still dripping wet.

"Get dry," Nick said.

He left the bathroom and went upstairs, flipping on lights as he passed. Something made him want to erase the gloom, lift the oppressiveness that seemed layered within this house like the stones that confined it.

He didn't know what to make of the little girl who was his daughter. What could have brought her out in this storm and down better than a mile of beach to stand on the terrace in the rain? She seemed to accept his presence here, at least for the moment. He supposed it made the situation easier; he might have had to deal with worse—tears, fear . . . Terrell.

In her bedroom he turned on the overhead light. The small pedestal table with the layout of stones claimed his eyes. Another enigma. Dismissing it, he went over to a chest and began opening drawers, selecting items at random, things that looked warm: a pair of sweat pants and a sweater, an oversized nightshirt. He spent a few seconds looking for socks, then opted for the pair of bedroom slippers sitting on the rug beside her bed. He picked them up. They had ears.

He took the clothes back downstairs, knocked at the bathroom door and handed them in when she opened it, careful to turn his head the other way. At what age did the female concern for modesty arise?

In the den next door he found the makings of a fire and lit it. All the comforts of home.

Heat began to bathe his damp body as the flames took hold. He shrugged out of the leather jacket and tossed it toward a chair, stripped off the shoulder holster and sweatshirt, then put both back on in reverse order. He thought he'd keep the Ruger handy from now on. Water still drained from his hair and ran down the back of his shirt. He wished he'd grabbed a towel for himself.

The wet jeans were becoming uncomfortable. Removing his shoes and the ankle rig, he unzipped

and peeled off the sodden denims, not especially
concerned with his own modesty. After all, he still
wore gym shorts. He tucked the nested Beretta inside his jeans and laid them on the floor to one side
of the hearth.

The chimney seemed to be drawing well. He put
another log on, stoked the fire, then stood before it,
leaving the fire screen propped to one side. Something mechanical began running in the bathroom;
he decided it was a hair dryer.

Nick watched the flames, contemplating tonight's
strange sequence of events. There seemed to be no
connection, yet some vague instinct suggested a tie-
in.

What had brought Sara here? She appeared content to be back at home. So far. She wasn't acting
the way one might expect—not even one familiar
with children, Nick guessed. She seemed all right
physically, though she hadn't said much.

He remembered the few words she'd spoken out
in the storm. What had she meant by "rock people"? Could she have been referring to the monks
who built this place, the ones the locals called "Ancients" and said drew power from the rocks? It was
highly possible that his daughter had heard the
tales, and children were particularly susceptible to
suggestion. Tack on a dark night, a storm, a recent
tragedy—it held all the elements of childish fan-
tasy. Surely enough to confuse a seven-year-old's
perception of reality.

Yet Sara hadn't seemed confused.

Had she actually seen someone? or could she be
hallucinating too?

Nick frowned. The thought that what had hit him
tonight could have also affected his seven-year-old
daughter from more than a mile away was ludicrous, genetics or not.

There simply was no apparent common denominator to the events happening here. Maybe that was the problem; maybe they *were* unrelated and he was looking for a link that didn't exist.

That didn't feel right either.

The hair dryer stopped running. He picked up the poker and stirred the fire. Glittering sparks and a smattering of gray ash spiraled upward, mingling with the smoke.

Carole had believed someone was trying to harm her and Sara. Apparently she'd been right. But why would anyone want to terrorize Carole, kill her and her family in such an elaborately brutal way? He couldn't equate his ex-wife with inspiring such viciousness; the very fact that she'd automatically thought it was him suggested a lack of enemies. And as for his own, their long-term estrangement made her a weak choice for exacting revenge.

Unless Sara had been the target. There were those who considered blood ties an absolute.

It was a valid point, perhaps the only one. Nick found himself confronting a very real possibility that the repercussions he'd sought to avert six years ago had finally caught up to him.

That still didn't explain tonight's episode. Or did it? Was whoever had been after Carole and Sara now after him? Had his ex-wife and daughter been used as a drawing card? was that the lure he'd sensed?

Nick wasn't satisfied with this explanation, not by a long shot. It was too sketchy, too full of holes. It left questions dangling: for instance, how had Sara escaped? That someone might—just *might* orchestrate such an elaborate vendetta he could buy; that it would include such bizarre, inexplicable special effects he could not.

He glanced up and watched the door open. Sara entered the room. She stood on the threshold, clutching her bear. From the looks of it, she'd used the hair dryer on them both. She'd dressed in the clothes he'd brought her, and looked a little bulky, but warm. She was carrying a towel.

Nick glanced at it, then back at her expression-less face. She walked over and handed it to him, then went and climbed up on the couch opposite the fireplace.

Coincidence.

He laid down the poker, swabbed the towel across his hair a few times, then looped it around his neck.

She watched him solemnly, feet stuck out in front of her, hands primly clasped in her lap.

The ears on her bedroom shoes flopped across her toes.

"I don't like them either," she said softly, and Nick realized they'd both been staring at the shoes.

Behind him, a log burned in two and fell into the coals. Outside, the wind was a low moan. He turned his attention to the fire, stoking it again; laid a fresh log across the dog irons. He could feel her watching him.

"Why are you here, Sara?" he asked as he set the fire screen in place. He knelt in front of it, his back to her, weight balanced lightly on the balls of his feet. He regarded the flames silently, and waited for her answer.

Silence lengthened; then,

"You know." The words were almost a whisper, but he heard.

He turned toward her slowly, keeping his move-ments calm, schooling his features into neutral lines. "No, I don't."

A flicker of some emotion darted across her face (*annoyance?*)—he couldn't identify it—and was im-mediately gone.

He maintained his crouch, at her eye level, rest-ing his arms across his thighs and lacing his hands in a parody of her own posture. He could feel the hardness of his corded muscles. The fire at his back grew warm.

"What happened here, Sara? What's going on in this house?"

She'd begun shaking her head with his first question, little spasmodic jerks that grew with every word until she was slinging her head back and forth, hair whipping the sides of her face. She'd closed her eyes, negating his inquiry, blocking him out.

Nick watched her a moment, then said, "All right, stop it."

He was mildly surprised when she obeyed immediately.

Neither of them flinched when the wind sent a volley of rain clattering across the room's only window.

Sara opened her eyes. They were back to square one: impasse.

Firelight danced around them, picking out the subtle colors in the thick hearth rug, tracing patterns on the stone walls. Nick watched the reflection in Sara's eyes, twin prisms of red on blue. What was she thinking?

The warmth on his back became uncomfortable. He stood, careful to keep his movements easy, not startle her. She transferred her gaze to the fire. A distant rumble of thunder penetrated the room.

It merged into the sound of knocking on the front door.

"Dani's here," Sara murmured as Nick stepped toward the hallway, his hand sliding beneath the sweatshirt.

He glanced back at her, frowning; she watched the fire.

Out in the hall, he slipped the Ruger from its cra-

dle—then shoved it back again and strode forward
as he heard, faintly,

"Vears? Goddamit, let me in!"

accompanied by a redoubled banging on the door.

With each step, east fistfall on wood, Nick's anger mounted. He'd had about enough tonight, and
this just might tip the scales. The check on his tem-
per felt marginal.

He swung the door open.

"Did you find her? Is Sara here?" Her husky voice
whipped past him with the sudden gust of wind.
"Tell me!"

She searched his face, one hand spasmodically
raking sodden hair off her forehead and water out
of her eyes.

"Vears—"

"She's here," Nick said, and her taut body sagged
with relief.

"Why the hell didn't you call and let me know?
Don't you realize I've been out of my mind with
worry? I've been combing the beach—"

But Nick was barely listening to her tirade, startled by the possessiveness he'd heard in his tone—
so much so that he'd allowed the Grant woman to
stalk nearly past him before he gripped her arm.

"Just a minute." The threat was there. It com-
pensated for his momentary lapse.

She glared at him, radiating outrage and defiance. "Take your hands off me! Where's Sara? I
want to see her. Is she all right? What have you
done with her?"

Nick took a slow breath, reaching for the control
that was beginning to fray—badly. "She's safe
enough. I've already killed my quota of kids this
month."

Their eyes locked. His grip on her arm hardened.
Nick felt like a gun that had been drawn, cocked,
aimed—but not yet fired.

Apparently she felt it, too. "Let go of me, Vears." Her voice was quieter, tight, but Nick knew she was afraid.

He clamped down on the raw fury moving him ever closer to the edge, remembering the last time he'd lost control: the last time he'd gone to the house he and Carole had shared. He'd waited two days to go home that final time, sat all night in their empty living room getting quietly drunk, then left . . . after putting his fist through a wall.

"Go away, Danielle."

"I'll be happy to. Just let me get Sara and we'll both be gone." She tested his grip, winced when he tightened it.

"Sara stays." He made the decision arbitrarily; it felt right.

"Not on your life, buster!" Fury blazed in her eyes again and fanned the flame in him.

With a small shove, he started propelling her backward, out the door, holding her upright when she stumbled, blocking her other arm when she tried to swing. He gripped it just below the wrist, continuing to advance, forcing her to retreat. She started to kick him then, and he thrust her out onto the walkway. She almost fell.

"You had your chance, Danielle. You blew it. Now let it go."

The storm attacked her from behind. Wind whipped tendrils of hair onto her face to be plastered down by rain.

"You may as well go ahead with your 'or else' now, Vears, it's the only way you'll get rid of me."

She stood there breathing heavily, her challenge reiterating itself with every ragged breath.

Nick took a step forward—

(Daddy . . . ?)

He swung around. Sara was standing in the hall. She glanced from him to Dani, then back to him again. Her face held a mixture of bewilderment and alarm. The stuffed animal was clutched tightly to her chest.

"Dani . . . ?" She spoke again, clearly this time, trying to see past Nick.

"I'm here, Sara," the Grant woman called from the doorway, and Sara took a couple of steps forward, then stopped and looked at Nick.

It was obvious that she wanted her aunt, probably to do all the things he hadn't. He suddenly felt hostage to the situation, ambushed by a child and an incompetent adult. But the white-hot anger of moments before was back under wraps, leaving only acute annoyance.

"Let me go to her, Vears." Danielle moved up behind him. "Please."

He continued blocking the doorway a moment, caught on his daughter's eyes, then stepped back.

Danielle strode past him into the house, crossed to Sara, and dropped to her knees beside the child, gathering her into a hug. Sara hugged her back, smiling with relief, seeking Nick's eyes over Dani's shoulder. He closed the front door.

"Are you okay, munchkin? Here, let go, I'm getting you all wet. Do you have a fever? What on earth made you go out in this storm? I was scared to death—don't *ever* do that to me again. And who put these clothes on you?"

Dani ceased her cross-examination long enough to hold Sara at arm's length, inspecting her ensemble of bright purple sweat pants, pink flamingo nightshirt, and blue-and-red bulky-knit rugby sweater, having apparently satisfied herself—through a succession of bone squeezing and temperature checks—that the little girl inside the hodgepodge was indeed all right.

They both turned to look at Nick, the Grant wom-

an's expression an indictment for—Nick as-
sumed—criminal bad taste.

Sara giggled.

The sound spread through the hall like the rustle
of leaves on a windy day, dissipating some of the
tension.

Danielle returned to her ministrations.

Nick observed the pair dispassionately, aware of
Sara's subtle attempt to link the three of them, but
resigned for the moment. It was natural, he supposed. They were all she had left. It wasn't going
to work.

He crossed the hall and headed down the corridor to the kitchen. Their being here presented a
problem, one he'd have to deal with. Eventually.
Right now he just wanted a cup of coffee.

Ignoring the elaborate Swedish coffee machine
that stood in a line of gourmet contraptions grac-
ing the countertop, he pulled a copper pan from a
wall arrangement, filled it with tap water, and stuck
it on the stove to heat. He found a mug in the first
cabinet he opened, set it down beside the jar of instant he'd brought with him, got out milk and a
spoon. The ritual of mundane actions began to re-
store his sense of balance.

"Is there any chocolate?" The Grant woman had
followed him into the kitchen.

Nick didn't look up from the chore of ladling coffee granules into the mug. "I have no idea."

He heard her step across the room, start rummaging through a cupboard. "Sara should have
something warm to drink."

He glanced up, saw Sara standing in the doorway. Without a word, he got out another cup. The
water began to steam. He waited for it to come to
a full boil, then poured it into the mugs.

Apparently Danielle had found what she wanted.
She came over, waited for him to finish stirring his

coffee, then picked up the spoon he laid on the countertop. The sleeves of her sweater dripped rainwater across the Formica as she fumbled with the small packet of instant cocoa. Her movements were jerky; she was obviously ill-at-ease, probably cold. She'd pushed her hair back off her face. It glistened under the fluorescents, as if she'd just emerged from swimming. She tried to control an involuntary shudder that might have stemmed from wet clothes or from her proximity to him.

He unlooped the towel from around his neck and tossed it to her. Catching it, she flinched as though she'd been struck.

Turning away, he picked up his mug with the intention of leaving. She stepped into his path.

"Look, Vears . . . can't we just settle this now?" Her hands gripped the towel, holding it in front of her like a shield. "You want me to apologize? admit I should have been more careful? call myself every kind of fool there is? I do."

"I want you out of here."

She stiffened. "Not without Sara."

He regarded her coldly as she took a shaky step toward him. "Dammit, Vears, I made a mistake. Can't you understand?"

When he didn't answer, she laughed, a bitter sound full of self-reproach. "You're really something, you know that? Mr. Sympathy himself." She dragged a hand through her hair. "But then, you don't make mistakes, do you? So why should you excuse them in others?"

"I'm tired, Danielle. I'm going to bed." He stepped around her, heard her mutter:

"Bastard!"

as he passed, then add:

"God*damm*it Vears! What are you going to do with a little girl? You don't even know how to dress her—just look at her—"

They both stopped, realizing at the same time that Sara was no longer standing in the doorway. Nick was already striding down the hall when Dani exited the kitchen. "Check the den."

He set his coffee cup on the phone table and headed up the stairs. He hadn't thought about where he was going; now he did.

At Sara's bedroom door, he hesitated, then opened it quietly. The overhead light was off. A nightlight in the shape of a clam shell glowed from an electrical outlet on the far wall. Hall light spilled across the room, illuminating the lower half of the canopy bed. A small lump rose in its middle.

Nick walked over, looked down on the sleeping child. Her hair appeared silver in the refracted light. Her stuffed animal lay nestled in the crook of one arm. She'd shed the sweater and sweat pants; they lay neatly folded across the end of the bed; the bedroom shoes were back in place on the rug.

Almost without volition, his hand reached down and lifted a strand of her hair, fingering it lightly. A thousand questions crowded his mind, but he let them all slip away unasked. There was only one answer; the only one possible for him. He turned to go.

"I called you," she murmured, checking his movement.

He studied her sleep-softened face, saw her eyelashes quiver as though caught within a dream. And then they fluttered open.

"I called you," she repeated, pinpointing him with her vivid blue eyes. "Didn't you hear me?"

Nick felt a brush of memory, as though a curtain was being held aside allowing him a glimpse: of blue sky; the recollection of a child's voice, down in the corridors earlier tonight. But that couldn't have been Sara; she'd been outside, on the terrace. She couldn't have gotten in.

"When did you call me, Sara?"

She simply looked at him, the intensity slowly fading from her gaze. A door being shut. Why did he feel as if he kept failing some sort of test?

Her eyelids fluttered down again—she seemed exhausted—and he stood there, watching her move back toward sleep.

She reached out her hand suddenly, fingers clenched as though holding something she wanted him to take. He held out his palm, and she released the object into it: cold, hard. His fingers automatically tightened around it, then he stuck it into the front pocket of his sweatshirt.

Almost immediately, she was asleep. He watched her another minute, lifted the quilt over a bare shoulder, turned toward the door.

The figure standing there caused only a minimal break in his stride. He had no idea how long Danielle Grant had been observing them. It didn't matter.

"I want you both out of here first thing in the morning," he said tersely, striding past her, not slowing his pace.

She'd backed out of his way without answering.

Nick went downstairs, taking the steps quickly, feeling a need for physical exertion. If he'd been alone, he'd have gone out on the beach for a run, despite the darkness and the rain.

Instead, he crossed to the great room, strode over to the open window, closed and latched it. The storm was finally abating. An occasional glimmer of lightning stung the distant clouds, a muffled growl of thunder.

Back in the entry hall, he bolted the front door, then headed down to the den, where he banked the dying embers and set the fire screen firmly in place. He stood there a moment, watching the red glow dwindle.

The restless energy persisted. He was tired, needed to sleep, but his body still felt keyed toward action. Taking several deep, slaking breaths, he moved into the discipline meant to relax tense muscles, taut nerves, a combination of isometrics and abstract thought. After a minute he stopped. It wasn't helping.

Gathering his damp jeans and the Beretta, he left the den and climbed the stairs, noting that the upper hallway was empty, Sara's door firmly closed. At least he wouldn't have to contend with the Grant woman any more tonight, and with luck he'd avoid them both in the morning. He still needed to talk to Sara, but he'd take care of that at another time.

Turning down the corridor toward the far bedroom, he detoured into the hall bath, tossed his wet jeans over the shower rod to dry, made use of the facilities. A hot shower might have helped him relax, but he decided not to bother. Either he'd sleep, or he wouldn't.

He left the bathroom, headed on down the corridor—and abruptly came to a halt. The door to his room was ajar. *Had he left it that way?*

The sounds of someone rummaging around inside were obvious.

Nick unholstered the small automatic and walked over to the door. He was sure who it was; he still didn't take chances.

He used his toe to inch the door wider, standing to one side, against the wall. "Find what you're looking for?"

She whirled around as he stepped through the doorway, glanced at the gun he held pointed toward the ceiling.

"Are you planning to use that thing?"

Nick moved on into the room. He reholstered the Beretta.

She turned back to the chest of drawers; Nick saw she was getting out dry clothes.

"You can have the room," he said.

"I don't want the room."

He shrugged, a gesture she didn't see since her back was to him. The wet cotton sweater molded her hips.

She slammed the drawer. "I don't think I ever want to sleep in this room again."

"Suit yourself."

"I know what you're thinking, Vears." She turned to face him. The damp sweater clung to her chest.

He let his eyes roam over her, hesitating on the outline of naked breasts beneath clinging cotton. "I don't think so."

A flush stained her cheeks. "You really are despicable." She walked past him out of the room.

Nick went over and closed the door. Apparently he'd found the key to getting rid of Danielle Grant.

Stripping off his sweatshirt, he heard something strike the stone floor. He remembered the object Sara had given him. He glanced down, caught a dark glitter to the left of the throw rug, bent and picked it up. It was a small black stone.

+ + +

From her safe spot, Sara watched the dream.

It couldn't touch her, couldn't get inside the warmth, but it chilled her just the same. It showed her things she didn't like.

It showed her a stone. A small black stone. Being gobbled up by light.

Sara shivered, hugging her Fuzzy.

That wouldn't happen—it was just a dream. A cold, bad dream. She wouldn't *let* it happen!

Like the glass, the darkness was her friend; and she pulled it tight around her, shutting out the bad.

The dream began to fade . . .

Sometimes it was hard keeping things away—outside—watching without being seen. It made her tired.

But it was better now. He was here. And she felt Safe.

Warm.

The dream was going away . . .

She nestled down into herself, pushing all thoughts aside, snuggling beneath the warmth.

The dream was gone.

+ + +

12

Lew Harris wasn't fond of late-night hours; nor was he fond of early mornings following them. He spent an inordinate amount of his professional time outside the nine-to-five arena, and putting in an eight-hour day was something to dream about. Yet an alternate life-style now seemed inconceivable.

He turned on his windshield wipers as a sudden heavy spattering of quarter-sized raindrops pounded the car, blurring his view. In moments he was out of the small shower, and he turned the wipers off again, along with his headlights.

Dawn had just rambled in from the east, and after a long night and a quick round-trip to Raleigh, Lew was feeling the effects of too little sleep and too much driving. He'd originally intended getting back earlier, at least in time to catch a few hours in the sack before beginning another round of on-scene investigation. Instead, he'd become involved in something he hadn't anticipated when he'd ordered that priority check run on Nicholas Vears two days ago.

Again he replayed the scene in Chief Martin's

smoke-filled office; again he felt the confusion, the gall of finding out the innocuous summons to headquarters for a "consultation" had been anything but. He was still trying to clear cigar fumes out of his lungs and come to terms with what had transpired.

A man of quiet habits and thoughtful nature, Lew could be voracious in his pursuit of the truth and dogmatic in his approach. It was a facet of his character that he'd long ago learned to live with, and if occasionally it turned on him, well, payment required.

He was making an installment this morning.

Lew turned the car off the highway and onto the beach road that ran past The Ridge, glad he'd taken time to stop by his Raleigh apartment for a shower and shave. That, and three large cups of coffee during the drive back, provided a reasonable facsimile of a full night's sleep.

When on a case, Lew became consumed with its vitals, eaten up with the need to pursue even the most obscure lead to its full explanation. It was the puzzle solver in him. He didn't like to cut corners, didn't like evidence based on spec, and was willing to concede extra hours to avoid both.

Lew saw a sheriff's patrol unit approaching from the opposite direction and pulled over to the side of the road. The deputy cruised to a stop as Lew rolled down his window.

"Any activity?" Lew returned the deputy's "Good Morning" nod.

The young man shook his head, a bit regretfully, Lew thought, speculating the kid had missed out on an initial tour of the great room.

"Nah. Things been nice and quiet on the hill." Stretching cramped muscles, the deputy stifled a yawn.

"Why don't you go get yourself some breakfast, call it a night. I'll be around for a while."

The deputy looked up at the breaking day, then down at his watch. "Yeah, think I'll do that. My shift's almost up anyway." He gave Lew a grin. "See you later, Agent Harris."

Lew watched him drive away, then did the same, remembering his own fledgling years on the force and the crapwork details he'd invariably gotten stuck with.

—a small, pristine circle in the middle of a room festooned with body parts impacted on the thought. *You're movin' on up.*

He turned into the driveway that wound to The Ridge and slowed to maneuver the long, uphill curve. About halfway up, he pulled the car onto a verge and eased to a stop, deciding to walk the rest of the way. He needed the exercise, and the fresh air would do him good.

The house looked drab and bulky this morning, slumbering in the half light of dawn. Morning air hung dank and misty; moisture stained the rough gray stones. Lew thought he could feel chill, dead air seeping from them as he neared. Cryptlike.

A fanciful thought. He pulled his raincoat tighter against the early-morning breeze.

At the top of the incline he stopped, stood regarding the silent house. Vears's four-wheel-drive vehicle sat in the parking area, but there were no signs of life.

Unease settled down on Lew, accompanied by that strange reluctance to enter The Ridge. Giving in to it for the moment, he circled around to the side of the house and walked out across the terrace, turning his eyes seaward and his thoughts to Nick Vears.

Two enigmas: The Ridge and Nicholas Vears. Evoking two entirely different reactions.

Where the house repelled him with its silence, made him want to board it up all the way around, the man piqued his interest, drew his professional nose like a dog to a bone. He should let it lie, leave it buried, Lew told himself as he gazed out over the rocky expanse. Especially now, after word had come down from on high to "Lay off Nick Vears."

But Lew could be tenacious when the bone demanded, and something told him the bone demanded. His lip gave a wry twist. Another day—another dogma.

He strolled over to the parapet and leaned against it, resting his arms on the cool, damp stone and casually linking his hands as he watched the constant shift of the sea. There was something soothing about the rhythmic motion, the sound of water rolling in to shore. Lew thought it had to do with prenatal memories, subconscious harmony with the womb. A tenuous umbilical that could never be severed.

Clouds banked the horizon and fingered the sky, remnants of last night's weather. They'd had a heavy rain, from the looks of it. A few miniature fishing boats rode the choppy waves farther out, late-night shrimpers who'd braved the squall, on their way back in to port. A hardy lot, these down-east clamdiggers.

Soft haze dazzled the air where the early sun was just beginning to break through and burn off the cloud cover. Later it would warm up. Right now it was pleasantly chill.

Lew didn't know how he was going to approach this new development yet. He just knew he wasn't backing off, wasn't going to be a good Nazi and *heil* on cue. If anything, the call-off made him more determined. It had never happened before. Lew frowned. It sucked.

Of course, he'd been hauled in on a few cases,

had his methods questioned; but these had always been strictly up-front confrontations with valid, if debatable, reasons; not this chickenshit "suggestion" with its implied threat.

The call-off in itself was an answer of sorts. Whoever Vears was, he had pull in high places. That could indicate a rash of possibilities, both benign and the red, itchy kind—Lew was a straight cop, not a naive one. If it was a case of the not-so-goods, he'd be making a mistake pursuing this, a *big* mistake, the kind of mistake that had terminal side effects.

At the least, he'd be jeopardizing his career, a step Lew didn't take lightly. But he *had* to follow through on this.

Not that he intended to be stupid about it. He'd made all the proper replies to his superior, offered a cursory argument, then bowed to the Powers That Be, indicating an unspoken awareness of the grief one could buy if one chose to buck the system. Was he losing proper respect for truth, justice, and the bureaucratic way? He'd left the SBI building seemingly pissed off, but resigned—

and gone right to work on calling in some outstanding markers.

It had taken most of the night, but when he was through, Lew had instituted a private checkout of Nicholas Vears that would no doubt eclipse what he could have expected from official channels.

He had particular hopes for Talmadge Reese, a hacker of uncommon talent who had electronic inroads to places Lew didn't want to know about.

So now it became a matter of waiting.

Conversely, Lew didn't really think Vears had anything to do with this atrocity. In fact, he wasn't sure *anyone* had—but *that* was a line of thought he wasn't quite ready to deal with. Yet here he was, possibly putting his career, or worse, on the line to satisfy a curiosity that had him by the balls and wouldn't let go.

"Perversity, thy name is Harris," Lew muttered, and turned from the parapet.

Something caught his eye. Movement on the rocks below. He turned back around, eyes narrowing as they scanned the cliff.

There it was again. Lew pinpointed the area, concentrating his field of vision to that spot. For a moment he could make out nothing but gray stone, with darker stains from ocean spray—

Then he saw the sniper.

He'd never have seen the man, camouflaged as he was in a gray coverall and mostly concealed by the shadow of an overhang, but for a sudden glint of sunlight and his own chance position above and behind.

Total concentration made the sniper momentarily blind to his rear. The slender-scoped barrel of the target rifle, with sound-suppressor attached, was already sighted up the beach to Lew's right.

Pulling his six-inch Smith & Wesson service revolver from its shoulder holster in a smooth, practiced move, Lew spared a glance that way and saw a lone figure jogging along the edge of the surf, totally unaware of the bead being taken on him. Vears.

An evaluation that didn't allow time for "whys" snapped Lew's body into the classic firing stance, both hands gripping the revolver, bracing against the parapet. His eyes reclaimed the rocks, calculating the down-line distance as just barely within range for the .357 Magnum. For a moment breath froze in his lungs when he didn't immediately respot the sniper—then he had him.

"SBI!" Lew yelled, "drop your weapon!" even as the sniper fired.

The cough of the muzzled high-powered rifle merged

with the pounding of the surf, the raucous screech of the gulls. As if in slow motion, Lew watched the sniper whirl around, swinging the gun toward him. Then the adrenaline factor kicked in.

Lew fired, bracing against the recoil as he squeezed off two rapid shots, aiming center mass. The least quiver could throw his aim wide, give the target time to scatter, or return fire in the split second before he could squeeze off the second round. The resounding explosion split the stillness of the morning: the acrid stench of cordite corrupted the air.

A bullet sang past Lew's head, a puff of wind. He heard a sharp, metallic *ping* as projectile met stone somewhere behind him. He squeezed off a third shot.

But the sniper had crumpled, tumbling off the rocks on the left side of the cliff to the beach below.

Lew held his firing position, following the body all the way to the sand. The rifle landed somewhere in the rocks, not visible from here, but away from the man who had held it. Only when a full minute passed and the body didn't move did Lew ease the hammer forward and automatically begin reloading the emptied chambers. Then he looked back to his right for Vears.

Vears was nowhere in sight. The man had simply disappeared. No body on the beach; no head bobbing in the water. That should mean he wasn't dead. What else this all meant was up for grabs. But Lew intended finding out—right now.

Holding the Smith & Wesson firmly in his right hand, he made his way down from the terrace and started across the cliff. There was no easy access to where the sniper had fallen; he'd have to climb over the rocks.

Innate caution coupled with the backwash of adrenaline kept his eyes constantly roaming as he scaled the rocky barrier, his breathing shallow and quick. He felt keyed to the moment, wired in to the slightest response. He had no idea if the sniper was dead, wounded, or just knocked senseless from the fall.

Lew recalled the first—and only—time he'd killed someone during his years with the SBI. The drug-pumped street punk had held up a liquor store, killing the owner, a patron, and a couple of bystanders in order to escape with three hundred and sixty-two dollars.

Acting on a tip, Lew and several of his fellow agents had followed him to a downtown sleaze-bag hotel where, as luck would have it, the punk had been shooting off his mouth, and his money. The desk clerk was only too glad to cooperate when Lew told him that though they weren't with vice, a visit could be arranged. The punk was being worked on upstairs by a couple of the house whores.

When Lew burst in the little creep had been well occupied getting a blow job from one of the hookers while the other one lolled behind him, cradling his head between her naked breasts and giving him a token massage. It hadn't stopped the bastard from reacting immediately with a .44 Mag exhumed from somewhere beneath the tangle.

The girls had peeled off to either side as the punk took his shot, and Lew would never forget the look of surprise on the guy's face as his own bullet crashed into the little bastard's chest, killing him instantly. The perp's shot had missed Lew by millimeters. He still had scars where splinters from the doorjamb had embedded in his neck and head.

A sudden pelting of the king-sized raindrops caused Lew to jerk around, then steady himself against the outcropping before continuing. The shower moved on. He started his descent.

Nearing the area where the sniper had fallen, he

ducked into the rocks, taking his time, leading with
the revolver. His feet found sand. He spotted the
fallen gunman. Slowly stepping out from the cliff,
he began his approach to the body, still holding the
gun cocked and ready; his reflexes were inching
back toward the safety zone.

The man lay on his back, spread-eagle, apparently wounded, breathing heavily. Lew continued
his cautious approach, darting an occasional look
around for Vears—where *was* he—not about to relax until he was sure this thing had played out.

At least one of his shots had hit on target, Lew
saw, but in the left shoulder, not dead center. It
was an acceptable hit, preferable, even—taking
down the man without killing him. Textbook procedure: "Always aim center mass," provide opti-
mum chance for bullet to find target and hope to
shit it would. Taking conditions, range, and variables into account, even the best sharpshooters were
lucky to put a shot precisely where they wanted it,
and in a field situation like this, one didn't take
chances.

Since he'd killed that little jerk-off nine years ago,
Lew had been involved in four shooting incidents,
all walk-aways. This looked like the fifth—

Suddenly, in a move that caught him completely
off guard, a figure materialized from the rocks next
to the sniper. Vears. He was dripping wet.

"Stand away from there, Vears," Lew shouted,
quickening his approach and swerving to an angle
that held both forms clearly in his sights. He wasn't
sure what was going down here, but he damn well
didn't like the looks of it.

Ignoring his warning, Vears bent over the body,
and before Lew could grasp his intention, the edge
of a hand cut down on the fallen man's neck.

"Get away from there! Back off—*back off!*" Lew
jerked the revolver forward as he quickly closed

the remaining distance between them, covering only Vears, now. Adrenaline resurged.

Vears glanced up at Lew, straightened, and did as he was told, moving a few paces away.

Lew's gaze darted between the two men as he reached them. He felt his face tighten with the raging emotions flooding to the surface.

A clean hit had stopped the sniper, neutralizing the threat and assuring Lew an opportunity for questioning. Blood still pumped from the shoulder wound, soaking the gray coverall, and the man had no doubt had the breath knocked out of him by the fall, but none of that should've been fatal. Yet he was writhing with convulsions, gasping for air like a fish thrown up on a pier. A horrible choking rasped the stillness. Glassy eyes searched the sky. Hands flailed helplessly at his neck, his face was a contortion of effort.

"Get back, I said!" Keeping Vears squarely in his gunsights, Lew reached down and ran a hand over the twitching body as Nick obligingly stepped farther back.

But there was nothing he could do for the stricken man; in the time it took to realize this, the spasms increased, the gasping grew frenzied. Lew felt nausea surge, helpless to stop what was happening or even alleviate the man's suffering. The gunman was dead—he just didn't know it yet.

For a moment Lew hadn't been sure, but now he was: the man had a collapsed larynx—he snapped his eyes back to Vears—and this asshole had done it. He remembered scenes like this in Nam, and a terrible anger consumed him at the reawakening of things long buried.

Anger trembled through Lew's body as he stared at Vears, and a stab of guilt that he hadn't locked this killer up when he'd had the chance. Well, that

was about to change. He gripped his gun firmly in
both hands again.

"Hands behind your head, Vears. Lace those fingers. Now get down on your knees."

He watched Vears comply with the first two orders, then stop. Tension crackled on the air between them, and a nebulous sort of assessment.

"Get down, goddammit, or I'll shoot you where
you stand." He rammed the gun forward, hardly
recognizing the harshness in his voice. The scene
had become ludicrous.

For a moment Vears remained motionless, and
the eyes that studied Lew were as smooth and reflective as the stones on Sara Vears's table. Lew felt
his finger tighten on the cold steel trigger, at the
same time wondering if he could follow through on
the threat—

and in that split second, he knew that if Vears
didn't drop, if the man took the slightest step forward, he'd do it, shoot him where he stood.

A gull screamed overhead; waves tumbled in to
shore. And Lew thought Vears almost smiled as he
dropped to his knees in the sand.

Sometime during this strange contest of wills, the
gunman expired. Lew felt the absurdness of the situation. He was standing in firing position, arms
stretched and rigid, holding a gun on a dead body
and a kneeling man. His mind raced with options.

Easing his stranglehold on the revolver, he
backed up a step. "All right, Mr. Vears, using your
left hand, I want you to lift that sweatshirt—
Slowly," he added, and watched the hand moderate
its downward course. "And if you're armed under
there, you'd best keep it nice and easy."

Lew followed the motion as with elaborately emphasized care Nick Vears pulled up the left side of
his shirt to reveal a snug body holster. Little rivulets of water ran down his naked torso and bare

legs from the sodden shirt and gym shorts. He'd obviously taken to the water after hearing the first shot, then climbed back through the rocks.

"Okay, now let's carefully remove the firearm and toss it to your left." His grip on the revolver tightened as Vears followed the order, giving no indication of doing other than as told. The big automatic went sailing across the sand, landing about a dozen feet away.

"Keep that shirt up."

Taking his time, and maintaining a respectable distance, Lew made a complete circle of the kneeling form, satisfying himself that no other weapons nested elsewhere.

"All right, hands back behind your head. Now stand up"—Lew gestured with the gun—"easy. First we're going to take a little walk, and then a little ride. Don't make any wrong moves—don't even think about it." There was no longer any doubt that Nicholas Vears was dangerous.

"I don't know who, or what, you are," Lew remarked grimly as his prisoner rose slowly to his feet, "but I'm going to do what I should have done two days ago and take you in—and I strongly advise you not to give me any trouble."

"I can't let you do that, Lew." Vears spoke for the first time, his tone quietly matter-of-fact, his manner politely conversational.

Sea wind ruffled the hair on his forehead and brushed Lew's raincoat against his leg. It carried with it the smell of salt, and dead fish.

He couldn't believe he'd heard right. "What did you say?"

"I'm going to have to stop you, Lew, and I'd rather it didn't get out of hand."

Lew stared at him blankly, still not taking this in. Could the man standing squarely in his gunsights seriously mean to resist?

"I really would prefer it if you'd just let me handle this." Vears's voice, like his eyes, remained calm, steady. "I have the credentials."

Lew looked at him, and a glimmer of knowledge peered from behind a door in the back of his mind. Cogs began dropping into place.

"I know you've talked to your people," Vears continued. "I arranged that. Remember what they told you."

His quiet words were having an almost soporific effect. Lew mentally shook himself. "Who the fuck *are* you?"

He thought Vears gave a small sigh, as if the question were an old one. A insane urge to laugh followed the sudden thought that he was trapped in a movie where the next line would be: "Bond— James Bond."

Instead, with deliberate care, Vears began unlacing his fingers and bringing his hands down from his head.

"I'm not your target." He spoke gently into the tenseness that grabbed the moment and moved Lew's finger a little closer against the trigger. "I'm on your side in this."

"Bullshit!" Lew's voice came hard and tight. He wasn't buying this line of crap. He gestured toward the corpse. "What about this little item? Am I supposed to believe that someone who just murdered a helpless man in cold blood is on my side? Do I even want him to be? And if he is"—Lew's eyes narrowed—"then maybe I'm the one on the wrong goddamned side."

"You're just going to have to believe me." Vears's arms had ceased their slow descent and now hung loosely at his sides. He made no further moves, but watched Lew carefully. "I think down deep, you already do."

Lew recognized that budding truth, tasted the

sour, gut-level instinct that had confused his deal-
ings with this man almost from the first. What
brand of undercover operative was he looking at
here? DEA? CIA? As if there weren't already enough
blind spots in this case, one of the principals had
to be 007. "Not without some answers. Who was
this joker, and why was he after you?"

Nick shrugged. "An unrelated consequence of
that little newspaper article. If you take the body
in, he'll eventually be ID'd as some imported hood-
for-hire with a string of hits to his credit."

"*If* I take the body in?" Lew picked up on the
most bizarre part of this bizarre statement. "You
have something else in mind?"

"How do you propose explaining this?" Nick indicated the sniper with a slight nod of his head.

Lew glanced again at the dead gunman. Flies had
begun buzzing around the man's lower body, where
no doubt the sphincter muscles had involuntarily
loosened. He looked back at Nick, who was regarding him calmly.

Lew felt anything but calm. His entire career,
every rule, every ethic, said haul this asshole in—
credentials be damned!—and every instinct
screamed just as strongly: *No.* There was no basis
for this; to the contrary, all the facts were stacked
the other way. He'd be letting a killer go. Period.
He knew this type of thing went on, even within the
system, but he'd never been forced to openly acknowledge it. Did that make him innocent by reason of disregard? And what if he was wrong? What
if Vears was not what he'd claimed? Could Lew deal
with the potential repercussions of such folly?

Lew couldn't believe he was arguing with himself
about hauling in a murderer—and losing. Shit!

"And just what do you propose doing with it? In
case you haven't noticed, the tide is coming in, and
I doubt the authorities—" Once more Lew had the

vague impulse to laugh at the way he'd said "authorities," as though he wasn't one. "—will believe it simply washed ashore."

"I'll take care of it."

"Jesus Christ." Lew stared at the man standing casually in the sand. What was he getting involved in here? He shook his head in disbelief, then again muttered, "Jesus Christ."

The faint sound of a car pulling into The Ridge's parking area sealed the dilemma.

"Time to decide." Vears turned toward the dead man.

For a moment, Lew held his ground, following Vears with his eyes and gun as his prisoner walked over to the man he'd killed and grabbed hold of the splayed legs. It was his move, now.

Holstering the Smith & Wesson, face grim, he decided.

Quickly he hefted the dead man's shoulders, grunting under his breath as the head rolled against his knee. He didn't look at the man's face, or Vears, or anything but the rocks they headed for. He didn't listen to anything but his own breathing and the sound of the car coming to rest in the drive. He didn't let his mind think about what he was doing—just do it—*do* it.

Sunlight beat down on his back as he struggled to climb the slippery rocks with his burden. He felt spotlighted by the sun, center stage. The cool morning mist had departed—like the man they were carrying. Sweat began trickling down the sides of his face, the back of his neck. He didn't need the pounding in his chest to tell him he was dangerously near his stress limit.

"Where?" He jockeyed the grip of his right hand; it kept sliding on the blood-soaked sleeve.

Vears nodded toward a narrow opening between two rocks.

Together they maneuvered the body into the slot, shifting it sideways to manage. Lew turned from the sight of Vears grasping a handful of the dead man's hair to help jerk the torso in farther. When they were done, the body was reasonably well hidden.

"Now what?" Lew wasn't at all sure he really wanted to know.

Vears moved past him. "Clean up." He cast a suggestive glance.

Lew looked down. His right hand was streaked with the sniper's blood. Some had gotten on the cuff of his sleeve, and a smear daubed the front of his raincoat. Silently he climbed back down to the beach and headed toward the water's edge while Vears went to retrieve his gun.

Using damp sand, he managed to blur the stains on his raincoat enough to pass muster. He kept washing his hands in the cold water even after the blood was gone, a pseudo Pontius Pilate making himself metaphorically clean. He washed until his hands felt raw and deadened.

When he turned around, Vears was casually erasing evidence. He'd kicked sand over the bloodstains and now began smoothing away their tracks toward the rocks.

Lew watched him work, not quite believing he could allow this to happen, actually take a hand in it. This wasn't what the good guys were supposed to do. This hadn't been covered in the hero's handbook. He started to open his mouth, say, *Wait a minute. Wait a minute. We can't do this. This isn't right—*

"Hey there! Agent Harris."

The hail came from above. Lew snapped his head up.

Someone stood on the terrace waving. It was Chief Glenn—Curly.

"Need some help?" the chief's cheerful voice boomed.

"Christ," Lew muttered, then quickly yelled. "No—no thanks. Everything's fine." *Just fine. We're all fine.* He smiled up at the chief, though he knew the man couldn't see the gesture. The imbecilic smile felt plastered on his face.

"I can come down," Curly shouted. Helpful Curly. Friendly Curly. *Get lost, Curly.*

"No need," Lew returned, losing the smile. "I'm coming right up. Just take a minute."

I can't handle this, he thought numbly as Curly waved and ambled away from the parapet.

Breathing deeply, he turned back toward Vears, more than half expecting to find him gone. But he was crouched there among the rocks, out of sight from the terrace, arms casually resting on the bunched muscles of his thighs, hands lightly clasped. He looked perfectly at ease, like he could hold the position for days.

"I need you to do something for me," Vears said before Lew could speak. Just as well; he had no idea what he'd been about to say.

"Sure. Anything to help a colleague." Lew knew he was babbling but couldn't stop. "Just name your poison and good old Lew will provide." He heard the sarcasm that laced his tone, felt it drip like acid from the words and sizzle to the sand. Strangely, he felt better.

"Sara and her aunt are up at The Ridge. Don't let them leave."

Lew felt an eyebrow lift in surprise. The Danielle Grant he'd talked to was downright rabid on the subject of Nicholas Vears.

Vears smiled faintly, but his eyes stayed distant.

They looked at each other a moment, and Lew reexperienced some of the same familiarity that had insinuated itself into their first meeting, the feeling of like for like. Part of him responded on a professional level; part of him felt like throwing up. But they were in this now, together. Comrades in arms. Partners in crime.

Turning away, Lew headed toward The Ridge.

Darkness in Sara's bedroom gave way to the sweet, clear light of dawn. Something had woken Dani. An airplane? She remembered there was a naval air station not too far away and decided it must have been a jet. It had sounded like a couple of sonic booms.

She slipped from the bed, quickly donned her clothes, and moved silently out of the room. The sleeping child didn't stir; Dani glanced back once, then closed the door.

Her eyes felt like sandpaper; her head throbbed as though she'd spent the night in a bar drinking rotgut. Not that she ever had. But she thought this was how it would feel.

The corridor was Stygian, untouched by morning sun, all the bedroom doors closed. What light there was had filtered in from below. Dani thought about the long expanse of windows in David and Carole's bedroom, the glorious openness of his studio. She thought about Nick Vears.

Nothing moved at the far end of the hallway. No glimmer pierced the gloom. Was he still asleep? She hoped so. She didn't think she could handle another face-off so soon.

Heading on down the stairs, she turned toward the kitchen, studiously avoiding a glance at the closed great room doors. What she needed was a cup of coffee, strong and black, the kind you could stick a spoon into and have it stand upright. Maybe that would chase the boogeyman away.

If only it were that simple.

She detoured into the downstairs bathroom, felt

better after she'd splashed her face with handfuls
of cold tap water.

In the kitchen she turned on an under-the-cabinet
light, not wanting to advertise her early rising, and
started Carole's espresso machine brewing. Mud. A
caffeine mud-pack for her head. She inhaled the
smell that was already beginning to smooth the
wrinkles from her skull. Lovely.

Last night hadn't been lovely.

Thoughts of Nick Vears again intruded, stirring
her anger and sending her pulse rate climbing. He'd
scared her last night—badly. He seemed to have a
knack for it. But she wasn't going to let him scare
her off. For a minute there in the rain, she'd been
certain he was about to strike her. Maybe he would
have if Sara hadn't come forward. He'd been angry
enough.

She remembered that anger, still winced at its
strength. He'd been furious, as furious as if he really cared about Sara. As furious as a real father?
She remembered him later, in Sara's bedroom, the
dark image of him gently fingering a lock of his
daughter's hair, lifting a blanket to cover her shoulder. The two images didn't mesh.

"He's a monster, Dani, remember?" she muttered, pulling her cup from the espresso machine
with more force than was warranted. "Carole told
you so. And you've got your own scars to prove it."

She tried to picture her sister-in-law with Vears.
That image wouldn't come. Yet they'd produced
this beautiful child, so there had to have been some
sort of closeness between them once. What had
happened to change Carole's mind, make her hate
Vears so? Another woman? Dani didn't think so.
Her response had gone way beyond so facile an explanation. It had held revulsion and fear.

What kind of man was Nick Vears? The kind who
would coerce and intimidate? The kind who would

kick small puppies and murder children? Yes to the first two. But what about the last?

"The man's a psycho," she muttered again, raising her cup. "He might have strangled you last night if it hadn't been for Sara. He's no fit person to have custody of a child." She washed the ultimatum down with a swallow of espresso, finding one bitter and the other strangely harsh.

The memory of that final set-to in his bedroom flashed to mind. She'd thought he had run the gamut with her, but that last thing had come way out of left field. She remembered his eyes on her, the look in his dark eyes. Primitive. Carefully controlled and utterly impersonal, but there all right. What was the term: post-ammo letdown?

And that, Dani realized, seeing the moment as clearly as if it were being replayed, was what scared her the most . . . because she'd felt an involuntary response.

"That's *sick*, Dani," she told herself, setting the cup down in disgust. "Sick.

"I've got to get out of here. Now. Right now."

Leaving the kitchen she thought she heard somebody shouting outside, and went over to the front door to look out. Sure enough, an old green Vega sat next to Vears's four-wheeler. She didn't recognize it, didn't see anyone around.

She started to open the door; thought better of it. This whole situation was making her paranoid. Maybe it was simply that jerk reporter, though she couldn't quite picture him in the beat-up car. Maybe she'd better get Vears—

Again she caught the muffled sound of conversation. Taking a cautious peek out one of the viewports, she spied Agent Harris and that local cop walking toward the house. A sigh of relief became hesitation. Was Vears with them?

"—and it sounded important," the smaller man

was saying. "Said his name was Tal and you'd know what it was about. Said he'd try to call you again at the inn around noon. Kept stressing that he *didn't* want *you* to call him."

Dani stepped back out of sight as the SBI agent reached the walkway. There was no sign of Vears; he must still be sleeping. The other man had gone toward his car.

"I appreciate the message, Chief—ah, Curly. And don't worry about things here. I'll be around all day." Harris's voice sounded strained.

"Okay by me. Wanted to go fishing anyway. See you later."

The sound of a car door being slammed. A motor starting up. A car driving away.

Dani jumped as a heavy knock landed next to her. Her heart began to pound a response.

Without hesitation, she flung the door open. The cavalry had arrived.

Lowering her voice and hoping Vears hadn't heard the knock, Dani grabbed the agent by the coat sleeve and propelled him inside. "Agent Harris, I'm so glad to see you. Sara and I need a lift to the beach house and I don't have my car. It won't take a minute. Just let me run upstairs and get her. I won't be long, I promise."

During this recital, he stood solidly in the center of the entry hall, looking so dependable that Dani felt safeness settle down around her. He wouldn't let anything deter him; would hold the boogeyman at bay. "Wait right here," she added, and started to turn toward the staircase.

"Just a minute, Miss Grant . . ."

"*Shh,*" Dani interrupted her headlong dash and turned back toward Harris. "Please, Agent Harris, keep your voice down."

"I'll be happy to take you wherever you want," he whispered, "but not right now."

"Why not?" Dani felt queasiness return to her stomach. Didn't he realize any minute that monster was going to wake up and hear them? She just wanted to be out of this house and away from here before then.

"I have"—again he lowered his tone as she gave him an exasperated gesture—"business with Mr. Vears."

"Surely that can wait the few minutes it will take to drive us down the beach. It's only about a mile."

But Harris was shaking his head. "I'm sorry, Miss Grant. You'll just have to wait."

Did he look a little grim beneath the polite facade? Had he somehow connected Vears to the deaths after all? The queasiness turned into acute nausea. All the more reason to grab Sara and get the hell out.

"Please, Agent Harris. I really need to leave *now*."

Dani thought she saw a glimmer of sympathy in his eyes, but his face was stony. "I simply can't take you at the moment. There are some . . . matters that need to be straightened out first."

"What matters?"

"Let's just wait for Mr. Vears."

"I don't *want* to wait for Mr. Vears," Dani hissed. "I have nothing to say to Mr. Vears!"

"I believe he has something to say to you." Lew glanced toward the open front door.

Dani followed his gaze, almost expecting Vears to materialize in the opening. "Well, I don't want to hear it."

"Good morning."

Both of them turned toward the voice. Vears was standing at the door to the great room, holding the bifolds apart. Beyond him the ocean sounded, an echo effect. A soft breeze wafted through the entry hall and out the front door.

He walked toward them.

Dani averted her eyes, from the great room, from the man. She couldn't take another scene. But she had an ally now; Harris would reinforce her position. "I was just about to leave. Agent Harris will give us a ride. I'll get Sara—"

"Sara won't be going."

Dani heard the words and instantly closed her mind against the finality of his tone. This couldn't be happening. Repulsing the lump of nausea vaulting toward her throat, she snapped her eyes back to him. "You *said*—"

"The situation has changed."

"*What* situation?" Dani felt the sting of frustration prick her eyes and blinked the revealing weakness away. She wouldn't let him get to her like this.

"Look, Danielle." Vears sounded almost human as he regarded her dispassionately. "You can stay here with her."

"No!"

The hardness came back into his eyes. "Talk to her, Lew." He shifted his gaze to Harris, and something seemed to pass between them in the look.

"Come on, Miss Grant. I'll drive you to the beach house." His voice was steady as a rock—but what she needed was some backup.

"Not without Sara." Dani turned toward the stairs, knowing she was making a fool's stand. She couldn't hope to go up against Vears and win, at least not alone. Would Harris help her?

Somehow Vears had anticipated her move. He now stood between her and the staircase. She stepped toward him—

"Dani?" The child's voice came from above.

Dani glanced up, startled, sensing both men do the same.

Sara stood at the balcony looking down on them solemnly. The shocking pink nightshirt hung to just below her knees. Her feet were bare. She clutched her Fuzzy.

"Sara, honey—"

"It's all right, Dani. I want to stay."

Dani felt the lump of nausea congeal in her chest. A pain that had nothing—and everything—to do with Sara tore at her gut.

"Come along, Miss Grant." Agent Harris gently took her arm.

Dani let him lead her from the house and down the driveway to his car. She got in calmly, said nothing, made no further dissent. Why bother? It was obvious what had happened, though she'd never have believed it possible. But there was no question about it, none at all.

Both Harris and Sara had gone over to the enemy.

13

Dani swung the Buick station wagon off the highway and onto the beach road, turning left toward the house that loomed in the distance. She made the final decision even as she made the turn. What else could she do?

So far it had been a day of decisions, anger, frustration. First she'd watched the child she loved dearly slip willingly and innocently into a situation she couldn't possibly understand. What was this game Vears was playing? Moving them like chess pieces from square to square. Dani didn't play chess, and she'd never been good at subtle mind games, never seemed to grasp the rules, or the pleasure. She didn't know how to fight him.

Then there'd been Agent Harris's defection. He'd spent the better part of an hour at the beach house listening to her protests and not being swayed. "The situation has changed," he'd repeatedly stated, sounding too much like Vears. Beyond that he wouldn't explain.

Finally she'd accepted the stalemate because there was little else she could do.

"After all, Miss Grant," Harris had reminded her, not without sympathy but firmly putting an end to the matter, "It is Mr. Vears's decision to make. She's his daughter." Then he'd gotten up to leave, adding rather grimly, "I can't believe he'd let her come to harm."

Dani's hands tightened on the steering wheel. "He'd better not," she muttered through clenched teeth. "Because if he does . . ."

She left the sentence dangling as she slowed to make the turn onto The Ridge's drive. For a moment she thought the sun glinted off a car coming behind her down the beach road—had that damned reporter followed her here from town? She'd seen him watching her.

She glanced back, not seeing anything now. It could have been anyone, or no one at all. And if the creep did come . . . Dani found herself smiling at the thought of Russell Reikert accosting Nicholas Vears.

"Couldn't happen to a nicer guy," she murmured, applying the sentiment to both of them.

The grocery bags in the back seat shifted, and she lifted her foot farther off the accelerator pedal as the car arced around the first curve. She should have put the bags on the floor, along with her and Sara's things. They'd been threatening to fall off the back seat ever since she'd left the convenience store.

The house on the hill drew nearer as she wound the car slowly up the drive, and she remembered the first time she'd seen it, a visit not long after David and Carole had bought the old pile of stones. David had stumbled upon it during a leisurely stop-and-sketch trip down the coast, and been captivated by the visual antithesis it presented to its surroundings; yet it had seemed intrinsically part of the natural setting, he'd said, almost as though it had been here first and nature had molded the seashore around it. He'd wanted to capture that spectral essence on canvas. It was a recurring theme in his work: the study of harmony in opposites.

Yet he'd never incorporated the old stone house into any of the paintings she'd seen, Dani realized, and wondered why. Now she'd never know.

She pulled the car into the parking area and got out, feeling not so much reluctance now as curiosity. What had Vears and Sara been doing all morning? How had he treated her? Had he talked to her? Fed her breakfast?

Dani doubted very much if he'd done either. Vears was not one for making small talk, and what he did have to say usually fell into two categories: unpleasant and more unpleasant. And a man who used a sauté pan to heat water for instant coffee probably didn't cook.

Thus the groceries. She might not be the gourmet Carole had been, but she could make a decent lunch for herself and Sara—let *him* eat beans.

The soft breeze off the ocean blew her skirt against her legs as she grabbed the bag of perishables off the back seat and headed for the house. She'd always loved it here; loved the wildness, the tranquillity—David's harmony in opposites. Until now.

Dani quickly switched thoughts.

What was Vears going to say about her returning? she wondered.

A seagull screeched in the distance. Waves beat rhythmically against the cliff, and Dani felt her heart beating faster as she neared the front door. She hoped they could avoid further unpleasantness, especially in front of Sara, and resolved to do her part to keep the peace. After all, he'd agreed to let her stay here . . . Or had that situation changed too?

At the door she shifted the bag of groceries to her left arm, then hesitated.

What should she say to him? What if he wouldn't let her in? Surely Sara would want her here. But Sara hadn't said anything this morning. Was the child still blocking out the tragedy she'd witnessed, trying to insert her father into the gaping, empty hole tragedy had left? Dani knew she couldn't fight them both.

"What am I *doing* here," she muttered, feeling a sudden urge to turn and run. Exasperated, she raised her hand to knock—

An arm clamped down around her throat, jamming against her windpipe, forcing the jaw closed. Her head slammed backward, breath all but cut off. Something hard jabbed her ribs.

"Do *exactly* what I tell you and you'll live a little longer," a harsh voice whispered in her ear.

Dani couldn't even nod "Okay."

Lew Harris looked at his watch, then the telephone for the twenty-fifth time in as many minutes. It was ten past noon and he'd been sitting in the lobby since fifteen till.

"Around noon," Tal had said. Well, it was around noon and Lew was getting antsy having to linger here when he should be—

Out doing cop stuff? Like hiding dead bodies and coercing innocent citizens? All in a day's work.

"Shit," he muttered, sprawling back in the leather chair with the splits in the arms and raising a hand to rub away the beginnings of a tension headache that could turn into a beaut if this kept up.

"Fish not biting this morning?"

Lew gave a start and glanced up at the grungy

angler who looked like he'd rolled in with the tide. Probably a lawyer or bank executive on vacation; a fishing community tended to bring out the slouch in even the starchiest professional—the way the events of this morning were bringing out the cynic in him, Lew realized, not liking the sarcastic tone of his thoughts or the caustic one-liners that kept coming to mind.

Like *Hooked a croaker but I had to throw him back* and *the really big one got away*.

Bad sign. A sign his attitude was getting bent out of shape—and when the attitude bends . . .

The fisherman shrugged and walked off, saving Lew the effort of trying to formulate a nonhostile reply.

Twelve: eleven.

Lew stared at the silent phone on the end of the desk, one of those old heavy black jobs with rotary dial. They didn't have in-room extensions here, though they did have TVs. Apparently one's time was well spent fishing, drinking, eating—he could attest to that—sleeping, watching television, and playing cards—Lew had noticed an ongoing poker game in the back parlor. No need for room phones. Gave one a valid excuse for not calling the wife; offered a plausible excuse for her not to call you. Business be damned. Problems can wait.

Gone fishin'.

Twelve: twelve.

Since depositing Danielle Grant at the beach house several hours ago, Lew had been anxious to get back to The Ridge. He wanted to talk with the little girl, and he didn't like the idea of leaving her with only Vears for protection, despite the man's "credentials." Not now; not after this morning. There was still no explanation for what had happened to the Grant family, and now Vears had added his own pieces to the puzzle. That little girl shouldn't be in the middle of it—Danielle Grant was righter than she knew. But Lew's hands were tied.

He wasn't through with Vears, though, not by a long shot. Lew knew he could still blow this thing wide open, whatever the personal cost, and he'd do it in a heartbeat if Tal's information didn't jive.

If Tal ever called.

Twelve: thirteen.

At least he'd gotten some necessary detail work out of the way: checking in with the sheriff's office, collecting preliminary investigation reports. They'd all been local, nothing from Raleigh yet.

On a chance, he put in a call to Kathleen Boyce and got her to pull up Pathology's file on the case and read him the notes they'd entered so far, to wit: "Eruption of (there followed a list of medical terms that condensed to 'body,' times four): Cause or causes unknown." Pathology was running the entire battery of tests again just in case they'd missed something, which wasn't likely. And Kate still wasn't making any guesses.

Lew glanced at his watch once more, frowned. His anxiety was increasing with each moment that limped by—for Tal, and the potential taint-by-association he could acquire should the wrong people find out what he was doing for Lew; and particularly for the situation left pending at The Ridge.

He stood to stretch tight muscles, repelling the sluggishness that kept trying to creep up on him the longer he stayed still.

The telephone rang.

Lew had it in his hand in two strides. "Harris."

"Lew, is that you?" Tal's voice sounded quivery and somewhat muffled, but the kid was always a bit fluttery around the edges.

"Yeah, Tal, it's me. I think we've got a bad connection—"

"You've got a bad connection, all right. Listen,
I'm at a pay phone and I haven't got much time.
And hear me good, Lew, this better *not* get back to
the department. I'm just hoping I didn't leave any
tracks getting in and out—"

"Just give me the data, Tal, and not in machine
language, please." Lew had a feeling he wasn't going to like what he was about to hear.

"Oh shit, Lew. Why'd you get me into this? What
did I ever do to you? Shit-shit-*shit!*"

"Calm down, Tal. Jesus! Just tell me what's—"

"It was that license tag that did it, legit enough
through the rental agency itself, but keep peeling
away holding companies and blanket corps and
there it is. *Shit*, Lew. Don't ever ask me for help
again. We're even, understand? Don't even fucking
call me—"

"There *what* is, Tal?" *Come on, get it over with.
Tell me I've screwed big time.*

"I ID'd the bottom-line organization. The one
your man's tied to. It's the NSC, Lew. Do you read
what I'm saying here? The fucking NSC!"

The line went dead.

Lew stared at the buzzing receiver, slowly placed
it back into its cradle. Well, it certainly wasn't
what he'd expected. No wonder Tal was having flut-
ters. It was enough to send him raveling in all
directions. Lew shook his head. The NSC. Vears
was connected to the NSC—the National Security
Council.

Shit.

The old chapel was dingy with the residue of de-
cades and the gloom of inadequate lighting. Nick
stood in the silence watching dust motes swim
across the few slatted sunbeams that managed to

penetrate thin embrasures lining the far wall. The meager openings gave little ventilation, and the long room smelled musty and felt uncomfortably dank.

He glanced down at Sara, wondering if she had on enough clothes.

The child stood quietly by his side, holding her—

"Fuzzy," Sara murmured, and Nick frowned.

"What?"

But Sara had stepped away from him, leaving his side for the first time since he'd brought her down here. He suddenly had the absurd idea it was the other way around.

"Have you been here before, Sara?"

She shook her head *no*.

"Does being here bother you?"

She didn't respond, just kept walking up the aisle toward the altar, yet Nick sensed that the answer to this question was *yes*. He was beginning to wonder about these odd flashes of insight between them. He was beginning to wonder about a lot of things.

He'd decided he might as well spend some time checking this area more thoroughly, see if he could find an explanation for last night. He didn't like not knowing what had affected him, whether it was due to extraneous causes or something more insidious. Wasting time waiting for Terrell to strike again was pointless, and playing bodyguard to a seven-year-old was wearing thin. Of course it could have been worse: the Grant woman might have elected to stay.

He stared at the back of Sara's head as she walked, started to say "Watch your step" or something of the like, decided it wasn't necessary. She was handling herself all right. Better than he was.

This morning's event had stung him, even if it hadn't left an open wound. He'd committed a cardinal error: underestimating his opponent. And his growing involvement here was an encumbrance he couldn't afford.

And now those circumstances were preventing his leaving, at least temporarily. Nick knew he was courting disaster every hour he stayed, and not just his own. He'd already revealed too much to Harris, made an alliance that suited neither of them and could have unfortunate repercussions for Lew. The overzealous agent might have gotten himself killed this morning by something that was not his concern. And for a moment Nick had doubted his ability to talk him around.

Everything was getting out of hand. Nick felt control spiraling away from him. The quicker he could settle things here and remove himself, the better for all concerned. Particularly Sara. He watched his daughter thoughtfully.

Having her with him was something Nick hadn't foreseen and didn't like. So far she'd told him nothing, and he was having to expend excess time and thought on her safety and care, now that the Terrell situation had merged into this one and she'd become part of the package. He was discovering he didn't much care for that.

Under other circumstances, his error could have become an adequate solution: let the situation come to him. But he wouldn't be free to act on it fully until she could be gotten out of the way. Which would be soon, though not as soon as he'd have liked.

She glanced back at him, her face a shadow, hiding expression, then continued her trek toward the altar.

He started up the aisle behind her. She'd stopped and was studying the large stone dais, her ... *Fuzzy* cradled in one arm.

Nick studied her. He planned to send her out

with the pickup team tonight, let them take her
to a safe house and get her out of trouble's way—
and his. Too many events were taking place simultaneously, too many distractions. What if he had
one of those hallucinatory episodes with Sara
here? He'd counted himself the best protection
she had at the moment, but in view of what had
been happening to him, was that decision ques-
tionable?

Unexpected events were affecting his ability to
deal with things, and that could be dangerous to
them both. He needed total concentration if he was
going to handle this business, turn it around. He
didn't need innocents getting in the way.

She looked up at him as he joined her, then
pointed at the floor to the left side of the altar. He
bent down and, using his flashlight, was able to
make out where faint scrape marks swung an arc
away from the rectangular stone base.

Pivot of some sort?

"You have good eyes," he remarked matter-of-
factly. The scrapes wouldn't have been noticed in a
cursory police search.

Sara didn't reply.

Nick stood and began making a slow tour of the
dais. A thick layer of dust and spiderwebs coated
the entire structure, including the pedestal column
and the two-tier support base. No hands had
touched this altar in years.

Yet the scrape marks looked relatively recent.

Nick bent down again, turned the light underneath, searching for knobs, levers. He tried manipulating various parts of the structure, but nothing
gave way, no hidden gears, no secret pulleys. He
ran the light over the slanted surface, then his hand,
tracking dust.

Backing off from the altar, he studied it thoughtfully and noticed Sara doing the same ... or was he parroting her?

Nick shrugged. Maybe he should try things the hard way.

Leaning a shoulder against the right-hand side of the altar, he gave the column a test shove—and felt it move. Another push, and with the scrape of stone on stone the altar swung aside, revealing a dark cavity with stone steps descending into blackness.

A breath of sea air floated into the room, chasing away the staleness and seeming to hold a hint of burnt tar.

Memory shimmered across Nick's mind, a flicker of vision as though through dark glass. He glanced at Sara and saw she'd backed up a few paces.

Probing the hole with the high-intensity beam, he played it down the stairs to where a bend circled out of sight. There'd been activity on the steps; footprints shone starkly in the light. But it had been a while. Dust had begun to resettle over the depressions. Still, this could be the answer he was looking for—a way in.

For whom?

He started to go down the stairs, stopped. He couldn't leave Sara here alone while he checked out the tunnel. He didn't want to take her with him. He'd have to wait for tonight, after she was gone and out of his—

A small hand tugged his sleeve. He hadn't heard her move.

He turned and glanced down. Sara placed a finger to her mouth in a gesture of silence, then pointed at the door.

Nick nodded. Quickly he picked her up and moved silently back down the aisle they'd just used. He deposited her on one of the stone benches, motioned her down, and quietly continued toward the door he'd closed and latched behind them.

Glancing back to make sure she was out of sight, he pulled the Ruger from beneath his shirt, feeling it meld with the palm of his hand. Attaching the suppressor, he tested the grip, released the safety. One safety feature the customized weapon lacked was a magazine disconnector. A chambered round could still be fired, even minus the clip, and made initial cocking unnecessary. Nick always kept a chambered round.

No sound penetrated the heavy wooden door. Nick took his time tripping the latch, waited a moment, then slowly eased the door open. The darker gloom of the corridor stretched silent and empty.

He widened the crack. Nothing shifted. Nothing stirred. Yet he could feel the prospect tremble on the air—

A faint sound drifted to him, a whiff of breeze. Someone had entered the old section of the house through one of the side doors, probably the same one the Grant woman had used that first night. But it would have taken more than a key this time.

Nick had made it a point to improve the locks on all the doors. Whoever was coming in uninvited knew something about the art of forced entry.

Sparing one quick backward glance, he stepped into the corridor, closing the chapel door soundlessly behind him. This morning's sniper had been a calling card—formal visit to follow. He'd hoped it might wait for evening. It hadn't.

Nick wondered how many had come, and briefly reviewed options, taking alternate numbers into account. He still saw it as one-on-one.

The key was logistics. The probable choice would be to converge wide from opposing entries, post a staggered front. Terrell was cautious, and deploy-

ing a net held strategic advantages. It also held a
potential flaw: misjudging perimeters.

Nick spotted the intruder. The man was edging
along the wall toward the branching corridor, carrying what looked like an Auto Mag, silhouetted by
the pale light seeping in through a salt-encrusted
transom. His attention was concentrated forward,
away from these deserted ruins, concerned only
with the quarry in the main house as that quarry
slipped up silently behind him.

The Ruger's barrel slammed into the back of his
neck. A hand smashed sideways across his face,
breaking his nose, then rammed home, sending
splinters of bone upward to his brain.

Nick controlled the man's slump, made sure he
was dead, and left him on the stone floor. He'd recognized him as one of the pair that had flanked
Terrell at the warehouse.

Moving along the corridor, he listened for further intrusion into this wing. Nothing alerted him,
and he stepped up his pace toward the bisecting
branch, certain he was now alone in this area.

At the branch he held position, standing silent in
the gloom. The archway door was closed, as he'd
left it. He had no way of knowing for certain
whether the main house had been breached. But it
was likely, and that was how he intended to play
it.

Easing back into the darker part of the corridor,
Nick settled down to wait.

Dani closed her eyes against the blackness swirling at the edges of her vision. A dual ringing echoed
in her head and ears. She could feel the man's hot
breath on the side of her face, smell the sour odor
of his unwashed mouth. His gun dug brutally into
her side.

"Pass out on me, lady, and you're dead," the

nightmare voice growled softly, and he gave her head a little jolt.

Dani's eyes flew open. She tried to focus through the sparkles of light swimming up to join the black. She'd been a *fool* to think the danger began and ended with Nick Vears. The real murderer had come back! He was *here*! He'd come back to kill Sara. What should she do?

The arm on her throat loosened marginally. "Don't scream."

Dani doubted she could.

"We're gonna play this nice and easy." The body against hers shifted, allowing her some leeway to move. "Set the bag down."

With a start, she realized she was still gripping the bag of groceries. The bread was smashed. She did as told.

"Now knock on the door and call out that it's you."

She tried to swallow, and couldn't. What was she going to do? Where was Vears? Harris? The local law? Here was the man they were looking for! Where *was* everybody?

"Come on, lady . . ." The gun barrel raked across her ribs, making her gasp.

She lifted her hand toward the door, seeing it move in slow motion. Sara was in that house. She couldn't just let this murderer in. He'd killed David and Carole—and the babies. And now he'd come back to finish the job, get rid of the only witness—

A sudden sharp click sent her heart plunging—he'd cocked the gun! The man tensed reflexively, jerking her sideways, away from the door. She sucked in a breath, waiting for the shot that didn't come . . . then realized it had been the doorknob releasing. Someone had tripped the latch from inside. The door had swung open about three inches.

He squeezed her back against him . . . and Dani nearly fainted then, from the chokehold, from the pain in her side. She heard herself moan.

He shook her roughly, whispered: "Call out to Vears!" Pressure on her neck again lessened.

Vears? How did this man know— He shook her again. She dragged a ragged breath into bursting lungs and cried, "Vears—?" It came out a croak.

But the door was swinging backward . . . slowly . . . as if blown open by the wind . . .

He shook her again, and she managed, "Vears, is that you?" a little stronger this time.

The door continued to swing open. She didn't see anyone. There was nobody there.

She could see into the entry hall, bright and empty, doors to the great room standing wide. Sunlight dappled the gray stone floor.

Behind her she could feel the man's uncertainty. He shifted positions again, moving his back to the outside wall, jamming her in front of him, coiled to strike. His head kept swinging right, toward the open doorway, then left, toward the terrace.

Oh please don't look that way, Dani prayed as he seemed to settle on the terrace opening as the point to watch. Vears must have created a diversion with the door and was even now slipping around through the great room to sneak up on them from the rear. But the man suspected. *Create another diversion, Dani!* She tried to think.

"Inside."

Pulling her with him, the man edged into the house, forcing her along by the arm still wrapped around her neck, the gun violating her ribs. She felt like a rag doll in the grip of an angry child.

Where was Sara? Dani glanced up the stairs. *Please, munchkin, don't come down. Where was Vears? Why didn't he do something?*

In a sudden burst of violence, the man kicked the

door backward, sending it careening into the wall. Satisfied that no one was hiding behind it, he dragged her forward and shoved the door shut, still using his foot. For just an instant, he removed his arm from her neck, just long enough to throw the bolt into place.

Dani knew it might be the only chance she'd get—to slap the gun away, to kick him, to run. All the TV cop shows she'd ever seen came flooding back to her, all the movies, all the books. This is where the heroine proves her worth, takes it on herself to save the day.

Except she couldn't move. She simply couldn't bring her muscles into motion. They were frozen in place.

The heavy arm went back around her neck and the man began propelling them backward into a corner of the entry hall. Dani moved with him, doing nothing to impede his progress. She felt mentally numb, physically blank. Things were going hazy in her brain; lack of oxygen, she supposed. The gun in her side was a dull ache, the arm on her throat an anchor.

In the corner he stopped, eyes roaming the area. His chin grazed the top of her head. He was tall, big; she felt encased by him.

The silence was unnerving. Tension knotted the muscles in his arms and body.

"Manetti—?" He waited for an answer that didn't come, then swore once, foully, under his breath. He'd begun to sweat; she felt a drop land on her cheek and trickle down her face. It made her want to vomit. His stench corrupted the air, the stench of a cornered animal.

He shifted nervously. "Vears? I know you're here. I've got the woman." He jabbed the gun and she groaned on cue. "If you want her alive you'd better show yourself."

There was no reply.

Dani felt like laughing, felt like saying, *You're going to have to come up with a better threat than me, old buddy, if you want to interest Vears.* Then she thought of Sara and didn't feel like laughing anymore.

Who *were* these people? Why had they killed David? What did it have to do with *Vears*?

"Come out, Vears," the man shouted, tightening his grip. "I'll break her neck."

A gull screamed in answer, its cry borne on the wind that gusted through an open window in the great room. A windowpane rattled, as though it had been lightly jarred—

Nick readied his shot. He wouldn't get but one attempt, if that. It would have to take Terrell out. The thought was not intimidating, merely there.

He'd been mildly surprised to recognize the man with Danielle. Displeasure within family ranks must be critical to send Frank himself from the fold. Was he on the run?

Nick steadied his aim. There'd be little time for choices once the opportunity presented itself, and the odds that it would didn't look good. His control factor extended only as far as the gun.

It was fortunate he'd chosen to move out of the older section and take up a position inside the house—fortunate for Danielle. Maybe.

For the first time, Nick questioned what had made him leave his excellent vantage point and slip into the main house prior to Terrell's entry. He hadn't heard anything—couldn't have from that distance and with everything shut up tight—and yet he'd moved. Intuition? Maybe. But Nick found he wasn't quite as satisfied with that explanation as he had been in the past.

He'd entered the great room in time to see Terrell duck past a window and, after waiting a moment, had followed. He'd watched Frank grab Danielle, then melted back from the edge of the terrace and reentered the house, leaving the window ajar.

During Terrell's attempt to draw him out, Nick had slipped the door latch and let the draft do the rest while he positioned himself in the dining room. A mirror over the sideboard gave him a clear view of the entry hall. He'd watched the pair's elaborate entrance.

Holding a hostage tended to restrict movement, however, and Nick wasn't too concerned that Terrell would search him out. Terrell himself had answered Nick's question of numbers by calling out only one man's name. It became a matter of waiting for a clear shot—and for Terrell to shift the gun from Danielle's side. If he did.

A windowpane in the great room rattled, as though it had been lightly jarred. Terrell shifted that way, pulling Danielle around to face the open bifolds, and for just a moment swung his gun toward the sound—

Something popped.

Dani felt a powerful momentum rip the man's body sideways, away from her. The gun in his hand went off and she screamed as the sound ricocheted through her head like fire. A chunk of stone wall beside the staircase blew apart and all Dani could think about was how David's body must have exploded like that. Outside, the gulls burst into a cacophony of screeching. Pieces of stone rained across the floor. The stench of gunpowder joined the stench of sweat and fear and something else she couldn't put a name to.

The arm about her neck was suddenly leaden, pulling her backward, dragging her down. She fought it, grunting with exertion and fright, wrenching her body out from under the clinging weight. At any moment she expected to be grabbed again, feel the gun jab her ribs, a shot blow her into a million pieces. Her feet tangled in his. She kicked frantically, struggling to crawl away.

Then Vears was in front of her, gun in one hand, grabbing her with the other. He jerked her toward him, behind him. She scrambled to her knees, fighting for breath, gagging, tried to shake her head, clear the fog. Everything around her was becoming blurred . . .

Maybe she did black out then, crouched on the hard stone floor, gasping in lungfuls of burning, rotten air.

When at last she managed to push back the darkness, she spotted Vears stooped over the man who had grabbed her, unceremoniously flipping through his jacket pockets and examining the contents. He shifted the body to get at the back and the man's head lolled to one side, giving Dani her first glimpse of the face that went with the nightmare voice. She winced at the sight, yet couldn't drag her eyes away. It seemed to scream accusations at her: mouth open and twisted, eyes staring and wild, cursing her with a silent, predatory malevolence that would haunt her in the nights to come.

But he was dead. Irrevocably dead. An ugly hole marked his left forehead, just above the temple at the edge of a heavy brow. Not a savage wound. A small trickle of blood leaked from it.

Her eyes flinched from the sight, shifting upward to a stain that decorated the wall right about where his head would have been, just above and behind hers. The dark patch oozed toward the floor, small rivulets making their way solemnly downward.

Pieces of bone and flesh glistened obscenely in the refracted sunlight.

Dani felt her stomach lurch, swallowed heavily. She shut her eyes. *Get hold of yourself, Danielle. Don't lose it now.* The imprint refused to fade.

She heard Vears leave the body. She opened her eyes and watched him come toward her, watched him draw to a halt at her side. He did nothing to shield her view, just stood looking down at her and his eyes were hard and black and cold.

She focused on them. "Where's Sara?"

"In the chapel. Safe."

"Safe?" Nausea retreated. Anger sprang to life. Dani couldn't believe the ease with which he was dismissing this carnage and what might have happened to his daughter. "Did you know this could happen? Did you keep Sara here with that murderer still at large, knowing something like this could happen?"

He stood there, not denying it, not saying anything.

"How could you do it? How could you risk Sara's life? Doesn't *anything* matter to you?" She looked at the dead man sprawled in the corner, and the horror of it struck her anew. "You shot that man with me standing there. You could have killed me."

"You'd rather I let him blow a hole in your side?" His words grabbed her unmercifully, tightening her throat as though the man's arm were still around it. She remembered the stab of the gun in her ribs and shivered violently.

"He would have, you know," Vears continued, each word impacting on her anger like hot coals. "The minute I stepped out he would have put a bullet in your gut and tossed you to the floor between us, thinking to shake me, make me careless. It takes time to die from a gut-shot, did you know that, Danielle? Lots of painful time."

She glared up at him, breathing heavily, wanting nothing more, now, than to rip that calculated mask from his face and draw blood. "Nothing shakes you. That's why you can blow a man's brains out with the same cool indifference with which you risk your daughter's life."

For a moment Dani thought something flickered deep within his eyes, something savage and not quite sane.

"It's what I do for a living," he replied, and his tone and expression were as hard and unrelenting as his eyes.

They regarded each other in silence. Then he put out his hand.

She let him pull her to her feet. Only when she was actually standing unaided was she certain her legs would work.

He turned back to the body and Dani turned away, taking a deep, shuddering breath. The man who'd killed David was dead. Vears had shot him. Case closed. *"It's what I do for a living,"* he'd said, which meant he *was* some sort of cop. The sort who could shoot a man in the head from ambush with a hostage in the way. Maybe that was how it was done in real life, maybe all the TV shows and novels and movies were just so much fiction where the good guys always prefaced their heroics with: "Drop your gun, this is the Law!" Give the baddies their fair chance before you shoot them, and ride off clear-conscienced into the sunset.

And he probably had saved her life . . .

"Forget it," she thought she heard him murmur as he walked past her and headed down the corridor, the body balanced across his shoulder and back. He'd pulled off the man's suit jacket and tied it snugly around the shattered head.

Dani stared after him, caught by the sight of the dangling, turbanlike head joggling against Vears's back, a wet stain already seeping through the dark brown silk. She barely made it to the bathroom in time.

14

The sound of retching followed Nick down the corridor. He swung Terrell's body sideways, pulled open the archway door and stepped through into cool gloom. Once again she'd gotten in the way, and he didn't feel sorry for her now.

Nick frowned at the foreign thought of "feeling sorry" for someone. One thing the Grant woman didn't evoke in him was sympathy. And if she kept thrusting herself in his way she was going to get hurt.

He turned right, toward the east passage and its row of narrow cubicles. One of the old monks' cells would make an adequate morgue for now. He dropped his burden in the first, then went to get the other body. The pair would join the sniper later tonight.

Nick wondered who else in the organization might know about him. The fact that Terrell had come here himself, and with only two men, indicated a certain lack of family sanctioning. Apparently they were settling back into the status quo, leaving Terrell to his own battles now that his attempted coup had failed. Failure carried the mark of Cain. Killing Nick Vears might have satisfied a personal vendetta, but it wouldn't have redeemed Terrell in the families' eyes.

And that had made him vicious. And careless.

Unless Nick was misreading the situation—again—this project was over.

When he passed the open archway door, the retching had stopped. He heard water running faintly.

"You could have killed me," Danielle had said. She was right.

But with Terrell it wouldn't have been a tossup.

Hoisting Manetti's body, he remembered Sara. She'd been alone in the chapel for some time. Was she all right? The question hovered in Nick's mind, growing sharper as he retrieved the Auto Mag and headed back toward the temporary morgue. He thought about the open tunnel. He didn't like the thought.

A breath of cold wind brushed by him as he dumped Manetti's body next to his dead boss and laid the big pistol in the corner with Terrell's .45.

He'd told Sara to stay put. Was she a child who did as she was told?

He left the tiny chamber with its grim contents and started up the passage toward the branch. With every step the picture of that gaping hole grew clearer, more defined. It beckoned him with a lure akin to worry, drawing him, whispering to him *come see . . . come see.* Would it also whisper to a child?

"Vears?"

The Grant woman was standing at the end of the corridor leading from the main house.

He glanced at her and kept walking. "Not now."

"Vears, wait a minute. Please!" She stepped into

his path, breaking his stride. "You *can't* get Sara yet."

Her face was pale in the dimness, shiny from splashing. Tendrils of damp hair had been raked back off her forehead. She was breathing heavily.

He started to move past her but she refused to budge. "Dammit, Vears, do you want her to see that wall?"

He heard her, but he was listening to something else . . . *something* . . .

"I can go stay with her while you get rid of it."

Nick didn't want her in the chapel. "No."

"Vears, for God's sake—"

"Be quiet."

She surprised him by lapsing into silence.

He didn't know what had alerted him—instinct again? Motioning her into the passageway and up against the inner wall, he unholstered the Ruger and glanced toward the archway.

Someone had entered the house. Nick felt it on the back of his neck. Had there been another man with Terrell, then?

Nick felt his jaw tighten at the possibility that he might have misjudged yet another situation. He checked his back. Nothing. Danielle stood in the shadows, hollow-eyed and motionless, jammed against the wall.

Dismissing her from his conscious thoughts, he began tracing his earlier route: through the archway . . . left, to the wall . . . use the recessed doorways . . .

The ocean droned steadily in the background, waves thudding on rock. An occasional gull shrieked; sea wind roamed the house

and something else.

Nick pinpointed the minute sound—like the rustle of cloth on stone.

He swung out from beneath the stairs, going low, gun raised—and almost squeezed the trigger.

"Freeze!" Lew Harris shouted from the doorway of the great room. He was crouched in firing position, gun leveled at Nick.

They hung there, locked in place, holding each other at bay.

Nick was the first to move. He slowly relaxed his muscles, stood, reholstered the automatic.

Harris followed suit, except he did not return the six-inch Smith to its cradle. Instead, he took a couple of steps forward. "What the hell did you bring in here with you, Vears—a goddamn war?" He glanced around at the chunk that had been gouged from one wall, the gory splatter on another, then back at Nick.

Nick decided it was time to draw some lines. "I don't have to explain myself to you, Harris. Stay out of this. It isn't your concern."

Lew regarded him steadily, and a subtle resolve flickered, then hardened in his eyes. "It can be." He took another couple of steps forward. "And I don't give a fuck who you are."

So, Lew had heard from his hacker. For a moment Nick didn't answer, then he said: "This war's over. Put away your gun or use it."

Harris remained static, studying Nick with an expression that had probably greeted sundry felons and low-lifes through prison bars and across interrogation tables over the years. Then he holstered the Smith.

"Just tell me one thing, Vears." Harris straightened his jacket over the holster. "Could your 'war' have encroached on the Grant family?"

Nick didn't waver. "It's possible—not probable. Do I get your help on this?"

Harris's expression was tight. "I thought it was cooperation you required."

The misnomer startled Nick, then he realized he did want more than just cooperation from Lew Harris.

The sound of hesitant footsteps in the hallway behind broke their deadlock. Harris tensed, reaching for his weapon, and Nick said, "Danielle Grant," then louder, "it's all right."

She came forward, looking first at him, then Harris, avoiding the wall. "If you two are all done with your Crockett and Tubbs routine, there's a little girl who needs attention."

Nick heard her concern beneath the brittle sarcasm, and something inside him shifted focus. He felt a prick of disquiet. It was as if part of his mind was receiving sporadic transmissions, subliminals garbled and mutated—of the chapel—the gaping tunnel—and something beyond . . . something cold and bright . . .

"Stay here."

He brushed past Danielle without giving Lew a backward look. If they followed him, so be it.

The old passageway felt colder than before, darker, the air heavy and thick. Nick felt a small muscle pulsing in the side of his jaw as he reached the chapel door; he realized his teeth were clenched.

Without a pause he shoved it open, eyes scanning the room. "Sara?"

She didn't respond. He stepped inside, closing and latching the door behind him. Quickly he moved between two benches and up the aisle to the spot where he'd left her. She was no longer there.

He looked toward the altar. Nothing had changed. The steps still yawned from its base, merging into darkness and offering a sudden, flagrant premonition of danger.

Nick bolted forward, jerking out his flashlight as his feet ate up the distance, flipping it on. The beam raked the tunnel, spotlighting the steps as he dropped to a crouch at the edge of the hole.

All was as before. There were footprints, not child-sized and covered with a dull patina of dust.

He started to rise again—

Distortion claimed his vision, as if blood had rushed to his brain. He shook his head to clear it and the humming in his ears. Wavery light seemed to hover at the bend in the stairs, like heat radiating off a metal surface. Yet the air from the tunnel felt cold. It touched his hair, his skin, silken fingers that spread like the liquid feel of cool, scented oil. The sense of danger subsided; a strange harmony took its place. He heard a faint whisper—of the sea? the wind? He leaned forward—

(No!)

Nick jerked around, the sound of her voice cutting through the distortion and bringing him to his feet. Her cry had come from behind him.

He strode back down the aisle, not bothering to check each bench he passed.

In the rear of the chapel he found her, bundled into a corner, looking small and afraid. She had a stranglehold on her stuffed animal. She winced in the beam of his flash—and for a split second Nick thought something in front of her had refracted the light, like a mirror or glass.

He turned it off, pocketed it, bent down. *(Sara?)*

She didn't answer, but Nick sensed fear ebbing and thought he detected the ghost of a smile.

He picked her up and went back to the door, wondering if Harris and Danielle would be waiting outside. No, he decided; the Grant woman would have been banging the door down by now.

He locked up the chapel and pocketed the key. He was going to check out that tunnel just as soon as he could get back down here—

Small arms tightened around his neck. He had a sudden contradictory impulse.

He frowned. "What is it?"

She said nothing, just held on tightly—to him, to her Fuzzy.

Pressing her face against his shoulder, he carried her through the archway door, past the pair standing silent in the hall, up the stairs. Someone followed them, the Grant woman.

Then they were in Sara's room and he was sitting her down on the bed. Danielle came in and he left them and went back down to Harris.

Lew had shed his coat, rolled up his sleeves, and was cleaning the wall. A bucket of sudsy water sat by his feet. It reeked of ammonia. The set of his jaw was grim.

Without a word Nick picked up a dry towel from beside the bucket, doused it thoroughly, and went to work. Within minutes, most of the litter produced by the special-design hollow point bullet had been removed.

Harris gave Nick a disgusted stare as he tossed his towel into the bucket. "I suppose you'll take care of this too."

Nick threw his towel on top of the other one, picked up the bucket. Hostility didn't concern him—as long as it didn't get in his way.

"I wasn't exactly talking about the bucket." Harris followed him down the hall to the bath. "I was talking about the rest of what was on that wall."

"I know."

"Shit," Lew muttered, then loomed in the doorway while Nick emptied the contents of the bucket into the john and flushed it. He watched him wring out the towels, then wrap them in a plastic trash can liner for disposal. "Have you got any information about the Grant thing you'd like to share?" The question came grudgingly.

Nick rinsed the bucket with alcohol, stashed it beneath the sink, then washed and dried his hands. Pulling out his cigarettes, he turned, shook one out and offered it to Lew, who declined. "Sara said something about seeing 'rock people' from the terrace last night." He put the cigarette in his mouth, lit it.

"Rock people?" That obviously had not been the reply Lew was expecting.

Nick leaned back against the sink. "Said they came out of the rocks."

"Ghost stories, Vears?"

"Maybe."

Lew frowned. "I take it you're aware of the local legends?"

Nick nodded, thoughtful. "Something was frightening Carole." He drew deeply and slowly blew out the smoke.

Tabling that line of thought for the moment, Lew asked: "Has she said anything else, anything about that night?"

Nick shook his head. He was going to have to have that talk with Sara.

Lew returned to the previous topic. "So, unless you've started to believe the tales about The Ridge, what you're suggesting is that someone around here could be playing ghost."

Nick took another draw, exhaled heavily and looked at Lew. "It's a valid point."

Lew thought a moment. "If someone was using this old house before the Grants moved in—say for drug running or as some sort of secret meeting place—they might use that method to try and scare them away."

"And kill them if they didn't go."

Lew's expression became rigid. "They chose one helluva way to get their point across."

Nick shrugged, meeting the look. Neither of them

were naive about the things people could do to one another.

But Lew was right. It was not a choice designed to avoid attention. He took a final draw and dropped the half-finished butt into the toilet. It hissed and died. A small curl of smoke trailed upward.

A number of questions still remained unanswered, chief among them how Sara had escaped. "Any explanation of that circle or what killed them?"

"Not yet." Lew's eyes narrowed slightly, and he looked away. "I need some air."

Nick followed him out to the terrace. The sun was warm, the wind had fallen. They stood in silence, watching the sea.

He lit another cigarette and thought about that circle in the middle of the great room floor. Everyone seemed anxious to avoid the subject, yet he felt more strongly than ever that it was a key. He thought about the tunnel, decided he wasn't ready to share that knowledge yet, not until he checked it out himself. Somehow he felt he held a proprietary interest in what was happening here.

He turned to see Danielle step through the French window. She'd regained some of her color, but her face was still drawn.

"Sara's sleeping." She answered the unasked question as she joined them—had it been in his eyes?

"Tell me, Miss Grant." Harris claimed her attention. "Did your brother or sister-in-law, or the child, ever say anything about the 'rock people'?"

She seemed startled by the question. "Not much that I recall. Carole made a joke once about the girl with the orange hair, said she looked like one of David's paintings run amok. Why?"

Nick and Lew stared at each other.

"What has that got to do with anything?" Danielle insisted, glancing from one man to the other, settling on Lew. "Who *was* that bastard, anyway? Why did he kill David? I want some answers, goddammit! And where are your people? Are you just going to leave that body lying around here someplace?"

"Mr. Vears will explain," Lew said quickly, ignoring Nick's frown.

Nick watched him walk away without a backward glance. His cigarette tasted suddenly flat. He flicked it toward the rocks.

"I don't understand. Where's he going?" She moved up to the parapet, facing him. Tiredness and confusion dulled her eyes. Nick decided he preferred the spark of anger. The thought annoyed him.

"I didn't ask."

"And I suppose that means I shouldn't either?" Her voice mocked, but the husky tone had lost its bite. She studied him a moment, then turned to gaze out over the ocean. "Look, Vears, I don't want to fight with you. Explanations can wait. I'm too tired. Just tell me what you're going to do about Sara."

"Not now, Danielle." Was he trying to provoke a fight? He lit another cigarette.

She turned back to face him. "When? The nightmare is over. You killed the man responsible, didn't you?" Her eyes searched his face and suddenly clouded with doubt. *"Didn't you?"*

He glanced at her, saw the dark circles from stress and lack of sleep, saw the laugh lines well etched from frequent use.

His annoyance deepened.

"Answer me, *dammit!* What's going on here?" Her voice was hoarse with emotion, choked with the memory of what she'd been through.

He took a deep drag from the cigarette, exhaled sharply. "Nothing—"

"Liar! Can you promise me Sara's not in any more danger? Can you guarantee she'll be all right?"

Nick tossed his cigarette over the wall. The wind had died, the sea was calm. Afternoon sun spread warmly across the terrace.

But the look in his eyes was chill. "I don't make promises. And there are never any guarantees."

The hands at her sides tightened, the eyes that met his held disdain. "Then I'm taking Sara out of here."

"That choice isn't yours."

"Dammit, Vears." Pain quivered behind the dark anger in her voice, her eyes. "I want to trust you— you saved my life. Why do you have to be such a bastard?" She turned around and went back into the house.

He watched her go, feeling stillness settle down in her wake. It should have erased his annoyance. It didn't.

Lew sprinted down the driveway to where he'd left his car, jumped in, and backed it out onto the beach road. It was a hell of a lot easier coming down that hill than climbing up it, he reflected, particularly with the sound of gunshots ringing in your brain and not knowing what to expect.

He'd heard the shot almost immediately upon making the turn into The Ridge's drive, and had decided that a one-man cavalry stood a better chance sneaking in than charging. Why hadn't he radioed for backup?

Lew gunned the car forward on this thought, realizing the consideration hadn't even been made. "Sliding in deeper and deeper, aren't you, Lew?" he muttered. "Learning the rules of CYA." Except in this case it was Vears's ass he was covering, not his own. Wasn't it?

"Shit."

He tried to clear his mind of unpleasant thoughts, of sarcasm and name-calling and self-flagellation. Forget about compromises and scruples. Forget about what was in the rocks and on that wall and how you almost shot Vears—or maybe the other way around. Just think about doing your job, about checking out this new lead and maybe solving this case while you've still got something left of yourself. Or the self you thought you were.

He rolled down his window and let the wind blow hard against his face as the car sped down the road at better than sixty miles an hour. Perspiration filmed his forehead and upper lip, cool in the breeze.

The old two-story house Set Reynolds and his group rented was coming up on his left. Lew slowed, passed a dark gray Chevy going in the other direction—looked like that rag reporter—and braked for the turnoff. The routine ID checks on these kids had been relatively clean: some minor traffic violations, a misdemeanor charge on Michaels for possession, nothing on Reynolds. And Curly had vouched for their behavior since they'd moved here.

Had they missed something important?

"Rock people." The ghosts of a little girl's nightmare, or a group of punk rockers?

"Let's find out." He pulled the car in behind a new Toyota van—the Gerrard girl had money—parked, and got out. Music pounded in the background, though not as loudly as he'd expected. Stereo or live band? he wondered, surprised at the quality of the sound. It had a jazzy sort of beat he liked.

His question was answered when, after climbing

the stairs and knocking on the door once, then harder, he heard the music grind to a staggered halt, followed by a couple of serious curses and complaints about more interruptions.

"Cool it," he heard someone masculine say. Footsteps approached the door, which swung open to reveal a tall, blond-haired youth with clear green eyes that seemed to look past Lew rather than at him. "Can I help you?"

"Possibly." Lew felt bypassed by those eyes. "I'm Agent Harris with the North Carolina SBI—" he flashed his shield—"investigating what happened at The Ridge—"

"Oh, sure," the young man said, and the look in his eyes became direct and sincere. Had Lew just imagined that faraway gaze? "Come on in. I remember seeing you up at The Ridge." He ushered Lew inside.

The room was a jumble of musical instruments connected to amplifiers and microphones by a tangle of wires. How did these groups keep from electrocuting themselves? Standard furniture was at a premium, but Lew roughly guessed there was thousands of dollars' worth of equipment in here. He noticed a large, computerized board up against one wall.

"Sorry to interrupt. This shouldn't take long." He eyed the other members of the band as they eyed him. Expressions ran the gamut from annoyed to cautious to bored. Lew's gaze rechecked the kid with the cautious look.

In appearance, they didn't veer far from any number of clone groups he'd glimpsed on MTV while switching channels—except for the little angel in the middle that looked like she should be decorating the top of a Christmas tree.

And Set Reynolds himself. He turned back to the tall, slender youth whose relaxed pose seemed completely honest, nothing ventured, nothing feigned. Unless Lew missed his guess, the clothes were designer quality. Generous girlfriend, or profitable sideline?

"Hey, no problem, man. We were just rehearsing for our gig tonight. At Hot Tamales down the beach. Ocean Pier, you know?"

Lew shook his head. "Sorry. From out-of-town."

"Yeah, well . . . What can we do for you?"

"Just routine checks of the residents in this area. See if you heard anything, saw anyone, things like that. Were you at home that night?"

"Sure were. Like, we already talked about it, and none of us saw or heard anything. Man, when we're into the music, that's all there is. Totally. Know what I mean? You have to bang on the door to get our attention."

Perfect fit; just like the Valley rap. "So you were practicing at home that night. All night?"

"Well, no, man." Set smiled indulgently. "Not *all* night. But probably till three or four o'clock. Like, that's not unusual." He didn't ask the others for confirmation. He hadn't even glanced at them once.

The leader of the pack. For sure.

It didn't really matter. They'd back one another up under cursory questioning. And Lew didn't have enough to haul them in. Yet.

"I appreciate your time." He turned to smile his thanks at the silent group and get one more look at the skinny kid with the glasses. It paid off. That kid was scared.

Satisfied, he walked to the door. "Oh, by the way," he spoke loudly enough for all to hear. "Chief Glenn received an anonymous tip that night about something going on at The Ridge. Any idea who it might have been?"

"Anonymous tip?" Set murmured, glancing straight at the kid with the glasses, then back at

Lew. "Why, no sir. No idea at all. You guys?" He polled the group with his eyes, then shrugged. "Sorry." He grinned.

"Thanks anyway." Lew stopped outside and the door shut behind him.

He stood there a moment, hoping to catch some careless remark, but none were forthcoming and he descended the stairs. Halfway back to the car he heard the music start up again, a fast, syncopated piece that made you want to beat time to the rhythm. These kids were good. Real good.

Lew wondered what else they might be.

Russ Reikert drove back into town, satisfied with the way his story was shaping up so far. All sorts of tie-ins were possible: from this hokey shit the locals kept laying on him about "Ancients" to those punkers he'd just left, who'd make great fodder for the readers who thought rock records were demonic spells cast backward. A few suggestions here, couple of references there—he'd have the Jesus-freaks believing this whole thing at The Ridge was step one in some Satanic master plot to rid the world of family and the bomb.

And for the sex angle, there was this little shack-up between the kid's old man and that Grant bitch, he'd seen her doing the Harriett Homemaker bit and followed her out to the house. He'd known she'd checked out of the inn, and had finally managed to get the low-down on that jerk who'd passed himself off as a cop. That was one motherfucker who was gonna be sorry he'd crossed Russ Reikert.

Only one thing still nagged him: what those kids had been up to last night. He'd tried to trip them on it without luck. They'd probably rehearsed their story the same way they rehearsed their music. No way were they going to talk about their little night jaunt up to The Ridge, and Russ wasn't about to say he'd seen them. Not yet, anyway.

He recalled the strange apparition on the beach, still not certain it had been one of the group. But if not—who? Was there something else going on at that house, something that could add a blockbuster touch to an already sensational story?

Russ planned to pay another visit to The Ridge tonight, check out those old ruins where he'd seen the kids go. Could be there *was* some devil worship going on—what a headline that would make: SATAN-ROCKERS CLAIM HUMAN SACRIFICES WHILE RELATIVES HOLD DEATH ORGY. He could see it now.

He wished he could go ahead and search the place while it was still daylight. But he didn't want to take the chance. He had a feeling that dude in the house could get mean.

He flipped on the radio, got nothing but static and some redneck music, and flipped it back off again. Actually those kids hadn't been half bad, from what he'd heard when he'd driven up. They'd mentioned a gig tonight down the beach. Maybe he'd stop in later, after he'd finished at The Ridge, see what the local night life had to offer, he could use a little beach action.

Yeah. Sounded good.

Russ began whistling a riff that had stuck in his mind, realized it was what those kids had been playing. Catchy tune. He whistled it again.

15

Dusk drained the beach of color. Murky waves folded over dingy sand. Oblong clouds drifted across the fading edge where the sun had lately sunk from view. Above, an occasional star glimmered weakly in the darkening sky.

Set's feet kicked up small sand showers behind him as he jogged, intent on the rocky cliff growing nearer with each step. A flock of gulls circled lazily above one section of the rocks, taking turns swooping down to peck at something that must be providing their evening meal. Their calls raced out to chase the surf away, then seemed to ride back to shore on the wind.

Set loosed the leather thong that held his hair and shook out the strands as he ran, letting the wind blow the mass away from his face. There wasn't much time; they had to start packing the van soon. He was taking a chance coming here this early.

But he'd had to come. He needed the stone tonight, needed to feel the Power.

Shit was rolling in on him. They couldn't stick

around much longer. Soon they'd be out of here, hit the tour circuit—maybe book a few one-nighters at first, but then . . .

That cop showing up this afternoon had cracked it. The fucker had a look about him, and Set knew they'd be seeing him again.

Spinning around, he jogged backward, searching for signs of life. The beach was deserted; faint light from the house he'd just left twinkled in the distance. He could picture the scene, the others bridging time until the gig: Mitch laid back with a joint; Vesper laid back with Mitch; Twyla sorting through clothes and deciding which earrings to wear; and Hump . . .

Set swung back around, made a sprint for the rocks.

. . . good old Hump, who had to be the one who'd tipped the law, retreating to the anonymity of his stereo headphones.

The unspoken accusation burned inside Set like a smoldering bed of fire. He'd withheld the words because it was not yet time; they had a show to do tonight. And nothing was as important as a show—nothing could compromise his music. They were moving, now—fixing to fly. He couldn't take a chance on anything getting in the way.

"They're gonna love us," Set whispered to the wind and felt it nod. He smiled. *They're gonna love us.*

No one stirred in the house on the cliff. A couple of lights had been turned on, and a flickering light, like from a fireplace, lit one downstairs window, but there was nothing to indicate that anyone was watching the beach. Set stayed low, merging with the rocks, angling a little farther away from the house than usual, just in case.

A breaker hit behind him, drawing a clamor from the gulls. The tide coming in.

With the wind a steady hand at his back, Set scrambled through the ruins to the tunnel entrance, quickly scanned the area one final time, then shoved the stone aside just enough to squeeze through. Once inside, he levered it back into place and made his way forward, not bothering to grab a lantern when he reached the cave.

The soft glow hung in the distance, seeming to pulse slightly as he moved along the path, then grow stronger, as though it recognized him, drawing him on. Set's breathing quickened; he'd been right to come.

Wind followed him in: sliding around and past him, almost pulling him along. He felt like he was coming home.

He reached the inner cave, and for a moment stopped to fill his senses with light. It was still here. Whatever had gone wrong with the ritual last time hadn't affected it. The Mindstone was still here.

Only now did Set acknowledge the fear that had been hiding deep within him: that he'd return to an empty cavern, an empty dream; that there'd be no light, no stone, no music; that it would all have vanished, or perhaps never been.

He gazed at the stone lying before him in the sand. Its light reached out to him, comforting, reassuring. The Power stirred. He could hear the crowds whispering his name ... louder ... louder ... He could taste the excitement, feel their adoration.

Tonight he'd show these little people what he could do—make them gasp beneath the touch of his music. And after tonight there would be no more waiting, no more falling short.

And no more dreams. They were done with dreams.

Laughter frothed out of him like sudden orgasm. Brightness touched his mind.

He squeezed his eyes to hold it deep inside. The light would go with him tonight, *be* with him, like the parting caress of a lover.

He stood embracing it, quivering from the tingle on his skin, drinking it through his pores. Every nerve, every sense, vibrated to bursting, making Set grasp this moment of life as keenly as a person must in the instant before death.

And suddenly he wanted to stay like this forever, poised on the very edge of all he'd ever hoped for, seeing his dream spread out before him like a glittering array of footlights and fans. It would never be this way again.

Sadness touched him, softly, fleeting, as though glimpsed from childhood memory; then it was gone.

But the light remained.

He opened his arms wide, stretched them outward and upward and for a moment thought he glimpsed another vision, another Light. Then it, too, was gone.

Tonight—after the gig they'd come back here, complete the rituals. He'd make them come, *all* of them, even Hump. And there were people upstairs in the house again. He'd use them too, if that's what it took. Whatever he had to do, however he had to do it, he'd make it work this time.

Leaving the cave, Set followed his track through the narrow tunnel, out into the starlit night. The soft breeze traveled with him, stroking him gently as he rolled the concealing stone in place and headed back across the sand.

Russ had known that his luck was bound to change. Part of being a good investigative reporter was trusting your instincts, and being behind the right rock at the right time. He'd known something was squirming under the surface of this place—metaphorically, he'd thought, not literally. But what the hell. Whatever it was, he was about to find out.

Leaving the tumbled pile of stones, he made his way as quickly and silently as possible across the ruins to where he'd seen that kid emerge. He'd gotten here just in time, apparently. Another drink in the bar—he'd have missed the whole thing.

A fast glance around, couple of grunting shoves, and he rolled the circular stone away from the mouth of what looked like a cave or a tunnel.

Tunnel from the looks of it.

Russ shone his small pocket flashlight around inside the opening, squatting to probe the light forward as far as it would go. The damn thing looked like it got narrower farther in, but marks in the sand indicated recent passage and hell, if that kid could make it, so could Russ.

He listened for a moment, heard nothing stir, and squeezed into the tunnel.

He'd been smarter tonight in his choice of attire: jeans and a cotton sweater. Of course they were quality threads, to the combined tune of several hundred bucks, but they could both stand a drenching, though it didn't look like rain. Still, these little beach squalls could come up in a heartbeat.

He considered rolling the stone back and decided against it. The thought of being shut up in here was suddenly claustrophobic. He'd rather take the chance of someone happening by.

Shining the flashlight ahead, he inched farther in, steering his thoughts away from things like rats and bats and snakes and booby traps—

That stopped him cold. He roamed the light around the tunnel. What if those kids had the place wired—and Russ didn't mean bugging. There'd been four exploded bodies up in that house. Was he taking an unsmart chance here?

He thought about it, decided he was psyching

himself out again, began moving once more. Those kids didn't strike him as demolition experts, and he doubted they'd risk the tunnel. Apparently this was their way in and out.

It wouldn't hurt to take a little extra care, though. Never know what might be lurking behind a rock.

Russ grinned, then shivered as a breeze tickled the hairs on the back of his neck. A rash of goosebumps grazed his arms. Getting colder in here? Probably. Being inside a cave meant lower temperatures. But the air felt unusually heavy. Close.

He moved ahead slowly, almost on hands and knees, patting the sand in front of him and shining the flashlight back and forth with each step, grunting softly with the effort. Just when he thought he couldn't go any farther, he spied the tunnel's mouth. Immediate reassurance. He wouldn't have wanted to back out of here.

Heaving his body through the opening, Russ found himself in a large chamber. He looked around, shining light into all the nooks and crannies. The cavern was bigger than he'd imagined from outside, and apparently extended even farther; he spotted a couple of exits. Was this whole cliff honeycombed?

Spying two lanterns, he decided to take one. Might need more light up ahead. Better be prepared.

For an instant, a feeling of dread washed over him, scary, eerie, like maybe he'd tunneled into somebody's crypt and maybe he shouldn't disturb it. He remembered that the house above him had once been a monastery, and the thought crossed his mind that he just might have stumbled into the monks' old burial chambers.

He felt for the small camera that swung from a strap tucked inside his sweater, fingered it as though it were a talisman. *Quality points for grisly pix*. That got him moving again.

One larger passage led from the cave, branching left and right after only a few yards. Tracks led right; it looked to be a well-traveled path. Russ considered the possibility of becoming lost in the catacombs. Not a pleasant scenario. Then he saw the fishing line. *Bingo*.

Right.

Just for an instant, he thought he heard people whispering, the low hum of conversation. Was someone still in here?

Quickly Russ turned off the lantern, pocketed the flashlight, and stood silent in the darkness. As his eyes adjusted to the lack of light, he became aware of a faint glow.

Oops.

What should he do now? Initial thought: Leave. Come back later. He did *not* want to get caught in anything sticky down here.

A current of cool air flowed gently toward him.

On the other hand, how bad could it be? He was already in, and traveling that narrow tunnel too many more times held no appeal whatsoever. Maybe he could just take a quick look, see what was going on. Might even get a couple of shots.

Pulling out the camera, Russ eased forward, moving toward the light.

The air current swirled around him; it had a liquid, oily feel. Not unpleasant.

He'd be careful. He wouldn't get caught.

The air seemed to finger him, glide across his skin, cold, thick. Inviting.

It would be all right . . .

Nick placed another stick of wood on the growing fire and sat back on his heels, idly watching the flames take hold. Behind him, Sara sat quietly on the couch, observing—the way she'd done all afternoon.

She'd hardly been five steps away since he'd come inside, intending to go check out that tunnel, and found her standing, staring down at him from the balcony. Danielle had been nowhere in sight, though he'd heard sounds coming from the kitchen.

He'd decided the tunnel could wait. It was time to get the answers to questions that had been pending much too long. He'd changed directions and gone upstairs, meaning to lead Sara slowly toward remembering, willing not to rush her. He'd gotten nowhere. She'd countered every probe.

He'd sensed her studying him, as she had the night before, and recognized the potential situation: lose one parent, find another. Something he could never be. Still, he didn't want to push it.

Later they'd eaten a meal the Grant woman had prepared, something with chicken in it, sitting silent in the kitchen as day gave way to night. Danielle had surprised him; she'd stopped the questions. It was almost as though they were all waiting for something to happen, himself included. But what?

Harris had called, more to see if Sara had said anything else than to give the terse report that Raleigh was running thorough checks on her "rock people" and he was going to stop by their gig tonight. Nick had almost smiled, recalling Lew's first visit to him at the beach house. Being stalked by Harris was not without its downside risk.

If those kids were responsible, Harris would soon find out.

But how had they done it?

Probably nothing more than a minor drug ring operating out of this old house, and David Grant had unknowingly gotten in their way.

and what about the circle?

They'd find the paraphernalia down in that tunnel—no doubt it led out to the beach—stuff brought in by boat.

and those hallucinations?

Nick prodded the fire and wondered what it was about this whole thing that kept throwing it so totally out of context. There was a wild card here. Did Sara know what it was?

She stirred slightly, and he put the poker down and turned to look at her, catching a glimpse of uncertainty in her eyes—and something else that had hovered there ever since he'd found her squeezed into the far corner of the chapel: fear.

"What is it you're afraid of, Sara?"

She winced.

He laced his hands loosely in front of him, arms balanced on his legs, watched her study him. The fire on his back was warm. "Tell me."

She squeezed her eyelids closed, then opened them again.

Her eyes seemed huge and shimmery and deep in the small pale face. Firelight glittered in them, reflecting off the corneas as if they were made of polished blue glass, like the black button eyes on her Fuzzy.

She hugged it to her.

"You've been stalling me all afternoon." He watched her fidget beneath his gaze. She looked tired. But this time he wasn't letting up so easily. "Why?"

Her words came muffled from behind the Fuzzy. "It hurt Mommy."

Nick felt his heartbeat quicken. He kept his voice soft. "What did, Sara?"

Her voice trembled. "It wants to hurt you, too."

He frowned. Was he understanding this? Was Sara's fear for him?

"I won't let it," he said quickly, reassuringly, attempting to get them both back on track.

She looked up at him then, eyes blazing in the tightly drawn face. Nick felt stripped by her gaze, laid bare to the bone—and for just a moment felt some sort of role reversal take place, as though he were the child and she the parent.

Her voice came low and intense. "Promise!"

He started to give the lie, say *I promise;* wasn't that what parents were supposed to do for their kids? The words he'd spoken to Danielle bruised his mind: "*I don't make promises, there are no guarantees.*"

"I can't," he said quietly.

She continued to look at him, but the piercing quality slowly drained away. Behind him, flames crackled in the fireplace. A log popped, sending a shower of sparks spiraling toward the chimney; he could see them reflected in her eyes. She seemed to suddenly droop with fatigue.

He should send her out of here tonight, or at least back to the beach house with the Grant woman, give himself room to move. He saw the fear still clinging to her eyes, felt it trigger a vague sense of alarm in him, and for an instant thought he could see something swimming, like an undercurrent, just beneath the surface of that thought.

The moment stretched between them like a tenuous bond—and Nick realized he couldn't allow this net Sara was attempting to weave around them to take too firm a hold. Soon he'd be gone, out of her life like he'd never existed. She didn't need another loss to contend with.

She frowned.

He welcomed the Grant woman's interruption. They both turned to see Dani at the door—except the door was closed. Then it opened.

"I think it's time Sara took her bath and got ready

for bed," Danielle said from the threshold. She didn't enter the room, just stood in the doorway and waited.

Nick glanced sharply at Sara, but she wouldn't look at him now.

Clasping her Fuzzy to her, she slid off the couch, small shoulders straight and determined as she walked to the door. There was something about the set of those shoulders that made Nick feel rebuked.

He watched them leave the room, relieved to be alone. Being around them was ... unsettling— something he rarely felt. He had no explanation for whatever this thing was between him and Sara. It kept throwing him off balance—*as though a door was being opened just slightly, just enough for him to get a glimpse, then slammed in his face.*

And he was oddly annoyed at Danielle's continued reserve.

She was walking an emotional tightrope, Nick realized, afraid of the questions she wasn't asking, afraid of the answers that might come if she did. He could have told her not to worry, that he wasn't going to take Sara. He hadn't. She wouldn't have believed him anyway.

He rose, picked up the poker and began stirring coals, clearing his mind of extraneous thoughts. By tomorrow this thing might be over, or far enough along to leave it in Harris's capable hands. He could be gone from here, back to the pocket of existence he'd created for himself.

Nick laid the poker aside, went and stretched out on the couch. The pickup team was due sometime after midnight. They would arrive by boat. He had two more bodies to add to the one on the beach before then. And there was still that tunnel to be checked out.

But it was too early, yet. With Sara and Danielle awake his movements were restricted. He'd wait awhile, let night settle in, get a couple of hours sleep.

Then he could take care of things.

The wind was blowing stronger, skimming through the tunnel in a steady current that seemed to sweep Russ along the path. It felt cold, clammy on his skin. It seeped through the porous sweater to his naked chest and sent another rash of goosebumps down his arms. He wished he'd worn a jacket.

But how could he have known spelunking would play a role in tonight's jaunt?

There must be another opening up ahead, Russ decided. Another opening causing the draft.

Light hazed the distance, like a giant's breath blown on frigid air. It sparkled as though filled with minute ice crystals. There was a sort of sepulchral radiance to it. He wondered if he'd find a crypt or shrine being tended by these kids, the residue of one cult forming the basis for another.

Good press. He crept forward.

He was nearing what looked like another cavern, where a rockslide or cave-in congested the walkway. He glanced up at the ceiling, not liking the thought of being buried in here himself, but it appeared sturdy enough. Apparently the falling rocks had come from that inner wall, the one where the light was shimmering—or had they been blasted away? Russ noted how the stones had fallen and the gaping hole they'd left. Which renewed his suspicion of a tie-in with the deaths upstairs.

Not a happy thought.

He began to have reservations about this, serious reservations. The kind of reservations that had R.I.P. carved on them.

Tentatively he moved forward, craning his neck to see into the inner chamber without revealing any more of himself than necessary. Little by little he made his way across the sandy floor, feeling his spine contract as he left the relative security of the passageway behind and entered the gaping exposure of the large outer cave.

But there was still the camouflage of darkness here; the light was centered in the chamber—like a stage, with him as the entire audience. Reassurance flooded him as he came to a standstill just beyond the rim of light. There was no one else in here, he was all alone—

"My God . . ." Amazement gripped him as he stared into the chamber. It was dazzling—theatrical. Russ's eyes traced spidery scrawls that covered the walls like hieroglyphics etched in gold. Unlit torches hung in ancient iron bracers set into the rocks, casting long, slender shadows among the sparkling stones. It was the backdrop for a Conan flick, he could almost hear the voices chanting, see the dancing acolytes.

"Ho—ly *shit*! What a story!"

Russ aimed his camera, remembered the lens cover, jerked it off and focused on the scene.

And saw the stone.

Slowly he brought the camera down from his eyes. "What the fuck—?" He took a couple of steps forward . . .

Something trembled on the air.

He glanced around. Didn't see anything. Looked back at the stone—or whatever it was. He'd never seen anything like that. Puddles of crystallized sand encircled it, small frozen channels ran from them and cut across the floor.

And the *light*.

Russ was almost blinded by the brilliance; it hurt his eyes, yet he couldn't seem to pull his gaze away. Cold tears shimmered across his vision and trickled down his cheeks like drops of melting ice.

His hands released the camera, and he felt it drop against his chest as he stepped closer to the stone.

Not a crystal. Too dense. A jewel, maybe. But what possible kind of jewel had such incredible radiance—

"Wait a minute . . ."

Uranium? Did uranium look like this? Oh, shit— Was he being nuked?

He started to step back, but his feet felt numb, frozen to the sand.

What was going on?

"Wait a minute!"

Fingers of light were spreading toward him, reaching for him, touching him. His skin began to tingle, like ants crawling over his body—an army of ants! They were crawling through this pores—

Inside!

A strangled cry spewed out of Russ, a cry of revulsion and disbelief and fear. His insides were on fire! Fire, in a shell of thick-ribbed ice.

Light poured into him from the stone—through his eyes, his nose, his mouth, held open now in a silent, frozen scream. It was invading every part of him, spreading through the nerves and cells like liquid flame!

A sudden burst of light flared from the stone, like a flashbulb going off in his face, searing vision from his screaming eyes. Still it flowed into him like a steady stream of blistering current, twitching, jerking him, as though he had hold of a naked wire and couldn't turn loose. He was burning up inside!

He tried to run, and couldn't; tried to scream— his mouth was filled with fire . . .

The snap of a log breaking apart woke Nick, a sudden flash of light. Sparks from the small eruption danced up the chimney. He swung his legs off the couch and sat up, staring into the flames. For a moment they seemed to reflect his eyes.

He ran a hand through his hair and stood, feeling a residue of unease prickling the back of his neck. Had he been dreaming?

Nick glanced at his watch and saw that only a few minutes had passed since he'd stretched out on the couch, hardly the nap he'd wanted; yet he felt totally alert. He frowned. Something was wrong.

His unease increased.

Leaving the den, he hesitated in the hallway, listening to sounds from upstairs that assured him everything there was as it should be, then headed down the corridor toward the archway door. Firelight seemed to accompany him, flickers of orange-red flames darting along in his path like huge snake tongues licking at the stones. They merged with the shadows, casting strange shapes on the walls and floor.

Nick unbolted the door into the old section, entered, and closed it behind him, leaving the flickering shapes behind. A finger of cool wind played across his skin.

Soft murmuring permeated the corridor, seeping from the stones with the damp night air. He'd never heard the ocean down here before. It was like holding a shell to your ear, the distant roar of unseen waves . . . cold . . . black . . .

Something *was* wrong in this house. Every instinct, every sense, came alive with it. This was no mirage, no illusion. He could taste it.

Taking the small flashlight from his pocket, he switched it on.

Particles of dust swam lazily on the chill air, sparkling like tiny ice crystals caught in the beam. A sudden gust set them swirling.

He pulled the Ruger from his shoulder holster and made the left turn into the passageway that led toward the chapel entrance, footsteps falling silent on the cold, hard stones.

The door was closed, as he had left it, padlock still in place. He listened, heard nothing, then slowly unfastened the lock and loosened the hasp. Using his foot he pulled the heavy door open, careful to stay on the wall's inward side. A rush of cold air flowed out to greet him.

Nick swung the beam around the chapel, searching for signs of an intruder. Emptiness stared back from the somber rows.

The light came to rest on the altar. He switched it off. A faint halo hovered in the air above the gaping hole.

Pocketing the flash Nick started forward, never taking his eyes off the glow as he edged between two benches, up the center aisle. It was time to find out just what was going on here.

He crouched at the lip of the cavity. The coating of dust on the stairway remained undisturbed. Whoever was down in that tunnel had not yet discovered this rift.

(Wait . . .)

For a moment Nick thought he heard somebody whisper, but it could have been the wind. He listened intently, keeping his senses focused, and caught another murmur from below.

Slowly he began his descent, holding the gun in his right hand while he braced against the wall with his left. The curve in the staircase inhibited his field of view. Every few steps he stopped, listened. The light was growing brighter; the murmur had become a muddy rush of sound.

Wind coiled around him, cooling the sweat that filmed his neck and upper lip. It seemed to nudge him gently, attach itself to his skin. Clammy. He wanted to reach up, peel it away.

He felt it recede.

Light greeted him as he stepped off the final riser onto a packed sand floor. A passage wound forward then twisted left. Nick followed it, slowing as he neared the turn. The light grew brighter.

It seemed to be moving, weaving toward and around him like the flame-shapes on the upstairs wall—undulating ribbons curling outward to meet him, bringing him inside—

Someone touched him!

Nick jerked around, shoving the hand aside. His eyes raked the passageway. There was no one there. Nothing lurked within the shadows; no one waited in the dark.

The murmuring of unseen voices mocked him. The empty darkness taunted his perceptions.

Was he having another hallucination?

Yet he'd felt that touch . . .

Grimly Nick began walking again, toward the light. Whatever was happening here, whatever twist of reality was being played out, he had to know its source.

The passage opened into a large cavern. Light spilled from a ragged hole in the far wall—brilliant, blinding. Nick moved forward, feeling a sudden urgency take hold of him. The air was crisp, excited. Energy hovered like a heavy charge of static electricity. It crawled across his skin, lifting the hairs on his arms and tingling his scalp and neck.

A whisper-chant vibrated his eardrums; its echo seemed to swell inside his head, fill his brain with coiling images, burning light.

A rush of wind moaned past, trailing a faceless shadow-image, scrabbling hands made of bone. It carried the sound of agony, and hate. He could smell the stale, burning stench of rotting flesh, feel the cold emptiness of despair. And through it all, an avid, hungry gasp for life.

Nick shook off the apparition, stepped into the opening—

And came to an abrupt halt.

A blur of incandescence and dazzling colors swirled at the center of the inner chamber. The blur became a body—a body embraced by light.

A small wince of reaction was the only betrayal that what Nick was seeing went beyond anything he'd seen before. The body was twitching uncontrollably. Fingers of light roamed and stroked it, entering in a thousand places, flowing out again.

He recognized the reporter that had visited him at The Ridge, though the face was distorted almost beyond recognition. Streaming light swept around and through the jerking torso; jagged, crackling wires of raw energy danced across skin.

Nick's eyes narrowed sharply. What was it? Some sort of spontaneous combustion? The man was a mass of crawling, sparking light—

The light spun toward Nick.

He felt it come; felt the heat of it, the searing cold, the tingle lick his skin. For a moment he stood mesmerized, watching it hurdle forward, unable to move—

He shoved it aside—*moving back . . . not moving at all*—and saw the light impact on the air in front of him, split apart and swirl to either side. It was as if he were suddenly encased in glass. Streams of light coiled around him; cold, glistening waves pounded to get in.

Nick hardly breathed, stunned by the reality of what was taking place. His mind tilted crazily. He could hear, but not feel; see, but not touch. He dragged air into his lungs and felt his chest constrict, as though oxygen had been sucked from the cave and he would have to fight for every breath. His movements felt sluggish, retarded. His thoughts fused.

(I'm coming—)

Sound roared outside the glass; muddied, distant. His ears felt stuffed with cotton. His mind had gone numb.

Beams of radiant energy zigzagged and whipped the air, crackling, popping through a maelstrom of blinding colors and brilliant light. He could still see Reikert's body at the center of the storm, buckling with the forces screaming through it.

He saw the skin begin to shrivel, crack apart as though a furnace raged inside, scorching the outer coating from within. Blood seeped through the cracks, bubbling in obscene patterns and dribbling onto the flow. A viscous, yellow substance erupted from the mouth and nose; bulging eyes liquified, spilling down the cheeks in wormlike rivulets that crawled onto the light. The body was evacuating itself, flooding from every pore and opening like molten rock from a volcano. Colors swam and bled together, running down onto the sand.

Nick's vision blurred—the glass encasing him wavered and thinned. Whatever he had done, whatever this barrier was, he was losing it.

Lightstreams darted across the air toward his eyes, licking at the weakness, trying to come in.

He pushed them back . . . barely.

Tiny cracks began to appear in front of him, spreading, growing, crazing outward like a windshield hit by a rock. He could still see Reikert—or what was left of Reikert—a hollow, glowing shell bleeding rays of light that quickly became tentacles reaching toward him

. . . back

spinning closer, wanting inside, wanting to touch, to join—

(NO!)

A glass wall crashed down in front of him.

Nick gasped long, slaking breaths of healing air,

shoving back the blackness that had been corrupted with dancing, sparkling light. He could see the cave again . . . see the withered, melting body that had been Reikert draining toward the sand.

Gradually strength returned. The cracks and fissures in the glass began to mend.

Outside, the cold light raged. Inside, Nick felt stronger than he'd ever felt in his life.

Slowly he turned around, feeling her presence before his eyes found her.

(Sara?)

(Come back)

She stood, small and seemingly defenseless, at the rear of the cavern, her eyes on him, not the light.

Could she be doing this? Could he?

(Come back COME BACK)

Nick stepped toward his daughter, a hesitant movement at first, then firmer, steady. It was as if a current of force flowed between them—from her, to him, then back again—some vital element that had lain dormant within him suddenly springing to life. The wall stayed in place, separating them from what was happening beyond. Strength seemed to radiate from him like waves of heat off a desert.

Another form took shape. Behind Sara. Danielle. She came toward them like a sleepwalker, eyes gripped by the horror Nick had put on hold. Was this *wall* protecting her too?

He glanced back and saw it shimmer, felt it tremble, grow thin—

(Sara?)

Her eyes had shifted to the light.

(Don't look!)

Had he spoken it? thought it? screamed it?

Again he felt the wall quiver and shoved his new-found strength against it, feeling them merge. The trembling stopped. But for how long?

(Sara!)

With difficulty, she dragged her gaze back to him and he felt the tremendous effort she was expending, realized his own.

He took charge then, running on adrenaline and raw nerve, knowing that whatever they were doing wasn't going to last.

"Go!"

He turned them back toward the passage, feeling an almost physical rending as Sara dashed on ahead, slinging Dani around and propelling her along—she seemed shellshocked. Sara was already scaling the steps when Nick reached them and boosted Dani up behind. He stayed with her, catching her once when she stumbled and would have fallen.

Dani came to herself as they sprinted across the chapel, light pouring in their wake from the gaping hole. He saw her grab Sara's hand and let them go on while he swung around and ran backward, scanning their rear for whatever might follow. Realizing he still had the gun in his hand, he thrust it in his belt.

Light spread after them like groping fingers, clutching at the dark, at them.

Nick dashed through the corridors to the branch and back into the main house, trailing the woman and child.

"Outside," he shouted—

and then they were all outside and running for the truck.

He snatched Sara up, disconnecting her from Danielle's hand, yelling: "I've got her. Go around."

Wrenching the door open, he thrust Sara inside and jumped in after her, firing the engine to life as Dani scrambled into the passenger seat.

He had the truck in motion before she'd shut the door, headed down the drive and out onto the beach road, gathering speed. His only thought was to get away. Everything else could wait.

"What was that thing—what *was* it?" Dani exclaimed. Her voice trembled on the brink of hysteria.

Nick shot her a look. "Get hold of yourself." The words came out hard and steady and had the desired effect. He rolled down his window and cool night air poured in, acting like a draft of elixir.

Danielle had wrapped her arms around Sara and was cradling the small body against her heaving chest. She glared at Nick over the child's head. "Of course *you're* taking this all in stride. What's another corpse, more or less? You kill people for a living!"

Nick glared back. "Not that way."

Their eyes clashed across Sara's head. Then Nick returned his attention to the road and Dani hugged the child who was softly whimpering.

The whimpers became words, whispered at first, then louder:

"It was the bright thing, the bright thing that killed Mommy and David and Karen and Jeffy, and it tried to get me too but I wouldn't let it in, wouldn't let it through the glass, and I watched it grow, saw it touch Mommy—and I tried to put her behind my glass, I really did, but I couldn't make it work right—and then it got loud and cold and the light hurt my eyes, and it made Mommy come apart and there was red swirling all around and sparkles hitting the glass and it wanted in but I wouldn't let it—*wouldn't let it*—"

"*Shh*, honey. Sara, it's all right. It's all right." Dani rocked and soothed the crying child, her tortured glance meeting Nick's eyes across the darkness.

Nick looked back at the road, beginning to slow for the turnoff to the beach house, drawing every ounce of discipline to keep his sanity intact. His hands felt welded to the steering wheel. His mind felt laid open, ripped bare from the separation in the cave.

That this was really happening he accepted. How it could be explained—or dealt with—was something else entirely.

Sara's crying quieted as he made the turn, blending with Danielle's softly crooned repeated words of comfort. The floodgates had opened for her, whatever good that might do. She now had all her horrors vividly at hand. His gut twinged at the thought of what his daughter had been carrying all this time, and would carry for the rest of her life.

He pulled the GMC into one of the slots beneath the beach house, not concerned with logistics at the moment. The past half hour had seen a number of priorities change.

They climbed the staircase, Nick carrying Sara. They didn't have a key. He handed the child to Dani and picked the lock—welcoming a problem he could deal with—then took her again and led the way into the house. They'd come away without anything, he realized, thinking grimly of the ECCO sitting on a shelf at The Ridge. Yet, if he had it, who would he call? What would he say? There were no requisition lists to deal with this.

Dani turned on a lamp in the living room, then followed them into the bedroom, pulling back the covers so that Nick could lay Sara on the bed, switching on a lamp. He smoothed the blankets back in place, bending over his daughter, brushing a strand of hair back from her tear-streaked face.

The child looked exhausted. Her face was pinched, white. Her eyes were deep holes beneath quivering lids; but the vivid blue that gazed up at him still glittered.

"Make it go away," she whispered, pinning Nick with those eyes when he would have risen.

He studied her closely, reexperiencing an awareness of the bond they'd shared in the cave. Just a touch. It was enough.

He was out of his depth, yanked from his controlled little world and thrust down in a totally alien environment where all his experience and training counted for nothing.

Make it go away?

How? How could he do that?

"I'll try." Nick hardly credited the words even as he heard himself say them.

But she nodded once, and was immediately asleep.

He felt the tautness that had gripped him lessen.

Straightening, he turned to Dani, who was standing nearby, white-faced, arms wrapped tightly around her. "I don't understand this. I don't understand any of this." Her voice was hushed. Her eyes held confusion, fear. And the horror of what she'd seen.

Nick released a slow breath. "Neither do I." He heard the exhaustion in his own voice. He needed to think.

"That . . . *thing*. That's what killed David . . . Carole . . . ?" She searched his eyes.

The answer must have been there.

"My God . . . We were staying in that house, *sleeping* there . . ." She shivered violently, clutching her arms tighter. "We could have all been—"

"We weren't." Nick took a step forward, put a hand on her arm. She didn't flinch. "We'll be safe here—"

"How can you know that?" she demanded.

He strengthened his grip. "I know."

Her eyes held his a moment longer, then, like Sara, she nodded once. Her body slowly relaxed.

"Try to get some rest," he said, and moved pas
her, out of the room. He needed to be alone.

Turning off the living room lamp, he went ove:
to the sliding glass door, unlocked and opened it
and stepped out onto the deck. Tangy salt winc
blew against his face and he drank it in, filling his
lungs with the fresh night air, opening his mind tc
the discoveries he'd made tonight—about The
Ridge, about himself . . .

There'd been a moment when he'd seen the truth
as clearly as it had been obscure before. Revelation
had come when he'd turned to Sara, looked into her
eyes. It was as if a door had opened, letting him see
the child behind the child, letting him glimpse inside himself. She'd known this about him all along,
that's what he'd sensed from her; known he possessed this . . . *ability*. He couldn't explain what it
was—maybe that would come later—but now he
knew it existed, had seen what it could do. And the
power was even stronger in his daughter. That
could not be denied.

A million questions still remained.

Nick pulled out a cigarette, lit a match. Wind ruffled the hair across his forehead and buffeted the
flame. He had to light another one.

What had they done, he and Sara? Formed some
sort of mental bond that generated physical barriers? Whatever that *thing* was at The Ridge, they'd
managed to protect themselves—and Dani—from it.
But how?

And what was it?

Nick's mind was a morass of questions. Questions without answers. He couldn't seem to pin
down his thoughts.

Tonight he'd entered a realm he hadn't known
existed. He was of course aware of on-going studies
in psychic phenomena, but it had always seemed a
bit too surreal for his well-grounded logic, and to

ate even the most promising results were akin to
minor card tricks. He pictured himself as a test
subject. He pictured Sara.

His eyes narrowed at the thought.

Taking a deep drag from his cigarette, Nick exhaled sharply and sent it spinning to the sand with
more force than necessary; a shower of sparks followed it down. There was no way he would allow
that to happen.

Make it go away . . .

Did that mean it was all up to him?

He breathed deeply of the crisp, salt air, trying
to regain some semblance of rational thought. The
night was still, hushed, like the eye of a storm. He
remembered the feeling he'd had earlier tonight,
the feeling that they were waiting for something to
happen. It was still with him.

Nick lit another cigarette, stood smoking, watching the waves roll in to shore. They spread onto the
sand in staggered coils, leaving a trail of foam to
dissipate as they drained back toward the sea. His
thoughts were becoming lost in their rhythm, scattered, whisked apart like the fragile bubbles on the
wind.

He sensed he was reaching his saturation point.

Tossing his cigarette to the sand, he went back
inside, glancing in on Sara as he passed the open
bedroom door.

She was deeply asleep—Nick recognized the
vague sensation that told him so. She'd sleep
through till morning. Then they would talk. He
could decide what to do.

Danielle lay beside Sara, stretched out on top of
the covers. She was still awake, and she looked at
him until he left the doorway and went into the
other bedroom.

He turned on a small table lamp, pulled the Ruger
from his belt and laid it on the bed, stripped off his

sweatshirt, then the shoulder harness. He was about to sheathe the gun when he heard the sounds of someone getting up, walking toward his room. He slid the gun into the holster and placed it on the table, then turned to see Danielle standing in the doorway.

"We've got to get Sara away from here. Surely now you realize that." Her voice was strained. He recognized the anxiety, the hesitation. And something else.

He studied her carefully. The muted lamplight warmed her skin. "I realize that whatever's going on needs to be resolved."

"Resolved?" She took a step forward. "How can you *resolve* what happened tonight? Tell me, Nick. What's the answer to that *thing* we saw? Hold a seance? Call a priest?"

"Maybe. Whatever it takes."

She stared at him in disbelief.

Nick was a bit surprised himself. His logic centers had undergone radical surgery in the past hour.

"So you're still willing to take a chance with Sara's life?" Her voice came low and hard, and he felt the prick of anger she seemed able to provoke at will.

His eyes narrowed. "Listen to me, Danielle. Whatever's going on at The Ridge has to be stopped."

"Surely not by Sara." Her eyes flashed stubbornly, momentarily chasing away the ghosts.

Nick didn't want this. He really didn't want this. What did he want? "Go to bed."

Turning away, he picked up his cast-off shirt, fished the pack of cigarettes from the pocket and impatiently shook one out, noticing—ignoring—the almost imperceptible trembling of his hand. He didn't hear her leave.

"Vears . . .?"

Nick wondered if he'd be hearing that in his sleep. Tossing the unlit cigarette to the table, he turned around. "What?"

For a moment she didn't answer, standing silent in the muted light. The stubbornness had fled, leaving a hollow plea for reassurance and the knowledge of what had been building between them for a time. He sensed her hesitancy warring with that reckless bravado. Hesitancy lost.

"I need to feel someone's arms around me tonight," she whispered, "even if they're yours."

She began walking toward him and he saw her need, a hint of urgency. Recognized his own. He allowed his eyes to roam her, seeing the natural grace with which she moved, the lines of her firm body; small breasts, slender hips, long legs.

Arousal stirred, more deeply than he'd anticipated. She stopped in front of him and stood, matching his silence, in an unassuming pose of utter sensuality. He lifted a hand to lightly trace a finger down the line of her jaw, moving to the buttons at her throat, but she brushed his hand aside and began undressing herself, abandoning her clothes to the floor.

Molding his hands to her naked shoulders, he moved her against him, fitting her length to his. She remained motionless as he slid his hands across her back, up into her hair, arms held loosely at her sides. His hands tightened and he slowly tilted her head back, holding her eyes as he guided her mouth to his, deepening the contact quickly.

She came alive then, in his arms, and he picked her up and carried her to the bed, stripping off the rest of his clothes, moving into her almost immediately as the heat built between them.

The first time he took her more roughly than he intended, giving way to the emotions churning inside him, and the sudden desire that had gripped him as she moved into his arms. Again she surprised him, meeting his terms—making them hers.

When she claimed the initiative, he found himself relaxing, letting her set their rhythms, until passion seized them both and he pulled her body to his, finishing what she'd begun.

Night moved toward dawn, and at last they lay, passion spent. After a while, she slept.

Nick held her naked, sweat-damp body, felt her breathing soft against his chest. It had been a long time since he'd held a woman while she slept.

PART THREE

The Crossing

16

Nick came awake with the suddenness of long-term conditioning. He'd trained himself to maximize a minimum sleep period.

Soft lamplight lit the room. He glanced at his watch. 2:37 A.M. His body felt rested, his mind clear. The jumbled thoughts he'd put aside earlier were now organized and relevant. He knew what he had to do.

Beside him Danielle still slept, curled onto her right side, her back to him, but nestled within the crook of his arm. He eased away.

She didn't stir, and he lay for a long moment staring at the pale expanse of ceiling above them, then got up and began pulling on his clothes.

He had to go back to The Ridge, check this thing out, evaluate it from a nonemotional level if he hoped to develop a criterion he could act on. Last night he'd allowed emotions to override training, make him slack. It wouldn't happen again.

The pickup team had been due to come in after midnight. They might have walked into the problem he'd conveniently distanced himself from. They might have been and gone. If not, there were two more bodies to be gotten out to the rocks—a job that needed taking care of, a job he'd arbitrarily shelved.

He stopped the thought, glancing at Danielle, then picked up his shoulder harness from the bedside table and shrugged it on over his sweatshirt.

The gun might be useless. Then again, it might not. Somewhere in the recesses of his mind a thought was forming that maybe, just maybe, a custom-designed exploding bullet could have relevance, even in the insane parameters of that cave.

He pulled out the Ruger, removed the clip, sighted it toward the lamp, then methodically slid the clip back in place, hearing the *snick* that told him it had locked.

Apparently Danielle heard it too.

She shifted restlessly, turning toward where he'd been lying, coming slowly awake. He sensed initial confusion, then saw her body stiffen with memory—of what had happened, of him. She looked around, and pulled the sheet to her in an unconsciously protective gesture as her eyes found his.

"What's wrong? What are you doing?"

He put the gun in his holster. "What I should have done before."

She sat up, holding the sheet in front of her, oblivious to the oddly vulnerable quality of the act. "Nick—?"

"Stay with Sara. I'll be back soon. And Danielle— keep her here."

"*Nick.*" She scrambled off the bed, tugging the sheet with her. "Nick, you can't mean to go back down to that house?"

He ignored her, turning to leave.

"Nick—that's *crazy!*"

But he was already out the door.

Placing the keys to the GMC on the dining room table, he let himself out the sliding glass door, closed it behind him. He'd considered calling Harris, but dismissed the idea. Harris would require explanations. He didn't have the time—or the explanations.

A stiff breeze was blowing from the northeast, bringing a distant growl of thunder and the smell of rain. Clouds blotted the moon. Waves beat restlessly against the beach as though shuddering from some violent schism taking place far out to sea.

Nick started to run, feeling a kinship with the night, a dichotomy of thought and mind, fact and reason. He paced himself to the rhythm of the waves, drawing energy from the familiar action, experiencing the physical exhilaration of well-toned muscles engaged in controlled exercise. His gaze remained steady on the approaching cliff.

He passed the house the rock group rented. Inside it was dark. Outside a single light burned above the door. Their van was gone. Harris had mentioned attending their gig and Nick wondered if he'd done so. Only a few hours ago it had seemed a viable lead.

Barely winded, he reached the rocks, scaled them to the spot where the sniper's body had been. Not a trace remained.

Apparently the team had experienced no trouble; they'd come and gone without an imprint, done their job. While he had *not* been doing his. Leaving the rocks, he made his way along the sandy path that led up to The Ridge.

The house sat silent and chill in the predawn

mist. A light wind swirled ground fog around his feet. He stopped walking, regarded the old house intently. It was almost impossible to believe what had happened here last night. For a moment logic asserted itself, suggesting possible alternatives, raising contradictions. There had to be a rational explanation.

It happened.

A tingle of awareness brushed the hairs of his arms and the back of his neck.

It happened.

Nick resumed his approach of the house.

The front door stood open, as they'd left it, inside lights still on. He entered and stood just past the threshold, scanning the interior. The house smelled moldy, stale. It felt cold. The dank, sweetish hint of decay and old stone hung on the stagnant air. But he sensed no immediate danger.

Leaving the front door open, he headed down the hall, turning off lights, moving silently and fast, feeling the coldness stir with his passing, like the ground fog outside.

Pushing your luck, Vears?

You don't believe in luck, remember?

You didn't believe in ghost stories, either.

Through the archway door. Right, not left. Not to the chapel. Not yet.

Using the flashlight, Nick traced his way to the cell where he'd left the bodies.

At first he thought they were gone. The light found only crumpled clothing where the pair had been. He stepped closer.

They were still here. But he wouldn't be needing the pickup team.

Two dark, curdled pools lay beneath the rumpled clothes. With his foot he shoved a shirt aside. It didn't want to move. A mass of gumlike residue had soaked through the back and begun to solidify, pasting it to the stones.

Nick stood looking down at what was left of Terrell and Manetti. He stood there for a while. Then he left the cell.

Tracking his way back along the corridor, he was suddenly anxious to be done with this, get out of here. Awareness honed his senses; cool air stroked his flesh. He didn't like the memories it provoked.

But he had a job to do, like it or not, ready or not. And he'd already wasted too much time.

Lew hadn't spent an evening like this in years. His social life had evolved into marathon movie weekends in front of the VCR, where he could stretch out and relax with his beer and bag of microwave popcorn, sleep when he wanted to (the beauty of a VCR was you could play back the parts you slept through), and put aside the pressures of his job.

Or he would read, enjoying the solid blocks of time when he could immerse himself in a good thriller and not have to break the flow of chapters with anything more distracting than a pause to pay the pizza delivery boy.

He dated some, but evenings out generally consisted of a quiet dinner in a classy restaurant, or a quick hot dog and a hockey game, ending at his companion's house or apartment if the mood was right, and a couple of solitary nightcaps at his own place if it wasn't.

Going out alone to bars or late-night clubs was not his style. Loud music and slam-dancing were not his thing. And the beach scene that existed about fifteen miles down the coast from the sleepy little fishing village of Spiney Point was not where he'd normally choose to spend time.

Still, he'd rather enjoyed himself tonight—discounting the slight headache from four hours in an overcrowded room breathing other people's smoke and sweat. Or was it the music that had made the evening other than the affliction he'd anticipated?

KAFKA had been hot, playing with a maturity and professionalism that rivaled some of the well-known groups Lew had seen. They'd blended ability and showmanship in a performance that had brought the crowd to their feet and kept them there through three sets. The songs were first-rate; original stuff, Lew guessed. The sound was good, *damn* good. And they knew how to play the crowd—particularly Set Reynolds—manipulating the audience the way they manipulated their instruments and equipment.

Lew had been impressed. Without doubt, these kids could go far if they kept at it, got the right breaks or made them. Unless they were involved in what had happened at The Ridge. Then it would turn out differently—for them, for the people who would never get to hear them play.

Why did potential so often fall victim to human frailty?

Because humans *are* frail, he thought as he climbed silently across a scrub-studded sand dune, following the group of five young musicians as they headed up the beach toward The Ridge.

Also suspicious. Lew wasn't quite sure what had made him tail the kids back to their rented beach house after the gig instead of calling it a night and grabbing some much-needed sleep. Instinct? Expectation? Pheromones? Could one actually "smell a rat"?

The group had begun playing their first set around ten, and finished the final one at a little past two. Though the crowd had clamored for the music to continue, the club manager had vetoed their demands; the club was supposed to close at two A.M., and it *was* Sunday morning.

Lew had left with the grumbling crowd, then watched the musicians load their equipment into a van from his car across the street. Instead of displaying signs of exhaustion from the intensely physical show they'd performed, the group was hyper, keyed to a fevered pitch.

Set Reynolds seemed to go even beyond that— standing a head taller than the others, above it all, yet seething with impatience and excitement, intoxicated with the sheer ebullience of the night. His eyes held the same faraway look they'd had through all the music, every song. Several times he'd stared straight at Lew, though Lew doubted he'd even been given identity, much less credence. A faceless fan among many. To be courted, captivated, and cashed in at a later date.

Now here he was, trudging up a beach at twenty past three in the morning, getting sand in his shoes and wondering what the hell was about to go down. He hadn't even called for backup—standard, by-the-book procedure—was it getting to be a habit? But he hadn't wanted to risk scaring them off, and he had no real working knowledge of what he could expect from backup here. Still, someone in your corner was better than no one at all when the odds were five to one.

Of course, Vears was at The Ridge. Wouldn't that even things out? *Possibly*, Lew thought without sarcasm. *Just possibly.*

He tucked in behind a sand dune as he neared the rocks, waiting until the kids scrambled over the crest before following. It looked like they were headed into the ruins at the far end of the house, and not the house itself, Lew saw as he carefully made his way up and over the jagged outcropping. Hesitating at the edge of the terrace wall, he watched them circle out of sight, filing down and around the tumbled stones that littered the base of the old monastery.

Glancing up at the dark house, Lew wondered if he should wake Vears now . . . then decided he'd better see exactly where those kids were going before he took the chance of alerting them, or losing them in the dark. He circled around the terrace wall and caught sight of them again beyond and below his position. They seemed to be working with one of the rocks.

What gives?

Cautiously he descended, approaching from their left rear and using the piles of tumbled stones as cover, intent on getting just close enough to determine what they were up to.

He never saw the blow coming. Only a shattering white light, an explosion of pain on the back of his skull, then nothing . . .

"Is he dead?" Vesper whispered as the group reconvened around the SBI agent's prone body. She came up behind Mitch, who was still gripping the rock he'd used on Harris, looking ready and willing to use it again should the man stir.

Hump stood a little apart, hands nervously swabbing the sides of his jeans; a jerky, abstracted motion. His eyes filled the round, horn-rimmed glasses he wore, owlish in the puckered face, locked on the crumpled form.

Twyla appeared to be holding her breath, still as the porcelain figurine she resembled. Wind lifted her hair and played with the delicate clusters of tiny silver bells that dangled from her ears, feathering the night with a tinkle of music, the faint, crystal-clear shiver of windchimes.

"Why don't you take those damn earrings off," Set muttered under his breath, "and no, he's not dead."

Slowly Twyla lifted a hand to her ears, one at a time, and did as told while Set removed his fingers from the pulse point in Lew Harris's neck and stood.

He looked at Mitch. "Let's get him into the tunnel."

Mitch tossed the rock aside, like a doctor would a surgical instrument that had been sullied, and bent to grab shoulders while Set took legs.

Wind seemed to gather around them as though attempting to help them lift the dead-weight body, lighten their load. A low rumble lumbered across the cloud-ridden sky, bringing with it the pungent smell of incipient rain and an ominous flicker of lightning. Moisture clung to the heavy air.

"He's bleeding." Twyla's voice was hushed, childlike, seeping from her like the mist that churned restlessly in small scabrous patches across the ground.

"Of course he's bleeding!" Vesper hissed, sounding defiant and scared at the same time. "That's what happens when you bash somebody's head in with a rock." She brushed past and started trailing after the two and their burden.

Twyla watched them go, murmured, "Please don't let him bleed to death," then lapsed into silence.

"Why'd you have to hit him so hard?" Hump's voice quivered anxiously as he stumbled after the group. "He's a fucking *cop*, f'chrissake."

Mitch snapped him a look. "Shut up before you alert the whole goddamn county."

Set ignored him. "Twyla?" His eyes reached across the widening distance to where she stood. "C'mon, babe."

She began walking forward.

They reached the spherical rock and the entrance to the tunnel, and again Set's mind hardened on the knowledge that had greeted him just moments ago: Someone had found the cave. The stone had been rolled aside and left that way. Their secret place had been violated. Their privacy destroyed. By this major asshole?

Set almost wished they could have kept him conscious long enough to find out. But they couldn't take chances. Not now. Not with a cop. And particularly, Set judged shrewdly, not with *this* cop.

He studied the face of the man they carried, noting how the skin appeared gray in the moon-poor light, seeing the flatness that unconsciousness brought to normally sharp features.

For a moment he visualized the electronic blip of a heart monitor with the bleating rhythm lined out to one long hum, like feedback from a microphone, its spastic jumping planed to an eternal bone of light. Until someone cut the power off.

The Power.

Set breathed deeply. He could feel it now, filling him as it had all evening. Tonight he'd been on the mountaintop, gazing down to the valley of shadows while scenes unfolded like stop-action frames on a video.

He'd seen himself running back down the beach, watching as they'd loaded the van, driving to the club.

He'd seen them take the stage—the *crowd*, make the night sing with the words and music he gave them.

He'd seen Richard Cranium here, tagging along

behind them afterward, laughed to himself as the stupid fuck slogged on toward the waiting rock.

All these things he'd seen from his mountaintop, from the crest of the wave like the sun through haze ... and now he was ready to sweep the haze aside. Now he would see with new eyes, *renewed* eyes—eyes that held perfect vision—

(for Mine *is the Power, the Glory)*

—True Light!

They set the cop's body down and stripped off his raincoat, tying its sleeves securely around his legs. Motioning the others into the tunnel, Set crawled in behind Vesper, Hump, and Twyla and began pulling the unconscious man along. Mitch followed, pushing against the man's shoulders and keeping the body from snagging on rough sections of rocks. It took them about twice as long as usual to maneuver the tunnel, but they managed, and once in the cavern Mitch removed the cop's gun and stashed it behind a rock while Set tugged the knotted sleeves off over Harris's feet, jerking his shoes off in the process.

He tossed the shoes to the sand beside the cast-off raincoat as the group continued on into the passage, headed toward a throbbing pulse of light. It didn't really matter. This was one cop who wasn't going to be walking his beat anytime soon. If ever again.

Just stay alive a little while longer, Set thought, extending a benevolent finger of Power to touch the unconscious man. *Then you can go where all the good dickheads go, because I won't need you anymore.*

If numbers had been their problem, then this time they'd have it right: the five of them, the three upstairs, this asshole—and his other Self, gazing down from the mountaintop, watching this mo-

ment move toward the final joining, the true beginning of eternity.

Again Set breathed deeply of the charged air,
feeling its energy spread through him like a sudden burst of adrenaline, a powerful infusion of
blood.

The passageway seemed to crackle with the life
force flowing in and around him. Excitement tin-
gled his skin. Aliveness effervesced the air.

And Light—like shimmering, billowing curtains
of spun silver and ice—parted for him at the touch
of a thought and spread a crystal carpet in their
path.

Light grew as they neared the inner chamber, filling Set's mind with vibrant, ripening images.
Voices sang to him, enchanted songs. Chill anticipation sped through his veins.

This time it would be right. He could feel it—*see*
it. The rituals would be complete, the gateway
opened. And all he'd ever wanted would be his—
His!

He felt himself moving toward the center of a
swirling mental universe
    (almost there)
the nucleus of vision, of Light and Life.
    (almost)

"Set—!" Vesper's cry ripped across his vision
with the jagged slash of a splintered nail.

Dumping Harris's body he strode forward, a red
flush of anger rimming the scene as he reached
the opening to the inner chamber. She stood, staring down at something in the sand, her outland-
ishly clothed body framed by luminescence, a
cartoon caricature silhouetted in a corona of
flame.

"Shut up!" he snapped, gazing almost indiffer-
ently at the pool of charred clothing and mottled,

jellified flesh that had once held human life. The bone structure, though twisted and fused, still retained a semblance of normalcy, not distorted past recognition. Portions were as smooth as candle wax. Others looked like congealed fat. The stark skeleton threaded through the mixture like a dribble of white paint, blending into the morass in places, webbing outward in others.

Set absorbed this in the mere fraction of a second it took to shift his gaze to the real focus of his concern. Beyond the body, a constant heartbeat of light throbbed like distant thunder and pumped icy radiance through the sharpening air. Familiar fingers touched his mind, his fear. The sudden tilting of his world righted itself. The Mindstone was safe. Nothing else mattered.

"Who is it?" Hump choked on the words, heaving them out as though trying to fight back the urge to vomit. "What *happened* to him?"

Set glanced again at the clotted, wormlike thing lying pockmarked and spilled across the sand like a puddle of child's fingerpaints. "Who knows— or cares? Shouldn't have been mucking about in here."

"But—"

Swinging on the group Set pinpointed each one in turn, smiling inwardly as their eyes shifted from his. He modified his voice, making it almost pleasant, controlling the passions that seethed beneath the surface of his anger.

Control. Of course that was all there was to it. Nothing could go wrong now. Nothing could take away this moment. He was in control.

"It doesn't really matter," he remarked, allowing the smile its freedom. "Nothing is going to harm us—that's what you're really interested in, isn't it? And no one—particularly not this asshole—will be causing us any more problems. Will they?"

He glanced at Mitch, whose eyes glittered fiercely in the refracted light;

at Vesper, who was regarding the curdled mass in frozen fascination;

at Twyla, with her waif's eyes that clung only to him;

at Hump . . .

"Set, man, I don't like this . . ." Hump backed up a pace. He'd begun to shiver.

Set bestowed his total gaze on the drummer. "It was you." The accusation eased out of him like the chill radiance of his smile.

Hump looked confused. "What—?

"You made that anonymous phone call to the police."

"No!"

"Always whining, always afraid." Set took a step toward him, still smiling, still certain.

Beyond them the Mindstone pulsed impatiently, pervasively. And suddenly Set experienced a fierce intolerance for these petty annoyances, and an overwhelming need for haste.

"No, man! I didn't—"

"It was me, Set." Twyla's trembling words floated across the cave and brushed Set's mind like a feather of unreality, causing him to momentarily lose the urgency that had gripped him.

He turned to her, disbelieving, stunned.

"I did it," she stammered in her little girl's voice. "I called them, not Hump." Her eyes pleaded for understanding.

He gaped at her, not understanding at all. A soft humming buzzed his ears.

(Set . . . Set . . .)

"What?"

A tear rolled down her cheek as she started walking toward him. "There were *children* up there, Set.

Little *babies* . . . I didn't mean . . . I didn't know . . ."
She began to cry.

The buzzing in Set's ears spread to the base of
his skull. "Twyla . . . ?" *What* . . .

Thunder shuddered through the cave. A rush of
wind. *Or was it in his mind?*

"It doesn't matter," he murmured, touching her
as if in absolution as she burrowed her head against
his chest. "It's okay . . ."

Waves of urgency and impatience flooded him.
"We have to get on with the ritual." He glanced
sharply at the group.

Vesper quailed, "I don't know . . ."

Pushing Twyla aside, Set swept a hand toward
Harris's crumpled body lying motionless to one
side of the chamber entrance. "In case you've all
forgotten, we're committed now. There is no turning back. We have to go on."

One by one, he touched their minds with the
Power.

One by one, they began moving toward the Circle.
First Mitch, who strolled nonchalantly past the
spongy remains, then Vesper and Hump . . . gathering around the stone, taking their places silently,
fearfully. But fear was all right. The wonder and
awe of what was to come *should* fill them, cleanse
them, make them pure.

Taking hold of Twyla's unresisting arm, Set
guided her to her place, stepped into his own.
There'd been enough waiting. Too much. The moment had

(Come!)

Slowly, relentlessly, he began the joining

(Closer . . . closer)

pushing past meager resistance to grip their
minds with the totality born of

(I am the Light . . .)

Never had he felt so full—so whole.

(Flesh of My *flesh . . .)*

Reaching out with the Power he blended their thoughts, leading them deeper into the journey that would see them all reborn, lifted from these ashes to the life that would be theirs—*His!*

Swiftly he took them past their tiny fears, guiding them forward, inward, replacing doubts with dreams, dreams with visions, filling them with the joy of perfect oneness,

True Light!

Light sped around the Circle, the Light of their own minds, linking them with a radiance they had never before achieved. Taking their radiance with him, Set fastened his eyes on the Mindstone, extending the bond, reaching out his mind

to touch—to join . . .

A slender strand of purest Light began threading its way from the very heart of the stone, weaving a path through the pulsing glow, separating into even more delicate tendrils reaching out

(to Touch—to Join!)

spanning outward from the stone like the spokes of a wheel to curl around each head, form crystal-white circlets—*halos!*—connecting them to the glowing hub. He could feel the cold beauty of his own. A silver crown—

The crown became a vise!

Power engulfed him, swamping his mind with the thrumming, buzzing tide of a thousand locusts, a hundred-thousand. A tiny bud of pain blossomed in his head and began spreading through the brilliance, as if a small blood vessel had erupted, sending countless hairlike tracers streaking outward in a network of stark red lines. Dizziness washed over him, tingeing his vision crimson, splitting it apart as if he were seeing through a prism of colors and light.

Help me! he cried to his other Self, plunging his

gaze into the fiery heart of the stone, seeking the mountaintop that had somehow shifted beneath his feet—

And then it was there—*He* was there—supporting, holding, calming Set's screaming mind. *He* was of them, of the bond—but not yet here . . .

(the Circle must be complete!*)*

Eyes within eyes. Vision beyond sight.

Set could sense a dusky warmth beyond the brightness: the tepid blur of the man they'd carried in here, the surprisingly pungent heat of other, stronger, minds.

And through it all, the swelling, frigid brilliance of the One True Light.

Softly the incantation rose

"O Divine Light . . . O Power of the One . . ."

New strands sprouted from the stone, seeking the minds still cowered in darkness, seeking to draw them toward the Light.

(the Circle must be complete!)

Set felt his body growing weightless

(Mind of My *mind)*

felt his thoughts spiraling far beyond this night, this place, as he gazed into the stone . . .

"Show us the bridge . . ."

The Crown of Light shed fire and ice. Shivers of delicious ecstasy wove their magic through him, taking him deep . . . deeper . . .

"That we might cross . . ."

sinuous fingers playing across his body—*within it*—bringing him to the verge of a climax he had never before attained—holding him there.

(The Circle must be complete . . .)

Voices sang inside his head, joining their songs to his

and the music was a part of him as if it were his soul!

Tears streamed down Set's face as he deepened

his contact, drawing Power from the minds, the
stone, spiraling out on strands of purest light, seeking to touch the others beyond them—as he himself
was being touched—bring them into the Circle of
One . . .

Warmth.

Snugged around her.

Keeping away the Cold.

She lay there, eyes closed to the outside world, seeing just the same.

Where was her Fuzzy?

She stirred slightly, and small hands searched the darkness, gathering a vision that was faint but growing stronger as she moved into the void.

She didn't want to go—*knew* she wouldn't like it here, yet someone wanted her, she could hear them calling her name . . . over and over . . . like a chant, or a song . . .

She was in a cave.

Dark. Lonely.

Fireflies flickered through the air. Shadows skulked in the corners.

Something glistened up ahead.

Slowly she entered the endless hall, drawn by the light that knew her name, holding onto the warmth. The Bright Thing. It couldn't hurt her—not as long as she stayed within her safe place.

Strange, she wasn't afraid yet. Always before she'd been afraid, fearful of the dreams that visited her, pushing them away.

Different now.

Now there was enough warmth to keep her safe.

The glistening thing took shape: like her pedestal table, standing in the center of the room. She walked toward it, seeing the stone that rested on the smooth white top. Just one. Bigger than hers. Full of light.

Her steps slowed as she reached the table and gazed down into the stone of light. There were stars inside; and sparkles and mist like spun sugar candy; and sunshine and . . .

the stone began to pulse and shift, expanding outward to meet her . . . humming softly . . . humming . . .

She saw a staircase taking shape. It was beautiful, shining, let down from the sparkling sky like a carpet of snow-white clouds. It spread out at the bottom, spilling into the vast room that surrounded it. The banisters were made of gold.

Around the room, the shadows danced; but they were silver shadows now, not black, their eyes twinkling like stars at night, not scary at all. Tiny, glittering creatures darted among the shadows; but they were fairy things, not monsters. And she was not afraid. They sang to her, a soft, humming song that smelled like summer rain.

At the top of the staircase was an ivory gateway, swirling with the clouds that covered its huge doors. The doors were closed. She moved closer, wanting them to open, to let her see the treasures on the other side . . . and not wanting it at all.

Coldness began seeping in with the light.

Her daddy was there. Standing just in front of her, not looking at the light, not seeing. He didn't see her yet, nor the stairway, and she tried to move toward him—but something held her away, the Cold! *Daddy*, she tried to call to him—but he couldn't hear her. And now the light was growing brighter, she could see it glittering around his body, harder than before, she could see the light *through him* and again she tried to shout *Daddy!* but the Bright Thing was too close—and she was too far away . . .

Waves. Cold, black.

She shivered as the scene began to change
Lashing at the edges of her consciousness.

like the night she'd stood behind the glass
Nightmare visions swirling all around.
watching the thing that was
*Badness! Roaring, shrieking badness! Wanting to
get her—come inside—*
(No!)
She backed up a step.

She could see other shapes taking form: a circle,
someone standing in the middle with arms held out
and burning eyes that turned her way. She could
hear other voices, calling to her, telling her to come
... *come* ...
(NO! Get Back!)
She stood her ground and watched *it* hesitate this
time—as if *it* were afraid—and she smiled a secret
smile.

It couldn't have her. She realized that now.
Couldn't take her unless she let it. She knew. *It*
knew.

The burning eyes refocused.
But it could take her daddy.
Fear came then, a sudden burst of afraidness like
That Night—
Mommy ...
But Mommy wasn't here anymore. The Bright
Thing had taken her. And David and Karen and
Jeffy, and now it wanted her daddy, too, wanted to
take him away and she wouldn't let that happen,
not again, not to her daddy, *Not my*

+   +   +

"Daddy!"
Dani nearly jumped out of her skin as Sara bolted

upright in bed and began frantically beating the covers aside, trying to get up, screaming

"Daddy!"

over and over again.

The child was hysterical. Dani scrambled across the bed and grabbed her before she could untangle herself.

"Sara. *Sara!* Please, honey, calm down. It's okay. Everything's all right. I'm right here. Don't—"

She tried to quell the flailing arms that whipped mindlessly at anything holding her back, grunting now with effort and emotion, the screams becoming hoarse.

"Sara, it's me, it's Dani. Baby, please wake up, you're having a nightmare. *Sara . . ."*

Dani shook her gently, then harder when that seemed to have no effect at all.

"Honey, for God's sake . . ."

She realized she was crying; both of them were crying, stung by the incredible frenzy that had seized Sara in the midst of sleep and wrenched her into something wild.

Slowly the cries subsided, the body stilled.

The child's skin was like ice. Dani clutched Sara to her, pulling blankets back around them both. She was shaking, herself, not so much from the cold coming at her in waves from Sara's rigid body, but from a nameless dread that was seeping in with it. She was frightened. Terrified! She'd never been this scared before, not even last night. And she didn't know why.

She began rocking the frigid body, on her knees in the center of the bed, forcing herself to think abstract thoughts—inanities like *I wonder where I put my shoes* and *What am I going to say to Nick the next time I see him?*—anything to banish the fear.

(We have to go, now)

We have to go now . . .

"What—?" she murmured, shaking her head as sudden confusion spread over her, a voice, Sara's voice in her mind, "What did you say?"

(It's time to go)

"Go . . . ?" The voice was stronger now. *Yes. They had somewhere to go.*

Dani unwrapped her arms from Sara, peeled back the quilts. Together they got out of bed. Sara took her hand.

"My shoes . . . ?"

"Here." Sara stooped down and picked up Dani's Reeboks— *Of course, she'd taken them off in here before . . .* She put them on.

"Where are yours?" She focused on Sara's bare feet beneath her pajamas.

"At home." Sara drew her gaze. *(We have to go home now)*

"We have to go home . . ." Dani walked slowly through the house to the door, holding Sara's hand, stopping to gather Nick's keys off the table as they passed. *Should she drive his—?*

(It's okay)

It would be okay, he'd left her the keys, hadn't he? . . .

The night air was cool and for a moment her confusion cleared—"Sara? What—?"

(Open the door)

Dani opened the door to the four-wheeler, let the child climb in first, then got in after her. She started the engine, backed out of the drive. Thunder rolled across the sky. The big GMC lurched forward.

Wind began pouring in the open window. Dani shivered. But she didn't roll up the glass. It was too much trouble.

The beach road was deserted. Their headlights

swept the blacktop like huge beacons. Small sand crabs occasionally scuttled from their path.

She slowed for the turnoff to The Ridge, drove carefully up the drive. They came to a stop beside David's station wagon. *Why wasn't she driving that?*

"Why—?"

(Park the car)

Dani parked, turned off the engine and sat looking out at the sea, remembering the time she'd spent here writing that article on ospreys—"fish hawks" the locals called them, not at all excited that a species that had been endangered in the 70s was now producing more than were dying. DDT had been the culprit, robbing eggs of calcium and making them so soft they'd break when the mother sat on her nest. But then the environmental people banded together and fought to make the authorities aware that heavy spraying for mosquitoes in coastal areas was poisoning the birds. David had even agreed to do some sketches for the piece— she'd had the originals framed and they were hanging on her wall at home.

Lost in contemplation of other, happier, times, Dani didn't even hear the door being opened . . .

Sara's footsteps were firm as she entered the dark house and headed up the stairs. She could feel the throbbing in the air, taste the dampness that smelled of caves and basement dirt.

Wind came with her, flowing over the banisters and crisscrossing her path. She adjusted the space around her so it couldn't get in, couldn't touch her. She wouldn't be stopped this time, wouldn't let it make her afraid.

She was doing things she'd never done before, never known she could. It made her feel stronger, older somehow—not little and afraid.

If someone could have seen her face at that moment they would have recognized single-minded determination in the jut of her chin, would have seen purpose gleam from her startling blue eyes with an adult-level intensity and a totally childlike stubbornness.

If Nick could have seen her, he might have recognized something else.

At the top of the stairs she turned left, toward her room, never faltering in the nearly pitch-black hallway as small bare feet slapped the cold stone floor. She didn't feel the chill. And she wouldn't hear the humming.

In her room she went straight to her bed and fished beneath the covers for the old worn bear that seemed to find her reaching hand. Gripping it she turned to go, then found her eyes drawn to the pedestal table where she'd spent so many hours arranging and rearranging her small collection of stones. A faint glow hovered there, like sparkling mist.

She walked over to the table, looked down . . . The center stone was swirling eerily, threads of gold entwining misty white. As she watched, a shape began to appear in the mist—a strange, glowing shape on a mountain of ice, with glittering red-coal eyes that swam in pits of burning yellow. The eyes began to grow, finding hers, locking on and holding them, wanting to pull her into their light—

With one furious backhand motion, Sara swept the stones from the table, smiling tightly as she heard them skitter across the floor.

"You can't have me . . ." she whispered, gripping her Fuzzy hard as she watched the mist dissolve. *And you can't have my daddy.*

17

Voices came from the cavern up ahead, echoing hollowly down the narrow passageway toward Nick. *Sounded like chanting, maybe half a dozen participants engaged in some sort of ritualistic ceremony?*

Gun drawn, he edged along the rock wall, listening to the incantation rise and fall, reverberating outward like the light that shone in the cavern beyond. Waves of kinetic energy seemed to dart about the tunnel, stimulating the air and making the hairs on his forearms and the back of his neck bristle. He hadn't liked this place the first time he'd come down here, and he didn't like it now.

Thin mist floated at the end of the passage, sparkling as if flecked with mica; a rippling miasma of light. For a moment each particle became a twinkling silver eye, blinking and staring and watching him come.

Nick swept the bizarre illusion aside.

At the end of the tunnel he checked his forward motion, standing silent and alert in the heightened air. As with most things, it had come down to a matter of two-edged choices: go or stay; play or pass; win or lose. He could not estimate odds, no precedents to draw, no rules to apply.

Yet one thing was certain: If people were involved here, then so was the potential for error. And where there was error, it could be capitalized on.

Nick just had to make sure it wasn't his error.

Slowing his breathing, he readied his move. The mind-set was simple: He'd either come out of this or he wouldn't. In case of the latter, someone else would inherit the problem.

Before coming down here, he'd taken the time to transmit a report via the ECCO—apparently there *was* a requisition list to deal with such things—a code he'd never expected to use, but that did exist. Maybe it had been his thought of psychic experiments that had triggered memory. Whatever. In essence, he'd sent a twelve-hour delayed priority message under a digital code that transcribed to: Unexplained Event Phenomenon—Confirmed Lethal. He'd sketched out details, added a personal tag concerning Sara's custody, and keyed it through to a way station where it would be held until countermanded by him or until the twelve hours were up.

Play or pass.

Nick eased into the cavern, flattening himself against the rough stone wall. He could see into the chamber beyond—enough to confirm that the voices he heard were coming from human throats, and that those throats belonged to Sara's rock people.

They stood in a circle at the center of the inner chamber, the tall blond kid presiding over them, arms stretched high, a look of mindless ecstasy and the sheen of sweat glazing his face. His eyes glittered with refracted light, and Nick saw madness there. He was swaying with the rhythm of the chant, seeming to exert almost a physical hold over the circle swaying with him.

They rocked, trancelike, apparently oblivious to his presence. *Yet someone knew he was here.* Nick could feel it in his gut.

Light came from the circle, an irregular glow, spilling outward and highlighting Russell Reikert's mortal remains lying where they'd fallen in the sand. But the snaking, deadly beams that had whipped the air were nowhere in evidence.

Another form took shape on Nick's right: Lew Harris; sprawled half in, half out of the entrance to the inner cave. The motionless body was turned away from him, but Nick took note of the dark pocket of blood that had soaked the back of his head and collar. He didn't consider crossing to him. If Harris was dead, there was nothing Nick could do to help. If he wasn't, there was still nothing Nick could do, and he'd be risking unnecessary exposure.

He inched along the inside wall, trying to gain a better perspective, gun ready, still willing to hedge his bets with proven advantages. The light seemed almost to pulsate, expanding and contracting with the rhythm of the chant. And beneath the surface of the sound Nick thought he could hear a deeper undertone, a more atonal drone that fell just a fraction of a beat off rhythm, but swelling, as though one chant was beginning to overlay another.

A mist had risen, swirling eerily around the circle, shrouding the forms in shimmering gray fog and connecting them in some sort of nebulous whirlpool effect.

Wind buffeted the cave. Thunder vibrated the air. And one by one the chanting figures dropped to their knees, except for their leader. He was staring into something in the center of the circle.

Nick's eyes narrowed. He stepped closer

(Closer . . .)

and saw the stone, lying in the sand like a glowing jewel of crystallized light. A single luminous thread was lifting from it, and as Nick watched, it began to ravel into separate strands, each reaching out to a member of the group—

(to touch—to join)

and then one was coming toward him

and Nick thought he'd never seen anything he so wanted to touch

It seemed to *open* . . . holding images that were like nothing he had ever seen before

(closer . . .)

offering fulfillment of deepest desires, secret wants.

An archway appeared, a bridge spiraling into the heart of the stone, drawing him forward, sucking him in—

Nick wrenched his gaze from the erotic dreams being spun at the heart of the stone; the wrench was like pulling back from the edge of climax. Beads of sweat popped out on his forehead. The inside of his mouth was dry.

What *was* that thing—?

(Come—)

(The Bright Thing—Don't Look!)

For a moment confusion gripped him, yanking him in two different directions. Immediately the light intensified, *blossomed*, breathing outward like a huge diaphanous lung . . . cold . . . colder . . . pressing . . . against him . . .

—and then strength returned, stronger than before, and he shunted the light aside, dragging in deep, slaking breaths until he felt the coldness ebb, the shadow-images start to fade.

Somewhere at the edge of vision he registered other movement: Harris. He'd stirred; he wasn't dead. A strand of light began converging on the body, a slick finger of whitewashed bone sliding across the sand.

Nick stepped forward, shoving his new strength into the breach, and saw the light recede.

Whatever this *ability* of his was, he was learning how to use it.

Waves of dizzying nausea greeted Lew's return to consciousness. Blackness gave way to blinding, killing light. His fingers groped feebly at the sand, trying to find purchase, get some leverage so he could move—if he was able to move. His body felt like lead.

Droning, muddied voices in cadence impacted on his eardrums, vying with the roaring wind; an ocean of sound crashing over him, driving him down, holding him under. The beat of his heart kept exploding in his head. It hurt. His mind was numb.

Where was he? What had happened?

He opened his eyes, and immediately shut them again as dizziness and nausea rolled over him with a wash of light, drilling into his eyeballs and drenching his body in cold sweat.

Tentatively he lifted a hand to the back of his head where hammer blows of pain kept relentlessly jarring his skull, sending dull shock waves coiling around his forehead. Fingers encountered stickiness, incrusted at the edges and filled with grit, but he could move, he realized, withdrawing his hand.

He opened his eyes once more.

And wished he hadn't.

For a moment the distortion threatened to plunge him back into unconsciousness. Or was *this* the unreal state—this nightmare vision? The howl of the wind joined the swirling madness that met his gaze, pulling his mind toward a centerpoint of light, like one of those crazily spinning targets that spirals in on itself and makes you feel you're being drawn inside.

Darkness wheeled around him, sucking in rainbows and shadows and flame, channeling it all like some kind of giant whirligig. It was as if he were looking down the length of a revolving funnel toward a dazzling white light—

Was he dead?

Was this what people who had near-death experiences saw?

Shapes rose and fell within the light, like horses on a carousel. Voices swam apart and collided, a calliope of sound. The pounding in Lew's head became a steel fist, beating on his brain like an angry hand banging against a door . . . *Let me IN . . . Let me IN . . .* He struggled to sit up, fighting the pain, denying the unacceptable, *refusing to open the door*, and finally managed to turn his body away.

Through the fog another form appeared, this one recognizable as human, coming from the mist.

Vears?

A sort of . . . iridescence seemed to surround him, shimmering like glass.

What he was seeing couldn't be real.

As he watched, Vears stepped forward, moving slowly and with great deliberation, edging into a line between Lew and that . . . *light.* Something was taking shape within the light, or from it, he couldn't tell; something that looked like a huge gateway, a bridge with stairs at the top, an arch fitted with beautiful doors, all white and silver and scrolling clouds.

Not real.

Someone—the Reynolds kid?—was climbing the stairway. He heard singing, saw the doors begin to swing open. Like the Pearly Gates. Lew smiled.

All a dream. Just a crazy dream—
or

Heaven? Was this Heaven? Was he really dead and had all his momma's stories been true after all . . .

His head rolled back against the sand as if the muscles in his neck and shoulders had suddenly turned to water. Pain erupted at the base of his skull, sending needles of fire punching though his brain and spangling his dimming vision with red and white stars . . .

Then darkness rose up, cool and quiet, pouring in from the sides, the top, taking him down where he couldn't feel the pain, see the madness . . .

Not real, Lew . . . none of this is real . . .

Dani's head hit the steering wheel with a painful thud. For a moment she saw stars.

What . . . ?

Raising a shaky hand to rub her forehead she leaned back against the seat, eyes closed, hearing the roar of the ocean ringing in her ears, feeling cold salt air pour against her face.

Had she left a window open . . . ?

"Sara—?"

She opened her eyes then and looked around, re-alizing she was sitting in Nick's four-wheeler—she glanced about wildly—at The Ridge!

"—th'hell . . . Sara?" OhmyGod! "Sara!" Where was she? What was going on?

Snatches of memory bombarded her as she threw the door open and scrambled out. Sara had been here—she'd gone inside! But how could that be? She couldn't even remember driving down here. Was she dreaming?

No. It was real. Too—real.

Dani caught her breath as she dashed across the house's threshold, pulling up sharply in the dark-ened entry hall. Which way? Where? Confusion blotted her mind . . . and something else something . . .

She opened her mouth to yell for Sara and darkness rolled toward her, rising out of the corners and emerging from the stones like heavy mist.

(Danielle . . .)

The whisper-voice curled around her like a wisp of wind; cool, damp . . .

"Sara . . . ?"

She shivered, alone in the silence, rubbing her arms against the darkness that was touching her all over—

(Turn around, Dani! Turn around and run!)

She swung back toward the door—

"Sara—?"

She didn't want to go. Sara was in here. Dani hesitated. How could she have brought Sara here?

She remembered Nick leaving the beach house . . . she'd dressed, gone back to Sara's room, stretched out on the bed beside the sleeping child . . . must have dozed . . . then Sara had shot awake, screaming for her daddy.

Dani realized it had been the first time she'd heard Sara call Nick anything at all. But what then?

She faced into the house once more, shedding some of her confusion. Vears was in there. That's why Sara had come. To find her daddy.

She darted a look upstairs, scanning the pitch-black balcony that seemed to stretch into an infinity of darkness where not even a glimmer of light could reach. Was he up there? Was Sara?

Again Dani opened her mouth to call out

and the blackness plunged toward her, descending like a giant bird swooping down with wings spread wide and burning red eyes and glittering silver talons reaching—

(To touch—To join)

She screamed. Dropping to her knees. Scrunching down. Covering her head with her arms. She could feel the wind whoosh by, a ripple of laughter as it swooped past, then

Nothing.

Whimpering with confusion and fright, Dani slowly unfolded from the floor, pushed herself upright, got to her feet. She slung her head right and left, searching for the specter that lurked within the darkness.

Nothing moved. Nothing showed itself.

Yet something was here

(Danielle ...)

"Sara? Is that you?" It was Sara's voice—and yet not Sara's voice. "Who's there ... ?"

A faint glow caught Dani's eye, a shiver of light at the end of the corridor. The archway door was open—

(Come to Me, Danielle ... Come to Sara ...)

There was

something

about that voice ...

light ...

Forcing her feet forward, she began moving down the corridor, slowly, fearfully, closing on the light.

She didn't want to.

She had to.

"Sara ... ?" Had she whispered it? screamed it?

Her skin puckered with goosebumps. She could feel them tightening her scalp, racing up and down her spine.

Could she do this? Could she face the horror that had sent her screaming from this place only hours ago? Could she make herself go back down in that pit—if that's where Sara had gone?

(Don't be afraid ...)

Light greeted her as she stepped through the archway

but not the savage, blinding light that had chased them through the darkness—not that light. This was kinder. Softer. Glowing. It made her body tingle

with pleasure. It almost felt like . . .

Gentleness stroked her mind, brushing away the jagged thoughts, the brittle edges of her fear. Her feet felt weightless as she threaded the silver pathway.

(Danielle . . .)

Someone was calling

Set reeled. A voice was chanting

(Set . . . Set . . .)

He staggered toward the radiance that was becoming deeper, stronger with every step he took.

The bridge was there, forming within the Light, shining like a beacon at the end of an endless tunnel. Swirling toward a gateway that was beginning to open, a huge aurora splitting apart at the center, swinging outward at the top of the bridge.

They were going across. *He* was going across.

Set closed his eyes at the marvel of the path he was about to walk—as Divinian had before him . . . becoming one with the Circle—the stone . . . flowing past darkness to embrace True Light.

Thunder echoed from his footsteps. Wind screamed wild and free. And within his raging mind pain built as he opened to the Light and the doors were flung aside—

Something filled the gateway—some*one* was standing in the portal.

Set tried to shield his eyes, his mind, from the dazzling vision. So he could see. Make out the form standing there to welcome him across, take them past the final boundary

Hair the color of midnight sun blew about the wizened head and shoulders. Eyes like bottomless fire pits blazed within the ancient face. Hands spread high above them, hands more bone than flesh. Robes billowed about the skeletal form.

Who . . . ?

Pain wracked Set's thoughts, voices sang inside his head and still the Power climbed, ascending in waves from the Circle, through him, to the stone—reaching past the stone to the figure who stood at the gateway.

Breathing became a labor . . . the figure demanded all—sucking Power, pulling it in

the Mindstone was expanding—opening—

Coldness gushed into the chamber, pouring from the stone like air rushing back into a vacuum. Quicksilver pools curled about the sand. Set could feel the others shudder as the coldness claimed them, and he pulled their warmth around him with all his remaining strength.

Power drove into his mind, blinding, tearing, threatening to rip him in two.

Power danced through the nerve centers in his brain, jolting the back of his neck and the base of his spine until he felt like a marionette on a palsied wire.

He was coming apart!

Twitching uncontrollably, straining to hold on, Set clung to the bond as a crackling, frenzied shock wave of Power surged through him, tearing him loose from himself, wrenching away his control . . .

and for the instant that exists between two heartbeats he could see all he had ever wanted slipping away, falling into the bottomless pit even as he himself was falling, crystal visions dropping from his eyes like tears

then the Light was taking him up . . . up beyond

the pain, the promises ... to the One who towered
above them all

and there was nothing else that really mattered
nothing but the

Eyes

eyes the color of fire and sun, drawing him into
a radiance that was

Beautiful! Wonderful! Filled with visions he had
never known could be. Granting him Light and Life.
Eternity! Making *Them*

(One!)

"IT IS DONE!"

The words exploded with a mighty rush of thunder as He stepped through the gateway, and their
crashing echoed down the corridors of time itself.

"At last, My children. It is done."

He looked down upon them, scattered before Him
like the grains of sand. So long had He sought this
pathway, borne the endless night alone. And now—
at last—the Light was—

HIM.

HE was the Light. HE *was the One True Light.*

He spread His gaze upon the world once more,
basking in the glory of

"Dominion."

He savored the feel of the word on His tongue.

"Dominion!"

Laughter filled the cave like savage rain as He
touched His children, reaching them easily now,
claiming their minds with the voraciousness of
raging hunger, unquenchable thirst. He was oblivious to their tiny cries. What matter if He left them
empty, hollow shells writhing on the ground?
There were others yet to claim. Stronger. More
worthy.

Soon all would know the joy of perfect union. All would worship the True Light.

He spread His arms and Power burst forth, filling the world with Light and Life.

His world. His Light.

All His.

Below Him the Mindstone shone like a single glittering star in the void of new creation. He stretched out His hand, wanting to hold its beauty, feel its might. The bond had not failed Him. It had become His pathway, His arc across the void—

Something pushed His hand aside . . .

Nick sensed Sara's presence before he saw her. A door swung open in his mind and her image came inside. Grimly he forced down useless questions, too-quick anger—

softly glowing light began to seep in after her, bringing visions, sensations . . .

Nick slammed the mind-door shut. To let down his guard, even for an instant, would be to lose his edge, the *whatever* was giving him the strength to resist.

The light was like a powerful drug, trying to control him, overpower his mind and will. And like a drug it wove insidious, seductive promises, making him want to give in to it even as he fought. It was a battle unlike any Nick had waged before. And he was having to fight harder than he'd ever fought in his life.

Her small form appeared at the corner of his vision. Clad in pajamas. Feet bare. Clutching her Fuzzy.

Nick felt his gut tighten as she moved in front of him, his seven-year-old child. Yet another part of him, perhaps the most inarguable part observed:

Sara is the key. He remembered having that thought—a million years ago.

(We have to make it go away!)

Her words hardened in his mind, became his. Her strength flowed into him, making him stronger, making them both stronger. He could feel Lew on the periphery of their consciousness; and someone else . . . coming . . .

Sara gazed into the stone, and he was part of that gaze, looking across into another cosmos. Someone was walking toward them from the mist.

(the wizard from that book of scary tales—the monster I dream sometimes at night!)

Light and darkness clashed around the grotesque form. Vision blurred, overlapped

Nick forced the superimposed images from his mind and vision became his again.

An old man in a tattered robe.

Matted tangles of hair blew wildly around his head and shoulders. Eyes ablaze with triumph, cankered with madness, burned in a face scarred by time and zeal. Thin lips stretched in a rictus meant to be a smile as he looked down on them, offering worlds within his gaze . . . magnetic . . . compelling—

Nick pulled his eyes from the glittering pits.

Not this time.

Stepping up beside Sara, he reinforced their bond, drawing confidence from the familiarity and warmth that flowed over and through him. Whoever this old man was—*what*ever—Nick felt more equal now.

Light had spread to the forms scattered about the sand. One looked unconscious; two were trying to crawl away; another was beating his head against the rocks, shrieking uncontrollably. Light touched the figures, playing over the convulsing bodies, flowing into eyes and mouths.

Halfway up a shimmering staircase, their leader stood bathed in light, glassy eyes fixed on the stone in the center of the cave—and the old man with outstretched arms who passed him was descending toward them

and then the specter was stepping into the circle, reaching for the stone—

Sara shoved his hand aside.

The unexpected move recoiled on Nick like the repercussion from an underwater detonation. He'd been part of it, but Sara had initiated the action. Totally.

An isolated thought flashed across his mind: Was their success subject to the strength and desires of a seven-year-old child?

He looked at the aged face as it turned toward them, and again felt the power of those eyes—

The glass between them shimmered. Shrill laughter chilled the air.

Laughter grew, pealing with the thunder, soaring with the wind, becoming a great cauldron of churning sound pouring down around them.

"*I am the Light!*"

Energy flowed from the specter's hand. Lightning leapt across the cave, arcing randomly between the four helpless forms, outlining their spasming bodies with rabid blue fire.

Eyes never straying from Nick and Sara, the specter twisted his fist and the bodies seemed to shrink, then swell, bloat with swarming energy . . .

and begin to rupture.

Memory—*his? hers?*—of

(*badness—roaring, shrieking badness*)

(*redness swirling all around*)

Their glass existed at the center of a screaming maelstrom—

but they were not being touched!

Nick found and held Sara's thoughts, trying to

block the savage visions, blunt the brutal memories— And then she was moving away from them— *all* of them, concentrating solely on the stone.

Fury replaced the creature's twisted smile. Nick could see the cold fury, the black hunger corrupting the eyes that fell on Sara. It wanted her— *badly*—

(Go BACK!)

Sara shouted . . . and maybe he had shouted, too . . .

But the specter wasn't going back. It hadn't moved at all. Light curled from the long, gnarled hands to form a cloud—a dazzling ball spinning tight . . . tighter . . . coming toward them . . . coming—

Nick rammed his strength against their glass as it hit with a force that nearly drove him to his knees. Adrenaline flooded his veins, bracing him for another onslaught. His mind touched Sara touching him and he could feel her strength, her resoluteness. There was no uncertainty in her—and maybe that was the key. But if so, it was her key. He could never match that child-pure certainty.

His eyes fastened on the specter's face

except it wasn't a face anymore, but a death's-head floating on a shroud of light, and the hands lifting slowly were skeleton hands, not hands at all. A cunning smile spread like thick, sweet honey, and Nick felt his muscles tense—

"Dani!"

Sara's scream snapped his gaze to their left. He saw Danielle Grant stumble from the tunnel.

"Dani!" Sara shouted again, and Nick felt her certainty waver. "Get behind the glass!"

Danielle turned toward the shout, eyes dazed, confused. It was as if she heard but couldn't quite comprehend. Recognition flickered, then died as

Light curled around her, leprous fingers reaching
out
(To touch! To join!)
Maniacal laughter ripped through the cave until
the air reeked with it—
and Nick felt Sara extend their wall, attempting
to thrust it around Danielle, pull her to safety. He
reached out with the child and for a moment
thought they'd make it. Then everything began to
blur. He could feel his thready link with Lew
stretch almost to breaking. Strength weakened.
Shards of blazing light impacted and shattered
against the glass. The glass began to crack, growing
thinner.

Light poured from the stone and wrapped around
Danielle. Her hair shone as if wet. Her skin seemed
almost transparent with luminescence. Slowly she
started moving again, toward the stone, a dream-
walker, staring ahead, not seeing, not knowing—
Sara pushed—hard!—and Nick saw Danielle hesitate.

A cold blast of rage filled the cave. Lightning
rained against the glass.

Sara was gathering everything they had, plunder-
ing Nick until he staggered beneath the suction,
draining already critically depleted life force from
Lew, shoving everything toward the stone—
(GO BACK!)
They were going to lose it.

With blinding clarity, Nick realized they were going to lose it.

They couldn't protect Danielle. It was too much.
It would destroy them all
(Sara—)
(No—I won't!)
She'd read his thought, was rejecting it—
"Dani! Take my hand! *Dani*—!"
—refusing to give up the fight . . .

And it *was* her fight—but not entirely.

(Sara. Move back!)

(NO!) "Dani!"

(Sara. Let Go—)

The glass had weakened to the thinness of tissue paper. It had to be

(—NOW!)

The wall snapped back in place as, almost simultaneously, a bolt of searing energy shot toward them from the stone. It splintered into a thousand tongues of fire, licking furiously at the glass.

"Dani! Come back!"

Sara was nearly hysterical, trembling with horror and fright.

But Danielle was walking toward the stone again, oblivious to her situation, totally immersed in light.

(GO AWAY . . .)

The thought came from Sara, with more intensity than Nick had ever felt. She was focused on the stone. Her gaze bored into it, drilled into it, aimed for its heart. She was pitting everything she had against the glowing rock. He could feel her pulling strength from him, pushing it at the stone.

(Go AWAY . . .)

A new beam of energy appeared—radiant, pure—flowing from Sara, through the stone, to the stairs.

The magnificent staircase quivered.

(Go AWAY . . .)

The energy beam spread, expanded. Its heart rose to meet the cold. It was curling up the trembling stairs now, finding the second step . . . the third . . .

The bridge began to dissolve, retract. Splinters broke off, fell away. "I *Am The Light!*" the specter roared, and for a moment the dissolution began to reverse itself.

(Go AWAY . . .)

Sara stepped forward, drawing Nick with her, pushing all their strength against the stone, through it. Fury swept the cavern. A red splash of pain. Nick felt as if he were being dragged into some gigantic whirlpool, spinning beyond sight, beyond time—

"*I AM*—"

(*GO*—

AWAY!)

A sudden ball of energy flew from Sara to the stone—bursting through it—streaking outward to the bridge. It struck with a thundering impact, and the concussion shook the air.

The stairs were swirling into mist, the bridge collapsing; the specter whirled to see darkness rising up to claim the light. The gateway was closing in on itself, the doors swinging shut.

Waves of fury leapt toward Nick as he shoved his last ounce of strength against the dwindling light.

But the skeletal hands had gripped the doors, were holding them apart. Darkness circled the wasted form, dilating, opening like a huge spiraling maw. Desperately the specter held onto the meager light, anchoring himself to it, wrapping himself in what remained.

"Dani!" Sara screamed as the maw engulfed Danielle—she was being sucked in!

Sara started to dash forward—

Nick grabbed her shoulder and held on as a vicious jolt, like a powerful electric shock, nearly set his arm on fire. *What manner of thing was this that possessed his daughter?* Relentlessly he tightened his hold.

"No!" She tried to shake him off. "We have to save her. *Help me!*"

The specter was coming toward them—closer—

closer—a prism of faces swimming within the light: the Reynolds kid—Danielle—

For just a moment Nick thought she saw them—

"Dani! We're coming! *Dani*—" Sara strained against his grip.

Choices. Win or lose.

Grimly, Nick reached down into the coldest part of what he was and withdrew what was needed to see this done. It was almost more than he could do to jerk Sara back as the specter lunged down in front of them and

Vanished.

Disappeared.

Taking everything and everyone inside that spiraling maw with him.

Frantically Sara slung her gaze back to the stone.

Nick felt a mighty rush of energy—from her?—from beyond?—A final blitzkrieg of wills.

In a great explosion the stone disintegrated, blown into a nothingness as final as the silence that suddenly descended, ripped into oblivion by whatever ultimate battle had—for a frozen moment—raged within it.

The glass wall winked out of existence. The cave seemed to waver, then return. Darkness swallowed up the light.

"Sara, stay where you are." Nick heard the sharpness in his voice as he released her and pulled the flashlight from his pocket, fumbling slightly. His hand was shaking. He realized he'd dropped his gun. Sometime. Somewhere. Did it matter?

He thumbed the flashlight on. Raked the darkness. Stooped to gather Sara against his chest. "Dani," she whimpered, and he felt such a wash of pain and grief flood from her that for a stark moment it seemed to be his. He held her shivering body close, then picked her up, shoving the phantom pain away.

The beam from his flashlight fell on Lew Harris. The SBI man's eyes were dazed. He was trying to rise. One unsteady hand rose to the back of his head and Nick saw him wince. He reached over and helped Lew to his feet.

"Vears—?" His voice reflected confusion, disorientation.

"Let's get out of here."

Carrying Sara, guiding Lew by the arm, Nick led the way down the passageway toward the stairs to the chapel. Lew moved drunkenly, and once Nick thought he would collapse. Then they were at the stairs and Nick boosted Sara up them, pushing her once to get her started. Somehow Lew made the climb.

They worked their way through the chapel, through the winding corridors, Nick half carrying, half dragging Lew, Sara walking now, but clinging to Nick's arm.

With every step, Nick drew coldness to him like a purge, feeling it settle back down inside him, harden his gut. He needed to feel that hardness.

They crossed into the house.

He herded them into the den, depositing Harris on the couch, Sara in a chair. Pale gray light penetrated the room. Abstractly he noted that glass had been blown from the window.

He unfolded a lap quilt and wrapped it around Harris. Found a smaller throw and did the same to Sara. His movements were precise, impersonal. Controller to subject.

Both Harris and Sara seemed in shock. Harris was unconscious again.

Nick left them and went out to the alcove where he'd used the ECCO. The phone line was dead. Taking the small gray case, he headed on outside, where he hoped he'd find the truck.

Glass crunched on the walkway beneath his feet, blown from the small viewports in the front doors. He paid scant attention to it, focusing only on whether the mobile phone would be operational. He wanted this over with. Over and done.

Sliding into the driver's seat, he quickly tied into the line. The light came on. The connection went through.

He keyed in a code and requested an emergency medteam and some additional backup. They'd arrive by helicopter in less than half the time it would take an ambulance to get here from the hospital.

No questions asked.

It was the best he could do. For Lew. For them all. Take it out of local hands and have his people make the necessary . . . adjustments? Was that what they'd do? Adjust things?

Changing the code, he canceled his earlier dispatch, then left the ECCO on the seat and went back inside. To wait. To be with his daughter. To face her grief and, maybe, her blame. He didn't know how to assuage grief. But he was learning about blame.

Nick felt the coldness well up inside him, filling the spaces he had dug within himself so long ago, the gaps. Years had been added to his life tonight. Years and emptiness. He hadn't recognized the emptiness before.

Sara wasn't in the den.

The familiar twinge stabbed his gut. He closed his mind to it.

The sooner this was done and he was out of here, the better.

Going back down the hall, he crossed the great room and stepped through the shattered window, knowing where he'd find her. The first faint rays of sunlight had begun to score the eastern sky.

She stood a little to his left, cradling her Fuzzy, leaning against the terrace wall and staring out at the sea. He approached her, prepared to say what had to be said, unwilling to prolong this final meeting. It would be better this way.

At her side he stopped, looked down at her small body, watched a soft breeze brush hair back from her face. The words hardened on his tongue.

He pulled the coldness tighter. "Sara?"

She turned then, stared up into his eyes, and for a moment Nick knew she was gazing somewhere only she could see.

Then her vision cleared.

"Don't worry, Daddy." Her hand found his— *warmth spread up his arm, flooding his body, chasing away the cold*

She almost smiled. "I won't let the cold back in."

THE BEST IN HORROR

THE BEST IN SCIENCE FICTION

THE BEST IN FANTASY

THE TOR DOUBLES

Two complete short science fiction novels in one volume!